DEADWOOD BURNING

DEADWOOD BURNING

Bring the morning with you.

JULIA ROSEMARY TURK

Lost Island
——— P R E S S ———

Deadwood Burning
Copyright © 2025 Julia Rosemary Turk

All rights reserved. No part of this book may be reproduced or used in any manner without written permission of the copyright owner except in the case of brief quotations embodied in critical articles and reviews.

Library of Congress Control Number: 2025919415

ISBN 978-1-962876-12-4 (paperback)
ISBN 978-1-962876-13-1 (ebook)

This book is a work of fiction. Names, characters, places, and incidents either are the product of the author's imagination or are used fictitiously. Any resemblance to actual events, businesses, companies, locales or persons, living or dead, is entirely coincidental.

Cover design by MAD Book Covers
Select interior illustrations by Nikki Kahl

Lost Island Press LLC
Oro Valley, AZ
lostislandpress.com

DEADWOOD PLAYLIST

CURATED BY THE AUTHOR

♪ MY VALUABLE HUNTING KNIFE - GUIDED BY VOICES ♪

♪ DEADWOOD - DIRTY PRETTY THINGS ♪

♪ COLDBLOODED - DUKE GARWOOD ♪

♪ WOODEN HEART - JASON MOLINA, WILL JOHNSON ♪

♪ BACK FROM THE DEAD - BABYSHAMBLES ♪

♪ I'M NOT COMING BACK - HUSKY ♪

♪ FALLING MAN - BLONDE REDHEAD ♪

♪ ALABASTER - ALL THEM WITCHES ♪

♪ GODLESS - THE DANDY WARHOLS ♪

♪ HAMMER SONG
- THE SENSATIONAL ALEX HARVEY BAND ♪

♪ DESERT RAVEN - JONATHAN WILSON ♪

♪ CALL IT A RITUAL - WOLF PARADE ♪

♪ KAUFMAN'S BALLAD - MEGAFAUN ♪

♪ FURNACES - ED HARCOURT ♪

♪ KINGDOM OF RUST - DOVES ♪

♪ OH LIGHTNING - VALLEY MAKER ♪

♪ WORKHORSE - ALL THEM WITCHES ♪

♪ SWEET HEAT LIGHTNING - GREGORY ALAN ISAKOV ♪

♪ JAGGED - THE OLD 97S ♪

♪ HAMMER SONG - CRIPPLED BLACK PHOENIX ♪

♪ IT'S THUNDER AND IT'S LIGHTNING
- WE WERE PROMISED JETPACKS ♪

♪ 6705 - KELLERMENSCH ♪

♪ SHUFFLE YOUR FEET
- BLACK REBEL MOTORCYCLE CLUB ♪

♪ NEON RUST - FRANK CARTER & THE RATTLESNAKES ♪

♪ THE DARK DON'T HIDE IT
- MAGNOLIA ELECTRIC CO. ♪

♪ AS BLUE AS INDIGO - TIGERCUB ♪

♪ (DIG, BURY, DENY) - CRIPPLED BLACK PHOENIX ♪

♪ BROKEN FINGERS - BLUENECK ♪

♪ STOP BREATHIN - PAVEMENT ♪

♪ BROKEN EYES - TWO GALLANTS ♪

For those who wield my shovels
when I cannot

PART ONE
RUST

Saturday, March 5

I think our planet is being roasted on a spit.

Everything is melting. The sweat on my skin. Ice cubes in the puddle of spilled soda I step over. Gray coins of bubblegum plastered on the pavement. The cone of mint chip ice cream in my hands, and the diminishing wad of cotton candy in Beau's.

A white sun cooks the fairgrounds around us. Even through my sunglasses, I can tell it drenches everything in a blinding haze, warping the ground and buzzing in my ears. Carnival rides glint in the light. The air feels sticky with sucrose—like we're walking through syrup instead of asphalt, dead grass, and litter.

Beau strolls at my right, staring at his cotton candy like he's won the lottery. "Dude, you've gotta try some of this."

Pieces of it stick to his auburn hair and freckled cheeks. If he weren't getting on my nerves, maybe I'd tell him. I take a cool lick of ice cream instead. "No."

"Here." He rips off a wad and tries to shove it in my mouth. I swat his arm away. "Oh, come on! Just one bite."

"We've gotta be strategic here, alright? I'm saving space."

"For what?"

I point to a man gnawing on a turkey leg. "One of those."

"You'll have room, trust me. This stuff is like air." He takes another bite. "I could eat fifty of these and never get full."

"You're the one who's been begging to go on the Zipper all day, not me." I raise a hand. "If I have any more sugar, we both know how it'll end."

I shudder as I remember what happened when we snuck out here last spring—how all this sugary food and motion sickness had me hurling the entire drive home. We grow our own food at the Cut, and since it's impossible to cultivate artificial sweeteners and cotton candy machines on trees, my stomach isn't used to the diet of chipped civilians. Beau had to pull over so I could vomit. Our trip before that ended similarly.

I take another lick of ice cream and hope I won't regret it later.

"It's all part of the fair experience, alright?" Beau devours more cotton candy. Unlike me, he grew up building a tolerance to this stuff. "You're the one always begging to tag along whenever I sneak out. If you want an authentic adventure, you've gotta let me show you the ropes."

"I don't *beg*."

"Fine. You *whine* about how bored and lonely you are. Better?"

He tries to feed me again. I swat him harder.

My shades slide down my sweaty nose again, and I push the frames back up. I'd love to get a break from wearing them, but it'd be pretty stupid to reveal my scar in a crowd full of Chips.

They'd kill us both if they figured out what we truly are.

"How's the ice cream?" Beau asks, jolting me out of my thoughts.

"The things I'd do to have mint chip ice cream back home." I shake my head and take another lick. "God *damn*."

"Murder?"

"Absolutely."

"I'll help you hide the body."

"I'll bring the shovels."

A passing man wearing all white stops dead in his tracks, brows pinched in our direction. Beau notices and gives him a wave. "We're kidding."

The man scowls and moves on.

Beau places a hand on my back and pushes me forward. "Walk quickly."

"What? Why?"

"Are you stupid?" he hisses, glancing over his shoulder. He lowers his voice to a whisper. "That was a *Chaser*, dumbass."

My eyes widen. I look behind us and watch the man disappear into the crowd. "No way."

"Don't look at him now! That's suspicious." Beau nudges my arm, and we glue our gazes to the pavement. "Only Chasers can wear all white like that."

"Why wasn't he in full uniform?"

"They need to look more subtle when patrolling crowded events like this. So they can watch you better." Now that the Chaser's farther away, he looks over his shoulder again, shuddering.

I can't ignore the twinge of guilt in my gut when I see the paranoia on Beau's face. I've gotten so used to having him around that sometimes I forget he grew up like this—out here with the Chips, always worried about saying the wrong thing or making a mistake.

Maybe I know what that feels like.

Beau scarfs more cotton candy. "So do you really think burying the body is the most efficient way to cover up this murder we're planning?"

"It's convenient. The body will decompose easy enough. No one goes out to the woods anymore, anyway." I bite down on a chocolate chip. "Plus it's good for the ecosystem. Circle of life and whatnot."

"Burying won't work. You've gotta burn it. That way nothing gets left behind."

I pause to think about that. "That's depressing."

"What is?"

I kick an empty soda can as we walk. "Getting reduced to nothing in the end. Just... ash. Or worm food."

He crinkles his nose. "Gross."

"What? I'm not wrong."

"But that's such a weird thing to say." He narrows his eyes at me. "You definitely need to be socialized. You're starting to sound like your dad."

I glare. "Say that again and *you'll* be the one decomposing."

Beau laughs. Maybe I'd give him shit for it, if there weren't such an undeniable ring of truth around his teasing. That *is* something Dad would say.

My hands clench into fists. *Which is exactly why I need to get out more.*

I shake my head and observe our surroundings again, taking in the crowd we weave through. The brightly colored rides that hurt my eyes to look at. The smell of fried chicken and corn dogs and funnel cake. The sound of children screaming and spinning on swings, or laughing with friends at the petting zoo.

We walk past it—the fenced-in patch of dead grass, organized in stalls with pigs and goats and sheep. I spot a mother goat with her kid in one stall, where two young boys reach down to feed them pellets. *Brothers.*

I walk slower, eyes glued to the baby goat with its mother. Then the brothers, who laugh and grin. Something in my chest aches. *Everyone looks so happy.*

No one here is alone.

I finish the last bite of my ice cream cone and wipe my hands on my pants, then nod toward Beau's pocket. "Still got some money left?"

"A little, why?"

"Enough for some turkey legs?"

"Just barely."

"Good. I think it's about time we indulge in a few."

He can't fight a grin. "Agreed."

We sit on a bench and scarf down two legs each. They're juicy, greasy, and definitely too salty for human consumption, but I'd eat five more if I had the stomach for it. I think it's the best food I've ever tasted. Beau agrees.

So we sit, and we enjoy the world's best turkey legs. For a moment, I feel like part of the crowd.

Until Beau elbows me in the shoulder.

"Look," he whispers.

He nods toward the bench across from us, where two girls our age sit. One of them wears her black hair in two neatly woven braids, and a white knit sweater that looks too thick for the weather. She holds a to-go cup of tea in her hands. The other has dark brown curls and an olive-green hoodie, sipping iced coffee with a frown.

The girl with the braids snickers and whispers something in her friend's ear, pointing subtly in our direction. Her friend rolls her eyes and shakes her head.

My face heats up. *Do I really stand out that much?* I glance down at my black t-shirt and tattered jeans. I've had these pants for years, since before my legs were long enough to fit in them. The shirt too. They're worn and ripped, but when I check the crowd, I see about a dozen other Chips wearing a similar style. On *purpose.* I even spot a few kids our age wearing boots like mine.

Then what are they looking at? My brows furrow. *Is it the sunglasses? Are they really that weird?*

"You should go talk to them," Beau says.

A twinge of fear flickers in my gut. "Why the hell would I do that?"

"Because they think you're cute."

"That's stupid."

"Oh, come on. It'll be good for you."

"Talking to strangers I'll never see again is a waste of energy."

"One, that's pessimistic. Two, I thought that was the whole point of me letting you tag along. A change of scenery. Having fun. Connecting with people."

I look away. "That's easier said than done."

Just because I want to experience life outside the Cut doesn't mean I know how. *And it doesn't fix the real problem here,* I remind myself.

Sneaking out once in a blue moon isn't the same as Dad trusting me to go out on my own.

Beau smirks. "You're nervous."

Heat spreads over my face. "I'm not."

"Look. You know a total of *three* Unseen girls your age."

I nudge him and mutter under my breath. "Lower your voice."

"You know three girls your age. One of them is your sister, and the other two were visiting from different camps. When do you ever get the chance to... you know, have a bit of fun?"

I toss the bone of my last turkey leg into the trash can, shoving my hands in my pockets. "I've met other girls."

"Oh really?"

"Why do you sound so surprised?"

"We've only snuck out like five times. All of them were with me, and I didn't see you socializing with anyone."

"That's because you were off *socializing* yourself."

Beau rubs his chin in thought, then snaps his fingers. "The boardwalk."

"No."

"The bonfire? At that one beach with the rocks?"

"This fair, last spring." I pick at my nails. "I talked to girls there."

Beau squints. "Plural?"

I glare and slouch further.

It's true. I did meet a girl once—the last time Beau and I snuck out. We waited for Dad's big spring foraging trip and took the same run-down car to this same overcrowded city and ate the same disgustingly delicious junk food. Beau was busy fraternizing with a few chipped students and I got bored, so I tried the Ferris wheel for the first time. I shared a car with a girl my age. I'd never admit it aloud, but I got pretty freaked out by how high up we were. My leg wouldn't stop shaking.

She noticed and held my hand without saying a word. When the Ferris wheel stopped, she gave me a kiss on the cheek. I never saw her again.

Beau laughs at my reluctance to answer. "Now I see why we need to run away more often."

It's quiet for a moment. I hear a distant stranger announce awards through a microphone, voice fuzzy, praising cows and pigs and sheep and alpacas.

He says something about the Nightjade Order. Our air is cleaner than ever. Our land is healing its wounds. Our soil is regenerating. There are no food shortages, no droughts, no wildfires—and they say it's all thanks to those damn playing cards. Our goats are fat and happy. Society is fat and happy. Balance is gradually being restored, because our country is *fair*.

I don't know what's fair about a world run by a card game you can pay to win.

I hear the baby goat receive an award I can hardly make out, somewhere far out of sight. It's just as fat and happy as the rest of them.

I vomit all the fair food into the garbage can.

I wash up in the bathroom. Beau laughs when I return to the bench, trembling. My head pounds and my skin is hot and sticky and my intestines feel like they're trying to strangle each other, and all I can do is sit with my head in my hands.

Beau pats my back with a burp, otherwise unscathed by his indulgences. "If we were back home, I'm sure your dad would know exactly what tea to give you."

I lean back and groan. "I don't care."

He shakes his head and stares down at his cotton candy. "He's not as bad as he could be, you know. There are worse dads out there."

Guilt knots my stomach, but I quickly shove it aside.

It's Dad's fault for never letting me leave the Cut, I remind myself. *It's not wrong to want more than what you have, is it?*

I'm too sick to glare, and the sunlight feels like it's drilling holes into my skull, so I close my eyes and sigh. As much as I hate to admit it, I know Beau's right. My dad isn't a bad guy. He's loyal and smart and he's done amazing things for the Cut, but that doesn't mean we get along well.

He and Dad must have had some sort of conversation. It's almost like Beau's *trying* to make me homesick.

I don't think that's possible.

"Don't forget why we're doing this, alright?" I say, opening my eyes to stare at the sky. "I just want one day without thinking about him, or his nagging, or his *teaching moments*. Is that really too much to ask?"

He raises his hands in innocence. "Okay, sorry."

I shake my head, bothered by the fact that I'm bothered when bothered is the exact opposite of what we came out here to be. Bothered that I can't *not* be bothered no matter how hard I try.

With Dad on his foraging trip, I know I'd get a break from him if I stayed home too. But there's more to it than that. A small part of me wants to prove that I can do this—that I don't need him around to experience the outside world and turn out just fine. *I can handle being out here by myself.*

Though I guess this won't prove anything to *him*, since he's never sup-posed to find out.

Beau and I sit still for a while, watching the commotion unfold around us. We place our hands behind our heads and stare at the clouds.

"Do you ever wish you could come back to this?" I ask.

"Sometimes." Beau glances at me. "Do you?"

I pause to think about his question.

It's stupid, really. I didn't spend as much time chipped as Beau did. He's been Unseen since he was fourteen, but I've lived at the Cut since I was five. My memories of chipped life are severed and hazy, just fractions. Climbing trees. Playing hide and seek with kids at school. Riding bikes. Eating sugary, colorful food, just like the kind that made me sick today.

And I'd still trade just about anything to get those pieces back.

"Then why *don't* you come back?" I ask instead of answering.

"Because going back doesn't exist. Just because all *this* is fun every now and then doesn't mean I'd choose chipped life over ours." Beau gestures at the crowd, then drops his hands in his lap. A gust of wind toys with his fox-colored hair.

"You really think living in the middle of nowhere with no one around and nothing to do is better than *this*? Having places to go? Things to do? People to..." My gaze drifts toward the girls on the bench, who no longer pay us any attention. "People to talk to?"

"No, but what you described isn't what we have," Beau says. "Our home is a great place to be. It's safe. Separate from..." He can't finish his sentence without triggering the mics. He shakes his head. "Living like this crowd isn't as glamorous as it seems, alright? Don't you realize how lucky you are?"

"Our life isn't exactly glamorous either."

"If that's really how you feel, then do something about it." He gestures to the girls. "You can't experience the world you're so desperate to know by sitting around and moping about your life."

I stare at them through my shades. The one with the coffee grins at something her friend said. My face warms.

I rise to my feet, cut across the pavement, and pause in front of them. "Hey."

The one with the coffee lifts a brow. "You lost?"

My heart drops. *Shit, do I really stand out that much?*

"No," I say a little too quickly, then clear my throat. I nod toward her sneakers. They're gray now, but they must have been white at some point. The sides of their soles are covered in bored doodles. I wonder if she did those in class.

"I like your sneakers," I manage, unsure of what else to say.

She nods. "I like your sunglasses."

The bridge of my nose heats up. I wave and turn to walk away. "Bye."

Coffee Girl's friend stands up. "Wait."

I turn around.

The friend holds back a grin. "Aren't you going to tell us your name?"

"It's uh…"

Should I tell them?

Dad always warns me to protect my name. Aaron Kabir is supposed to be dead. He disappeared at age five when his tracker went off, and no one's seen him since. Rumors say he was kidnapped by *Undergrounders.*

If the authorities somehow discovered I'm still alive—that my father and I abandoned our trackers and society to live with the rebels in the woods —they'd go after Mom and Lori. That's how the Runner's penalty works. We're *traitors.*

The Nightjade Order is unforgiving of those who can't pay for Immunity and become an exception to the rules. Even the Immune aren't fully safe from the consequences of treason.

Beyond that, Dad says my name is a symbol. It represents who I am at my core. Traitor, Runner, Undergrounder—they can call us whatever they want, but I'll always have my name.

I'll always be Aaron.

You're being overdramatic, I tell myself. *And Dad's not here, remember?* These girls seem harmless. I can trust them with something this simple.

Coffee Girl stands before I can answer, tugging at her friend's sleeve. "Stop pestering him. We have places to be."

"Alright, *fine.*" Tea Girl rolls her eyes. "Well, we better get going. It was very nice meeting you."

I watch them disappear into the crowd of strangers.

When I return to the bench, Beau is eating another spool of cotton candy with a smirk. "See? That wasn't so bad, was it?"

I refuse to look at him. "Finish your food."

Beau devours the rest of his cotton candy, still unaware of the crumbs on his face. We sit in comfortable silence, watching the sun set over a world that will never be ours again.

Something white flashes past our bench.

A tiny goat springs through the crowd, chased by an older man in a brown flannel.

Beau blinks. "That's the baby goat from the petting zoo."

"No shit."

"There's gotta be a good story behind that one."

I fight a smirk. "You thinking what I'm thinking?"

Beau winks.

Without another word, we jog after them, eager to see what's going on. The crowd gasps as they dodge the man and the runaway kid—then us.

The man in the flannel trips over a soda can. Beau and I leap over him and continue after the goat. It sprints through the crowd before disappearing in an alleyway between two brick buildings. We hurry after it and finally reach a dead end.

The goat has nowhere left to run. I scoop him up in my arms. "Gotcha."

I notice little nubs on his head where horns will grow someday. He reminds me of the goats we have back home, but much smaller. *A pygmy goat.* We don't have those at the Cut.

"Hey, little guy," I coo. He bleats. "Shh. It's okay."

He releases another loud cry. *He probably doesn't like my shades*, I realize. The goats back home always hate when I wear them. I glance over my shoulder. We're still alone in the alley, so I remove the sunglasses and hang them over my collar.

"I think he's calming down," Beau whispers.

The goat doesn't seem scared anymore. He looks me right in the eye. I can see my reflection within them. Only then do I realize they're different colors. One is an earthy brown, while the other is a pale, cloudy green.

My brows knit together. Heterochromia is rare in goats. I've never seen it before. I squint to study it closer—and my lips part.

His eyes aren't different colors. One is scarred. Blinded, maybe.

Just like mine.

"Oh, thank you! You found Gooseberry," a new voice says.

We turn to find the man in the flannel approaching, panting as he wipes sweat from his forehead. "He's a feisty one, alright. Does this all the time."

The man steps closer, and I offer him the goat. He's about to take him when he pauses, brow raised. "That's quite the scar you've got there. What happened to your eye?"

Shit. My shades are still attached to my collar.

"Wait a minute..." The man's gaze lands on Beau next. "They're looking for a boy with your description." He observes the empty paper cone in his hands—and the crumbs lining his face. "You're the kid who stole that cotton candy, aren't you?"

Beau hides the cone behind his back. "Uh... no?"

The man glares. "I think you two are due for a little chat with the authorities."

We petrify as my mind returns to the patrollers dressed in white. This place is swarming with Chasers. If we're reported for suspicious behavior, it's over. They'll figure out where we came from in no time.

We'll be *dead* in no time.

The man pulls a phone from his pocket.

I whisper quickly under my breath. "We need to bolt."

"We're turning this goat Unseen, aren't we?" Beau whispers back.

I smirk. "It's like you read my mind."

I kick the phone out of the man's hands and run for it.

Saturday, March 5

♪ DEADWOOD - DIRTY PRETTY THINGS ♪

Beau's fingers dance across the steering wheel.

He taps along to a song from one of Cecil's old Yesterday CDs, which we borrowed for our trip. It's quick and gritty and one we'd usually have lots to say about, but we haven't spoken for the past hour.

Dad's voice in the back of our minds has done enough talking for the both of us. He has a way of doing that—getting in your head, even when he's not around. I'd call it a superpower if it weren't so maddening.

It's easy to feel fearless when you're young and stupid, he likes to say. *Fear is wisdom.*

I hate how right he is.

What were we thinking? I stare at the sleeping goat in my lap. *This was a stupid idea, right?*

I don't know why I wanted to take Gooseberry with us. I tell myself we did it for his own good. He'll have a better life at the Cut. It's green and vast and far from anyone who would ever want to hurt him. I've read about factory farming—about the awful things Chips do to their animals.

They keep them confined with hardly any room to breathe and feed them terrible food to produce mass amounts of product as cheaply as possible. They exist only to work until they die, and the moment they stop benefiting the system, they're culled. Almost like what they do to Chips themselves.

He'll be better off with us.

Guilt tightens my throat when I think back to his mom. *But they'll never see each other again.*

I glance through the back windshield for the twelfth time. There's nothing but a long stretch of empty road behind us, lined with pines on one side and cow fields on the other. I turn back around, leg bouncing. "No one's following us."

Beau nods with a heavy swallow. "Good. That's good."

We drive in an old sedan from the Yesterdays, which is practically in pieces. I'm pretty sure there are weevils in the ceiling, and the fabric droops like lichen on a branch, but it's functional enough. It's one of the few vehicles we keep at the Cut. For emergency use only, of course.

We're dead if Dad ever learns we stole it.

And if Chasers are on our trail, I'm sure we'll meet the same fate.

"They would've caught up to us by now, right?" I ask. "If they were really after us?"

"They use new cars. Good cars. They're fast."

"Right."

My throat feels scratchy and my stomach is doing cartwheels. I keep my eyes glued to the road ahead, which starts to bend. I slouch lower in my seat and prepare for another wave of motion sickness.

Keep your eyes on the road, Dad tells me on our rare trips to visit Mom and Lori. *It'll help with the nausea.*

I stare through the window instead.

My foot keeps shaking up and down. All I want is a nap, but I can't stop thinking about what we've done. We can't hide a goat—especially a breed we don't have. Even if Dad doesn't figure it out right away, he'll question Gooseberry's spontaneous appearance in the barn eventually. As head healer, he's always giving our livestock checkups.

This will earn us a teaching moment, for sure.

I shudder at the thought of my most recent lesson, which occurred after I fell behind on my herbalism readings to play pool with Beau and Cecil. Dad sat me down and handed me two nearly identical plants. My job was to identify which specimen was the edible Queen Anne's Lace, and which one was its toxic cousin, hemlock. I had to consume whichever one I chose. I spent an hour making my decision—and the entire night regretting it.

Turns out, my dad gave me two cuttings of hemlock.

"The dose wasn't high enough to kill you," he argued. *"Now you'll never make the mistake of eating it again."*

It's true. But that's not the point.

It's quiet for the next hour as the woods start surrounding us on both sides, thickening by the mile. Even with the moonlight, I can barely see a thing. The air is heavy and clings to my skin. I fidget with the AC controls, but nothing in this car ever does what it should.

"I'm sick of old things that don't work right," I mutter.

Beau pats the dashboard fondly. "That's just the charm of Cut life."

"And I hate this heat," I add. "Wasn't the Pick supposed to help offset climate change? It's only March. I shouldn't be baking in Washington."

"That's what The Presidency tells you. But they're getting richer, and it's still hot as balls."

I lean forward and put my head in my hands. "It's making me nauseous. I've still got fair food in me."

"Want me to pull over?"

"No." I plant my face in Gooseberry's neck. He smells nice—like newborn kittens and hay and funnel cakes. My stomach stirs and I clutch it tightly. "We need to hurry home. When Dad left yesterday morning, he said he'd be back by midnight. *Tonight.*"

"We'll be at the lot soon. Then we'll park this bad boy, and it's just a quick one-mile hike from there."

I groan. "One mile?"

"You can do it. You're a big boy."

"I'll throw up on you." I fold forward and bury my face in Gooseberry's fur again. *Just a little longer.*

That gets uncomfortable after a while, so I try to readjust, but no matter how many times I shift in my seat, I can't find a position to soothe my churning gut. It feels like my throat is constricting and I can't take a full breath, and my head is pounding, and—

I lean forward and vomit.

"Oh, come on, man!" Beau shouts. "I asked if you wanted to pull over!"

I puke again. Gooseberry bleats in distress. Beau reaches over and grabs the goat with one hand before setting him in the back seat. I cough and heave, and the last of all that fair food finally meets the floor of the car we were never supposed to touch. Bile burns my throat. I taste mint ice cream and turkey legs.

"This shit's gonna stain! How are we supposed to explain *bright green vomit* to your dad?" Beau scowls. "Nothing we eat is bright green!"

"Just chill out, man! We'll wash it."

"With *what*?"

"Water." I squeeze my eyes shut, rubbing my temples.

"We don't park our cars at the Cut. Where the hell are we supposed to get a *garden hose* out in the woods?"

"I don't know, okay?"

I bring a hand to my mouth and try to exhale through my nose. My shoulders lurch and I swallow down more retching.

Beau shakes his head. "This is so stupid."

"Don't blame me!"

"I'm not the one throwing up in the car!"

"You're the one who asked me to go with you this time, alright? Don't act like this is my fault."

"And you're the one who won't stop complaining about how miserable you are!" His yelling takes me by surprise. The road straightens out, and he glues his eyes to mine. "Why do you think I take you on these trips, Aaron?"

Through the dark of the hour and faint tendrils of moonlight, I stare at him. My shoes are covered in vomit. I'm drenched in sweat. I smell like stomach acid and fried batter and metal. I still feel like my head might explode. And in spite of it all, Beau looks at me like I'm the baby goat in the back seat. Like I haven't done anything wrong. Like I'm the one who's always needed protecting, not the other way around.

And when a black-tailed deer leaps into the road, he doesn't even see it.

I open my eyes.

For a moment I swear I'm back at the fair, strapped in the seat of some ride. That's why I'm hanging upside down. *Why is it so dark?*

The illusion passes quickly when I realize the burning sensation in my left shoulder.

This is no carnival ride. I'm in a car.

My entire body aches. It feels like my head might split in two. My arms are numb, but I manage to bring a hand to my shoulder, then freeze. It's soaking wet.

Blood.

Everything floods back to me. The argument. The deer. The swerving —and the dipshit in the driver's seat who flipped us over.

My heart lurches. *Beau.*

I ignore the searing pain in my neck and look to my left anyway. Beau isn't upside down like I am. He's on the floor of the car—what should be the ceiling. His eyes are closed. He rests in a lake of shattered glass, wet with crimson and shimmering in the moonlight.

"Beau." My voice is raspy. His eyes remain shut. "Hey."

I reach over and nudge him. Still, he doesn't stir.

Even the smallest movements set my muscles on fire, but I manage to unbuckle, using my hands to brace the fall. My throat tightens, pressing every breath that tries to crawl through it back down into my lungs. I bring a finger to his neck.

The three seconds I wait almost kill me.

I feel a pulse, the faintest flicker of a heart still beating. Slow, but there. I crawl through the shattered windshield, wincing as my elbows scrape against broken glass. I rise to my feet and clutch my forehead when my vision darkens, holding onto the car to steady myself.

Something makes a noise. My eyes pry open. I turn around to see a little white goat standing a few feet away, perfectly unharmed.

I glare. "How are you fine?"

Gooseberry bleats again. He chews on a nearby bush.

I drop to my knees and pull Beau out of the upturned car. I prop him against the vehicle's side, patting his face. "Wake up."

He groans.

"Hey." I snap my fingers. "Come on, man."

Slowly, he opens his eyes, looking down at his side. A shard of glass the size of his fist protrudes from his abdomen. His eyes widen when he sees his shirt, soaked in blood.

"Aaron?" He trembles. "What's this?"

"Don't worry about it."

He can't peel his eyes from the wound. "Aaron..."

"Stop looking at that."

His breathing quickens. "Shit, dude. That's glass."

"Just stop thinking about it, alright? Get up."

I wrap my arms under his shoulders and help him to his feet. He winces, holding onto me for support as he stares at the ground. "My foot. I think it's broken."

I exhale sharply through my nose. *Of course.*

"Lean against the car, alright? Don't put any weight on it." I crouch down to take a look. It's swollen and bruised and twisted at an angle that makes my stomach churn. "I think you're right."

Beau reaches toward the glass in his side, arm shaking. I stand and swat his hand away. "Don't touch that."

"What?" He looks at me, eyes wide and glossy, breathing faster. "Why?"

"I'm pretty sure we're not supposed to take that out yet."

"But that doesn't make any sense!"

"I know it doesn't make any sense!"

"What do we do?"

"I don't know, okay?"

"Your dad's a healer, for God's sake! Shouldn't you know?"

"Probably!"

We both pause at the same time. Slowly, we turn around to face the car

—and I feel sick all over again.

"How the hell are we explaining *this*?" Beau mutters.

I swallow. "I have no idea."

My head is killing me and the wound in my shoulder burns, but I can still walk.

I wrap Beau's arm over my shoulder, whistle for Gooseberry, and start hiking.

I know these woods like the back of my own hand, or the sight of my reflection in the mirror. Some days it feels like they raised me. Tree branches were my cradle. The rocks I upturned to find isopods and worms were classrooms. The sound of wind whistling through leaves is the only lullaby I can remember. I can map every boulder, every stream, every gnarled oak or skyscraping cedar in my mind.

This hike should have taken thirty minutes.

We limp back home in two hours.

Gooseberry follows us into our cabin. To my relief, the lights are off—but the glowing red clock in the living room tells me it's well past midnight. Dad must be running late.

I'm too tired to go around and turn the lights on. Instead, I direct my last bit of strength toward hauling Beau upstairs and into bed. All I want to do is collapse, but his wound needs attention.

When my dad is gone, I'm the one who takes over his duties at the Cut. I'm nowhere near as skilled as he is, but he raised me to know more than most. I can hold Beau over until Dad returns.

I find a first aid guide in his study that I try my best to follow. I remove the glass from Beau's side, apply pressure to stop the bleeding, clean the wound, and bandage it sloppily. I'm unsure how we'll explain our injuries to Dad, but whatever scolding we get from our excuse will be much more pleasant than what the truth would bring us.

I scoop up Gooseberry and exit Beau's room, closing the door softly behind me. I can barely keep my eyes open, but I need to do something about my shoulder. And all this glass in my arm.

I walk downstairs, set Gooseberry down, and finally turn on the kitchen light. The water is cooling when I rinse the blood from my hands. I clean and bandage the gash in my shoulder, and I'm about to take a pair of tweezers to the shards in my elbows and forearms when someone clears their throat.

I freeze, then turn around slowly.

My dad sits at the table with his arms crossed. "Welcome back."

Saturday, March 5

I'm not sure how long we stare at each other until Dad speaks.

"Are you going to tell me why you look like shit, or keep standing there with your mouth open like a carp?" He nods toward Gooseberry, who nibbles on a dish rag. "And what the hell is that?"

I shrug. "Found it."

"Your arms are covered in glass."

I stare at the cuts and shards in my skin. "Huh."

Dad nods, pressing his lips together. He stands to rummage through a drawer before retrieving a roll of duct tape. He points to a chair. I sit.

He takes a seat next to me and tears a strip of tape with his teeth. I stare at the table as he spreads the tape over a section of my arm.

"A car is missing from the lot," he says plainly.

"Really?"

"And one of Cecil's CDs."

"Hm. Weird."

"*Waterloo to Anywhere*, to be exact," he adds, smoothing the tape over my cuts. "That's one of your favorites."

I clench my jaw and shut my eyes, suppressing a sigh. *I can't believe I forgot to grab the CD.*

And if Dad knows the album's missing, that means he and Cecil already had a conversation about what we've done. *So he wasn't late, after all.*

He saw us gone and probably went straight to Command.

My stomach drops at the thought of Noriko and the other strategists learning about our escapes. Their disappointment. I work so hard to get them to stop treating me like a kid—and the *one time* I let myself act like one, everything goes to shit. After this, it'll be months before they trust me to do anything meaningful.

I clear my throat. "It'll probably turn up eventually."

"Cut the bullshit, Aaron. I know what you did."

Before I have the chance to reply, Dad rips off the tape.

"*Ow*! What was that for?"

He sets the used tape on the table. Grains of blood-covered glass stick to it like sand.

"Effective, but unnecessarily harsh," I mumble. "How on-brand."

"I can be a lot harsher." He spreads more tape over my elbow. "Do you know how incredibly stupid that was, or do I need to spell it out for you?"

He tears off the tape again, collecting more glass. I wince.

"I work hard to provide you with everything you need." His voice is calm, which is somehow worse than if he were yelling. "You always have food to eat. Water to drink. Clothes to wear. Shelter. Medicine." He sticks a strip of tape to my other arm. "Yesterday books. Television. Music." He rips it off. I grimace. "You have no reason to leave without supervision."

I exhale heavily. *Of course he doesn't get it.*

I keep my glare fixed to the wall. Even when he holds out a hand and I give him the tweezers, I still refuse to look at him.

We sit in silence as he plucks the larger pieces of glass from my arms and shoulders. There are some lodged in my neck too. He checks my head. My eyes. He removes the last shard, then starts patting away the scrapes with a wet cloth.

"I know you're struggling, Aaron. I know you're feeling restless, and I know you're at an age where all you can think about is acting out. But I expected better from you. You're smarter than this."

I cross my arms and try to ignore the knots of guilt in my stomach.

Dad releases a drawn-out sigh. "We don't live the kind of life where you can get away with behaving like this. One wrong move—*one* mistake—and it's not just your ass that's on the line. You've put the entire Cut at risk."

"You don't, actually."

He pauses. "What?"

I rise to my feet. "You don't know."

"What don't I know?"

"What I'm *feeling*."

He doesn't say anything. I shake my head.

"I'm not acting out, alright? And I'm not stupid, either."

Dad's face remains stern. "Bring—"

"Don't say it."

"Aaron—"

"I swear to God, I'll lose my shit."

"Bring the morning with you," he says, firmer this time. "Take a deep breath and start over. Whatever you're feeling, we can talk about it calmly and reasonably."

I laugh bitterly. Of course he said it.

Bring the morning with you. That's been his motto for as long as I can remember. It's his weird way of saying you can restart your day whenever you'd like—as if there's some magic off switch you can press to simmer down and ditch a bad mood.

It's never too late to start over and be good, he'd say. I heard that every time I got in trouble as a kid, and I'm still subjected to it now.

I think it's bullshit.

If it were really that simple, no one would ever be in a bad mood. I would know. I'm in a bad mood all the time, and it's not exactly pleasant.

"Do you have any idea how unbearable it is to live like this? I mean, how could you?" I scoff, gesturing out the window. "You grew up out there, alright? And I've spent over half my life trapped here doing nothing. *Being* nothing. But you? You get to leave. *You* get to go out *there*, and you never take me with you."

"That's not true," he says, voice steady. "Asa and I take you to see your mother and sister."

"Only twice a year!"

"That's because you act like this!" He stands. "You're careless and temperamental. You can hardly manage the responsibilities you have *here*. I ask you to water the garden and you start sketching it instead. I give you a thorough lesson and you forget it an hour later. I ask for your help to prepare medicine and you screw it up, because you don't listen to me. These are *simple things*, and you don't have the initiative or the maturity to handle them properly. You're not ready to experience what life is like out there."

I clench my fists. *I do listen*, I want to scream. *I always listen.*

"That's because you keep me here." I raise my voice. "I'm seventeen. I'm not an idiot and I know how to handle myself, and if you would just let me go see them on my own—"

"We are not having this discussion again."

"I'm suffocating, Dad!" My voice cracks. He flinches, so I speak softer. "There is nothing for me here."

There's a pause. "Nothing?"

The way he looks at me stings, but I pretend it doesn't.

"I've been living the exact same day for the past twelve years," I say, "and for the first seven of them, I was the only kid here."

Dad's quiet. He knows I'm right. I'm an outlier. Every child that's been born at the Cut since it was discovered is still too young for me to be anything but a babysitter.

I don't have any friends.

I have Beau, of course—but he's three years older, and it's weird to call him a friend when he's been my brother for the past five years. While he's taking on greater responsibilities for the Cut, with less and less time to spend with me, I'm stuck doing Dad's busywork. Everyone else I'm remotely interested in being around is too old and too busy.

But that's not the point.

No matter how hard I pretend it doesn't exist, it's impossible to fully ignore the ache in my chest. The seed of a gaping void that Dad planted the moment he stole me away from Port Keys, that only seems to grow bigger with every passing day.

At the root of it all, it's my sister I miss. It's my sister I think about every waking moment of every single day—and it's my sister who isn't here. And I can't help but think that if she were, this life would be more bearable. I could tolerate the sameness and the isolation if I had her by my side.

But I know that's not feasible. She and Mom aren't ready to leave their life behind, and I get that. I know what it's like to be forced into this way of living, and I don't want that for them.

All I want is to see them once in a while.

I swallow the lump in my throat and look Dad in the eye. "Do you have any idea how lonely that is?"

He doesn't say anything.

I chuckle. "Of course you don't."

I leave the kitchen. Dad calls my name as I grab my jacket from the coat rack and storm toward the front door.

"Aaron, wait." He grabs my shoulder to stop me. I pull free with a glare.

"I understand that you're angry. I understand that you want to be alone right now, and frankly, so do I. But you're forgetting something."

He points at Gooseberry, who chews on one of Beau's shoes.

"You're the one who took that goat away from its home and brought it here. It's your responsibility now. You need to take care of it."

"I'll take him to the barn tomorrow."

I turn toward the door, but he stops me again. "Aaron."

"What?"

"I mean, take care of it."

My brows crease. "What are you talking about?"

Dad sighs. "Asa's family had goats when we were growing up. I'd help him with his chores sometimes. They're a lot of work. They all love chicken feed, surprisingly." He hesitates. "You know what else all chipped goats have in common?"

I shake my head.

"The microchip in their left ankle."

My face pales.

He nods. "You know what to do."

"But I've never debugged anyone before."

"When I debugged you, neither had I."

I glare and point to the scar on my face. My blinded left eye. "And look how that turned out."

"You wouldn't sit still."

"I was five and, and you were *cutting my eye open.*"

"I did what I had to do." He turns toward the stairwell. "Now you will do the same."

He walks upstairs and shuts his bedroom door behind him. I stand there for a while, too tired to do anything but stare at the wall. Gooseberry bleats behind me. I spin around and study him.

He's younger than I realized. So damn small.

I scoop him up in my arms, knife in hand. Every muscle in my body aches, and my head is killing me, but I hike another mile until there is only me and Gooseberry and the woods. I hope no one cares enough about one goat to follow his microchip all the way out here. It would be pretty stupid if I ruined everything for everyone over a mistake like this.

The goat's crying. Maybe he misses his mother. Maybe I know how he feels.

I debug him quickly. His flesh is soft. Now, he cries because of my knife. Blood stains his fur red.

The knife in my hands is the same exact color. It looks like rust.

When I get back home, I can't fall asleep. My eyes are dry and burn with exhaustion, but my brain won't shut off. To skip the torturous ritual of tossing and turning, I grab my bag and head outside.

I don't hate the greenhouse. I spend a lot of time here, pulling weeds and fixing things up for my dad. I like it almost as much as the woods—a familiar place where I can go to escape the noise and clear my mind.

I walk inside and shut the door. The air is warm and sweet. I close my eyes and take a deep, intoxicating breath. It almost soothes the ache in my head.

I find my favorite spot and take a seat. It's a bench surrounded by potted ferns, rosemary, and lavender. I love the smell of it. Sometimes I'll take a sprig of rosemary and put a few leaves on my tongue, or rub it on my wrists and neck so I can breathe it in. It tastes great in bread too.

Lavender tea just might be my favorite.

I pull out my notebook and start sketching. I like using pens when I draw. Sometimes when I'm feeling serious about it or doing lessons with Dad, I'll start with a pencil before going over it with ink. But I rarely take art seriously, because I love it too much to let it become another chore.

I like the freedom of a pen's restraint. It chains you to the idea of accepting your mistakes and being okay with making them. I make careless, sloppy sweeps, bringing the lavender in front of me to life on the page. When I get tired of that, I draw a deer with wide, haunting eyes. It can see the headlights approaching.

"Hey kiddo."

I snap the book shut. Cecil stands a few feet away, grinning slightly with his hands in his pockets. "I knew I'd find you here."

Cecil is a big man with brown hair and a bushy mustache. He lost his left eye when he was debugged sixteen years ago. He prefers not to have a glass one like my dad, so he wears an eyepatch instead. He says it looks cooler.

I open my sketchbook again. "Not now, C."

"You always say that." He takes a seat next to me and stares at the ceiling, observing the stars through the glass dome above us. He glances at my jacket. "You're still wearing that thing?"

I refuse to look up from the deer I'm drawing. I've started adding sharp teeth to it, and outlandishly large antlers draped in lichen and curls of ivy.

"Your mom got that for you years ago," Cecil says.

"So?"

"It's just getting a bit small on you, that's all." He chuckles. "You've grown a foot in the past year alone."

"I don't really care."

"If you need a new jacket, I can pick one up on my next trip to the city."

My jaw tightens. I don't say anything.

"Or you can find one on *your* next trip."

I close my eyes and sigh. "You heard?"

"Everyone knows, kiddo. You and Beau aren't exactly subtle."

I groan, leaning my head back. "I don't understand what the big deal is. We're fine." I think back to Beau's broken foot. "Mostly."

"That's not the point."

"If you're just gonna recite the lecture my dad already gave me, I'm leaving."

"Alright, alright. I won't mention it." We're quiet for a moment until he smirks. "Did you really steal a goat?"

I fight a grin. "Maybe."

Cecil laughs. "No way."

"They really do eat anything." I point to my leg, where a patch of fabric is missing.

"You'll be able to sew those up just fine." He gestures at my drawings. "You've got a steady hand."

I shut the book again and tuck it into my bag.

Cecil frowns. "Why don't you show those to anybody?"

"It's stupid, that's why. You've seen Dad's encyclopedias."

"Well, if it matters to you, I think they're ten times better than anything your old man could draw."

"Dad's look like the real thing."

"And you draw deer with sharp teeth. *He* doesn't."

I roll my eyes. Cecil stares at the sky again. I do too, studying the stars through the glass until I fall asleep. I don't remember heading back to the cabin. He must have carried me home.

Saturday, March 12

My palms are covered in blisters.

Most days, my hands don't mind the work. I've earned pretty good calluses over the years, but I've done more chores this past week than I have all spring combined. Dad's been a real stickler lately. I'm not sure he'll ever forgive me for the car thing.

I'm in the garden outside our cabin, turning compost with a shovel. It's swarming with flies that buzz obnoxiously in the heat. I'm surrounded by towering sunflowers, peachy snapdragons, and blueberry bushes that aren't quite ripe. The tomatoes look ready enough. *I'll have to pick those later.*

A butterfly dances past me. I almost mistake it for another fly and swat it, but I catch myself. It lands on a stalk of milkweed. Dad says the flowers won't bloom until May. Butterflies really like it. Monarchs specifically. They won't lay their eggs on any other plant.

I scoff. I can't imagine living *here* by choice.

Beau sits in the wooden lawn chair I made last year, watching me work while he holds Gooseberry in his lap like a kitten. He sips a glass of lemonade—made from lemons *I* picked and juiced, from the tree *I* grew, and honey from the beehives *I* keep. I clench the shovel harder. *And Dad says I'm irresponsible.*

My eyes widen. I forgot to check on the bees this morning.

I take a deep breath. *One thing at a time, Aaron.*

"Hurry on now, get back to work." Beau snaps his fingers and takes a sip. "The sooner you finish, the sooner I can become unbored."

"Right away, your highness," I mutter.

He blows me a polite kiss and somehow develops a formal accent. "What an honest, hard-working young man."

"I'll hit you."

"How *dare* you threaten me?"

I raise the shovel, and he lifts his hands in innocence. "Okay, okay. I get it. You're grumpy."

"No shit." I poke the pile of rotting fruit rinds and dirt, pausing to wipe a bead of sweat from my forehead. "I'm the one Dad's punishing for this whole thing."

"That's because *I'm* injured." Beau points to his foot. "And he said he's teaching you, not punishing you. Remember?"

I grit my teeth. "Is there really a difference?"

He rolls his eyes and returns to watching me in silence.

I finish my chores around the garden, check on the bees, and feed Gooseberry, who's staying in the backyard until the wound in his leg heals. I even do the dishes so Dad doesn't hound me about it later.

Then I make my daily rounds. I distribute honey, tinctures, lemons, fresh herbs, dried tea, tomatoes, and other assorted goods around the Cut. It takes twice as long as usual since I'm covering for Beau's share of the work too.

Since we manage most of the gardening around here, Dad keeps a running list of different goods he's promised people. I check items off for him while he's helping a family in the Block recover from food poisoning. I've been doing this my whole life, so I have most of the deliveries memorized by now. But sometimes he adds outliers to the list—specialized orders or gifts people *didn't* ask for. It's so generous it's almost annoying.

Luckily, this is the part of my routine I hate the least. I'd never admit it, but it's nice to talk to everyone and feel like I'm helping out. Tad Bentley always gives me fishing advice, even though I don't fish. Henry and Abigail Greer send me home with cookies. Miss Hart in the cabin at the end of the Block makes me tea and tells me about her late husband. Sometimes I'll fix things around her house when she's not looking.

When I'm done with my rounds, Beau and I walk to the church for a game of pool. It's a nice day out; birds chirping, sun glaring. Emerald grass and humming insects. It's a long walk, but Beau's managing it well with the pair of crutches Dad made for him.

I look them up and down as we walk. The design seems simple enough. I'm sure I could replicate it if I ever needed to.

Cut that out, I tell myself. *Stop thinking like Dad.*

I exhale through my nose and shove my hands in my pockets. *Healing is what* he *wants, remember?*

It's not that I'm uninterested in healing. I spend too much time in our library reading up on it when no one's looking. I like the idea of using plants as medicine. The science behind how our bodies work. Making tools and teas and tinctures—doing something therapeutic with my hands. But every time Dad gives me a lecture, or a *teaching moment*, or nags me for doing something wrong, that interest dissipates. It's like he *wants* me to hate what he does.

If I had it my way, I'd like to create things just for the sake of making them. Carvings, drawings, furniture, whatever. I've even picked up the guitar behind closed doors. I've tried explaining this to my dad, but he always looks for a way to make my interests productive or useful. Like if I'm going to make something, it has to serve a purpose or offer some return on investment. I want to draw, and he tells me to help with his encyclopedias. I want to work with wood, and he tells me to fix the broken baluster on our staircase.

I can never catch a break.

We pass the jackalope fountain. I help Beau up the church steps, but we pause before opening the doors. There are voices inside. Not the building's usual chatter and laughter—something hushed and tense.

Beau and I exchange glances and make our entrance.

The conversation dies down the moment the doors slam shut behind us. Noriko, Cecil, Viv, Hugo, and Dad occupy the round table, arms folded and faces somber. The strategists, we call them—Noriko's council. They watch us slowly walk to where they sit.

"Now's not a good time, you two," Cecil says. "We'll play our game tomorrow, okay?"

"It's alright," Noriko insists, adjusting her eyepatch. "They can stay."

"What's going on?" I ask.

The two of them swap looks. My dad won't peel his stare from the table.

"I'm sure you know we sent another Double out for training," Cecil says. "Lonny Foster."

I nod.

"Asa left another letter," Noriko says.

My heart races. *I wonder if he has any updates about Mom and Lori.* "What did it say?"

Cecil releases a long, drawn-out sigh. "Our Double is dead."

The words feel like a punch in the gut. I close my eyes, exhaling shakily. Knots form in my stomach.

We all expected this. But no matter how many times we try to plant a Double out in the field, it's still shocking when they don't come home.

"He really didn't make it?" Beau mutters. He's trembling.

Cecil shakes his head.

Beau slumps into a chair with his face in his hands.

Noriko's had an interest in planting Double Agents in the Chaser Corps for as long as I can remember, but no one we've sent ever made it past training. We still don't know the full extent of what it entails, or why no one makes it out.

Lonny Foster left for training last summer—a quiet man in his mid-twenties. He stayed in touch with Asa for a bit, giving us basic updates. We've gathered important information about Nightjade. We've confirmed we really do have trackers; Noriko figured that much out on her own a long time ago. But it's the final tests we know nothing about.

Foster went silent a while back. We suspected he was killed.

I guess Asa finally found a way to confirm it.

"We're trying to figure out who to send next," Noriko says. "Training only happens once a year, so we need to decide quickly. Summer's approaching, and it takes time to prepare a candidate."

"We talked about this," Dad says. "If our last five attempts failed, chances are the next one will too. Is the reward really worth the risk?"

Noriko's voice grows stern. "You know how important this is for us, Simon."

I let out a tired sigh. I've heard this argument before.

While the Corps grows stronger every day, we grow weaker. Our numbers are small. The Unseen groups in the Pacific are hardly united, and we're still the most organized region.

Whatever momentum we once had is failing—because we all know our chances are shit.

"We've stayed quiet for too long, hiding from the rest of the world when we should be helping it," Noriko continues. "We thought we could get away with building our numbers slowly by convincing desperate Chips and Runners to seek refuge with us. But without real purpose, there is no incentive. Our people are losing sight of what really matters, and if the Corps remains a mystery to us, it will stay that way."

No one says anything.

"If we want to reverse our odds, we need to learn how the Corps operates. That's the only way to uncover their weaknesses."

"Not to mention the opportunities we'll have if a Double performs better than expected," Cecil adds. "If they keep jumping ranks, we could have someone on the inside with enough influence to spark real change."

Dad's gaze hardens. "They never make it past training. We're sending them to their deaths."

"Then maybe we're doing something wrong," Cecil says. "Maybe we aren't preparing them enough. Maybe we're sending the wrong people. We need candidates with more experience. More... grit."

"So it's Foster's fault he got exterminated? He wasn't *gritty* enough?"

Cecil glares. "You know what I mean."

"Most trainees are under thirty. The younger they are, the easier they are to mold," Noriko interrupts. "That rules out more *experienced* candidates."

"And how can we prepare if we don't know what we're preparing for?" Viv adds.

"Maybe we need to change our approach," Cecil says. "The Chaser Corps isn't only made up of Officers and Agents. There are other divisions. What if we start small? Instead of focusing on physical conditioning, our next candidate could be... unimpressive. On purpose. Aim to be sorted into a desk job or something."

"Having a plant in the NOT division would be ideal," Hugo says.

Nightjade Operations and Tech, I remember.

Viv nods. "They might end up being more valuable than an Officer, anyway. They'd have access to the Corps database and wouldn't be risking their lives out in the field. We could get blueprints, names, locations. Maybe even more Nightjade samples for Simon."

"There are too few variables we can reasonably control here," Dad argues. "We don't know how trainees are graded or what determines division assignments. As of right now, we don't have a way to manipulate those odds. It all circles back to chance."

"Then what do you suggest?" Noriko crosses her arms. "We can't drop this operation altogether."

"And why not?" Dad shrugs. "You said it yourself. Our numbers are small. We're not ready to manage Double Agents. If we spend a few years gathering resources and building our numbers—"

"We don't have a few years," Noriko snaps. "Waiting to act isn't free, Simon. It costs lives."

Dad stays silent. *He knows she's right.*

"Look." Noriko sighs. "We can't deny the importance of a successful Double. All we can do is adjust our approach like Cecil suggested, and... try again."

"It's still a risk," Dad says.

"So is existing out there. Or anywhere, for that matter."

"Enough bickering," Viv interrupts. "Noriko's right. This is absolutely an obstacle, but there is no going around it. We have to find a way through it, and that begins with finding our next candidate."

"It won't be that simple," Dad says. "News circulates quickly around here. People are talking. They're scared of what this means."

"We won't corner anyone into it," Cecil assures.

Noriko nods. "We'll hold a meeting here and ask for volunteers."

"After this?" Dad scoffs. "Who in their right mind would ever—"

"I'll do it."

I don't realize I've spoken aloud until everyone freezes.

All eyes glue to mine. Even Beau lifts his head from the table, gaze wide and unblinking. If a pin dropped, we'd all hear it. No one says a word.

Until they all start speaking at once.

"Are you *crazy*?" Viv seethes.

Dad glares. "Absolutely not."

"Be rational here, Aaron," Hugo mutters.

Cecil folds his arms. "If he wants to do it, I support him."

Everyone goes quiet again. Even my lips part in shock.

Dad laughs cynically at Cecil. "You can't be serious."

"I'm completely serious."

A pallor spreads over Dad's face. "No."

"Simon—"

"Do you hear yourself, Cecil? Just look at him!" Dad gestures toward the leftover bandaids on my arms. "You know exactly what he did. What makes you think he can handle something this sensitive?"

"I also know how capable he is. And when's the last time you've seen him *wanting* to do anything?" Cecil sighs. "You're the one who wants him to find a sense of responsibility. Maybe this is what he needs."

"I mean doing the dishes without being asked every now and then. Taking a bit more initiative during our lessons. Understanding the value of healing and being Unseen. Not sending him off to the *Chaser Corps*. He doesn't have the maturity or the training for that."

"Maybe you underestimate him. We should at least hear him out."

"He's my son, Cecil." Dad's gaze darkens. "I won't allow it."

Cecil clenches his jaw. "Whether he realizes it or not, this kid is more Unseen than the rest of us. He's spent his whole life knowing nothing else, and he's smart as hell. He was practically raised by knives. He's been helping out around here since he was just learning how to read, but all you ever do is point out what he's doing wrong."

"Now is not the time for this discussion."

"I think it's the perfect time." Cecil's nostrils flare. "If he *wants* to do this for the Cut—for the Unseen—isn't that a good thing? Doesn't that mean we've raised him right?"

A muscle in Dad's neck feathers.

"All he's ever wanted is to prove himself to you, and it's never enough."

"It's not a crime to expect the best from him," Dad says. "Has it ever occurred to you that I have these expectations because I know he has it in him?"

"The least you can do is hear what the kid has to say. Did you even ask him why he wants to volunteer?" Cecil's shoulders relax. "He needs you to believe in him."

"This isn't about how capable he is."

"Then what is it about?"

"I'm not sending my son to get slaughtered!"

"That fear assumes failure."

"Hey assholes," I interrupt. They freeze. "I'm right here."

Everyone looks at me again. In the silence, I can hear Dad's slow, angered exhales as he tightens his lips to a seam.

"I can think for myself, you know. I'm good with knives. I know how to throw a punch. I practically live in the library. If this is about odds, let's face it. Mine are the strongest here."

Cecil nods, urging me to continue.

"Most Chaser cadets are my age anyway, right? Sending anyone older would draw attention. And I'm sure as hell not letting you put *him* in there. Especially not with that busted foot of his." I point to Beau, who averts his gaze.

"He makes a decent point," Viv mutters.

"And I'm not heartless, alright?" I sigh, then look at my dad. "Has it ever occurred to you that maybe I want to help? That I actually care about what we're doing?"

"Given your track record, no," he grumbles.

I clench and unclench my fists, steadying my breathing. *Stay calm. Don't prove him right.*

"Every time I ask to help on your trips, or to see Mom and Lori on my own, you shut me down. You tell me I'm not ready and you never explain why. Cecil's right. You underestimate me and I think that's unfair. You always say true learning is experience. How am I supposed to learn to be ready if you won't let me?"

"You don't know their world like I do," Dad warns. "There are reasons why I've kept you from it."

What reasons? I grind my teeth. *He just wants to control me.*

"Every time you leave the Cut, you're putting more than yourself in danger. You're compromising our entire operation. Hell, the entire Unseen. If you want to see your mother and sister more, perhaps that can be arranged when you earn back my trust. Volunteering for this position as an excuse to leave is—"

"That's not what this is about!"

"Then tell me, Aaron. What *is* this about? Why do you want to do this?"

My hands curl into fists. *Does he really have to ask?*

"Not a day goes by where you don't tell me how unhappy you are to be here," he continues. "If you truly hate it here as much as you say, don't expect me to believe you're doing this for the Unseen. Or that you'll suddenly learn to love it under interrogation."

The words feel like a stab in the gut. "What are you saying?"

"You're not ready for a job like this."

My throat burns. "You don't trust me, do you?"

He's silent.

"You're questioning my loyalty."

"I'm questioning your ability to make rational decisions for the greater good. You let your anger get the best of you, and if so much of it is directed here—toward us, and our home—how am I supposed to trust that you will protect it when you're out there?"

"I'm just as Unseen as any of you."

"I never said you weren't."

"But that's what you mean!"

"And what if you let something slip?" He rises. "We all know about your talent for saying the wrong thing at the worst possible time. For letting your emotions surpass your rationality and judgment. Will you still be Unseen when they beat the living shit out of you?"

Nobody speaks. I blink.

"Will you still be Unseen when they start pulling out your teeth?"

"Simon…" Cecil warns.

Dad steps closer, arms crossed. "Will you still be Unseen when they start peeling off your toenails? When they brand your skin with a hot knife or crush your knuckles with a hammer? When they saw off your fingers and toes and feed them to you one by one?"

"*Simon*," Cecil hisses.

"He needs to know the truth," Dad snaps. "We both know what I'm describing is nothing from my own imagination."

Cecil tightens his jaw.

Dad faces me again. "If you screw up and they realize you have information they want, they will do anything to get it from you. *Anything.* Do you understand this, Aaron? They will *hurt you.*"

I look him in the eye. My nails carve into my palms, breaking skin. "I am Unseen."

"Until you learn to truly accept your responsibilities—until you can say with pride, on your own accord, that you are Unseen, and the Cut is where you belong—I can't believe that either of those things are true."

My throat burns. It feels like my lungs are constricting and I can't take a single good breath. I'm so angry I feel like crying, and that makes me even angrier, because I'm not sad, and if I don't suck it in, they'll never let me go. So I don't cry. No matter how angry I am at my dad or how badly my shoulder hurts or how deeply I miss my mom and sister with every fiber of my being, I keep it all inside.

I need to prove him wrong. I need to experience the world for myself, on my own terms. And if I can get him to trust me again… maybe he'll let me see them more.

Cecil clears his throat. "I think we've all said our piece." He nods toward Noriko. "What do you think about all this?"

She studies Dad and me carefully. The seconds feel like hours until she finally releases a sigh. "I think it's up to Aaron. He's almost eighteen. Only he can decide what he's ready for." The one eye that isn't concealed by her patch is glossy as she gives me a small grin. "He's my godson. I'd trust the kid with my life."

"He's my *son*, and I hardly trust him with his own!"

"You forget your place, Simon," she snaps.

The sternness in her voice takes him by surprise. The others shift uncomfortably. Even I pause at the sudden display of authority.

Noriko may be our leader, but she rarely makes decisions without the input of her strategists. Their opinions are valued as much as her own. It's not often that she pulls the Commander card, but when she does, it always sends shivers down my spine.

"You elected me as Commander. *All* of you." She gestures toward the others. "Are you challenging my judgment?"

Dad's jaw feathers. "No."

"Do you really think I'd let Aaron do anything I thought he wouldn't survive?"

He bites his tongue.

"Right now, this is the best course of action for the Cut. The rebellion *you* dedicated your life to. Honor the oath you made when you became Unseen, Simon—because holding Aaron back would betray it."

The room falls quiet. Everyone turns to Dad, awaiting his response. When he finally talks, his voice is stone-cold. "Proceed as you see fit, *Commander*."

The title has a bite, but Noriko ignores it, facing me now. "No one is pressuring you into anything."

"I know," I mutter.

"But if you feel called to do this for the Unseen..." Noriko gives me a fleeting smile. Her good eye waters. "Who am I to stand in your way?"

"So what will it be, kid?" Cecil asks.

I look around. Viv gives me a saddened grin of encouragement. Hugo nods. Beau's expression is pleading as he shakes his head. Now Dad won't even look at me.

I close my eyes and drown it all out. I take a deep breath, focusing on the smell of wood and dust and old carpet. I think about the pool table in the corner, the rows of empty pews that stretch on forever in my mind, waiting to be filled. I think beyond them, to a different point of endlessness. The horizon through the window of my mother's coffee shop. So much gray as far as the eye can see, like a desert made of clouds.

What do I want?

The question takes me by surprise, and I don't know how to answer it. *Maybe that's the problem.*

My whole life, I've been told what to do and who to be—what I'm ready or not ready for. Maybe what I want is to find a solid answer to that question, all on my own. Maybe the answer is waiting for me out there. *Not here.*

And maybe, beyond my desire to do something good, I want to prove myself to my father after all.

I've spent my whole life trying to earn Dad's trust, and nothing I ever do is good enough. I need to show him I'm responsible—that I'm ready to go on foraging and smuggling trips with him. That I can handle visiting Mom and Lori as often as I'd like to. That I can make my own decisions for a change, without screwing things up.

I am just as Unseen as he is.

I open my eyes. "I'll do it."

Monday, March 14

For the next two days, the strategists tell me everything we know about the Chaser Corps.

We know the Corps is split into divisions. Officers are the most well-recognized—the ones who patrol the streets and carry out exterminations, clad in white armor with Nightjade guns at the ready. Other divisions like Sitters and NOTs occupy desks and labs, managing everything from press and Nightjade research to public surveillance. The classier Sitters of the Corps are high-society business people who attend elaborate dinner parties to discuss the Nightjade crop, extermination quotas, and the weather, among other pleasantries.

They are all Chasers.

We know what they know, to an extent. The public isn't entirely convinced us Unseen exist; most lower-ranking Chasers have their doubts too. They call us the Underground. Ghost stories and cautionary tales.

Agents, however, seem to have eyes everywhere. They know things other divisions don't. They watch carefully, waiting for us to make mistakes and lead them to our hideouts. They want another Harebell Hill—another Unseen camp occupied and harvested for information.

We also know the higher-ups in the Corps are well-versed in the workings of the Syndicate. Dad's mentioned them before. The intricate crime network of well-off chipped citizens, who have the Immunity and connections to get away with breaking the Nightjade Order for profit behind closed doors. They're bootleggers that operate the *real* underground of major cities. They're not technically traitors like us and don't usually mess with the Corps, so in return, the Corps doesn't mess with them. Some Agents even partner with the Syndicate to access their goods and feed their guilty pleasures.

And lastly, we know about the trackers in our left eyes. From insight gathered by past Doubles during training, we assume this information is Agent-exclusive. All other divisions are told the microchips are hidden beneath the Cards of our left wrists.

I slouch in a chair at the round table, staring at my own tattoos while Viv lectures me about something I don't pay attention to. Dad's here too. My leg shakes. The air inside the church is hot and stale and we don't have fans in here, so my skin glistens with sweat. Everything smells like wood and old carpet.

I rub my thumb back and forth over the 2 of Spades on my left wrist, then study the Joker on my right. Even after all these years, the ink is still crisp. I wonder what sort of tools the artists use. It's a shame no one sees tattoos as art anymore. Just handcuffs.

That would be cool, I think. Being a tattoo artist.

"Aaron," Dad says, pulling me out of it.

I lift my head up. "Hm?"

"You're the one who signed up for this. Pay attention."

"I am."

"What did Viv just say?"

I glare. I hate when he does that. I turn to Viv. "Sorry. Continue."

"This is important stuff, Aaron." Viv sighs. "Look. Why don't you go take a break? We've been talking for a long time. I wouldn't be able to focus for that long either."

"Thank you, Viv." I rise to my feet and resist the urge to toss Dad a dirty look on my way out. He shakes his head.

My first instinct is to track down Beau, but I doubt he wants to see me. He's spent these last few days holed up in the armory, taking things apart and putting them back together, like he always does when he's going through something. I think he's mad at me for agreeing to this whole thing.

I walk through the woods near our cabin to find my favorite knife-throwing spot instead. To my surprise, Cecil's already there. He chucks a hatchet at a target Dad pinned to a tree a long time ago. He almost gets a bullseye.

"Hey kiddo," Cecil says, retrieving the hatchet.

"Hey."

I find my own tree, pull out my knife, and ready my stance. Just as I'm about to throw, Cecil interrupts. "Check your feet."

I roll my eyes and adjust my stance.

"Relax your shoulders."

I grit my teeth and do as he says, then pull my arm back and throw. It misses the center by an inch.

"Not bad." Cecil stands beside me. "Your technique could use some work though."

I ignore him, retrieve the knife, and throw again. It hits the edge of the target.

"Your dad should be the one helping you with this. He's the knife prodigy, not me." Cecil pulls out his own blade and throws it at the tree next to mine. It misses too. "Simon never misses."

I frown at the suggestion. "Absolutely not."

I throw again. It's still an inch away from the center.

Cecil raises a brow. "So you disagree."

"No. I'm not stupid. I know my dad's a good shot." I pull out a second knife and throw with that one instead. It knocks the other down and takes its place. "But if I wanted to be around him right now, I wouldn't be out here."

Cecil watches me retrieve my blades and aim. "You can't avoid him forever, you know."

"I'm not *avoiding* him. He's just pissing me off lately. It's different."

"I don't know, kid."

I scowl. "Do you really want me to be upset with you too?"

"Alright, alright." Cecil lets out a long sigh. "I know you and your dad butt heads a lot—and I'll admit it, he and I have our fair share of arguments—but... he's a really good guy. One of the closest friends I've got. You know how you and Beau are." He pauses. "Simon's like my brother."

I avert my gaze.

"He's a good dad too."

"Unless you know what it's like to be his son, I'd tread lightly." I throw again. And again.

"I don't want you to spend your life hating the guy for wanting what's best for you."

I ignore him and gather both knives.

"He won't be around forever, you know," Cecil says. "You'll miss him someday, and when you do, I don't want you to regret anything."

"That's pretty grim, C."

Both my knives hit the target, still not quite in the center. Cecil collects the blades this time and hands them back to me. "Have I ever told you about my old man?"

"I don't think so."

"He was hard on me too." Cecil studies his hands, twisting his own blade between his fingers. "We had a falling out when I was younger. Eventually, I forgot what our fight was even about in the first place, but I still held onto that grudge anyway." He shakes his head. "I spent so much of my life hating him. Until he was gone."

"What happened?"

"He was Picked."

It's quiet. I avert my gaze and focus on a nearby crow instead.

"He wasn't perfect, but he wasn't terrible by any means. There are some really shit parents out there and he was never one of them." He stares at the bird too. "I wish it didn't take losing him for me to come to that conclusion."

The bird flies away.

"And then a year later, *my* Cards were Picked." Cecil throws his knife. Again, no bullseye, but it's close. He gives me a small smile. "And eventually,

I got to understand a bit more of my old man's perspective myself."

Cecil collects his knife. I throw. Perfect bullseye. He pats me on the back. "Nice going."

We keep throwing in comfortable silence. I hit three bullseyes. As a reward, Cecil promises a pool tournament with Beau and me, after I get back from wherever it is I'm going.

Twigs snap. We spin around. Hugo jogs up to us, breathless.

"What's wrong?" Cecil asks.

"He's here," Hugo pants.

Cecil pales.

My brows furrow. "Who?"

"Walter bloody Schneider," Cecil mutters, eyes glued to Hugo's. "He really came after all?"

Hugo adjusts his glasses and nods.

I frown. "Who's that?"

Cecil faces me. "You know about the Syndicate."

The crime ring Dad talks about? I nod.

"Ever heard of the Serpent?"

"Uh, no?"

Cecil sheaths his knives, picks up his hatchet, and starts walking away. "Well, you're about to meet him."

The woods are eerily quiet today, as are the four of us. The air tastes like evergreen and clouds keep passing over the sun, casting uncertain shadows over every dew-jeweled fern and root and mossy rock. I don't notice a single bird chirp. Even Cecil and Noriko seem nervous. A rare occasion. Cecil won't stop clenching and unclenching his fists. Dad doesn't even investigate the cluster of morels we walk past; I'm not sure he sees them at all. He's barely said a word since right before we left for the rendezvous cabin.

"You will not speak to him unless spoken to. You will not do so much as look him in the eye without permission. Understand?"

"What, is he in charge of the Syndicate or something?"

"No." He paused. *"But his brother is."*

I keep turning the situation over in my head. I'm not entirely sure who this Serpent guy is. All I know about the Syndicate is what I've gathered from listening in on hushed conversations over the years—and Viv's lecture back at the church, which I probably should have paid more attention to. They're on our side. I think. *Then why is everyone so tense?*

Why are we going to meet him? And how does this involve me?

I jog up to Dad and lower my voice to a whisper. "What are we doing?"

"We have negotiations to make."

Negotiations?

I shove my hands in my pockets. "Are you... afraid of this Serpent guy?"

"Of course I am. Afraid is the smart thing to be."

I swallow dryly.

He studies me for a moment, contemplating how much to say. He sighs and stares ahead again. "Grant Schneider. Ever heard of him?"

"No."

"He was the father of Walter and Francis Schneider. Married a woman named Yvette Chandler, who inherited the position Francis currently holds from her parents."

"Francis is Walter's older brother," I say. "And he's... in charge."

"Correct."

"So Yvette and Grant were too, once."

"Yes and no. Grant was a controlling man. Took over most of the Syndicate's operations after their marriage, which had been arranged by their parents."

"So he married his way into owning most of Seattle?"

"Essentially, yes."

"Lucky guy."

Dad shrugs.

"Walter always had an obsession with snakes, ever since his mother gifted him a rainbow boa as a pet." He lets out a one-note chuckle. "He found them fascinating. Started collecting them. He was like a walking encyclopedia. He could identify any species of reptile he saw. Knew all the best spots to find copperheads, rattlesnakes—you name it.

"But his father never approved of the obsession. He always found Walter odd and weak; favored Francis instead. His mother was the only one who seemed to understand him or care for his curiosity."

"And this is important because…"

"When Walter was seven years old, he found out his father was having an affair." Dad flicks a glance in my direction. "Can you guess what he did?"

I shake my head.

"Somehow, a rattlesnake found its way into Grant's bed." Dad stares forward again. "He was found dead the next morning."

My eyes widen. "Oh."

"Yvette was pleased with her son's initiative. The torch was rightfully passed to her, and she had control again." He looks at me. "You know what she did to reward him?"

"What?"

"She bought him another damn snake."

I stop in my tracks. A chill loops around my spine. "What's your point?"

"My point?" He glares, like it's obvious. "The man you're about to meet is a piece of shit, but you're going to respect him like your life depends on it—because it does."

"And you know all this how, exactly?"

He looks at me over his shoulder, then turns his head back around. "He told me himself."

I don't question it further and keep walking.

Monday, March 14

♪ COLDBLOODED - DUKE GARWOOD ♪

We reach the cabin and walk up the porch steps. It's a quaint old thing tucked between towering firs and pines, made of round logs and thick antique glass. Dust and moth-eaten curtains block our view of the inside.

Noriko knocks in an odd rhythm. Code, probably. From the other side, a different but similar knock cuts through the silence. She taps back.

The door opens. Not a second passes before a tall man wearing a worn brown jacket and a rancher hat steps outside and wraps his arms around her.

I grin when she hugs him back. *Asa.* My godfather. My father's best friend, my uncle by default, and the love of Noriko's life.

She buries her face into his chest. "God, it's good to see you."

He just pulls her closer.

The moment is interrupted when Dad barrels into them, joining the embrace on the porch. "Get a room, softies."

Someone clears their throat.

A slender man in a spruce suit stands in the doorway. Wavy salt-and-pepper hair falls just below his ears. I crinkle my nose at his tie, which is black velvet with an iridescent scale pattern. His eyes are a disarming shade of green, like peridot. Or bile. He holds his hands patiently behind his back.

I notice his ears are pierced with oddly shaped gold studs. *Are those... plated teeth?*

My stomach churns.

"Well I'll be damned." The stranger folds his arms over his chest, voice low and unsettlingly smooth. "Asa McLellan, Noriko Teshima, and Simon Kabir—all together in the same place. What a marvelous reunion. Almost brings you back to our university days, doesn't it?"

Dad's jaw twitches. He forces a nod in greeting. "Walter."

So this Walter guy is the Serpent? My brows knit together. *They went to school with him?*

"Oh, and hello to you too, Mr. Logan." Walter grins at Cecil, who clenches his fists. "I assume you've tamed your temper since the last time we convened?"

Cecil stays quiet.

The Serpent laughs. "I only tease. Always so serious. Worry not, that incident is far behind us. Now do come in, it's a bit chilly out here."

Walter waves for us to enter the cabin, like we're his guests and not the other way around. I think about the beads of sweat on my forehead and the sun that glares through wispy clouds. *It's not even cold.*

I lean over and whisper to Cecil. "What did you do to him?"

Cecil chuckles. "I punched that prick in the mouth."

We walk inside and gather around a small table in the center of the cabin's only room. Asa closes the door behind us. Flames crackle in the fireplace, where a wooden kettle hangs. It's uncomfortably warm. My shirt is already sticking to my skin.

Walter leans back in his seat, studying us with an entertained smirk. I follow Dad's instructions and keep my stare fixed to the table, not looking the Serpent in the eye. Noriko is the only one unafraid to look at him— and the only one whose eye contact *he* avoids. Asa keeps watch from afar, leaning against the door.

A shrill sound cuts through the silence, making me flinch. Walter stands with a smile. "Tea's ready."

He crouches besides the kettle, pouring what smells like chamomile and lemongrass tea into a tray of chipped teacups. I catch a hint of spearmint too. *All good for relaxation*, I note.

Walter returns and sets the tray on the table, taking a seat. "I found some tea in the cupboard and couldn't resist. I hope you don't mind."

"Not at all," Noriko says flatly. She waits for him to take a sip before taking her own. Reluctantly, Cecil follows her lead. Dad only stares at the table, arms folded.

"Is something wrong, Simon?" Walter asks. "I thought you loved lemongrass."

Slowly, Dad grabs a cup and takes a sip. He flashes a faux grin. "The tea is lovely, Walter. Thank you."

"You really think so?" The Serpent tilts his head. "I expected Nightjade to appeal to a more selective palate."

Dad and Cecil spit out their drinks.

Walter chuckles. "I'm only teasing. I thought the mood could use some uplifting."

No one speaks.

"What?" Walter places a hand over his heart, feigning offense toward my father. "You truly believed I would ever attempt such a thing? Now that's just hurtful."

"Wouldn't be the first time you poisoned a man," Dad mutters.

"You can cut the performance, Walter," Noriko says. "It's paper thin."

Walter's grin falls away. He lowers his eyelids, unamused. "Fine. You want to cut to the chase? Let's cut to the chase, then."

He leans forward, lacing his hands together.

"You've summoned me here because you desire a favor. I carved out time to make the trip when I could have easily sent a courier in my place, because I must admit, I'm rather curious as to what the Cut could possibly have to offer in exchange for such a bold request." He chuckles, then lowers his voice. "There are few who have the desperation and audacity to ask the Serpent for a good turn."

A shiver crawls down my back.

"We appreciate your willingness to meet with us today," Noriko says. "Due to these... unique circumstances, I thought it best to speak in person. Hiding behind puppets doesn't suit me."

Walter narrows his eyes at the backhanded insult. "What do you want, Noriko?"

"Asa filled you in on our operation?"

"Briefly, yes."

Noriko sighs painfully. "All of our Doubles failed to make it through training."

"Pity."

Dad glares.

Noriko glances at me briefly. "As you know, our next candidate is... different from the others. He needs to come back in one piece."

Walter studies me, but I keep staring at the table. My leg shakes. I can practically feel his eyes burning into my skin and ignore his curious grin.

He faces Noriko again. "My question remains unanswered."

"What we want is your guidance and protection," she says. "No one here is a stranger to your influence. Not only within the Syndicate, but among high Immune society as well. Your authority and resources could greatly improve our odds of success."

"Is that so?"

"During his operation, Aaron will need a place to stay. His back watched. Preparation for what's to come. This includes a false identity and a new tracker, as your associates have generously arranged for our previous Doubles, and introducing him to chipped life. He needs training long before he steps foot in any Corps facility."

"And you cannot simply send him off with Asa?"

"You know why that isn't an option."

Ren and Margot, I realize. *Staying with Asa would put them in danger.*

"And what about Aaron's mother?" Walter gives Dad a smirk. "How is Esmerelda, by the way? I haven't seen her in ages. Oh, wait—neither have you, from what I've heard."

This time, Dad looks the man in the eye. "She's fine."

"We're not risking our families' safety," Noriko intervenes. "Aaron must stay with trustworthy chipped contacts under the Syndicate's protection. If you were to arrange this for us, we would be very grateful."

"And what could the Cut possibly have to offer me in return?"

"We've discussed forming an alliance between us and your branch of the Syndicate in the past. I know our previous attempt... fell through, but we're willing to make this partnership official."

Walter chuckles. "That's quite the unbalanced offering. The way I see it, the Cut would be the main beneficiary of that outcome."

"How so?"

"A lot can change in fifteen years. We have arrangements with nearly every Unseen group in the Pacific Region. Even the smallest encampments harbor our *goods* in exchange for provisions. We have wealth, weapons, power. You have twigs and leaves. Oh, and those little herbs you peddle to desperate Chips in exchange for toiletries and hand-me-down clothing."

Noriko glowers. "Your point?"

"We've grown, but the Cut remains the same." His grin disappears. "Why would I agree to something so asymmetrical?"

"You were the one who proposed this alliance when we last discussed it," Noriko says flatly. "What changed?"

"I'm not *against* the idea. I just don't think an alliance alone is enough to cover the time and energy required to achieve what you ask of me. Not to mention the risk involved with harboring a traitor."

Traitor. The word makes me flinch. I clench my fists under the table.

"I didn't particularly enjoy your *hospitality* the last time we spoke either." He tosses Cecil a frigid glance. "The greatest advantage you have that I'm interested in is your lack of trackers. Cooperative rebels can be quite useful for our bootlegging operations. And yet, last time we met, you refused to play any part in it."

The last time they met... was that when Cecil punched him?

"That much remains the same," Noriko says. "We won't move or store your contraband. We want nothing to do with your business or the enemies that come with it. We already do enough of our own smuggling as it is just to keep the Cut fed and functional. Adding your goods to the mix is too much of a risk."

"Then what *are* you willing to do for me?"

"A tide is turning, Walter. I'm sure you feel it too."

He doesn't deny it.

"The Corps is growing increasingly aware of what the *Underground* truly entails. As restrictions increase, you'll need our support to keep your operations running smoothly."

Walter scoffs. "Need?"

"Change will arrive, whether you're prepared or not. And when it comes knocking, who would you rather have on your side? Those fighting for freedom, or control?"

The Serpent stays quiet.

Noriko leans closer. "We're the ones trying to turn that tide. Even if this country's Unseen are disconnected, we're all on the same side. We've got contacts in all six Regions. You rule Seattle, but we rule *everywhere*. We outnumber you by a long shot, and you know it."

He chuckles. "Is that so?"

"Think of this partnership as an insurance policy." She straightens her posture. "When the Nightjade Order is gone, we'll make sure not to throw you out with it."

The Serpent's eyes narrow. "You can't bargain with what-ifs, Noriko. Unless you have a tangible benefit to offer, I can't waste time and resources on the Cut's behalf." His smile has a cruel edge. "Not even for you."

Noriko pauses briefly. "There is one thing you're forgetting."

"Oh?"

She looks at me, then back to him. "You may have your Vipers, but you're not the only one with spies."

Vipers? My brows crease. *Is that what he calls his spies?*

Noriko takes a casual sip of tea. "A few of our chipped contacts frequent Prairie Pit quite regularly for more than drinks alone."

"You've been keeping tabs on me?" Walter leers. "I'm flattered."

"Prairie Pit?" I repeat. "What, is that a bar or something?"

Dad kicks me under the table, glaring. *Stay quiet*, he warns in silence.

Walter chuckles in my direction. "I suppose you could call it that. Why?

Would you like to visit sometime?"

"He appreciates the offer, but he'll have to decline," Dad snaps. "He's only seventeen."

The room goes still. Cecil shifts uncomfortably in his seat. Even Noriko's shoulders stiffen in fear.

The Serpent chuckles again, turning back to Noriko. "You were saying?"

"You have the same problem we do," she continues.

Walter squints in confusion. "Enlighten me."

"Half your patrons are Immune Chips and Chasers, but they aren't your allies. You don't have true partners on the inside, so you tried planting your own Double Agents."

Walter doesn't deny that, either.

So this guy wants a Double too?

It makes sense. The Syndicate isn't invincible against the Corps; Immunity can only stretch so far. While it protects individuals from being exterminated for petty crimes, any act of sabotage or espionage against the government counts as treason.

Having a drink or a smoke is one thing. Bootlegging is another.

Selling alcohol, drugs, and weapons under the Presidency's nose could be painted as conspiracy. It puts profit over loyalty, contributing to a breakdown of social order during times of hardship—especially as the Unseen's rebellion grows. All it would take is one *honorable* Chaser with enough evidence to deny the Syndicate's bribes and take them down.

If I were running a crime ring, I'd definitely want eyes on the inside—warning me about investigations and raids, informing me who I can or can't trust.

Of course he wants a spy. I smirk, studying our Commander. *Clever approach, Noriko.*

"You can guess what our contacts uncovered." She takes another casual sip. "Just like us, none of your Doubles made it through training."

"Most cadets do not, though it doesn't matter," Walter says. "I've had a few Chasers in my circle."

"But those partnerships don't last, do they?" Noriko tilts her head. "Eventually, they realize a promotion within the Corps is worth more in the long run than whatever you can offer them. Once they start distancing themselves, you realize they're contemplating turning you in. We all know how you handle betrayals. I can't imagine disposing of a Chaser inconspicuously to be an easy task."

Dispose of?

I shudder.

"It all boils down to loyalty. You need a Double who will be on your side from the very beginning—one you can truly trust. Given Aaron's connection to the Cut's leadership, we can guarantee his integrity. He will be just as much your spy as he is ours."

Something clicks behind Walter's eyes. Slowly, his lips creep upward as he realizes what she means. "A Viper of my own in the Corps? Now that does sound enticing."

Dad and Cecil exchange nervous glances.

"Anything he learns, you'll have access to," Noriko says cautiously.

Walter shrugs. "Information is easy enough to buy. The real value lies in the position itself. There is always room for growth in the Chaser Corps." He looks me up and down. "You seem like Officer material. I'm sure you could be more, if we play our cards right."

Dad's jaw tightens. He opens his mouth to reply, but Noriko beats him to it.

"He won't be in the Corps for long," she corrects. "We only want him out in the field for a few months. Once he's gathered enough insider information for us to better understand their weaknesses, he'll fake his death and come home."

Walter presses his lips into a tight seam, observing Noriko in thought. "Let's say he does make it past training." He pours himself another cup of tea. "He beats the final test, becomes an Officer, performs well on the job. After a few years, they might start promoting him."

"A few years?" Dad scoffs. "No."

Noriko lifts a hand, calming him before turning to the Serpent. "We understand your point, Walter. But taking down the Corps from the inside isn't our long-term goal. That would require more than one Double, and more noise than we can afford. We want him to remain inconspicuous.

Aaron should return home as quickly as he is able."

"I'm not suggesting the collapse of the Nightjade Order. Just imagine the value of having an Agent on the inside—one with *his* unique upbringing, who would never sell his loyalty over to the Corps. Tell me, are there any other Unseen around here who were converted so young, and are now old enough to be useful? You said it yourself. Life at the Cut is all he's ever known. He would never reveal anything he isn't supposed to—not with the fate of his entire community on the line."

Something about that makes me shudder.

"The more they trust him, the more he'll get to know," Walter continues. "The more valuable he proves to be, the more they'll invest in him."

Noriko's voice turns rigid. "As quickly as he is able."

"We'll see what Aaron decides." He grins in my direction, like I'm a prized goat at the fair. "Who knows? Maybe he'll discover he *likes* Immune life, after all."

Dad clenches his jaw.

"You clearly see the value in having a loyal Double to call your own," Noriko says. "Beyond that, this could serve as the beginning of a new partnership between the Cut and the Syndicate—one that both sides may benefit from equally. Is all this worth the cost of your resources? Your protection?"

Walter lifts his teacup to his lips, still observing me in quiet contemplation.

"And if these benefits aren't *tangible* enough for you, Walter, let me remind you of something." Noriko leans closer. "In the long run, being an enemy of the Cut would be *much* more expensive than being an ally."

He grins. "Is that a threat?"

"It's an offer."

The Serpent strokes his chin in thought. Dad's leg shakes under the table. Cecil taps his fingers, while Asa watches like a hawk.

The silence seems to stretch on for hours—until Walter speaks. "Have I ever introduced any of you to my niece and nephew?"

Noriko blinks. "Not that I can recall."

He retrieves a folded photograph from his pocket and slides it across the table. Not to Noriko, but to *me*. He waits for me to react. My heart pounds.

I look at him, then Dad, then pick up the photo carefully.

A younger version of Walter stands in the woods beside two small children. The boy seems like the oldest, maybe eight, with a messy head of chestnut-brown hair and a wide grin that makes wrinkles form at the corners of his eyes. His sister has the same hair, only neatly woven in two braids with pink bows at the end, which match the color of her skirt. She wears hiking boots and a white knit sweater with a cartoon cat in the center.

Then I find the soulless eyes of the dead deer she stands next to.

I realize she's holding a hunting rifle from the Yesterday's, which is almost bigger than she is. A chill runs through me when I realize who killed that deer.

She can't be any older than seven.

While hunting with Yesterday weapons is not *technically* allowed, with Immunity, Chips can get pardoned for almost anything that isn't treason. Money can buy you out of any trouble, Dad always says. I look up at Walter. *He's just as Immune as they come.*

I hand him the photo, which he tucks back into his pocket.

"Ansel and Lily live with me. It's safer that way, given who their father is. They will be pleased to have a new friend their age. We don't get many visitors—none they would be interested in, at least. They know not to get attached too quickly."

Noriko's brows pinch together. "What are you saying?"

"If you four were willing to risk further damaging our already fragile relationship by not only meeting with me in person, but *demanding* a Syndicate alliance—all to ensure the protection of this young man—then he clearly must be of high value to the Cut. You have genuine faith in his odds, don't you?"

"I do."

"Then I would trust no one else but myself with a task so sensitive. He'll be staying with me."

Cecil pales. Dad's eyes grow into saucers.

"We'll provide him with a new name and tracker, food to eat, a roof over his head. My associates and I will look out for him. I will see to it myself that he is most certainly prepared for training."

Noriko blinks in surprise before clearing her throat. "That's very generous of you, Walter, but we'd be more than happy with any—"

"It's already been decided."

She swallows nervously. "Is that... all?"

"We can work out the kinks of our new deal later. You're a smart woman, Noriko; you know the cost of not paying your dues in this line of work. Good business partnerships hinge on equality. I trust you'll return the Syndicate's generosity in full with time."

She hesitates, then nods.

"Consider this project a... trial run, of sorts. To see just how well we collaborate before making any hasty investments. And, when we are old and gray—or six feet under, if we fail to reach that point—*his* generation will be the one running the show." He nods in my direction. "Whatever seeds of alliance we sow now will eventually be tended by them. I think it would be wise to nurture these beginnings sooner rather than later.

"So what do you say, Noriko?" He flashes a chilling grin. "Are *you* willing to trust me?"

She studies him carefully for a moment, then glances at Asa. He seems more like a statue than a living person. She looks to Cecil next, who nods slightly—then my Dad. He locks his gaze with hers, jaw twitching.

She is the one who nods. He doesn't say a word.

She extends Walter her right and only hand. "To trust."

The Serpent takes it. "To trust, in the seeds we sow and a productive future."

We finish our tea in silence. Walter announces he should be leaving soon; Asa will escort him back to the city. He shakes our hands and we exit the cabin, but he stops when we're on the porch.

"I'd like to have a word with Aaron," the Serpent announces. "In private, if you don't mind."

My heart races. *What could he possibly want to talk to me about?*

The others swap nervous glances. Asa nods. "You all go ahead. I'll start packing." He walks back into the cabin, giving me a reassuring pat on the back. The door shuts, leaving Walter and I alone on the porch.

"I saw you eyeing my earrings earlier. Do you like them?" He pulls back his hair so I can see them better. "My niece made them for me. She's a very talented artist."

I force myself to speak. "They're... cool."

"Oh, don't worry. They're not *human* teeth. Only deer."

Only.

"Would you like a pair? Lily makes them for all my associates."

The question makes me blink. "Um... I'm good."

"Are you certain?"

Now I'm not so sure. *They're just earrings,* I remind myself. It's not like I'm rejecting *him,* is it?

"I'm not keen on the idea of running a needle through my earlobes at the moment," I say.

He arches a brow. My eyes widen. *Shit, did I offend him? Am I being too casual?*

To my surprise, he chuckles. "Understandable. There are other ways we display loyalty in my circle. I'm sure we'll figure something out when the time comes."

Before I can question him further, he pauses, bringing a hand to his ear. "Hear that?"

I shake my head. He crouches beside a pile of firewood on the porch—then his hand lunges out to snatch something.

When he draws it back, his fingers are wrapped around the throat of a snake.

It hisses and writhes in his grip with wide-open jaws, revealing a menacing set of fangs and a black forked tongue. It won't stop rattling its tail, an obnoxious clicking sound already getting on my nerves.

"*Crotalus oreganus,*" he says. "A western rattlesnake."

Daringly, he brings it closer to his face, inspecting it like it's a cool rock he found—not a living creature that could kill him almost instantly.

"Do you know what it means to be a pit viper, Aaron?" Walter turns the snake over. It squirms even more, but it's helpless in its cage of flesh.

"Not really."

"A pit viper sees more than we do." He points to a pair of pits in the snake's head, located near the eyes. "Do you know what these do?"

I crane my neck to see it better.

"Oh, don't be frightened. Take a closer look."

My hands shake. I step forward, flinching when the snake jerks in my direction. Walter tightens his grip around its neck.

"Are they uh... nostrils?" I ask.

He pauses. "How does a snake smell, Aaron?"

"They use their tongues."

"Their tongues do not taste. They pick up chemicals from the air and ground, from two different points. At the base of the snake's nasal cavity lies the Jacobson's organ, and attached to that are two ducts accessible at the roof of the mouth. When the snake retracts its tongue and touches both prongs to these ducts, the organ translates the collected chemicals into smells." Walter turns the snake over again in thought. It won't stop rattling. "They can smell in *three* dimensions. Is that not the most curious thing?"

"I guess."

"So, Aaron." He stares at me now, expressionless. "If you already knew snakes smell with their tongues, why did you suggest I was pointing to his nostrils?"

My stomach churns. *Why's he looking at me like I just punched him in the face?*

I shrug. "They look like nostrils."

"*Look like*. Such a detrimental assumption. Truth is never what it looks like." He huffs, then sighs. "I suppose your guess wasn't entirely baseless. Although rattlesnakes do have nostrils, they rely primarily on their tongue. *These* are pit organs. They allow the creature to perceive infrared heat."

"So... they see everything," I conclude. "Even in the dark."

Walter smirks. "Perhaps you are not entirely incompetent after all."

"Thanks?"

He observes me for a moment, then extends the snake to me. "Would you like to hold it?"

I flinch, stepping back. "Not really."

"He won't bite you, if you don't let him."

My heart thuds as I watch the rattlesnake writhe and hiss. My arms tremble. Its fangs look so sharp. The rattle continues to ring, an unending warning to those who tread where they shouldn't. *Why does this feel like a test?*

I glance at Walter, who watches me closely—just as he studied the snake before. Like I too am some *curious* specimen. I think back to Dad's warnings and shudder when I realize which threat would be deadlier to tread on.

I take a deep breath, ignore my buckling knees, and reach out.

A twig snaps just in time. My hand stills. I look over my shoulder to find Cecil approaching the cabin to fetch me. He sees the snake and freezes.

Walter notices his hesitation and smirks. He walks down the porch steps and crouches to let the creature go. Cecil jumps when the snake slithers by.

"Off you go, little viper." Walter rises and wipes his hands together, gaze still fixed to the foliage the rattlesnake disappeared into. "See everything."

"We really must be going," Cecil says firmly.

"So must I." Walter gives me a chilling smile. "You made the right choice."

He disappears back into the cabin. I whisper to Cecil. "And why do they call him the Serpent again?"

The question was rhetorical, but Cecil answers with a shrug. "He runs cold."

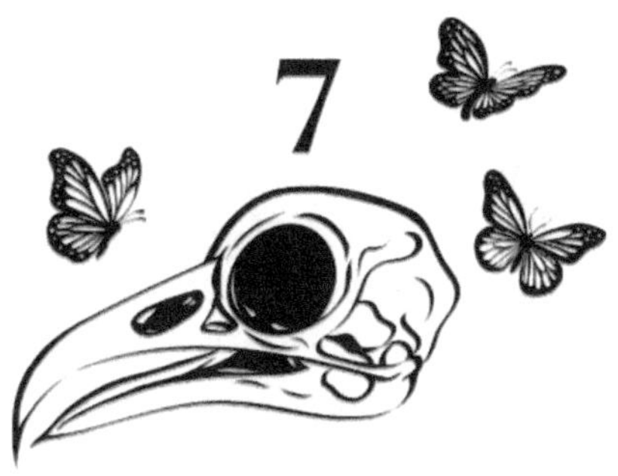

7

Monday, March 14

"You never told me you were turning my son into a *Viper*."

The words come from my father. They echo through the trees as Cecil and I catch up to him and Noriko, exchanging wary glances. We approach quietly.

Noriko keeps her voice low. "It was the only way to secure the deal."

"You're selling him to the Syndicate!"

"We're buying his protection," she corrects. "We're giving Walter a cut of our intel, that's all."

"Intel?" Dad huffs. "You heard the man. He bribes like he breathes. He wants a spy in the Corps long-term."

They haven't noticed us yet. I try to step forward, but Cecil stops me, shaking his head.

"The deal is done. We got what we asked for and manipulated our odds. You should be relieved."

Dad scoffs. "Relieved?"

"This is good news. We've spent *years* waiting for a breakthrough like this, and we got one. Just imagine what a real partnership with the Syndicate could mean—for all of us. Resources. Information. Weapons. Everything we need to put *real* change in action."

"In exchange for what?"

Noriko stays quiet.

"What happens if Aaron *does* make it past training, hm? What happens when he becomes a Chaser? Or more, like Walter wants?"

"He'll come back to us," Noriko insists. "We briefed him on the objective. Once he's gathered something of value, he'll return."

"He won't be here at the Cut anymore. He'll be off out there as Walter's pawn, *miles* from any of us. He's young and easy to manipulate, and that's what the Serpent does best."

I scowl. *What is he talking about?*

Noriko folds her arms. "He won't be a Double forever, alright? Just enough to—"

"And what if he doesn't want to quit?"

Quiet.

"Walter will promise him the world. He'll buy him nice things. Offer him money and drugs and women and all the other bargaining chips he uses to hold power among the Immune."

I glare, itching to interrupt—but Cecil places a hand on my shoulder, keeping me quiet. *Why can't I say anything?*

"Let them hash this one out, kid," he mutters under his breath.

"But—"

"Otherwise they'll give each other the silent treatment for a week, and I'll be the messenger."

I frown.

"And how could he resist?" Dad chuckles bitterly. "He says he's *suffocating* here. He wants to be out there, where it's new, and exciting, a-and..." He runs his hands through his hair, squeezing his eyes shut. "*God.* Does he have any idea what it took to build the Cut? What we sacrificed to give him this life in the first place?"

His voice cracks, taking me by surprise.

"I'd give it all up ten times over again just to keep him safe, and you're throwing him straight into a nest of vipers. *Literally.*"

Noriko glances in our direction now. "Simon—"

"They'll eat him alive, Noriko." I only know my Dad's shoulders as rigid, but they melt. Desperate. Shaking. "If he goes down that path, we'll lose him."

"*Simon.*"

She nods toward us. His lips part when he sees Cecil and me, standing a yard away. He stares for a long time.

With one last glare for our Commander, he turns to keep walking back home.

We hike in silence for a while. I trail with Cecil a few yards behind the others. They discuss something quietly. Somberly.

"Okay—tell me more about that punch," I say. "Or how you *survived* it. Dad was acting like the Serpent would skin me alive if I looked at him funny."

"Schneider would have done something much worse if Noriko hadn't convinced him to leave me alone."

"Back in the cabin..." I step over a root. "Why did he seem... afraid of her?"

"I think she's the one person on the planet who could ever sway the Serpent. Not by much, but enough to save my life, at the very least."

"Why is that?"

"They shared some university classes together."

"And?"

"He and Noriko may have had a brief... fling."

My eyes widen. "I thought she and Asa started dating in high school."

"They took a short break in college."

"Why?"

"Beats me. All I know is they were busy getting into all sorts of trouble with Walter and his friends."

"I can't even picture her with a guy like the Serpent." I shake my head, staring at our Commander as she walks with Dad. "Why is he so afraid of her, then?"

"As far as I know, she's the only living person who knows his worst fear. She hasn't even told *me* what it is."

"Then why doesn't he just..." I swipe my finger across my throat. "Take care of her?"

Cecil chuckles. "She also happens to be the only person he'll never have the guts to kill."

"A soft spot."

"We've all got one." He stares at Noriko as she walks ahead of us. "Unfortunately, that's the closest thing to an underbelly I know of. Like I said —he's untouchable."

"But you punched him."

"A few years after Noriko founded the Cut, she and Asa arranged a meeting with Schneider to discuss a partnership between his Syndicate network and the Unseen. That's when I met him for the first time."

"What happened?"

"You know how Simon is. He doesn't put up with bullshit and the Serpent's full of it. The alliance proposal fell through. Old wounds got rehashed, an argument ensued, and he threatened your dad."

"So you *punched him*?"

"I was only a couple years Unseen. Didn't realize how big of a deal it was until after the fact."

"Guys like that deserve to be humbled every now and then."

"Well don't get any ideas." Cecil sighs. "We aren't *enemies* with the Syndicate. We agreed to leave each other alone, which is why it's taken this long to even think about a partnership. But our standing is shaky at best."

"Because of the punch."

"Young me had a real habit of screwing things up." He shakes his head. "It sucks, but with enough money, some people are pretty untouchable. I'm lucky I still have my hand."

I nod, swallowing the lump in my throat. This man sounds terrifying. He *is* terrifying. And he's supposed to become my teacher?

I feel that shiver again, like my blood has gone cold.

What have I gotten myself into?

We're back by sunset. I continue learning about the Corps and basic combat training with Viv until nightfall. My knife throwing's getting better by the day. I head home and sit on the back porch, watching Gooseberry chew on tufts of dry grass.

The night air is hot and clings to my skin. It smells like the ripening blackberry bramble lining our property, the rich smoke of something grilling over by the Block. Crickets cry. Bullfrogs croak somewhere in the pond a few yards into the woods. Insects buzz and hum like electricity. There is so much noise, and Gooseberry doesn't seem to notice any of it.

I study the lonesome goat and the fence we're both trapped within. My throat tightens. *I've made him a prisoner here too.*

The back door swings shut. Dad walks out with two steaming mugs of herbal tea. He sits in the wooden chair to my right and hands me a cup. *Lavender*, I note. My favorite.

We watch Gooseberry in silence until Dad speaks. "He's quite the little menace, you know."

I nod.

Gooseberry gets bored and trots up to a growth of bright purple vetch, aggressively tugging at the leaves.

"He's been messing up the yard all day. Eating everything." Dad sips his tea. "I gave up trying to get him to stop a long time ago. Maybe he'll learn to settle for grass when he eats something he shouldn't."

It's quiet again. A soft gust of wind breathes through distant leaves, shaking pine needles and carrying their smell with it. I think the evergreens are something I could never tire of. The trees might be the only things about this place I'll truly miss when it's time to leave for the city.

"I had a friend once," Dad says, pulling me out of my thoughts.

"Okay."

"You know the story." He sighs. "Your mother and I grew up with Noriko and Asa in Port Keys. Eventually, we all went off to college—a small school in the next city over. We lived together for quite some time. Those were the best years of my life."

Dad smiles slightly for a moment, staring at something I don't see. Then the warmth fades, and he looks into his cup instead. "Until our trouble got the best of us."

"What do you mean?"

"We've always shared the ideals we hold now, long before we started the Cut. We were young and stupid and dreamed of changing the world, as you do in early adulthood." He takes a sip. "One day, we stumbled across someone who seemed to share similar beliefs."

Something about the way he says that gives me goosebumps. "The Serpent."

Dad nods. "That was before he and his brother took over the Syndicate. We got caught up in some things we shouldn't have, but... we earned a close companion in the process."

My nose crinkles. "Him?"

"Not Walter. Someone else." Dad stares at the pines. The parts where the light from our moth-ridden sconces don't reach. "His name was Cain."

He lets out a deep sigh. "Eventually, Noriko had the twins, got Picked, became a Runner, and started the Cut. She found Cecil quickly after that. For a while it was just the two of them, until Asa and I started bringing people over."

"Was Cain one of them?"

Dad shakes his head. "He was an important contact during our founding days. Every now and then he'd arrange for the Syndicate to send supplies to the Cut. He'd find people who felt trapped in the Syndicate or chipped life and helped them switch over to our side."

"Sounds like a solid guy."

"He was."

It goes quiet. "What happened to him?"

"I was in my early twenties. The Cut was small, but growing. I'd finally convinced your mother to marry me. I wasn't fully Unseen yet, but Asa and I were helping them from our side. Smuggling trips, supply runs, completing odd jobs for Walter in exchange for resources. We weren't partnered with the entire Syndicate, necessarily—just trading favors with the Serpent now and then. It felt like I was finally doing something worthwhile. Like I was really making change."

Dad takes a slow sip from his mug. He stares at Gooseberry, who's moved on from the vetch to a patch of grass. "Asa and I were on a smuggling job with this friend of ours when we were captured by Chasers."

My eyes widen. "You got caught?"

"We were far from Seattle's Agency headquarters, so they took us to an abandoned warehouse. They decided to run their own interrogations while waiting for higher-ups to arrive."

A knot forms in my throat as I recall everything Dad said about Chaser interrogations. The hairs on the back of my neck stand on end. "What did they do?"

"I was tied to a chair. Broke free with this." He lifts up his jeans, flashing me the scabbard tied to his ankle. He leans back. "Chairs make good weapons too."

I conceal a smirk. "Really?"

He shrugs. "Sometimes fighting back is as simple as using what you already have. And the element of surprise, of course."

"Good to know."

He chuckles, but it fades quickly. He takes a long sip of tea. "By the time I knocked out my Chaser and made it to Cain, I was too late."

His gaze hollows. I stare at the pines, thinking back to the torture methods Dad mentioned before I agreed to this job. "All those things you mentioned..."

Dad can only nod.

For a long time, the crickets do the talking for us. I watch Gooseberry play in the yard, so oblivious to everything around him. It's like he doesn't even feel trapped at all.

"Death is common in our world, Aaron. I don't want you subjected to the things I've seen. Why do you think I brought you here all these years ago?"

To keep me under your control, I want to say. *To force me to live the life you wanted for me, against Mom's wishes.*

"To keep you hidden," he says. "To keep you safe."

My jaw tightens. I'm still mad at him. *He's* the one who made me Unseen, and he had the audacity to question my loyalty? *Bringing me tea and pretending to be nice doesn't take any of that away.*

"I know I don't say it as much as I should, but... you mean everything to me, Aaron. And I don't want to lose you." When he looks at me, his eyes are glossy. "It's not too late to back out of this. No one will think any less of you."

It's quiet for a moment. I keep my voice calm, but certain. "You can't keep me here."

Dad nods again. The crickets sing for a long time until he heads inside. I stay in my chair, and I fall asleep to the hum of the cage I know so well.

The last sip of tea in my mug grows cold.

Tuesday, March 15

Milkweed is what did it.

I find Gooseberry next to a shrub of it when I wake, completely still. His fur is just as cold as my tea.

In April, the milkweed will bloom with clusters of pink stars. Their nectar smells sweet, like vanilla.

In April, there is a kaleidoscope of monarchs that seems smaller every year it passes through the Olympic Peninsula. They will drink the nectar, which makes things cold, and they will not lay their eggs on any other plant. Only milkweed.

In April, the grave I dug will be filled with worms.

Someday beyond April, beyond me, there will be no flowers. No monarchs. No eggs.

Just worms.

I spend three days locked in my room. I stay in bed and stare at the ceiling, unable to talk.

No one asks me to come out.

Saturday, March 26

The weeks pass quickly. Dad and I have a quiet goodbye. Cecil promises a pool tournament when I get back. Beau sobs.

I rise with the sun and meet Asa at the cabin. The woods are damp and blanketed in thick mist. We trek through tunnels of spruce and cedar, hemlock and pine. Every twisting branch holds drapes of lichen. The air smells like moss and amber.

For as long as I've known him, Asa McLellan has been a quiet man. It makes him unassuming, even with his noticeable height—and that worn brown Stetson he insists on wearing. Hats have always seemed impractical to me, but Asa argues it keeps the sun out of his eyes. Dad says it belonged to *his* father.

That's what I focus on as we walk—Asa's hat as he leads me farther from home with every step, possibly for good.

"How much longer?" I ask, stepping over a root.

Asa doesn't look back. "You'll know when we get there."

"And where is *there*, exactly?"

"Same answer applies."

I lean my head back, adjusting the backpack slung over my shoulder with a groan. "That's not helpful."

"Neither is complaining."

I kick a rock. "I'm just bored."

"Bored?" He gestures around him. "You've got all this to look at. You'll miss it where you're going. The city's got some trees, but it's no forest."

I frown and shove my hands in my pockets.

No one ever gives me good details, but I've gathered enough to know that Asa is escorting me to a rendezvous point. From there, someone will pick me up and take me to the Serpent's estate.

Apparently, I'll be attending the training center in Seattle, not the one outside of Port Keys; every time the Cut plants a Double, we alternate between the two to keep the Corps off our tail.

Preparation. I've heard that word a thousand times since this whole plan was put into place, and I still don't understand what that entails. All I know is that given my unique upbringing, I'll need to spend a month or two learning how to live like Chips before I go off to training on Saturday, June 18th.

Ninety-six days until I'll be putting my life at risk to complete a job no other Double has survived.

You're the one who signed up for this, remember? I remind myself. *You're doing this for a good reason. You're helping out.*

I stare ahead, watching Asa's hat.

And maybe I can finally prove myself to them.

"How are the kids?" I ask, trying to force a conversation out of Asa. If there's one subject that can get him talking, it's his family.

I can't see his face as I walk behind him, but I can hear the smile in his voice. "They're doing alright."

"How's that new tincture Dad made for Margot?"

"The *desmodium molliculum* and *pimpinella* mix?"

"Uh... yeah. That."

"She picked up a book the other day." Asa throws a pleased glance over his shoulder at me. "She's already read half of it."

I can't conceal my grin. "Really?"

Maybe I'm not as well-versed in my dad's craft as I should be by now, but I do know that for the past two years, Margot McLellan's health has been declining. She hasn't been able to read or write or do basic math. From what I've heard, she spends all day in bed. When school's in season, she sleeps as soon as she gets home.

This is the first sign of improvement we've seen in a very long time.

Asa's daughter has had chronic Lyme disease since she was little. It's a real tricky thing. Symptoms can come and go in waves. There is essentially no part of the body the disease can't reach, and antibiotics aren't always effective. Dad's been sending her naturopathic medicine ever since he first suspected she had it.

Margot isn't Unseen yet and doesn't even know we exist, but for years, Dad's been working with Asa to create a protocol for her. It's a difficult process that requires a lot of adjustment, because some medicines don't work. You have to balance killing off the disease with adequate detox, otherwise she'll feel sicker.

Treatment is a rollercoaster, and things often get worse before they get better. There are ups and downs, bad days and worse days. But Margot reading—for the first time in what feels like forever—is great news.

In spite of the excitement, something in me unsettles for a moment. I chew on my lip in thought.

I love plants. I love healing and I always have, but...

I pin my eyes to Asa's hat. *Do I really have it in me?*

Part of me is convinced that if I ever do give healing a real try, it'll only end in disappointment. That I'll never be good enough for Dad, or myself, or the people I'm trying to help. Nothing I ever do is good enough for his standards.

I stare at my shoes. *Maybe this job is what I'm meant to do instead,* I wonder. *Or maybe I'll never figure it out.*

Asa stops in front of a big shape covered in a blue tarp, twigs, and vines. He brushes off the debris and yanks off the tarp to reveal a boxy sedan from the Yesterdays—one I recognize instantly.

Asa's car is the only other vehicle I've ridden in, aside from the one Beau and I wrecked. It's the one he usually uses when he and Dad go on smuggling trips, or when they take me to Port Keys to visit Mom and Lori.

"We're driving to the rendezvous point?" I ask.

"Unless you want to hike for a week." Asa pulls out his keys and climbs in the driver's seat.

I shake my head and walk toward the passenger's side. My hand pauses inches away from the door handle. *Why can't I stop shaking?*

My breathing halts. For a moment, all I can do is picture a deer with glowing white eyes. It can see the headlights. *And it doesn't even move.*

"You coming?" Asa asks.

This is my last chance to back out, isn't it?

I think about Dad. Cecil. Noriko. Beau. My mother and the sister I miss more than anything. And beyond them, I think about what I'm doing this for.

The world is a real shitty place, but maybe I can make it better. Even just a little.

They all need me to do this.

I climb in the car and try to forget what it feels like to crash one.

Saturday, March 26

I wake to the sound of a car door slamming.

It's night. My neck hurts from leaning against the window for hours. I rub the back of it with a wince, right as Asa opens my door.

"Rise and shine," he says. "We're here."

I glare and stumble out of the car. Groggily, I put on my regular glasses, since Asa said I won't need to hide my scar. For now, at least. It's too dark for me to see much as my eyes adjust, but something smells familiar. I can taste salt in the air. Seaweed. The dusty, mineral scent of coarse sand, like stone after rain. I hear the faint whispering of waves. The creaking of a wooden sign swaying in the breeze behind me.

I spin around. We're in a gravel parking lot. There are no street lights nearby, no glowing windows. Just a moonlit sea in the distance—and the shop planted in front of it.

My heart stops. *Port Keys Coffee Co.*

I stare at Asa, unable to breathe or blink. I try to pinch myself, certain I'm dreaming, but my hands won't move.

Asa can't hide a wide grin. And I can't help but laugh.

I don't waste a second before running up to the shop's salt-eaten porch.

I reach into a potted plant, pull out the key, and unlock the front door. A little bell rings over my head and I don't even bother closing it.

The shop is empty, chairs upturned and resting on the tables. I hurry to the back and jog upstairs, then down the hall, until I'm standing in front of a closed bedroom door. I knock. And I wait.

A woman with long dark hair opens the door—pointing a Yesterday shotgun in my face.

"Listen here, pal. You've got two options and only one of them involves breathing." She adjusts her aim. "Leave, or I'll put a bullet in your head."

I smile. "Hi Mom."

She lowers the gun, eyes wide. Her lips part as the realization settles in. "Aaron."

I wave.

She pulls me into a hug so tight I worry my spine might snap. "You scared the shit out of me."

I wrap my arms around her. My heart sinks when I realize I'm a whole four inches taller. *Has it really been that long?* I bury my head in her hair and kiss the top of her head. She smells like coffee and rose oil.

"God, I'm so sorry, baby." She pulls away and holds my face in her hands. She's smiling so wide her eyes crinkle. I think they're watering too. "I don't have my contacts in."

We chuckle as a door creaks behind me. I turn around slowly.

Down the hall, my sister stands in a hoodie and bright red Christmas pajamas, rubbing her eyes. "What's with all the noise?"

Lori squints to make out the scene. Before I can blink, she's hugging me more violently than our mother. She laughs, bright and contagious. I do the same. She pulls away. "Is it Christmas?"

I point to her pajamas. "You tell me."

Her brows crease. "It's not my birthday, is it?"

"That's in July."

"And Mom's is in September."

"Uh, yeah?"

"So... what are you doing here?"

I open my mouth to respond, then pause. I glance at Mom and back down at Lori. If they figure out what I'm really doing in Port Keys, they'll never let me leave.

I think about prisons from the Yesterdays. We don't have them anymore, and the only ones left standing serve as the Tombs, but I've read about them. Sometimes they'd let you pick your last meal before execution.

I'm glad Asa knew what I'd choose.

I place a hand over my heart in feigned offense. "Do I really need an excuse to visit my annoying little sister?"

Lori rolls her eyes. Mom swats me in the shoulder and I giggle like a child. For the briefest of moments, I feel like one.

The four of us sit in a booth downstairs, sipping coffee at midnight in the light of a vintage stained glass lamp.

Well, I'm not drinking coffee. Mom knows I prefer tea. As much as I fight it, I am my father's son, after all.

"So." Mom clears her throat. "How's everything?"

"Good."

"I see you twice a year if I'm lucky, and that's your answer?"

"He stole a goat," Asa says plainly.

"He did *what*?"

Asa folds his arms. "Oh yeah. And a car."

Lori laughs. "A car?"

"Crashed it too."

Mom covers her mouth in disbelief.

I speak before she can scold me. "Okay, for the record, Beau's the one who crashed it, not me."

"You were in a crash?" She takes both my hands in hers. "Are you hurt?"

"I didn't make it, unfortunately."

She drops my hands with a frown, shaking her head. "Spare me the details. I don't even want to know." We sip our drinks silently for a while until she clears her throat. "How's your father?"

I nod, avoiding eye contact. "He's uh... he's good."

Mom does the same. "Good."

She doesn't ask for elaboration this time.

When she's not looking, I study her face. She seems so tired. She fidgets with the emerald ring on her left index finger. I can't tell if she's annoyed, or misses him.

Mom was livid when Dad first took me to the Cut. I can't blame her. I'd be pissed too, if my partner disappeared for four years—just to come back and turn my only son Unseen. The note he left behind was the only reason she knew it was he who took me. He didn't bring Lori with us because he didn't even know he *had* a daughter at the time. She was asleep in the other room.

The note contained instructions for Mom to join the Cut. She refused.

I went a whole year without talking to anyone. I didn't even know he was my dad at first; I thought he was just some *Undergrounder* who came to steal me away, like in the ghost stories. When I first got to the Cut, he couldn't even explain who he was. I'd just cry and hide from him.

He did debug me, after all.

For months, Noriko was the only person I wasn't afraid of. I warmed up to Cecil too, and then eventually—after many wooden jackalope carvings —my dad.

That's why it took so long for him to learn about Lori. We left for our first visit to Port Keys an hour after I first mentioned her in passing.

It took a few years for Mom to stop shouting at Dad for what he did. Throwing things at him. She wanted to take me back, but that was impossible. I had no tracker anymore. It was too risky. The first few trips, he'd just drop me off so I could visit with her and Lori, and then he'd come back for me a few days later.

Eventually, after enough arguments and Port Keys trips, she let him stay. They couldn't help but warm up to each other again. Little by little, like slowly thawing ice.

Even as a kid—even through the bickering—I always knew they loved each other. I caught onto their moments of vulnerability. The two of them dancing to Yesterday music in the kitchen. Stolen glances, soft smiles. Pancake breakfasts. Mom tracing the carvings of wooden animals he'd make for her. Dad brushing a hand against her back as he walked past.

Despite the hatred they pretend to feel, I know they still love each other. They're just... living on different sides of the divide, trying to do what they think is best for their children.

When I find someone I care about that much, I don't want to be like my parents. *I don't want to choose sides.*

We chat for a while longer until Asa and Mom shoo us away so they can discuss something in private. Probably stuff about Dad, or some other Unseen business they tend to leave me out of, as per usual. I doubt he'll tell her about my job. She'd never let me leave.

Lori and I sit on the roof, watching waves roll in the distance. It's a quiet and mostly windless night. We don't say anything. We don't have much to catch up on. Nothing really happens at the Cut, and Lori doesn't like talking about school.

Deep down, we both know we share a noteworthy lack of friends. The same way we share our father's resilience and our mother's attitude. Their dark hair and warm brown eyes. Mom's sharp jaw. Dad's dimpled, slightly crooked grin.

But that's the thing about Lori and me. We don't need to talk about our loneliness to understand it. We just do. And we've always been that way. Even with the separate lives we lead, there is no one on the planet who gets me like she does.

"I miss you," I finally say.

"I never miss you."

I frown.

She points to her head. "You're always up here."

I feel like crying. I don't have a witty remark—just a tightening throat and a knot in my chest that won't unravel. I force myself to change the subject with a smirk. "I think we're long overdue for a game of Shorebird."

She grins. "You're on."

We go down to the moonlit beach and wait for the waves to retract. When they do, we race to the shore. We fall to our knees and dig with our hands until we see little gray sand crabs burrowing deeper. We pluck them up gently, collecting them until the waves chase us away—only to return when the water retreats again. Back and forth, running and giggling like children. Whoever finds the most sand crabs in five minutes wins, and we keep time by counting the seconds aloud. Whoever finds the *least* has to wade into the icy water and dunk their head beneath the surface.

Three hundred seconds go by so much quicker than I remember. Lori has gathered seven crabs. I've only found five.

Lori snorts as I remove my glasses, set them on a log, and take the dreaded walk into the sea. The moment the water touches my skin, I let out a high-pitched squeal. She cackles. I don't waste any time dunking my head.

Someone splashes me when I resurface. I open my eyes to find Lori standing three feet in front of me, hair just as soaked as mine. The water is so freezing I think my toes might fall off. But we laugh and we splash and tease each other like no time has passed. Muscle memory.

After a while, it doesn't feel cold anymore. Even as my entire body shakes and my fingers turn blue, there is warmth here, and she could outburn the sun.

We head back to shore and sit on the driftwood log. We catch our breath and let our smiles and laughter die down. I stare at the pile of glossy, writhing crabs. A few of them scurry back into the sand.

"This game is kind of cruel, isn't it?" I ask quietly.

Lori shrugs. "We're gentle."

"They look confused."

"They'll find their way home."

Home. I stare behind me, at the whitewashed walls of my mother's coffee shop. I study the distant pines beyond that, picturing what Dad must be doing in our cabin. I wonder if Beau's still awake.

Then I look at my sister. She yawns and leans her head on my shoulder, where she falls asleep.

I'm not sure how much time has passed before Asa approaches. A single nod is all it takes for me to know it's time to leave.

I carry Lori to bed. Mom is already asleep in hers. I'm sure they think we'll be staying for a few days, as we usually do. I don't think I can handle saying goodbye to them.

I watch Port Keys Coffee Co. shrink through the rear windshield of

Asa's car. I think of the places and people I call home, and I wonder if I'll ever find my way back.

JULIA ROSEMARY TURK

Asa's car. I think of the places and people I call home, and I wonder if I'll ever find my way back.

PART TWO
DULL

Sunday, March 27

The Serpent's manor is a Georgian-style monster with beige brick scales, a dozen double-hung windows for eyes, and wrought iron fences like sharpened fangs.

It looks like it could devour me alive.

I'm in the back of a sleek black sedan, driven by a woman in an expensive green suit. Her inky hair is slicked back in a knot so tight I get a headache just thinking about it. Although her Card tattoos just barely peek out from her sleeves, I can see they are both crossed out with thick black *X*s. She wears gold-plated deer teeth earrings like Walter and is missing her right pinky finger.

Last night, Asa drove me to an abandoned parking lot to meet a woman who said her name was Ruth Harmon, and nothing else. Asa seemed to recognize her. He hugged me goodbye before I climbed in the car and fell asleep. Only when I felt the road shift from cracked and bumpy to smooth and soundless did I open my eyes.

Now I press my head against the tinted window at my left, taking in the sights as we drive through a guarded gate and over a long, twisting road lined with towering cypress trees. I don't wear my sunglasses at the moment.

Ruth said I don't need to for now, but I have them packed with me just in case. I wear my regular glasses instead and can't help but feel exposed with my scar out in the open. And in chipped territory too.

We reach a circular cobblestone driveway with a fountain in the center. Ruth parks the car and opens the door for me. I step out, slinging my backpack over my shoulder. I take one look at my oversized black tee, torn jeans, and dirty hiking boots before gazing up at the mansion in front of me.

"Good God," I mutter. "This guy's loaded."

Ruth doesn't say anything, but I swear I see the corner of her lip twitch.

The estate is perched upon a secluded bluff. In one direction, the sun rises over a glistening Puget Sound, dark blue and dreary. We must be on the west side, then—not far out of Seattle. In the other, the white-capped Olympic Mountains stand regal like gods. The sky behind them is a soft periwinkle, streaked with hints of lilac, blush, and peach.

It'd be pretty if I wasn't scared shitless.

Ruth walks me up the driveway in silence. The heels of her loafers click against the stone, echoing off the manor's monstrous walls. She leads me up too many porch steps and pauses at a set of dark doors to enter a code into a keypad.

The lock beeps. She swings the doors open and gestures for me to walk through. "Welcome to Whitestag Estate."

Of course it has a name. Rich people in movies always name their houses.

I take a deep breath and step inside.

The doors slam shut behind us, but I barely hear it. I stand in the entryway upon checkered black-and-white marble tile, rooted in place, unable to blink or breathe as I absorb the sight before me. Twin staircases covered in velvety red carpet spiral on either side of the foyer, intersecting at the second floor landing. The railings are wooden and so elaborately carved I can't fight a twinge of jealousy toward whoever crafted them. An elaborate crystal chandelier the size of a cow hangs above me, glistening with faux candlelight. A sculpted pair of two-headed cobras guard both staircases with their fangs bared. Their eyes look like obsidian. One of them is missing.

I've never felt more out of place in my life.

The manor is eerily quiet. I can't tell if that's because it's so early in the morning or if it's always this empty. Ruth leads me up the stairs and down an ornately carpeted hallway, which smells like wintergreen and the remnants of something smokey. The walls are spotted with bronze sconces in the shape of snakes, also with obsidian eyes. I can't shake the feeling that I'm being watched.

We reach a tall oak door at the end of the hall. Ruth knocks in an odd rhythm—the same one Noriko used back at the cabin. A familiar voice calls out from within.

"Come in."

Ruth opens the door. The Serpent sits behind a massive black desk, sipping coffee while flipping through a mess of documents. Ruth pulls out a cushioned chair with a towering back and gestures for me to sit. I do.

We wait in uncomfortable silence as Walter continues reading through the papers, not sparing either of us a glance. Like we're not even here. I take the opportunity to observe the room.

It's a large study with paneled oak walls and more bronze snake sconces. Elegant but efficient, with minimal decor. For the few decorative pieces he decided to include, Walter made sure to go bold. And weird. I realize this as I stare at the head of a white buck mounted to the wall behind him. It stares back with dead black eyes.

It's not the only taxidermied specimen in the room. All across the wall, the heads of hares, mallards, beavers, bobcats, and even some rats watch with the same soulless voids.

It makes me sick.

Walter finishes jotting something down and glances at Ruth. "Leave us alone for now. Thank you."

She eyes me suspiciously—as though *I* might be a danger to *him*—then takes her leave. Only when the door clicks behind her do I realize how small I feel in this chair.

"So." Walter knits his fingers together. "How was the trip?"

"Fine."

He spreads out his arms. "Enjoying the scenery?"

I look through the window and catch a glimpse of the mountains in the distance. I nod.

"I'm not talking about the mountains, Aaron."

My forehead wrinkles—then I realize what he's gesturing to. *The animals.*

"Oh." I clear my throat. "Uh... sure."

"My niece Lily is quite the artist, much like yourself. Taxidermy is a hobby of hers."

My brows crease. Before I can ask how he knows about my art, he nods toward a few leftover ink stains on my fingers. Even I hadn't noticed them.

"I do hope you two get along," he says. "Lily doesn't have many friends. She could use a healthy dose of socialization."

I can see why. I try not to make a face. "I'm sure we will."

"So, Aaron, let's cut to the chase." Walter leans back, arms folded. "Your father holds quite a bit of sway at the Cut, doesn't he?"

"I guess..." I glance around, unsure of who might be listening now that we're in chipped territory.

"No need to worry about mics. It's a privilege we pay handsomely for."

"Okay."

"You're close with Cecil and Noriko as well? Last I heard, your Commander's something like a godmother to you."

I nod.

He picks at his nails. "Is that why they're throwing you to the wolves? To toughen you up so you can fill their shoes someday, like some Unseen heir?"

"No one's throwing me anywhere," I snap, only to remember who I'm talking to. I lower my voice. "I volunteered."

"I see." His eyes narrow. "So you feel unproven."

"Sorry?"

"You're young. Inexperienced. To volunteer or such a drastic task... I can only assume you aim to prove something to someone. Your father?"

I don't answer.

"Your commander?"

I shake my head.

"Yourself, perhaps?" I still don't know what to say, and Walter chuckles. "You young folk are too easy to crack. So desperate for approval. Acceptance."

"It's not that deep, alright? I'm just trying to help."

He raises his hands in mock surrender. "If you say so."

I tap my foot. I don't want to look at Walter or the dead animals, so I stare out the window again. The sun has mostly risen now. *I wonder if Mom and Lori are up yet.*

"If it's acceptance you're after, then mine is all yours," he says lightly. "You're a guest here. Ask for anything and it will be granted. My staff will treat you as one of our own. But approval..." His voice flattens. "Approval is something you earn."

"Alright."

"You don't strike me as stupid, Aaron." He swivels slightly in his chair. "You understand there is more to this arrangement than your upcoming training alone, yes?"

"I do."

I think.

"The Syndicate is what the Corps likes to call us... less-conforming Immune folk. But like the Unseen, we're fragmented. My family holds Seattle. The Cut, meanwhile, is perhaps the most dominant rebel force in the entire Pacific Region. It is only natural to desire a partnership between our side and yours."

"You didn't sound so eager at the cabin," I say.

"Politics is theater. You will learn that soon enough. I had to maintain the upper hand. Draw out your commander's desperation to... sway the odds in our favor, if you will."

"So you want a real partnership," I clarify. "Not just a truce."

"Something like that." He shrugs. "If there is anything you will learn from me, it is that survival is persuasion. Power belongs to those who strike better deals."

"And let me guess." I fold my arms. "I'm your stepping stone to scoring something better."

"You are the first step in the right direction."

Why is he being this transparent? What deal is he trying to sway with me? I squint at him, trying to read his expression. To learn what he's *really* thinking.

He catches on and grins. I decide I'd have better luck with one of the animal heads.

"You're a guest," he repeats. "But make no mistake. We run a tight ship here at Whitestag. I am not generous nor forgiving. The safety and protection your Commander secured for you only extends as far as you are willing to reach. If you are useful, you will be treated as such. If I am going to invest my time and energy in preparing you for training, you will return that investment through your service. You will be my fox in the henhouse of headless chickens that is the Corps, but until then, you must navigate *our* world."

His fox? I thought I was the Cut's.

"Luxuries are deceiving, Aaron. Wealth is not always kind. You will learn things here that the Cut could never teach you. *See* things you could not have imagined during your quaint little life making tea with your father, or whatever it is you do. You will not put your nose where it doesn't belong, and you will keep your wits about you. Your name means nothing here. The moment you become an inconvenience, you will be dealt with accordingly."

I swallow. "Dealt with how?"

"Do you know how the Chaser Corps handles retirement?"

I shake my head.

"You are a Chaser until death, or retirement. One is involuntary, the other is a choice—but they both earn you the same fate. There is no leaving the Corps unless your heart stops beating. Do you know why that is?"

A chill spreads across my shoulders. "Because they know too much."

"Clever boy." The Serpent smiles. "See? You're catching on. So long as you behave, there is nothing to be afraid of."

"And if I don't?"

The question seems to take him by surprise. He opens and shuts his mouth in thought, then leans forward, lacing his hands together.

"Your assignment puts more than your life on the line. One wrong move could initiate the Cut's downfall—possibly the entire Unseen network in the Pacific Region. If you're reported, the Corps will interrogate you until you can't tell up from down or day from night, and before you know it, you've given them *exactly* what they need to destroy everything you love. All it takes is one person to say the right thing to the authorities." His eyes darken. "You do understand what I'm saying, don't you?"

I try not to look at the dead deer on the wall. I wonder what he did to piss Walter off.

"I understand."

"I'm only being considerate here. Do take my warning to heart. We wouldn't want you making any decisions you'd regret."

I clench my jaw. His *warning* feels more like a noose than a favor. I force a toothless grin. "I won't."

He chuckles. "Wonderful."

And just like that, the politeness returns. He pats the desk and rubs his hands together. "Well, I'm sure you must be tired and hungry from your travels. Sundays at Whitestag are for relaxing. Ruth will give you a tour and see to it that you are fed, and you'll have the rest of the day to settle in."

Relaxing? If he didn't just threaten my entire family, maybe I'd laugh. My dad would eat a doughnut before letting me spend a Sunday without a to-do list.

But Dad isn't here.

Ruth escorts me out of the office, down more impressive corridors until we reach a room even larger than Walter's study. My jaw drops at the four-poster bed, intricately carved from polished dark oak. Exposed beams cut through the ceiling, and the walls display detailed wainscoting and crown molding. Dad would lose his mind if he saw this woodwork.

Stop doing that, I tell myself. *He's around to get in your head anymore, remember? This is the break you've been needing for so long.*

Relax. Simple. I can relax.

I lose my confidence when I notice the framed bat specimen hanging on the wall above the bed.

"This room is yours," Ruth says. "Breakfast is ready."

I toss my bag into the room and let myself grin. A queen-sized bed, just for me? Breakfast I don't have to make myself? Soft bedding and mountains of throw pillows? Freedom to spend my day as I please, without my dad's nagging?

I could get used to this.

I grin on our way out. "You Chips have it *real* good."

Ruth doesn't say anything to that.

I'm escorted to a dining room downstairs with glossy parquet flooring, high ceilings, and elaborate chandeliers. Light spills in through two sets of French doors. Through them, I see a vast courtyard filled with stone fountains and perfectly manicured flower beds. I think back to my days spent shoveling compost back home and wonder who takes care of the gardens here. Definitely not Walter.

I almost smirk. *Or me.*

A large plate and a glass of orange juice waits for me at the end of the table. As far as I can tell, we're the only ones around when Ruth pulls out a chair and gestures for me to sit.

"What's this?" I ask.

"Smoked salmon Eggs Benedict."

"Egg who?"

She sighs. "Egg, toast, sauce, fish."

I frown. "I'm not stupid, okay? I just didn't grow up all *rich* and *fancy*."

"Neither did I."

I don't say anything else because I'm too busy eating what might be the best meal of my life. Just a few weeks ago, I thought nothing could top fried turkey legs and mint chip ice cream. I was wrong. This tastes clean. Fresh. Expensive. Like it won't make me throw up and crash a car.

"I think I'm in love with smoked salmon," I say through my last mouthful.

Ruth nods and takes my empty plate. "I'll let the chef know."

She returns with seconds and I eat it all.

After breakfast, Ruth gives me a tour of the estate. The manor is huge, filled with more rooms than I can count or pay attention to. Instead, I observe the detailed woodwork, the expert craftsmanship displayed in every nook and cranny. There is no inch of the house untouched by some sort of artistry. I never knew buildings could be so beautiful.

The gardens take even more of my breath away. Ruth's retelling of the estate's history fades to background noise as I take in the large rectangular pond in the center, flanked by potted pink tulips, flowerbeds buzzing with bees, and manicured lawns on all sides. Stone pathways circle the garden's perimeter, paved alongside thick hedge walls. A wrought-iron gate at the far end leads to the woods beyond, which plague the land-adjacent portion of the bluff in evergreens. I taste pine and cedar and salt in the air. The mountains loom far beyond them, still watching our every move.

After the tour, Ruth brings me inside and leaves to *run errands*. While I'm pretty used to the cold outdoors, I left my favorite jacket at home, and I don't see the point in going back outside with so much comfort here at my disposal. So instead of investigating the gardens further, as the first instincts drilled into me by my father suggest, I explore the manor. I peer into guest rooms, offices, and closets I probably shouldn't—until I open the door to a bedroom.

This one is occupied.

The girl is my age, with chestnut hair wrangled into two short, messy braids. She sits cross-legged on the ground in front of a low table, filing her nails. She wears a silky white collared shirt with a pink skirt and strawberry-shaped earrings. Her eyelids are smudged with smokey makeup. The table is covered in a mess of paper, each sheet scribbled and sketched on.

She's too busy to notice me just yet, and I'm too busy taking in her room to back out and close the door. I've never seen anything like it in my life.

It's a large room with pink floral wallpaper and bedding to match—and there are bird cages *everywhere*. There must be dozens, each one hanging from the ceiling at various lengths, holding finches and parakeets that preen their feathers and chirp gleefully. There are terrariums, too—an entire wall filled with live plants and reptiles I read about in our library back home. Coiled snakes. Bright green tokay geckos. Panther chameleons. Some of the smaller tanks hold tarantulas, scorpions, and millipedes. I even notice a towering enclosure filled with pale green White's tree frogs, and a few buzzing insect colonies.

Then I see the taxidermy.

Her entire back wall is covered in animal parts. Framed bats, pinned moths, antlers and spines, and other bones I can't identify. I squint to make out the contents of a bookshelf and shudder when I realize she's made *scenes*. Dozens of dioramas in glass boxes of beetles and lizards doing human things, like brushing their teeth or reading books.

I shouldn't be in here, I realize with a rush of dread. I step back to take a panic exit—then freeze when she speaks.

"Rude."

I blink. "Huh?"

She finishes filing her last nail and blows off the dust. It's sharpened to a point. She tilts her head at me. "You're not going to introduce yourself?"

I swallow nervously, trying not to think about the ways she could injure me with those nails. "Aaron."

"Lily."

She picks up a pen and continues sketching.

"So... can I go now?"

"If you want to."

A new voice materializes behind me. "Is my sister bothering you?"

I spin around. A young man with feathery brown hair and green eyes stares in the doorframe, wearing a navy knit sweater, dark jeans, and shiny black shoes.

"No." The word slips out a bit too quickly. I clear my throat. "Not at all."

"No need to be so polite." He nods toward the hallway, hands in his pockets. "Come on. Don't pay her any mind."

Lily keeps sketching.

The boy extends a hand. "I'm Ansel."

I take it. "Aaron."

He looks me up and down in something like disgust, then pats my shoulder with a fake smile. "Don't worry. We'll find you something decent to wear soon enough."

I force a grin and hold my tongue.

He leads me out of Lily's room, chuckling as soon as she's out of earshot. "Sorry about my sister. She doesn't take kindly to guests, let alone her own family, for that matter. If she was hostile to you in any way—"

"She wasn't."

Something about his voice reminds me of his uncle's. Smooth. *Too* polite.

"Good. I'm surprised she didn't threaten to turn you into one of her creations." He turns to me. "Have you had breakfast yet?"

"I did."

"What did you think?"

"It was pretty amazing, actually. Never tasted anything like it."

His brows furrow as we turn a corner. "Really?"

"Uh... yeah?"

"Hm. I suppose someone with your... unique background would think so. I can't even imagine spending my entire life eating only what I could scrounge up in the woods."

I try not to glare. We don't have the luxuries of Whitestag back home, but our food isn't terrible. We still have gardens and trees. Livestock. The bees I keep instead of *relaxing* like these guys. No smoked salmon Eggs Benedict—but we weren't destitute like Ansel's tone suggests.

Growing up like this doesn't make you better than anyone else, I almost say, but I decide against it when I remember who he is. Offending him seems like the kind of trouble Walter warned me about.

Keep your cool, I tell myself. *You're finally away from home, remember? Enjoy it while you can.*

"But can I be honest with you, Aaron?" Ansel continues.

"Sure."

He grimaces. "I'm not fond of our new cook."

"I thought the food was pretty good."

"It's tolerable, but pathetic in the shadow of our previous chef. He was the best of the best. Made a delicious steak."

"What happened to him?"

Ansel spares me a brief side glance and shrugs. "Off to greener pastures, I suppose."

Something tells me that isn't what really happened.

"Is that why you hate the new cook?" I ask. "Because they're not the old one?"

"I can't bring myself to respect a chef who isn't capable of making half-decent crème brûlée."

I laugh.

Ansel stops walking. "What's so funny?"

"Sorry. I thought you were joking."

"Why would you think that?"

"Because it's ridiculous."

My hand nearly flies to my mouth. *Shit. I didn't mean to say that.*

Ansel doesn't blink. I can feel my lungs pinching shut as I wait for him to say something. Anything.

What the hell is wrong with me? This kid's father is in charge of the entire Syndicate—the man who allegedly kicks puppies and skins people alive or whatever. And I just insulted that man's son. To his face.

I've known him for two minutes.

To my surprise, Ansel cracks a smile. "You're right. I was only joking."

He leads me to a library and we sit in red leather armchairs. He cracks open a book, but I can't bring myself to read.

He doesn't say another word the entire time.

Sunday, March 27

Dinner is a dead goose.

I've never eaten goose before, and I've never seen a cooked one resting on a platter either. A server in a white button-up shirt carves into it and heaps piles of meat, mashed potatoes, and grilled asparagus onto my plate. It's all pretty good when I ignore the carcass.

I sit at the end of a long dining table across from the Serpent, beneath dimly lit crystal chandeliers. Lily and Ansel occupy either side of me. We're joined by Ruth and a man I don't recognize, who wears a neat black suit and sleek sunglasses. He looks about ten years older than me, with wavy black hair and a neat mustache. He politely picks at his asparagus without a word.

"So, Tern," Walter says. "Enjoying your meal?"

The man, Tern, wipes his mouth with a napkin. "Very much, sir. Thank you."

"I for one think the goose is rather dry." Walter nods toward Tern's plate. "Is that why you've hardly touched it?"

Ansel chews in contemplation. "It *is* rather dry."

"Horribly dry," Ruth says flatly. I get the feeling she doesn't mean it when she takes another bite. Like she's used to saying whatever Walter wants.

"Not at all." Tern chuckles nervously. "I apologize if I've offended you, Walter. I've just been so distracted by these delectable dinner rolls. I'm loving this new chef of yours."

Ansel scoffs.

Walter takes an unamused sip of wine, staring straight ahead. "I assure you, Tern, I have greater things to worry about than taking offense to your dietary preferences. Do you think the goose is dry, or not?"

Tern opens his mouth, pausing in thought. He rubs the back of his neck. "In all honesty, I can't say I'm the biggest fan of goose. Perhaps I'm not the right person to ask."

I can tell the man holds his breath as he waits for Walter to respond, but the Serpent only stares. Even I feel goosebumps tickling my arms, and I'm not the one under the spotlight. *Does anyone ever know what he's really thinking?*

"There's no need to lie next time," Walter finally says. "I pay you to be honest, don't I?"

Tern only nods.

Walter sets his glass down with a chuckle. "But I'm afraid you've ruined your chance of ever winning another game of cards again. With me around, at least."

"How so?"

Walter grins. "Now that I've seen you lie, I've figured out your tell." He rubs the back of his neck, mocking the action from earlier.

Tern doesn't know what to say.

"So." Walter turns to Ruth. "How are things at the Prairie?"

Ruth nods. "Fine."

"There must be *something* noteworthy to share."

She shakes her head. "Everything is the same."

"No bar fights? Heated brawls? Bets left unpaid?"

"There are always fights, Walter." She takes a bored sip of her drink. "That's why you pay me."

So she's in charge of security?

Lily leans over and whispers in my ear. "Prairie Pit is an establishment of Uncle's."

"Huh?"

"You looked confused," she says. "I'm providing you with valuable insider information."

Is that an ounce of humor in her tone?

"Oh." I blink. "Thanks."

"Do you know what a speakeasy is?" she asks.

I think back to the Yesterday books I've read about the first Prohibition and nod. Now that the Nightjade Order enforces a new one, Dad says speakeasies—illegal bars—are common among the Immune who pay to be exceptions to the rules.

"Uncle bootlegs," Lily says. "That's how he brings in money for our family. Alcohol. Medicine. Weapons. You name it. Prairie Pit is one of his nightclubs."

She leans away and takes a casual sip from her glass.

"Well," Walter says, continuing his conversation with Ruth, "no news is good news. I have a feeling you'd let me know if the Corps finally decided to raid the place. Not sure it'd do them much good with half their ranks being permanent residents on our guest lists, anyway."

Tern scoffs. "They're headless chickens. The Corps couldn't find Prairie if they tried, and it's right under their feet."

"Then I suppose we have you and your red herrings to thank," Walter says.

Red herrings? Like distractions? My brows crease. *Does Tern have some sort of connection to the Corps?*

"The Agents who frequent your establishment are too fond of it to say a word, and even if they did, my higher-ups have bigger priorities at the moment," Tern says. "They view the Syndicate like a hornet's nest. Pesky, but not worth the poke."

"You almost sound frustrated." Walter chuckles. "If I weren't paying you a fortune, I'd believe it."

"My apologies, Walter." Tern gives a polite smile. "It's an exhausting line of work, that's all. Too much pettiness and infighting. It's all one big power struggle. Rank always outweighs reason. The higher your rung on the ladder, the more rules you can bend to match your own ambitions." He shakes his head. "They don't realize this makes them weak."

Walter takes a long sip of wine. "As long as it keeps them distracted, it's fine by me."

So Tern is an Agent?

A shiver runs down my spine. *Then what the hell am I here for?*

Lily notices my confusion and leans over to whisper again. "All sorts of Chasers and Immune folk visit Uncle's clubs. Most Chasers look the other way if they're paid well enough or get something good in return."

"Where is it?" I ask quietly. "The Prairie Pit?"

She taps her foot on the ornate rug beneath the table.

My eyes widen. *It's underground?*

I glance at Lily again, who pretends to busy herself with her meal. Maybe she's not as awful as Ansel wants me to believe.

"So, Aaron," Walter says, resting his elbows on the table and lacing his hands together. "How's the goose?"

"Good."

"Really?" He raises a brow. I nod. "You don't think it's... dry?"

I stare at the remaining shreds of meat on my plate, then back at him. "Doesn't taste dry to me."

He tilts his head. "Why don't you give it one more try?"

Reluctantly, I take another bite, unsure why I feel like I'm being tested. I chew and swallow. "Still tastes fine."

The Serpent narrows his eyes for a long time, deciding whether to believe me. To my surprise, he smirks. "It is seasoned rather nicely. Perhaps it isn't so bad after all." He takes another bite of his own, pondering as he swallows. "I think I'll keep this new cook of ours."

Ansel scoffs. "I doubt our guest knows what good poultry tastes like, Uncle."

"At least he's capable of original thought."

Ansel scowls and picks at his food. Lily hides a grin.

After a few more bites of mashed potatoes, something catches in my throat.

My eyes peel open wide. It's something solid, the size of a pea. I try to cough to get it out. It doesn't budge. When I breathe in, it only seems to go down further. And then I *can't* cough, and it's sharp, and it scrapes my throat, and I can't breathe, and I—I can't breathe.

I can't breathe.

I don't know what else to do but tap on Lily's shoulder. She sees me grabbing my throat and points. "He's choking!"

Ansel's on his feet before I can blink. He hurries behind my chair, wraps his arms around my torso, and begins an abdominal thrust.

Well—he tries. His arms move, but he's barely applying any force.

My head spins. I can feel the air seeping from my lungs as he attempts and fails another thrust. *Is he really this stupid?* I'd laugh if I could. I'm choking to death and the only one helping me can't even manage a proper Heimlich.

"You're choking," he whispers under his breath. The others don't notice.

I grasp at my throat, still wheezing as the edges of my vision blur.

"If I save you, you owe me."

What the hell? He fakes another thrust. I'm losing air. The room spins. My head pounds.

"Tap your neck three times if you agree," he mutters with another fake attempt.

This guy is clearly mad. But I can feel my consciousness slipping away, and I don't have any other choice. I tap my neck desperately.

This time, he saves me for real.

I cough up blood as the object lands on my plate. My spit stains the mashed potatoes red. All eyes are on me as I pick up the item and study it carefully.

A tooth. And it's certainly not mine.

"Lily..." Walter turns to his niece. "I believe you have some explaining to do."

"What?" she says. "It's not human, it's deer."

I glare. "You put a *tooth* in my food?"

"You weren't looking." She takes a casual sip from her drink. "It's not my fault you're such an easy target."

I open my mouth to retort, but Walter speaks before I do. "Thank you, Ansel."

Ansel nods and sits back down.

The Serpent turns to his niece again. "Do you really believe this is the proper way to treat a guest?"

"It was a harmless joke!"

"Aaron is staying with us for a reason," Walter says. "Beyond providing him with support and training for his operation, we are laying the foundation for a successful alliance between our family and his. And how will this alliance begin? With friendship, yes?"

Pouting, Lily nods.

"Do you think Aaron will want to be friends with someone who puts deer teeth in his mashed potatoes?"

"I would."

"Lily..."

She glowers with a sigh. "No."

"I don't think so either." He gestures to his nephew. "Ansel, on the other hand, acted quickly and selflessly. He saved Aaron's life without a second thought. Who do you think Aaron would prefer to respect as a leader of the Syndicate? Ansel, or you?"

She stares at her plate. "Ansel."

"Loyalty is currency, Lily. Your wealth and how you choose to earn it is up to you."

Lily picks at her food.

"Be more like your brother, dear." He takes a sip from his wine and stares at the wall. "It will do us all some good."

She sinks lower in her seat. Ansel gives me a smug look.

I know better than to say a word.

We have crème brûlée for dessert. I think it's the best thing I've ever tasted—even better than fair food or smoked salmon Eggs Benedict. Ansel says it's overdone. I eat the entire thing anyway.

Everyone drifts off for the evening, so I head upstairs, clutching my stomach. Something feels off. I'm not used to eating so much sugar. The sconces in the hallway are unlit. I've always been a bit scared of the dark.

"How's the stomach?"

I freeze. Ansel leans against the wall, arms folded.

I slide my hands into my pockets. "So this is how it's gonna be, huh?"

"I don't know what you're referring to."

"Cut the bullshit, alright? I'm not stupid. Neither are you."

"I'm flattered."

I inhale through my nose. *Keep it together. Stay calm.*

"What was that back there?" I ask.

"I saved your life."

"You used it as a bargaining chip."

"And you agreed to the bargain. Now you owe me."

"Okay, Rumpelstiltskin."

"That's a big word for an Undergrounder."

"I've got more."

He glares for a moment, then tilts his head with a snide grin. "You know what? I think I decided what my favor will be."

I try to walk past him. "I'm going to bed."

"You should know we take favors *very* seriously in the Syndicate. Especially when they're not returned. We even have a saying for it. *No promise left unpaid.*"

"I didn't ask."

"I could turn you in."

I stop dead in my tracks. Slowly, I turn around.

"I'm Immune. My father knows a few Agents. You even dined with one tonight." He shrugs. "I'm untouchable."

He's bluffing, right? He has to be. That's what I tell myself, but I can't shake the knot forming in my gut.

Something tells me the Schneiders treat their threats like favors.

"You, on the other hand..." He steps forward. "Giving up your little camp would earn me quite the reward."

My heart plummets. *He knows the Cut's location?* "And piss off your family."

He scoffs. "My father couldn't give a damn what I do."

"I meant your uncle."

That makes him pause. Then he chuckles, quiet and bitter. "Dignity is the one thing my uncle values over money. He won't lose sleep over a traitor who disrespected me—even if it means losing out on whatever deal he has with you Undergrounders."

I lean in. "Like I said, I'm going to bed."

"You think I'm joking?" He laughs again, tone darkening. "Would you like to test that theory?"

I clench my fists. *What's his motive?* I couldn't have pissed him off this bad so soon. Doesn't he have anything better to do?

I look at the walls, thinking about the size of this place. The towering ceilings. The endless hallways. The garden maze outside. The ridiculously long dinner table, and the noticeable lack of guests to fill it.

Probably not.

"You'll stay on my good side if you know what's best for you," he says, voice low. "Even if I don't make your life hell now, I could certainly do so later."

"This is about the cook, isn't it?"

His brows pinch together. "What?"

"No way." I scoff. "*That's* what insulted you?"

"I don't know what you're talking about."

"Dinner," I say. "I disagreed with your Uncle, he valued my opinion more than yours, and you're a kiss-ass, so of course you're pissed. I loved breakfast too, and now you're stuck with a cook who makes mediocre crème brûlée."

"That's a bold assumption."

"I'm a bold guy."

"You know what, Aaron?" He steps closer. "Maybe I am a little pissed."

"Aw, why's that?"

"Because my uncle let a filthy *traitor* under our roof," he hisses.

The words echo throughout the hall. He glances over his shoulder, quieting his voice.

"He could've chosen anyone for this job, and he chose *you*. An Undergrounder without a clue of what it's really like to live in our world. We'll be lucky if you don't screw everything up for all of us. You have ties to the

Syndicate now. That means more information to protect. More mistakes waiting to be made."

"I know the stakes."

"And now, he's choosing *our* cook based on who *you* like? When I clearly expressed *my* opinion? Of course an Undergrounder would think anything we cook is the best damn thing they've tasted." He laughs tiredly, running a hand through his hair. "You don't live here! He chose a stray over his own nephew. It's unfair, that's what it is."

I fold my arms. "If I didn't know any better, I'd say you were jealous."

Jealous. The word makes me scoff. *How could anyone be jealous of becoming a Chaser?* Even if it's just pretend—for the good of the Unseen and the rebellion my parents have dedicated their entire lives to planning— becoming a Chaser may as well be selling your soul to the Corps.

Who in their right mind would want that?

"I could never be jealous of a traitor like you." Ansel straightens his posture. "And if I remember correctly... that traitor agreed to a deal."

I lean my head back, closing my eyes. My stomach hurts, I'm tired, and I just want to go to bed. *I need him to shut up.*

"Whatever. Let's get this over with."

"Ah, yes. My favor." Ansel looks me dead in the eye. "Kiss my foot."

I blink. "What the hell?"

"You heard me."

"No."

"Remember what I said about breaking our deal, traitor?"

Keep cool.

"Are you really that prideful?" He tilts his head. "You would risk the safety of everyone you know and love, all to protect your ego?"

I dig my nails into the sides of my arms. *Keep cool, keep cool,* I tell myself, over and over again until it makes me dizzy. The corner of his lip twitches upward. "Now what will you sacrifice!"

We stare at each other for a long time. Slowly, I get on my knees. I kiss his shoe.

"There." I stand up, wiping my mouth. "Favor repaid."

Ansel chuckles. "Pathetic."

That's when I punch him in the mouth.

I don't realize what I'm doing until the sound of my fist cracking against his mouth echoes through the hall. A dribble of blood runs from his split lip down his chin. He touches the corner of his mouth and inspects his crimson finger for a long time before shifting his gaze to me. His eyes are so wide I can see how green they are, even in the dark.

"When I tell my uncle what you've done," he says coolly, "he'll ruin your life, if he doesn't end it first."

"I don't think you'll tell a soul."

"Another bold assumption."

"Allowing yourself to be disrespected like that? He won't pity you." I fold my arms. "He'll only be disappointed."

A muscle in his neck twitches. "You don't know what you're talking about."

"Is everything okay?"

We spin around. Lily stands a few feet down the hall. I hadn't realized we were in front of her bedroom. Despite the blood on Ansel's chin, she's looking at me—not her brother. Like she knows he did something to provoke it.

Ansel storms off, slamming his bedroom door shut behind him.

Lily and I stand in silence for a while, until I walk over to where she stands. I pull the deer tooth from my pocket and offer it to her. "You forgot something."

"You can keep it." She shrugs. "It was meant to be a welcome gift, you know. They bring good luck."

I turn it over in my hand. "Thank you."

She doesn't say anything before disappearing into her room. I shove the tooth in my pocket and disappear into mine.

Monday, March 28

The next morning, I wake up groggy with a bandage over my eye.

My head throbs. Morning light floods through my curtains. It's searing. I squeeze my eyes shut, massaging my temples. *What the hell is going on?*

It doesn't take me long to realize what happened.

I've had a bandage like this before.

I'm not sure what drug the Serpent used to knock me out or how he snuck it into my dinner, but someone must have finally given me my false tracker last night—the one containing the data for my new identity. A dupe like this must've cost him a fortune.

I try not to think about what it will cost the Cut to repay that favor.

Before I can drag myself out of bed, something tickles my forehead. Then my cheek. The bridge of my nose. I freeze.

There's a scorpion on my face.

I fold forward. The scorpion tumbles off. It takes me three seconds to retrieve the knife under my pillow and plunge it into the creature's armored back. Its blood stains the sheets blue. My nose crinkles in disgust.

I walk down the hall to Lily's room and knock. She tells me to come in.

I open the door. She's sitting at her drawing table when I toss the dead scorpion at her. It lands on the table with a slapping sound. "Brought you something."

"Thank you!" She inspects it with a wide grin. "This is gorgeous. Where'd you find it?"

"My bed."

Her brows crease. "That's odd."

"Oh, cut the bullshit. You put it there."

"No I didn't."

"It could've poisoned me!"

"It wasn't me!"

"You're the one obsessed with killing things. Who else could it be?"

"I'm not obsessed with *killing things*." She glares. "It's life I'm interested in."

I gesture to the decor on her walls. "You're surrounded by death."

"Why do you think people visit graves? Or have urns on their mantle? Put hunting trophies on the wall?"

I fold my arms. "I saw that photo your uncle carries with him. The hunting trip? You and the gun?"

"I didn't kill that deer."

"Then who did?"

"Ansel." She looks back to her drawings. "Uncle let me pretend in the photo though. He wanted Father to think I made the shot."

I open my mouth, then close it with a sigh.

She's probably been around a lot of death, given her family. She's weird, alright—but I understand why. *Maybe that scorpion did escape.*

"Sorry for bothering you." I'm about to walk out, but she speaks before I do.

"For the record? Nothing escapes my terrariums." She starts drawing again. "Someone put that scorpion in your bed, but it wasn't me."

Goosebumps prick my arms.

I give her one last look before leaving. I can't shake the feeling that despite the bugs and bones, Lily isn't the person in this house I should fear.

Saturday, April 9

My first two weeks at Whitestag pass like years.

Every morning at breakfast, Walter quizzes me on my new identity, as well as common Chip information any seventeen-year-old should know.

My name is Cedar Warren Beck. I'm a distant cousin of the Schneiders, from the Central Region. I grew up in Illinois where there is corn, sticky heat, and fireflies. My parents are teachers who sent me to live with my uncle and cousins, so I can go to a nice school and eventually become a Chaser. No one calls me Aaron, because he died twelve years ago when his rebel father debugged him. I'm only Cedar.

Cedar Warren Beck.

But I'm not around people much to be called *anything*. Even with Walter's quizzes, it's difficult to remember a name I have no attachment to, especially with all the other new things I need to remember—like how to use computers or tie a tie. Change the thermostat. Don't get me started on that damn espresso machine. He even taught me how to *milk* a snake, which is apparently what they call harvesting venom.

I don't know what any of this has to do with the Chaser Corps.

Every now and then, I'll get another surprise from Lily. No more teeth, just lots of moth wings and dried tree resin with bugs in it. She reminds me of the cats that roam the Cut, leaving dead lizards and rat snouts on your porch. They don't know any better, but it's still gross.

Lily has taken to decorating my room when I'm not there. Every day, I swear another framed bat or beetle specimen pops up on my wall, or a drawing of some animal hybrid with sharp teeth and antlers. Her art is actually amazing, but I don't tell her that. I get the feeling she already knows. She doesn't come out of her room much.

It's strange not having a routine and being around so many new things, but it's nice too. I haven't done a single chore. If I need anything, I ask for it. I've had crème brûlée for breakfast three days in a row. I have a closet full of soft brown, black, and gray sweaters I like more than I'd admit. My jeans don't have holes in them. My shoes fit me. I spend most days by myself, enjoying the quiet garden and big leather-bound books I pretend to understand.

No waking up early to water the plants. No hours spent taking inventory of our teas and medicines. No *teaching moments*. Just... me, doing whatever the hell I want to do.

I don't feel homesick at all.

Ansel doesn't want anything to do with me; my main source of socialization is at dinner when the Serpent gets home from work. Tern reports to Walter every other week, so it's usually just us and Ruth. She lives at Whitestag too.

Today is the only day I've actually *seen* Lily before dinner, ever since the scorpion incident.

I open the door to her room by accident, thinking it's mine. I'm still not used to the manor's maze. She kneels in front of her drawing table, sketching a scorpion and humming softly.

I don't close the door right away because I'm distracted by her technique. She draws with her left hand using an expensive-looking fountain pen, and colors with her right. I never thought scorpions could be an iridescent periwinkle color, but maybe she knows something I don't know.

"Make up your mind." Her sudden voice nearly makes me jump. "If you're going to stand there staring, shut the door behind you. Otherwise you can leave. Close the door either way, though. I hate when it's open."

"Hate's a strong word."

"The sconces are ugly, and I *hate* looking at them."

I don't have anything better to do, so I walk inside and close the door. "Nice pen."

"It is."

"Looks smooth."

She offers it to me. "Want to try?"

Reluctantly, I take the pen and sit across from her. She slides me a blank sheet of paper.

The pen is heavy, carved from some sort of stone. It glides effortlessly across the page. I glance behind her and squint at a moth specimen on the wall. I draw it quickly using careless, sloppy strokes. She cranes her neck to watch my every move. She doesn't look impressed, so I draw blinking eyes.

That makes her smile.

I hand the pen back to her. "I always thought I was a ballpoint guy, but now I'm not so sure."

"It's obsidian." She takes it back and returns to her scorpion. She begins drawing human eyes on its back, like the ones I drew on the moth. She draws lips too, blood red with sharp fangs. "Do you know how obsidian is made?"

I shake my head.

"It's volcanic glass. It forms when lava cools quickly." She stands to retrieve a small box, which she brings back to the table. She opens it, revealing a collection of jagged black rocks with sharp edges. "It's my favorite stone, you know. Though I guess it's not a true rock. You can find it out in the woods in some places, if you know where to look."

She finds a jagged piece and studies it closely. "Lava is viscous. Isn't it strange how it can turn into something like this under the right conditions? Something so... sharp?" She pricks herself on the edge with a chuckle. "The world is a weird, weird place."

Lily returns the obsidian to its box and closes it. She starts drawing again. I watch her add more blue and purple to the scorpion. *Maybe she's not as odd as she seems.*

"Next time you come into my room to spy on me, I'll turn you into one of those." She points to a stag head on the wall.

Or maybe she is.

I take that as my cue to leave. I can still hear her humming when I close the door on my way out.

For the first time since I arrived at Whitestag, dinner is at 4:00.

That's three hours earlier than usual, so it's still pretty light outside when we gather at the table. Tonight we feast on filet mignon with roasted rosemary potatoes. I don't know what the hell *filet mignon* means, but it's some sort of meat, and it's absolutely delicious.

We never ate this much meat at the Cut. We had some livestock, but not enough to butcher and consume on a regular basis. Sometimes Cecil and Beau would organize hunting trips, but aside from that, we kept a primarily vegetarian diet.

I don't think I could ever grow tired of eating meat.

"So, Ansel," Walter says. "How is school?"

"Fine. I did well on my chemistry exam."

"Score?"

"Ninety-six."

"Very good. Lily?"

"I got an A on my literature paper," she says.

"I meant precalculus, my dear." He takes a sip of wine. "You mentioned your exam last week."

"Ah. Well, I didn't do so well in math, since I was so focused on writing that—"

"Score?"

She bites her lip. "Sixty-two."

The Serpent nods slowly. Lily can't bring herself to look at him, or even touch her plate. He folds his hands and turns to his nephew. "Your school holds a carnival this time of year."

Ansel nods. "It's this evening."

The Serpent checks his watch. "Would you look at that? The night is still young."

"I guess."

"Why don't you take Cedar to the carnival?"

I nearly choke on my water. Ansel appears to be overcoming the same challenge. He clears his throat. "What?"

"You heard me."

"I'd like to go," Lily says. "They have those dart-throwing games where you can win goldfish, and—"

"Your evening is booked, dear," Walter interrupts. "Ruth will be tutoring you every night after dinner until your grade goes up."

"But—"

"Argue with me, Lily. I welcome it." The Serpent's gaze grows colder. Emptier. "Perhaps repetition is the learning style you respond best to...

because I'm sure I've taught you the consequences of talking back before."

Lily sinks lower in her seat.

The Serpent turns back to his nephew. "Ansel, you will take Cedar to this carnival."

"I have quite a bit of studying to do, actually."

"Nonsense. Go and enjoy yourself, you deserve it."

"But I—"

"Ansel," he warns.

The boy sighs. "Yes, Uncle."

"You will show him around and answer his questions," Walter says, turning to me now. "This is a great opportunity to practice socializing, and learn how to hold your tongue in certain situations. Consider this a test, Aaron." I flinch at the sound of my real name as he flashes me a faux grin. "How well can you hide in plain sight?"

I swallow. I've been to carnivals with Beau, but never for the point of socializing. I think back to how I interacted with the girls on the bench, and my face warms. I'm not used to being around people my age.

I study the Serpent's smug expression, and I can't shake the feeling that he knows something I don't.

What else am I being tested on?

I smell turkey legs again.

Ruth drops us off by the parking lot at Ansel's school. It's a large campus, judging from what little I remember about my old elementary school back in Port Keys. It reminds me of Whitestag. Towering brick buildings with ornate marble columns and fancy shutters. Endless green lawns. Fancy gardens. A distant view of Puget Sound, and a crisp night air thick with the taste of salt and evergreens.

The event is in the parking lot. The sun has set, but we don't need it to see; the colorful twinkling lights of carnival rides and noisy game booths illuminate everything in view. I even spot a Ferris wheel spinning in the center of it all. Just looking at it makes me dizzy.

I taste fried food and sugar in the air, which already clings to my clothes and hair. I wear an itchy black knit sweater with jeans and expensive white sneakers. They're not as comfortable as my worn hiking boots, but they look nicer than any shoe I've ever owned, so I don't complain.

I wear my regular glasses, not shades. Ruth concealed my scar with makeup and gave me a contact lens to hide my blind left eye. She taught me how to put the disguise on myself, so I'll be ready when it's time for training.

The second Ruth drives away, Ansel pulls me aside with a glare.

"Look. I'm here for a good time, not to have you following me like a shadow, alright? I don't care what my uncle says."

"I'm not exactly excited about our little date either."

Ansel frowns. "Just meet me here at the end of the—"

"Ansel!"

A high-pitched voice cuts through the air. We spin around. A girl our age with brown hair and blunt bangs approaches, wearing a light blue t-shirt. Her olive skin is dusted with freckles. "It's so nice to see—"

She pauses when she sees me standing next to him. A playful grin creeps across her face. "Who's this?"

"This is..." Ansel frowns at first, but his face shifts as his voice trails off. Like he's realizing something I'm not. My brows furrow. He places a hand on my shoulder, grinning. "Cedar. My cousin."

Her eyes widen with excitement. "I never knew you had a cousin."

"He's from out of town." Ansel pats my back. "Why don't you tell Mandy about life back home?"

Mandy twirls a strand of hair, waiting for me to say something.

"Uh... I'm from Illinois."

She gasps like it's the most interesting thing anyone has ever said. "I've never been to the Central Region! Is it nice?"

"No," I say a little too bluntly. Ansel gives me a threatening look.

Mandy chuckles. "You must be glad to be here then."

Ansel's death glare softens into something like a nod of approval.

We venture farther into the festival, walking past blinking game booths and food trucks serving funnel fries and giant cheeseburgers. Someone passes with cotton candy, which makes me think of Beau—but I'm quickly distracted by the man dressed in white who passes next.

I lean over to whisper in Ansel's ear, heart pounding. "Why are they here?"

"What do you mean?" Mandy asks. "They have Chasers at every school event. It's policy."

"He's from a small town," Ansel adds. "He's never been to a carnival like this. He's homeschooled."

"Then what do you do for fun?" Mandy asks, moving around Ansel to walk next to me instead.

"Roam around cornfields and set shit on fire, I guess."

Mandy laughs. "He's funny, Ansel."

At that, Ansel gives me an approving smirk.

I insist we stop by the turkey leg truck. I don't have any money, so I offer to pay for Mandy's, and that gets Ansel to step in and pay for all three of us. It's like I'm winning a game I'm not even playing.

We walk around a bit more and play a few games until Mandy's friends come over. Ansel's friends join us too—Marco and Dalton, who seem to know everyone we walk by. Ansel and his buddies give random students fist bumps, finger guns, and waves every two seconds. I've never been around this many kids before in my life.

Every now and then, Ansel leans over to whisper tips in my ear. Things like putting my hands in my pockets to act nonchalant, or teasing to show I'm interested. I ask why people don't simply say what they mean. He says that's the stupidest question he's ever heard.

Mandy and one of her friends won't leave me alone, but Ansel doesn't seem to mind, because her other two friends won't leave *his* side. Strangely, Marco and Dalton also appear to be more interested in Ansel's cousin from out of town than him. They manage to make me laugh a few times. Real, genuine laughter.

What surprises me most is that behind this mask—Cedar from out of town—I know what to say. I have a quick response for every joke, every question, every flirtatious line from Mandy and the other girls. Hell, I think *I'm* flirting with them a bit too. I use Ansel's tips. I subtly reference Yesterday romance books and make them blush like I've done it a thousand times before. It feels so damn easy.

I don't know what's gotten into me.

For a brief moment, I'm actually enjoying myself. I forget where I am or why I'm here or the place I came from. I have no responsibilities, no chores, no overprotective father. Just me, surrounded by real kids my age and fair food that doesn't make me as sick as it did before.

I could get used to being Cedar.

For the next hour or two, we play more games and fill up on junk food. I spot a dart-throwing booth and win two goldfish. I give Mandy one of them and keep the other. Mine is white with an orange spot on its head, swimming in circles in a water-filled plastic bag. *I'll give it to Lily when we get home.*

We eventually reach the end of the parking lot, beyond the last booths and rides. It's empty and unlit. A metal railing lines the edge of the pavement, blocking us from a cliff overlooking the Sound below. The carnival noise behind us is distant and muffled.

I stare at the water past the cliff, lips parted. We don't have views like this at the Cut.

"What do we have here?" Ansel says, pulling me out of my thoughts.

A boy I hadn't noticed sits against the railing, reading with a flashlight. I can tell he's our age, though he's a lot smaller. He has big round glasses and a messy head of brown hair.

"Not now, Ansel," he mutters without looking up from his book. "I'm busy."

"Oh, come on, Corey. Too busy for *me*? How impolite."

Corey sighs. "What do you want?"

"Just saying hello. Is that not allowed?"

Corey returns to his book. "We both know that's not true."

Ansel takes a step forward. Marco and Dalton do the same. Mandy and her friends snicker and whisper.

"I'm afraid I don't like your tone, Corey. A shame. I was really excited to see you, and now my feelings are hurt." Ansel crouches in front of him. "I think you owe me an apology."

I scoff. *This is ridiculous.*

Corey looks him dead in the eye. "I said, I'm busy."

Everything goes quiet. All I hear is the distant underwater sound of laughter and carnival rides, games that ring a dozen times to announce a winner. Beyond the cliff, waves whisper into the night.

Ansel takes Corey's book and throws it over the edge. Before I can say anything, he's lifting the kid up by his collar. "*I said*, apologize."

Corey doesn't say a word.

Ansel yanks the kid's face closer. "You don't want to go through this *again*, do you?"

He still doesn't speak.

"You should have learned your lesson by now, but you *still* continue to disrespect me."

Corey chuckles tiredly, like he knows what's going to happen next. "And you're still delusional enough to believe you actually deserve respect."

Ansel freezes.

"Let's just go, Ansel," Mandy says nervously. "I'm bored."

Ansel holds up a hand. She quiets.

"I'm going to give you one last chance to reconsider." The humor has drained from his voice. What's left is cold and empty. It reminds me of his uncle. "Ten seconds, Corey."

My brows pinch. *What is he talking about?*

"Nine," Ansel says.

"Come on, man." Marco nudges Ansel. "Do we really need to do this right now?"

"Eight."

Marco and Dalton exchange glances. I clench my fist, one hand still holding the goldfish bag.

"Seven."

"Let's go," Mandy mutters, corralling her friends. They hurry back to the carnival.

"Six."

"Just say you're sorry, dude," Dalton tells Corey.

Corey laughs. "The day I say sorry to a prick like him is the day I lose my mind."

Ansel doesn't even finish counting before pulling the boy into a choke-hold. "I warned you."

I run up to Ansel's side and try to pry him off. He elbows me away, hissing through clenched teeth. "*Not now.*"

"You're being stupid. There are Chasers here, you know."

It's like Ansel can't even hear me. He tightens his hold on Corey, who claws at his elbows, choking on his last bit of air. His face is already turning purple. I think back to what it felt like to have that tooth lodged in my throat, and I try not to throw up.

"Apologize, Corey," Ansel seethes. "Then I'll *consider* letting you breathe again."

"He can't even talk!" I protest.

"Then he should've done it while he had the chance."

That's it. I shove the water-filled goldfish bag into Marco's chest. "Hold this."

I yank Ansel away from Corey by the hair and lock him in my own chokehold. The other kid falls to his knees, gasping for air, coughing as he holds his neck.

"Stay hydrated, peppermint tea, rest your voice," I say to Corey as quickly as I can. He nods and hurries back to the carnival.

I let Ansel go and shove him away from me. "What the hell is wrong with you?"

He rubs his throat with a glare, voice raspy. "He disrespected me."

"You just can't stand not being the most important person in the room, can you?"

"It would do you some good to learn a thing or two about respect as well, *Becky*." Ansel steps forward. "Have you forgotten who I am? Or what my family is doing for yours?"

My jaw tightens. Dalton and Marco exchange confused glances.

"I know exactly who you are," I say calmly. "Corey said it perfectly."

This time, he's the one to punch *me* in the face.

His fist cracks into my jaw, snapping my head to the side. I don't waste a second before hitting him back, and before I know it, we're rolling around on the pavement swinging punches at each other.

"Break it up, you two!" Dalton shouts. We don't listen.

I kneel on Ansel's legs and throw my fist at his mouth, but he dodges his head and my knuckles slam into the ground. I curse when something cracks and shake out my hand, giving Ansel the perfect opportunity to pin me to the ground and punch the side of my face. Then I shove him aside and pin *him* to the ground by the shoulder, using the other arm to slam my fist into his nose. It drips blood.

Someone whistles and claps. I glance over my shoulder, eyes wide when I realize a crowd of students, eager to watch our fight, has migrated to our end of the parking lot. While I'm distracted, Ansel tackles me off him and pummels his fists into my face. I wheeze when he punches me in the stomach. Students cheer.

I knee him in the gut. He coughs, but it isn't enough to get him off me. Instead, it makes him hit me in the face again, this time knocking off my glasses. The world around me becomes a blur; everything is a hazy collection of fuzzy shapes, outlines of features I can't quite make out.

Beyond Ansel, I see the crowd break as two white shapes cut through. The students disperse. Even Marco and Dalton make a run for it as the shapes grow closer and closer. I put my glasses back on—just as someone yanks me up by the collar.

"You two are coming with us," a deep voice says.

I don't realize he's a Chaser until he spins me around and zip-ties my wrists together.

We're in an empty classroom on the far edge of campus. I can't hear the carnival from here at all.

It's dark. Soft blue moonlight seeps through one of the back windows. Ansel and I sit in two chairs, hands tied behind our backs as a pair of Chasers lean against a desk, studying us carefully. They haven't said a word this entire time.

"*Affray*—a public display of violence that disturbed the peace," one of the Officers finally says, voice low and rough. He could be my dad's age. "That's the crime you'll be punished for."

Ansel and I are too stunned to speak.

"We know these incidents are common at school events," the Officer continues, "which is why we're stationed here in the first place. It's an unfortunate truth, but truth nonetheless."

The other Chaser nods. He's only a few years older than us. "A real shame, exterminating young folks. But you two had to go and misbehave."

"It is our societal duty to weed out bad characters such as yourselves *before* they become a larger issue in adulthood." The older Chaser sighs. "You understand this, correct?"

I blink. *What are they talking about?* My ears are ringing and my head is still killing me from the fight. Everything feels hazy.

"We want to make sure you're aware of how this will benefit the years to come," the younger one says, "before we follow through with protocol."

"We'll make this quick." The older Chaser opens a shiny white case, retrieving a long syringe with a thick needle. It's filled with dark purple liquid. "There is no need to worry."

"I'm Immune," Ansel says plainly.

The Officers look at each other, then back at us. "Are you certain?"

Ansel glares. "Yes, I'm *certain*. Look me up in your bloody database before *following protocol*." He shakes his head. "Incompetent. That's what you are."

"Watch it," I warn under my breath. Ansel doesn't seem to care—and neither do the Chasers. The older one approaches me with his Nightjade syringe in hand, while the younger one does the same for Ansel.

"I've been in this line of work for a long time," the older one says tiredly. "I've heard every bluff in the book. This will be a lot easier if you just let us do our job and—"

"Let you do your job?" Ansel scoffs. "So you can do it wrong?"

The Officer doesn't stop. My pulse races. He stands behind my chair, bringing the syringe to my neck.

My eyes widen. "Whoa whoa whoa. Just wait a second, alright?"

He doesn't listen. I feel the tip of the needle against my throat, icy and sharp. The younger Chaser holds one to Ansel's neck too.

For the first time in my life, my tongue is completely tied. I try to speak, to protest, but no words come out. My pulse hammers in every vein. I stare at Ansel, pleading in silence for him to do something. *I'm Immune too, right?*

The Serpent paid for me to bypass the exam. My spot in training is already secured. *I have to be Immune if I'm going off to training.*

Ansel speaks again. "You seem so set on following protocol, Officer—what was it again? Bird Brain?"

The temperature in the room drops. The Chaser behind me freezes, slowly turning to face the boy in the chair next to me.

"*Riker*," he seethes. "A tone like that is enough to warrant your extermination with or without the Immunity you claim to have, young man."

"Officer Riker, you either don't know shit, or your *years* of experience have made you lazy. *Protocol* requires you to check for Immunity, whether you believe your target is telling the truth or not—and *protocol* condemns Chasers who fail to follow it. But you know what protocol doesn't say?" Ansel chuckles darkly. "The Corps rewards loyalty, and if Officer..." He looks at the other young Chaser.

"Proctor," the Officer says.

"If Officer Proctor were to report you for failing to follow protocol, supported by proof—such as the fact that I *am* Immune, which you would know if you *checked the bloody database*—he would be rewarded, and you would be punished. Or better yet, exterminated instantly, because the moment your higher-ups learn just *how* Immune I was before you ruthlessly murdered me, they will shit their pants and end your worthless little life the moment they recover, if my Uncle doesn't get to you first. If he does, he will not hesitate to slowly remove body parts I'm sure you are rather fond of and let you bleed to death. And judging by your *pleasantness*, I can only assume that Proctor would not hesitate to rightfully earn his reward and score himself a better partner in the process, if the opportunity presented itself. Have my points been made clear, Riker?"

No one says a word.

I think about the dried blood on Ansel's face. My sprained fingers and torn-up knuckles. The bruises already forming on his face and stomach. *I did that to him.*

If Ansel can threaten a Chaser and get away with it, maybe I'm in deeper shit than I realize.

Finally, Officer Riker pulls out a tablet with a sigh. "Name?"

A small bit of relief courses through me. Ansel's shoulders relax. "Ansel Walter Schneider."

The color drains from Riker's face. "Schneider?"

Ansel smirks.

The Chaser clears his throat. "Cards, left to right?"

"King of Diamonds, 9 of Clubs."

The man types something into his tablet. The other Officer peers over to look at the tablet, then they nod at Ansel. "You're all clear."

Proctor cuts Ansel's ties and starts walking him to the door. Riker brings the syringe back to my neck.

"We're cousins," I say.

"How unfortunate for Ansel," Riker mutters apathetically. "I lost a cousin once. He was Picked."

"I'm Immune."

Proctor stops by the door with Ansel, watching. Riker pulls out his tablet with a sigh. "Name?"

"Cedar."

"Middle and last?"

My heart plummets. *Shit.*

I can't remember my name.

My hands shake. I go over every meal I've had with the Serpent, scouring my memories for some sort of clue. I can't for the life of me recall anything else but Cedar.

I almost chuckle. *What a simple, stupid mistake.*

A simple, stupid way to die.

"Middle and last?" Riker repeats impatiently.

I glance over my shoulder at Ansel, who stands by the door next to Proctor in silence. He looks at me, waiting for me to say something. And then it hits me.

Ansel knows my full name. He said part of it to me before we fought— I know it. Once again, he holds my life in his hands.

And I just beat the shit out of him.

My muscles relax in defeat. He won't say a word. *This is the perfect way to finally get me out of the picture.*

I look to Riker, who wears a pristine white uniform, despite the blood he has cleaned from his hands, time and time again. He is tired, impatient, and he has done this a thousand times before. He will not hesitate to kill me if I don't have an answer.

No one is coming to save me.

"Cedar Warren Beck." Ansel crosses his arms over his chest. "Forgive my cousin for his hesitation. He has a hard time speaking when he's scared shitless."

"Beck?" Riker raises a brow.

"A maternal relation," Ansel says. "But as long as he shares blood with a Schneider, his name bears the same weight."

Riker swallows uncomfortably, then nods, making a note on his tablet. "Cards?"

"2 of Spades, Joker."

Riker types in the information. The seconds we wait last lifetimes, until he frowns and shuts off the tablet. "You're enlisting in the Corps?"

"I am."

Riker studies me with something like exhaustion or disappointment. "You don't seem like the type."

My pulse races. *Is he onto me? Does he know I'm a fake?* "How so?"

"You're not a killer."

I swallow. "I could be."

"I work with them every day."

There's a pause. "Then what am I?"

He shrugs and walks around to cut my bonds. "Something else."

I don't know what to say to that, so I keep my mouth shut.

Riker and Proctor escort us from the portable and back to the blacktop, where the last vendors and volunteers pack up their booths. The students are gone now, save for the few waiting for rides or lingering in small, whispering clusters. Wind carries candy wrappers past our feet.

"Be careful with your tempers, kids," Riker says. "Immunity can't save you from everything."

The Chasers walk away, leaving Ansel and me alone.

"Is Ruth on her way?" I ask.

He nods. I nod. More quiet.

"Thank you," I say.

Ansel shoves his hands in his pockets. "Don't thank me."

He wipes the last of the crusted blood from beneath his nose with his sleeve. It doesn't do anything to address the cut in his lip or the black eye he'll have tomorrow. "My Uncle would kill me if I let them exterminate you."

Something about the way he says it, and the shiver crawling down my spine, leads me to believe that he's not exaggerating in the least.

Maybe, I wonder, *this was a test for us both.*

Friday, June 17

On the night before my first day of Chaser training, Francis Schneider shows up late for dinner.

I sit around the table with the Serpent, Ansel, Lily, and Ruth. Strangely, Tern is here too, though he already had dinner with us last Sunday. He shouldn't be due for another report until the 26th.

I'm not entirely sure what these reports entail. They occasionally discuss Syndicate matters at the table. But usually, Walter, Tern, and Ruth chat in the study, where I'm sure the real business talk happens. I've heard them murmuring, voices low and mixed with thick cigar smoke that drifts throughout the manor. Sometimes they argue. Sometimes they laugh. Sometimes they play a card game called *Cobra*.

But tonight, there was no conversation in the study. No smuggled cigars. No cards. And for the first time since my arrival, Walter sits to the side of the head seat. That chair is empty.

It's strange, but my thoughts are pulled away from it when dinner is brought out. It's some sort of meat again. I pile heaps of it on my plate, along with a fancy salad and dinner rolls.

"So, Aaron," Walter says. "Thoughts on our main course?"

I nod with my mouth full. "It's delicious."

"Agreed," Ruth says.

"You've outdone yourself once again," Tern says.

There's a brief pause until Walter nods toward me. "Do you know what you're eating?"

I glance at my plate. "Chicken?"

He grins. "Goat."

I spit out my food.

The table goes silent. All eyes glue to me. I reach for my water and gulp it quickly, coughing to get the bit of food that went down the wrong pipe back where it belongs. I clear my throat and wipe my face with a napkin. "Sorry."

Walter studies me carefully. I can't peel my eyes from the platter in the center of the table.

I ate goat.

My mind goes to Gooseberry—the innocent little creature in that fair stall with his mother. The creature I escorted to his death.

They are the same species.

I cover my mouth to keep from throwing up.

"You seem uncomfortable. Is there a problem with the food?"

"The food is fine."

"Take another bite."

My shoulders stiffen. "I think I'm alright, thank you."

"Are you not feeling well?"

I shake my head. "I'm good."

He takes a sip of wine. "You're bothered that it's goat, aren't you?"

I shake my head again.

"Don't lie to me."

I swallow. "Sorry. I've never had goat before. It's a little weird."

"And how is a goat any different from a goose? Steak? Or that smoked salmon you love so much?" Walter leans back in his seat. "They are all animals. What puts one above the other?"

I try to smooth out my expression to hide my confusion, but I'm not sure if I'm successful, because the Serpent laughs. "Meat is meat, Cedar. Death is death, no matter how it's cooked. And it is a necessary part of life."

He takes another sip of wine. It looks like blood. He reaches forward to fork seconds onto his plate.

"The powerful prey on the weak, and the weak sustain the powerful." He saws at the meat and shovels a bite into his mouth. "Reminds me of the Agency division—doesn't it, Tern?"

Tern pauses. "How so?"

"The Agency is a food chain. A ladder, really."

"I'm afraid I don't understand what you mean."

"Every Agent exists to climb it. You only have as much power as the rung you're on. But once you start climbing, you realize how little you had before... and how much you'd gain if you could just get"—he stabs his fork into three different bites for each of his next words—"*one rung higher...* Sound familiar?"

Tern forces an uncomfortable chuckle, rubbing the back of his neck. "The excessive bureaucracy can be quite maddening. Rank over reason, as I say."

"Greed so often overcomes loyalty. To ourselves, to humanity. To those who helped us get on that ladder in the first place. Climbing it can be such a dangerous game."

"Dangerous?"

"The higher you get..." Walter pours more wine into his glass. "The farther you fall."

Tern flashes a constructed grin. "That's very wise, sir."

Walter turns to me, voice cold. "Finish your dinner, Cedar. You're thin. You'll need the sustenance for training."

Approaching footsteps snag my attention, sparing me from having to take another bite. A stocky man I don't recognize waltzes in, wearing a dark gray suit with white pinstripes. He has a thick beard and dark brown hair that's just long enough to be tucked behind his ears—like Walter's, but without the strands of gray. He chuckles loudly and takes a seat at the head of the table across from me.

"Sorry I'm late," he says. A server quickly rushes to pile food onto his plate and pour him a glass of wine. "Got caught up in a game."

"Dad!" Lily shoots up from her seat and runs to the head of the table to wrap her arms around his neck.

I freeze, eyes wide. This man is Francis Schneider.

And we're sitting at the same table.

He laughs and hugs his daughter. "I've missed you, my dear."

"I've missed you too."

He gives her a pat on the back, eyes crinkled with what looks like genuine joy. The crinkles fade when he looks at Ansel. "Son."

"Father." He says it like an insult.

"I've made something for you," Lily says, retrieving a necklace from her pocket. The pendant is a scorpion encased in glass, beneath a flat lay of fern leaves. It's strangely beautiful.

Francis releases an exhausted sigh. "Lily, we've talked about this."

Her shoulders slump. "About what?"

"Your..." Francis crinkles his nose, gesturing toward the necklace with his hand. "*Hobbies*."

"Is something wrong, Francis?" the Serpent asks. "You seem displeased."

"I suppose I am a little tired of repeating myself. I thought we discussed this too, Walter."

"I believe her skills and passions deserve encouragement." The Serpent takes another bite. "They enrich her mind and keep her busy. And they bring you joy?"

Lily nods.

Walter shrugs. "So I do not see a problem with it."

"It's just... odd. She should be honing skills that will be of good use to her. Not *this*." He gestures to the necklace again. Lily hides it behind her back.

My hand curls into a fist in my lap. Something about that statement feels familiar.

"And what *skills* do you propose she sharpen?" Walter takes a sip. "Your children attend the best school in the city. They perform well and receive private tutoring from Ruth in areas they need to strengthen. For children their age, they are well-versed in history, science, mathematics, literature—you name it." He cuts another slice of meat. "They also understand politics. Leadership. The most fatal places to insert a knife. How to fire a Yesterday gun, skin a deer, filet a fish. How to survive in the woods for a week with no tools. How to... clean up certain messes, if the need arises."

Ansel and Lily flinch at that last one.

"So, Francis." Walter swallows his bite. "What skills would you like me to add to their list?"

"Those skills will suit *Ansel* well." Francis takes a tired sip of wine. "Lily should be socializing with other girls her age. Participating in school clubs. Attending debutante balls and dinner parties and making connections. *Those* skills will suit her well."

Lily's eyes lower to her shoes. I dig my nails into my palm.

Before I get the chance to chuck a spoon at this man's head, the Serpent scoffs. "Don't be archaic, brother."

"They're *my* children."

Tern and Ruth busy themselves with their meals uncomfortably.

"And yet I am the one you entrusted to raise them as I see fit," Walter says.

Goosebumps prick my skin as the two men study each other in silence, taking slow, careful sips of wine. There is no glaring in their gazes. Only a cold, perfect politeness.

After what feels like ages, Francis leans his head back and laughs. He reaches over to pat his brother on the shoulder. "Oh, Walt. I've missed bickering with you. I suppose you make a fair point." Francis turns to Lily again, extending a palm. "The necklace, darling?"

Reluctantly, Lily hands it to him. He places it in his pocket.

"You're not going to wear it?" she asks.

He forces a smile. "I'm saving it for a special occasion."

She nods, then returns to her seat. Ansel stares at the wall boredly. He's seen this happen before.

"So." Francis leans back. "This is the Unseen boy you told me about?"

I freeze.

"He is indeed," Walter says.

"*This* is who you're sending off to the Corps?"

"Training is the goal. And the Cut is the one sending him, not me," the Serpent corrects. "I'm just... *preparing* him. Doing them a favor, really."

Francis squints at me. "He's scrawny."

I hold back a frown and bite my tongue. *I'm right here.*

"Our new chef will fix that. Training will help too."

"He was raised at the Cut? By Unseen rebels?"

"Your point?"

"That seems... risky." Francis's nose twitches slightly. "Putting a teenage boy with that upbringing under so much pressure. Pinning so much responsibility on *any* child is asking for a mistake."

"Plenty of young people go off to Training," Walter says.

"Not with his background."

"He may not look like much now, but I see potential in Aaron. We all have our dark sides. Sometimes harnessing that darkness is just a matter of... receiving the right nudges."

Francis shakes his head and returns to his food. "The Cut is sending a lamb to the slaughter."

I swallow. *Comforting.*

Dinner continues. I still feel a coldness in the Serpent's voice, but I'm not sure Francis notices. Everyone chats politely about the weather and how delicious the goat is—until the conversation shifts.

"So, Ruth," Walter says. "Tell me about the trouble at Prairie."

"We had a situation last night, as I'm sure you've already heard," she says casually, taking a bite of her salad. "There's talk of a raid."

Walter laughs in disbelief. "A raid. In Prairie Pit."

Francis keeps eating, as unfazed as Ansel.

Ruth nods. "There will always be rumors, of course, but one of our Vipers found a man checking out our entry and exit points. He was taking notes, too. After giving him a good *talking to*, he revealed he was paid to scope it out."

There's that word again. I remember it from the cabin.

"Vipers?" I ask aloud.

Ruth glances at Walter, who grants her a nod of permission. She turns to me. "Walter's inner circle. We keep an eye out for him."

Ruth plucks at her green suit, then rolls up her sleeve, revealing her crossed-out Cards. I stare at her gold-plated teeth earrings and think back to what Walter said back at the cabin about displaying loyalty. *Is this what he meant?*

Ruth stares at her missing finger. I shudder. *I hope that's not part of it too.*

"You mentioned this man was paid," Walter says.

Ruth nods.

He scoffs. "By who?"

"A man who calls himself Laridae."

"How interesting. And... familiar. I swear I've heard that name come up before." Walter glances at Tern. "And what are your thoughts on the matter?"

Tern looks up from his food. His hand is shaking. "Hm?"

"This man, Laridae. Have you heard anything about him at HQ?"

Tern rubs the back of his neck. "I'm afraid I have not, sir."

Walter studies him for a moment, then nods.

"So, Ruth," he says, eyes still glued to Tern's. He knits his hands together. "Tell me more about this man you caught."

"He's never worked with Laridae before. This is the first time we've heard that name. Laridae doesn't show his face. He just hires Prairie regulars desperate for cash to collect information."

"Information that's small enough to gather unnoticed, but revealing when brought together," Walter clarifies.

Ruth takes a large bite. "Mhmm."

"What kind of information, exactly? Aside from entrances and exits?"

"Names of our servers and dealers. Our food suppliers and their routes. Laridae even tracked down the guy who delivers our napkins."

"And you gathered this information from the man you caught last night?"

Ruth nods.

"So this Laridae is trying to protect his identity," Walter says. "Save his own *skin*."

Tern brings a sip of wine to his lips with a trembling hand.

"Yep." Ruth reaches over to grab another dinner roll. "But, after our *conversation* with the man we caught, we got more names. Tracked down other nobodies he's hired, had a few good chats, and now we know who Laridae's working for."

"And who might that be?"

Ruth picks at her dinner roll. "He's an Agent."

Walter's eyes widen, but something about it almost seems ungenuine. *What is he up to?*

"From what we gathered, a group of Agents is trying to orchestrate a raid against Prairie," Ruth says. "There are rumors that we conduct business with traitors there. Laridae's higher-ups advised against the raid to keep the peace, but his group is betting on asking for forgiveness instead of permission."

Walter nods, stroking his chin. "This Laridae must be a regular at the Prairie, if he feels the need to be this cautious."

"I think you're right, Walt."

Tern stares at the platter of goat meat.

"So, Ruth." Walter leans forward. "What happened to these *nobodies* you caught? The ones spying for Laridae?"

"We gave them a good shedding."

"Shedding?" I mutter.

Ruth peels the thin outer layer from her dinner roll, revealing soft white flesh beneath.

My stomach lurches.

We continue eating in silence, nothing but scraping forks and the sound of chewing cutting through. I can't bring myself to take another bite.

Walter clears his throat and nods in my direction. "Cedar."

"Hm?"

"Do you know anything about *Laridae*?"

A chill courses through my veins. "I don't know anything about Laridae."

"*Laridae* is the scientific name for a family of seabirds. There must be about a hundred species that fall under this umbrella."

"That's... interesting."

"Isn't it? Can you name any of the birds in this category?"

"Gulls?"

"Yes. What else?"

"I dunno."

Walter lifts his chin. "Noddies."

"Skimmers," Ansel adds tiredly.

"Kittiwakes," Ruth says with a mouthful of food.

"And..." Walter's gaze shifts. "Tern."

The Agent spits out a bit of his drink.

He coughs, hands trembling. He grabs a napkin and pats at the dribble on his chin. The table falls silent again.

He clears his throat with a fleeting grin. "What a peculiar coincidence."

"Peculiar indeed."

Walter strokes his chin for a moment, then looks at me again. "Cedar, I understand you grew up... *differently* than the rest of us, but it's time you learned a valuable lesson." He sets down his glass and leans back, grinning almost excitedly. "A young man oughta learn how to root out a snake."

I blink. I don't think I've ever heard him speak so casually. "A snake?"

"A rat. A *traitor.*" He picks up his drink again and swirls it gently, watching the blood-like liquid spin. "A wolf hiding beneath the sheepskin of integrity."

Tern doesn't look up from his food.

I nod slowly. "Alright."

"There is a list of boxes to be checked in a very particular order," Walter continues. "Do you know which to mark first? Assuming you've already known about your pest problem for some time."

What is he saying? My forehead scrunches. I glance at Tern again, who pretends not to pay attention.

"I'm not sure," I mutter.

"Evidence, Aaron. You plan how you'll dispose of the evidence before you have any to begin with. You'll learn more about this step later."

Evidence?

"Then there is suspicion. Even if you have arranged a way to avoid the eye of the law, that doesn't conceal you from friends, allies, higher-ups. There are masks to be worn and they must be worn well. You must find your own sheepskin to hide behind." He takes a large bite of goat. "Do you know how I deter suspicion?"

I shake my head.

"Geofencing is a method I'm rather fond of."

"Whitestag is geofenced?" Tern swallows so loudly I can hear it. "Our trackers don't work here?"

"Why do you seem so surprised?" Walter asks.

The Agent adjusts his sunglasses, but his hands are shaking so violently it doesn't do much to correct them. He looks like he might throw up. "No reason."

"I'm not following," I admit.

"You see, Cedar," Walter says, "by removing the nuisance of mics and tracking throughout Whitestag—an expensive but worthwhile privilege—I am planning ahead for the next step."

"The next step?"

"Inviting the snake to dinner."

Tern shoots up to his feet. Ruth pushes him back down in his chair.

That's when the realization hits like a truck.

Tern is the Double Agent. He's the one planning the raid.

And Walter knows.

"Extermination is the most nuanced phase." Walter is still picking away at his food. "Although I do enjoy the thrill of the hunt—the adrenaline rush of catching a snake with your own two hands is *euphoric*—there is value to being cautious. Remaining a sheep as the wolf that you are."

I think back to standing on the cabin porch—the rattlesnake he held like it was nothing.

"When you're handling a snake, the cleanest way is to use a hook and observe from a distance. Even the most competent people make mistakes. The best method would be the one that gets your hands the least dirty." He takes a sip of wine. "Do you know the cleanest way to kill a man?"

My heart stops beating. Lily won't look at me. Francis and Ansel lean back with their arms crossed, watching closely.

I clear my throat. "Sorry?"

"The cleanest way to kill a man." He repeats it like it's a common question. "I like to be efficient, and I don't want to get blood all over our table."

My hands quiver. "Nightjade, I think. It's cheap. Grows like a weed. Works instantly."

"That is the obvious answer, I suppose. But it's so... *unoriginal.* And not very practical if you don't have your own supply."

I blink. "Anything that won't leave blood behind."

Walter nods.

I glance at Tern. He stares at me without blinking, pleading in silence. My pulse reverberates in my ears. The room spins and the lights are suddenly too bright, because I know what he's asking.

He's asking how Tern should die.

My mouth goes dry. *Why is this falling on me? This isn't my decision to make.*

I'm no Chaser. I'm no god. I'm just Aaron.

But you aren't supposed to be Aaron anymore, are you?

I look at Tern—an Agent, the worst kind of Chaser. I wonder how many people he's played god with to earn the right to wear that suit. How many lives he sacrificed for his greed. He's still human somewhere, right? *Meat is meat.*

What gives me the right to answer?

Walter taps his fingers impatiently. I have to say something.

I think carefully, going over every human weak point I learned about with Dad. There's the heart, of course, but that gets messy. There's the liver, but a stab to the abdomen poses a similar issue. The eyes are a quick window to the brain. The ears too. But that sounds so... painful.

"Some other kind of poison, then," I mutter.

Walter shrugs. He stares at the watch on his wrist. He's getting impatient, and I haven't given him an answer he likes.

My hands curl into fists. No matter what I say, Tern is going to die— there's nothing I can do about it.

My gaze flickers around the room, snagging on one of the snake sconces. "Venom."

Walter's lips curl into a grin. "I like the way you think."

All at once, everyone but Ruth stops eating. Ansel and Lily reach for their waters in unison and gulp them down at lightning speed—like they've gone through this before. Even Francis stares at his plate with suspicion.

"I suppose there is no harm in poking at the snake before skewering it. Just for a bit of fun." Walter sips the last of his wine. When he sets it down and stares at Tern, something darkens behind his eyes. "*Laridae?*" He scoffs. "You couldn't have picked a more idiotic code name, Gene."

Gene must be his real name.

"You can take those off," Walter says. "There is no use in hiding anymore."

Slowly, the Agent removes his sunglasses. Ruth extends a hand. Tern sets the shades in her palm. She pops out the lenses, crushes them against the table with the blunt end of her steak knife, then snaps the frames in half. She crushes those, too.

"There are trackers in our glasses," Tern mutters, barely able to get the words out.

"We know," Walter says.

"The one you just crushed." Tern swallows. "They'll know it went off right here, at this table."

"No, they'll know it went off in the woods fifty miles from here," Ruth says. "Or in an alley out in the city."

"What do you mean?"

"*Geofencing.*" Ruth grins. "Remember?"

The Agent freezes.

"The moment you step foot on this property, your signal remains locked at the far edge of the property. Out in the woods, acres away from the manor." Ruth takes another bite from her roll. "If any tracker is disabled within twenty miles of here, it will send false location data to the Corps database."

Walter folds his arms and tilts his head. "Do you know what that means, Gene?"

Tern's entire body quivers. "A tracker can be disabled here."

"And?"

Tern stares at the table. His eyes are so wide I wonder if they might roll out of his skull. "And no one in the Corps can do a single thing about it."

Walter chuckles. "There we go. See? A bit of honesty never hurt anybody.

Perhaps you are not as dense as you seem. In fact, I now feel inclined to be... more *merciful*."

"Merciful?"

"Don't worry about what happened to your contacts, Gene. Your betrayal hasn't earned you a fate like theirs. You can keep your skin."

"I... thank you." Tern's shoulders relax. "I-I have a safe house in Vermont. I'm sure I can arrange a transfer to the Northeast Region. I'll be out of your hair and we can forget any of this happened. By the end of the week, at the very latest—"

"What are you talking about?"

Tern's body goes rigid.

Walter laughs. "You aren't going anywhere."

The Agent's eyes flicker to meet ours. He lets out a confused chuckle. "But... you said..."

"I said you can keep your skin."

Tern's smile fades.

Before he can say anything, he begins to cough. Mildly at first, then stronger. He clutches the tablecloth and covers his mouth with his other hand. When he pulls it away, there is blood on his palm. The Agent's eyes are wide as he stares at the Serpent one last time.

He grabs the left side of his chest. His body stiffens, and he falls out of his chair with a thud.

My knuckles whiten. My arms won't stop shaking and I can't look away from the man on the floor who is so still. Unblinking. My dinner rises up into my throat, but I swallow it down.

"Pulmonary hemorrhage," Walter says, staring at the crimson drops on the tablecloth. "Uncomfortable, but I believe cardiac arrest is what took the final blow."

Bleeding in the lungs? A heart attack? What causes that?

"In high enough doses, viper venom can initiate rapid death in under forty five minutes." Walter lets out a fascinated chuckle. "Convenient, but I suppose it did get a bit of blood on the table after all."

Ruth reaches for Tern's abandoned wine glass and knocks it over. A pool of red liquid seeps into the cloth, swallowing up the drops of blood until

I can no longer tell where they once were. "Oops."

"A tragic waste of good wine." Walter shakes his head. "It's a shame Tern knocked it over during his... heart attack."

"A shame indeed," Francis adds.

"In another scenario, if his body needed to be found, or displayed at a funeral for more *strategic* purposes, we'd rinse his mouth of the blood. Wipe it from his lips. That way it really would seem like a death as simple as cardiac arrest. But in this case we are better off letting the body go... *undetected*."

I bring a hand to my mouth.

This man is dead. *Dead.* If I were to go over and touch his skin, it'd still be warm. *And Walter's already talking about covering his tracks?*

Why is he explaining this to me like it's something I need to know?

"Very well done, Walt." I flinch when Francis claps loudly. He folds his arms with a sigh. "You always excel in putting on a good show."

"I won't stand for disloyalty." Walter stares at Tern's plate. "There is nothing that disgusts me more."

Ruth rises and approaches the Agent's lifeless body, but Walter holds up a hand. "No need, Ruth. I think I'll let the boys handle this one."

She nods and returns to her seat. A chill runs through me. *What is he talking about?*

"Glad to have one less snake around," Francis mumbles, shoveling more food in his mouth now that it's in the clear. "Let's just hope our next Double takes this lesson to heart."

This is why I'm here, I realize. *They've suspected Tern's disloyalty for a while, haven't they? That's why they want a new contact on the inside—a trustworthy one.*

That's why they want *me*.

"He will." Walter eyes me carefully. "I'll make sure of it."

"I don't know what we'd do without your vigilance," Francis says. "I had no idea."

"Ah, yes. Without me around to clean your messes, you'd be walking around with blood on your hands and shit on your trousers." Walter refills his glass. "Then you couldn't attend those elaborate parties you love *far* more than your responsibilities, because you'd lose all the respect I've helped you earn over the years."

Francis freezes, then laughs. He wipes his mouth and stands up, flicking a crumb from his suit. "You and your humor. So much like our mother."

Walter takes a generous sip of wine. He doesn't laugh. "And you're just like our father."

A server hurries over to bring Francis his coat. He slides it on swiftly. "Dinner was delightful, but I'm afraid I have matters to attend to."

He walks around Tern's dead body and gives Lily a kiss on the forehead. Her arms are shaking like mine.

"Goodbye, my dear. I'll see you at the Glasshouse Gala in August, yes?"

She forces a smile and nods.

"Good." He gives her a pat on the back before walking away, not even bothering to spare Ansel a glance.

The moments of silence following the leaving of Francis last lifetimes. Lily won't look up from her plate. I can't peel my eyes from Tern, or the blood crusting his bottom lip.

"You know what to do, Ansel." The Serpent rises from his seat and exits the dining room. "Make sure Cedar does too, by the end of the night."

Walter leaves. Ruth and Lily do the same. Ansel and I remain silent for a long time before he stands. "Follow me."

He walks away. I give the remaining food on my plate one last glance before following him out of the dining room.

Meat seems less appealing than it did yesterday.

Friday, June 17

Three hours. 1,400 degrees Fahrenheit.

A brick oven, tucked away in the tunnels beneath Seattle. That's all it takes to become a pile of ash.

Ansel and I sit on the ground against a grimy stone wall, waiting in silence.

We haven't spoken a word since the burning started. I don't think either of us can. I try to ignore the sweat on my skin, and the smell, but it's difficult to focus on anything else in this quiet.

I stare at the floor, going over everything Ansel told me.

Death is busy in today's world. There's too much of it. We can't process corpses the way we once did in the Yesterdays. That's why the Tombs exist —facilities designed to manage dead bodies, while forcing prisoners to do the labor.

In rare cases, if a criminal isn't a high-risk traitor, the Tombs serve to dispose of them efficiently—far out in the desert sand, where no one is around to mind the smell, or the air pollution, or the sea of graves dug by prisoners too healthy to go to waste. Too healthy to receive the mercy of an injection when they could easily pay back the debts of their crimes by working themselves to death.

The dead who never crossed the rigid lines of the Nightjade Order are treated more fairly as corpses. If you can afford it, private funeral homes ensure your loved ones get a nice, respectful transition into the afterlife.

Or you can take the cheap way out and send them to the Tombs, where they'll disappear into the desert sand forever.

Most people take the latter option. If you have the money for a funeral, you're better off spending it on Immunity.

Eden's Remembrance. That's the name of Walter's private crematorium, and one of the many businesses he runs for his family. The real thing is above us. There's a locked door across from where Ansel and I sit, with a staircase leading up to it. The oven in the tunnels—the *Den*—is for personal use only.

That's how he gets away with it. And his fortune, I presume.

"This isn't usual."

Ansel's voice startles me out of my thoughts. But I don't look at him. I don't even have the energy to clench my fists.

None of this is usual, I want to scream. *None of this is right.*

He leans his head against the wall. "My uncle told me to make sure you know how things are done by the end of the night. He's a literal man, so I should make something clear."

"Alright."

Ansel glances at me, then back at the oven. Flickering flames cast his face in an amber glow. I can see the fire mirrored in the green of his eyes. It makes me sick.

"This oven is for emergencies only. It's efficient enough. We haven't been caught for it yet, but it's still risky. The smoke has to end up somewhere, right?" Ansel stares at the oven's venting system and sighs. "But there is a... cleaner way of doing things."

My body goes rigid. "And what would that be?"

"The real Eden."

I expect him to take me to the official crematorium—the facility above our heads. But instead, he takes me down another hallway, dimly lit by flickering Yesterday lights that buzz and hum. The floors, ceiling, and walls are damp stone, sleek with something green. Cobwebs lace the rotting wood posts that support the ceiling. It smells like pavement after rain, but with something slightly rancid too. Something mildewy. But it's hard to fully make out with the stench of burning flesh still crammed in my throat.

We eventually reach a long corridor with a dark metal door at the end. Ansel slides its panel open, revealing a viewing window. "Look inside."

There isn't much light beyond the door, but there's enough to make my eyes squint as they adjust.

It's... a forest. There are real logs, real plants, real rocks, a real stream of running water—all cramped into a small room the size of my own back home.

It's not a forest, I realize, remembering the tanks in Lily's bedroom. *It's a terrarium.*

In the center of the room, coiled upon the leaf litter and soil, sleeps the biggest snake I've ever seen. It's white and freckled with black spots, digesting a lump the size of a dog. Maybe even bigger.

"Uncle is fond of Eden," Ansel mutters. "His cow retic."

"Cow what?"

"A reticulated python. She's as old as I am." A pause. "He loves her more than anything on the planet."

I can't tear my eyes from the snake. The lump in its stomach.

"What does a snake have to do with..." I can't finish the sentence.

"Tern had viper venom in his bloodstream. That wouldn't be very good for Eden to consume."

My heart lodges in my throat. "What do you mean?"

"Even if she weren't busy digesting, at the moment, she wouldn't be interested in Tern anyway." He turns back to the window, studying the sleeping creature. "She only eats live prey."

My eyes grow wide. I bring a shaking hand to my mouth and try not to vomit.

"Twenty feet. That's how long a reticulated python needs to be to consume a full-grown human." He shoves his hands in his pockets and turns back down the hall. "Flesh and bones and all."

He leads me back up to Whitestag. We pause in front of my bedroom door.

"Ansel?" I say.

"Hm?"

"Where do the ashes go?"

He stares out a window, studying the moon-drenched garden below. Purple rhododendrons sway in a breeze too gentle for a night like this. "Get some sleep, *Officer Beck*. I'll take care of it in the morning." He starts walking away. "Wouldn't want you messing things up for Uncle."

I step out of my clothes and into the shower. No matter how thoroughly I scrub my skin and tear through my hair, I can't wash out the smell. When my fingers are wrinkled and the water's gone cold, I give up.

I fall into bed and stare at the ceiling. I don't think I've ever been this tired in my life. I need rest for tomorrow, but I can't fall asleep.

Tern was an Agent. Maybe he did unspeakable things, but he was still human. *And I didn't do a thing to save him.*

I think back to Dad's warnings—everything he said about Walter and his family.

Maybe there was nothing I *could* do.

I'm going off to Chaser training tomorrow. Not a single one of our Doubles has made it back alive. And still, as I lie in bed, unable to close my eyes, I can't help but wonder if the worst of my dangers are sleeping under this same roof.

Survive training, gather information, make it back home, I tell myself. *That's all I need to do.*

Survive training. Gather information. Make it back home.

Survive. Make it back home.

Survive.

A knock on my door startles me forward.

I drag myself out of bed to open it. Ruth stands outside, holding a glass bowl with a goldfish inside.

"I forgot to mention," she says, "you had a visitor today while you were out in the garden. And then dinner happened, and you and Ansel were... busy."

Marco, I realize, remembering how I passed him the fish bag before interfering with Ansel and Corey. *I forgot to bring the goldfish home from the carnival.*

"It'll need a bigger tank. Unless you want it to be oxygen deprived. Or not have room to grow while its internal organs don't *stop* growing, so they'll get too big and push against its—"

"It's for Lily," I cut in.

"That's very kind of you. I'll take her to the fish store tomorrow."

It's quiet for a moment. "Why did he go out of his way to return it?"

"I asked him the same thing."

"What did he say?"

"He told me someone's gotta be stupid enough to stand up to Ansel every now and then." She turns away. "He's just glad it didn't have to be him."

She's about to close the door, but I stop her. "Ruth?"

"Yes?"

"Do you agree with everything Walter does?"

A pause. "No."

"Then why do you go along with it anyway?"

She looks over her shoulder. "Because I'm not stupid enough to try anything else."

Ruth leaves. I return to bed and think about what she said.

Maybe Dad and Ruth are right. Maybe it is smart to keep your mouth shut sometimes. That's the safest option—the one that doesn't involve bruises or Chaser confrontations or making enemies with the wrong people.

But then I think about what Marco said.

Maybe we do need stupid people doing stupid things sometimes. Maybe speaking up isn't always as stupid as it seems.

I haven't made up my mind by the time my eyes finally close, but I do decide on one thing.

I will never stand idly by and let someone hurt an innocent person again.

Even if it's stupid.

Saturday, June 18

♪ I'M NOT COMING BACK - HUSKY ♪

I don't realize there's a tooth in my pocket until I'm standing in line at the Training Center, watching a girl's necklace get crushed by the scanner in front of me.

I was told about the scanners. I was also told not to have anything in my pockets, but I didn't notice the tooth when I groggily slipped into my jeans this morning. Perhaps it's a consequence of getting a whole two hours of sleep.

I've been carrying the deer tooth around ever since Lily told me it was good luck. At first I thought she might ask me about it, and I didn't want to hurt her feelings by accidentally losing it, so my solution was keeping it on my person at all times. Now it's a habit I hardly think about.

My heart races as the girl in front of me walks through the scanners and into the lobby. I stand still, unsure of what to do now that it's my turn.

If they detect something in my pocket, what if they do more than just confiscate it? What if I lose points or something?

Are there even points in this whole training thing? How are we graded?

Is there a grade?

I rub my face with both hands, exhausted and confused and entirely unprepared.

The Serpent was supposed to make sure I was ready for this. All he did was educate me about manners, feed me rich people food, force me to hang out with his bratty nephew, and show me how to get rid of a body. None of that is doing me any good now.

Please step forward.

The robotic voice comes from the scanner.

I reach into my pocket, feeling the tooth's smoothness between my calloused fingers. *I could just drop it on the floor, right?* No one would notice, and I could pass through the scanner while remaining on this passive aggressive robot's good side.

But for some reason, I don't feel like leaving it behind.

Please step forward or exit the line. This is your last warning.

I pause. *This is my last chance to turn back, isn't it?*

I glance over my shoulders. A line of impatient cadets glares at me, arms folded. Now I really can't get away with dropping the tooth. Not without drawing unnecessary attention to myself.

My throat tightens, and my breathing shallows. This is it. Now or never. Good luck or bad luck. Forward or back. *Tooth, or no tooth.*

I think about my goal—the reason why I'm here in the first place, and the footsteps of death I am filling. I am the next in line in a sure sequence of failures. I need all the luck I can get on my side, whether I believe in it or not.

I put the tooth under my tongue and step forward.

I feel a slight buzz in my left eye—the machine is reading me. I can't keep my foot from tapping nervously. What if my new tracker was put in wrong? What if it senses the makeup and contact lens covering my scars? *What if they know I'm Unseen?*

It lets me through without detecting the tooth.

I spit it out and shove it in my pocket. Maybe it is good luck. I can't help but smirk as I walk through the lobby toward the buttonless elevators. *Maybe the Corps doesn't know everything after all.*

The elevator swallows me the moment I step inside. And when I watch the Training Center's front doors disappear, my smirk is quick to fade, and I can't help but question just how lucky I really am.

The elevator leads me to an underground room the size of a school gym, with seamless white walls and black floors. The Officer in charge of training is an older man named Frank Gilbert, who has cropped gray hair and a rough face that always seems to be pinched in some state of displeasure.

It feels weird to introduce myself as someone else. Every time I tell a fellow cadet my name or hear someone call me Cedar or Beck, I expect them to do a double take. To narrow their eyes at me and say something like, *That's not really your name, is it?*

But they don't. They smile, shake my hand, and move on, accepting everything they're told without a single questioning doubt.

They're Chips, I remind myself. *That's what they do best.*

Gilbert goes over everything I learned with Dad and Viv about the structure of the Chaser Corps. Although I've heard this same lecture about a dozen times, hearing it now feels... different. Wrong. Because now I have to nod and pretend to be amazed by this *incredible* organization I feel nothing but hatred for.

But I'm here for a good reason. The information I gather will help the Unseen. And when we get our uniforms, even as I stand in a sea of people dressed exactly like me, I know I am not like them.

I am not like them, I tell myself, over and over and over again.

Wednesday, June 23

Conditioning is a hell I've visited before.

Oddly enough, I find it much more preferable to turning compost. The chores I did back home make this feel like child's play, but it's still not my cup of tea.

We run races carrying other cadets on our back. We do push-ups until I feel like vomiting. We spar with wooden weapons, which I pretend to be less practiced with than I actually am. Lunges and planks, mountain climbers and squats, anything to make our muscles set themselves on fire —and we do it all with Gilbert screaming in our faces.

I decided I didn't like him the moment I saw his uniform, but his nagging doesn't bring him any closer to my good side. And for some reason, he *really* likes picking on me.

I'm not as scrawny as I used to be, but I didn't grow up with the kind of food these cadets did either. I didn't have constant access to grocery stores, junk food, or that disgusting protein powder Ansel uses to make milkshakes. I've eaten more meat as Cedar Beck than I have in my entire life. Even with the grit I earned from my chores back home, I'm barely keeping up with the other cadets.

My back isn't straight enough during a push-up? I have to do an extra fifty while everyone else moves on. I'm the last to finish a lap? I have to run five more. Because for whatever reason, Gilbert has chosen me as his favorite example.

It's like he knows I'm itching to talk back to him. This whole thing seems like another one of the Serpent's tests. The pressure of being monitored weighs heavier when you don't even know what you're being tested on to begin with.

But despite the yelling, provoking, and public humiliation attempts, I keep my mouth glued shut. I prove Gilbert wrong and do everything he tells me without a complaint.

Until today.

It's my fifth day of training. We're warming up with laps around the room. We've been running a mile every morning, and my legs still aren't used to it. They're sore and weak and feel more like jelly than flesh and bone. When I came home after my first day, I wouldn't stop throwing up.

I don't feel sick anymore, but I'm still unhappy and jogging with a frown.

"*Beck*," Gilbert yells from the center of the room, arms crossed. "Wipe that face off or I'll do it for you."

I bite my tongue and try to relax my expression, but it's hard to do while jogging with my limbs on fire.

"Ignoring me, are you?" he shouts. "The Corps won't stand for attitude, Beck. At least act like you're here by choice, because you are."

I grind my teeth. *Keep it cool.*

If he wants me to fix my face, fine. I'll fix my face.

I force a smile. The most obviously posed expression I can muster—a grin so big it makes my eyes squint and dimples come out. I even give Gilbert a little salute as I jog past.

He scowls. "Now hide that stupid grin."

It takes everything I have to make my face as neutral as possible.

He addresses the whole group now as we keep running. "In the Corps, all must be uniform. Everyone must be the same, from what you wear and how you speak to the way you hold yourself—including your expression. Even if you are upset, even if you are in pain, you must hide your emotions. Because the Corps will not stand for anything that goes against their grain.

"You are a tool now. A machine. And machines feel *nothing*. So you will either force yourself not to feel, or pretend until it becomes true." He glares as I jog past him again. "And machines most certainly do not have attitude."

I refuse to look him in the eye.

"Beck."

"Sir?" I shout back.

"Unclench your jaw, relax your brow, and run another lap. You will run another for every reminder."

I bite my tongue to keep from saying something I shouldn't. I look at the trainee running beside me and huff. He looks more miserable than I do, and Gilbert hasn't said a word. But I do as he says and run my extra lap.

The other trainees have already started sparring with each other, as we've done every morning after our runs. I can hardly breathe by the time I finish and jog up to Gilbert. Every muscle is sore and my eyes droop with exhaustion. "Am I cleared to join the others now, sir?"

He looks me up and down. "Run another."

My brows furrow. "Why?"

"Because I said so." His voice echoes throughout the room. A few cadets glance at us over their shoulders. "Now you will run three more instead for questioning my command."

That's ridiculous, I want to scream. *No one else is running extra laps.* My nails dig into my palms and I clamp my mouth shut.

"I see that look on your face, Beck," he spits. "And perhaps you are right. Maybe some things are unfair, but that is how the world works, and you will learn to follow orders anyway."

My mouth opens reflexively, ready to give him a piece of my mind. But I pause. For a moment, I swear I see the Serpent's face plastered over Gilbert's. *They're just the same, aren't they?*

This guy could have me exterminated with the wave of his hand. I *should* be afraid of him. Maybe I don't agree with him, but if I don't learn to control my emotions, I could easily fail training. And they've already made it clear that failure means death.

Even though I'm itching to argue—even though it feels like my entire body might fall apart—I run another lap.

By the second lap, the anger has only grown.

And by the time I'm finishing my third, I'm so exhausted and frustrated and glad to be done that I feel delirious. I'm *laughing*.

Without thinking, I cup my hands over my mouth and shout at Gilbert from across the room. "Am I pretty now, Officer?"

Shit.

I stumble to a stop, bringing a hand to my mouth. That is *not* what I meant to say.

All cadets in the room freeze, holding their breath as they watch me with wide eyes. Like they're waiting for me to get an injection.

No one has talked back to Gilbert before. And here I am, making yet another example of myself.

The Chaser stares at me across the room for a long time, posture rigid, hands locked behind his back. The seconds feel like lifetimes until he speaks, voice so low I can hardly hear it.

He points behind me. "You will walk through that door."

I turn around slowly, noticing a faint outline carved into the wall.

"You will head straight down that hall. When you return, you will be better."

I'm in a long, narrow room without my uniform. A corridor, really. The walls are a searing white. The floors are black and glowing red.

The entire floor is made of hot coals.

My head pounds. I can barely breathe. The stench of burning flesh chokes me, sending me back under Eden with Ansel, when we watched Tern's body turn into something like the ash and rocks beneath me. The room spins. It's so damn hot in here.

The only way to keep my skin from melting off is to keep running. Even though my muscles feel like lead, I run. Too slow, and the coals will burn my feet.

But jogging doesn't feel great either. Instinct urges me to be quick, but the faster I go, the deeper my feet sink. Pieces of coal and ash stick to my heels and singe my flesh.

There must be a better way to do this, but I can't think about that. I can't master being swift and weightless in this lead-limb panic. All I know is moving forward.

The walls are closing in on me. There's nowhere to turn, nowhere to go but in an endless jog to one wall and back. If I stand in one place to take a break, my feet will get charred.

But the ground is still hot, and I burn anyway.

I don't know how long I've been in here by the time I fall to my knees.

I can't run anymore.

My eyes squeeze shut. I let out a pathetic cry as the coals eat right through the fabric covering my legs and burn my flesh. I can hardly hold myself up. I hang my head, clutching my hair in fistfuls. I'm still sobbing when two uniformed Officers in their fireproof boots pull me up and escort me out.

My head cartwheels. I'm hardly paying attention when they bring me to another white room I don't recognize. A pair of Corps healers introduce themselves and rub a stinging ointment on the bottom of my feet. I'll be ready to run again tomorrow, they say.

When I limp out of the infirmary, the other trainees are on their lunch break. I don't feel like eating. I sit against the wall in a corner, staring straight ahead. I don't notice Gilbert approaching until he speaks, standing in front of me with his hands behind his back.

"I am rough because I need to be," he says.

I can't look at him.

"There is no other way to file you down to your sharpest point." He turns to study the other cadets. "You should be grateful for your potential and my acknowledgment of it."

My hands clench into fists. *Potential? That's what this is about?* The thought makes me want to tear my hair out. I'm too weary to laugh at how ridiculous he sounds.

"Imagine you are presented with a box of tools. There are three that are polished and sharp, and a dozen others that are dull and rusting. What would you wield?"

It's a dumb question and I feel even dumber for answering. "A sharp one."

"And where do the others go? They aren't useful anymore. What point is there in crowding the box?"

"They get tossed out."

"So what will it be, Beck?" He looks at the sea of chatting cadets like they're a line of ants. A nuisance. "Are you going to sharpen, or rust?"

I stare at the trainees too. They look so young from far away. I wonder if any of them have seen a man die at the dinner table, or smelled the stench of burning flesh. "I haven't decided yet."

Gilbert observes me for a long time, then turns to walk away. "Decide soon, Officer. I'd hate to see such potential wasted."

Officer? My brows crease. *But we won't be sorted into our divisions until training's over.*

An Officer is the most esteemed division in the Corps, second only to Agents. Even most Agents start out wearing that white suit of armor before earning a promotion.

A chill runs through me. *Maybe I'm doing better than I thought.*

Maybe I can survive training after all.

I can't tell if I should feel relieved or sickened

15

Wednesday, June 23

Gilbert lets me sit out for the rest of the day. Ruth picks me up from training as usual. I don't say a word. I just head straight to my room. Collapsing on my bed has never felt so relieving and painful at once.

A knock on the door cuts through the silence.

Lily walks in, pausing when she sees me staring at the ceiling. She shuts the door, pulls up a chair, and sits. "Thank you for the goldfish. I really like him."

I don't say anything.

"Ruth took me to the fish store the other day. We have a whole tank set up just for him, with a dojo loach and everything. They're great bottom feeders. They act really funny too. So spastic."

I turn onto my side and look at her. I want to say something—that I'm glad she likes the goldfish, and that I'm happy to see her happy, because she's the only one in this house who seems to give a damn about me. The only one I could call a friend.

But my mouth is cemented shut. The words are there, but I've forgotten how to say them.

"Did you know a goldfish can grow over twelve inches long if you put them in a pond? Imagine that! They get real fat too. The trick is giving them the space to grow, not restricting them to one little bowl."

I can't look her in the eye.

"Can you hear me?" she asks quietly.

I nod.

"You're not going to say anything?"

I shake my head.

"Don't worry. I know you're not ignoring me."

I glance at her.

"I get like that too, sometimes." She stares at her thumbs. "When everything is too much, and you just... can't talk. Even if you want to."

It's quiet for a while. "Do you want me to keep talking?"

I nod again.

So she does. For an entire hour, I stare at the ceiling while she tells me about the ponds she'd like to have someday, big enough for her goldfish to grow. And I listen, because everything hurts, and I like her voice a lot more than the one in my head.

Until someone knocks on the door.

"Come in," Lily says.

Ansel opens it. "Dinner's ready."

"I don't think Aaron in the mood for—"

"You know he won't care."

Aaron. She's the only one who still calls me that.

Lily sighs, then faces me again. "Can you stand?"

I force myself to a seated position, squeezing my eyes shut. Every time I move it feels like my burns might crack open.

"Do you need any—"

"I'm fine." My words return a little harsher than I meant them to.

Lily nods. Despite the pain, I follow the siblings downstairs, limping all the way.

Dinner is uneventful. Walter quizzes me as usual, asking about poker tactics, hand-to-hand combat, rattlesnake anatomy, and other topics I find useless.

I answer monotonously, eyes glued to the food I pick at. He tells me that an octopus has a donut-shaped brain and neurons in its arms, that the world is full of strange things we cannot understand and secrets we never expect. He says gathering information about everything you can is one of the best tools a man can wield.

It's really annoying.

Heading back upstairs and walking through the hall feels like setting myself on fire all over again. I'll need to put more of that ointment on my feet soon if I want to run again tomorrow. *All I want is sleep.*

Just enough moonlight shines through the corridor to make something glint in the corner of my eye. Ansel leans against the wall in the dark, skinning an orange with a peeler. He scoffs at the sight of my limp. "What happened to *you*?"

I ignore him.

"I don't understand how a bit of physical conditioning resulted in *this*. Are you really that weak?" He shakes his head. "Those who aren't used to pain always crumble at their first taste of it."

I stop walking.

"I'm going to give you some advice, Becky." He tosses a peel on the ground, not caring about the mess. Someone else will clean it for him.

I turn around with an exhausted sigh. "I'm really not in the mood for this, alright?"

He tosses an orange slice into his mouth. "If you want to survive this job of yours, you'll need to shed your skin for something thicker."

That's it.

I pin Ansel against the wall, taking his peeler and holding it to his throat. "My skin's thicker than yours will ever be." I lean in. "And I'd *really* like to test that theory."

"I was only teasing, though my advice was genuine." Ansel chuckles, but the sound falters quickly, fading into something like boredom. Maybe disappointment. "So easily provoked. Another sign of weakness."

"Weakness?" I snicker bitterly, pressing the blade firmer against his neck.

"You've never had to work a day in your life. You've never been without food. Comfort. Safety. You have *no idea* what it's like to live every single day worrying that it might be your last. That your entire world could crumble beneath you in an instant because you're not supposed to exist. All you've ever known is Immunity, and believe me, it shows."

Keeping the peeler at his throat, I use my other hand to yank his palm to his face. "Look at your hands. Soft. *Weak.* Because you'll always have someone to clean up your messes, won't you?"

His expression remains calm, but his tone sends a chill through me. "You know nothing."

I laugh tiredly. "You're not a mystery, alright? You're so damn easy to read."

"Is that so?"

"You're an asshole because dear old dad doesn't give a damn about you."

"Excuse me?"

"I'm no idiot and neither are you. We both saw the way he looked at you on Friday night. Hell, he hardly noticed you. Your weakness disgusts him, doesn't it?"

He tries to break free, but I push him back.

"You've never been deserving of his attention or admiration. So you act out, and you try to force people to respect you, because you're desperate to make up for the one person who never will."

His entire body is trembling now.

I think about that photo with the deer—what Lily said about pretending to be the one who shot it to impress her father. I saw the way he treated his children at dinner. They hardly see him, and when they do, he dismisses them. No wonder they're so eager for his approval.

"You've despised me since the moment I got here, and I've been racking my brain to figure out what I did wrong," I say. "I think I get it now."

"You know nothing."

"You were supposed to be the Serpent's *fox in the henhouse*. Not me."

That makes him freeze.

"You don't deny it. Am I wrong?"

He clenches his jaw, not saying a word.

"Oh, come on, Ansel." I lift his chin up with the peeler. "What are you so afraid of?"

"*Yes*, alright? It should have been me!"

His words bounce off the walls. He lowers his voice to a harsh whisper, teeth clenched.

"I was supposed to be the Chaser," he seethes. "That was *always* the plan, long before you came along and screwed everything up. Uncle needed someone loyal. I was going to become an Agent and work my way up the ranks. Climb that damn ladder he's always going on about."

"Supposed to." I tilt my head mockingly. "So you failed."

His face reddens. "That entrance exam was rigged. I wasted days—*nights* of my life preparing for that damn test. I memorized every equation and principle in my textbooks. Trained for hours with Ruth. Stopped eating to make weight for the physical. Studied psychology to ensure I passed the psychiatric evaluation. I did *everything* right, and they still failed me." He scoffs, shaking his head. "It's because they know who my father is, that's what. They saw my name and failed me because they didn't want a Schneider in their midst."

"Or maybe you just failed."

He lurches forward, but I push him back. "Get your filthy hands off me, or I'll—"

"If they bribed a proctor in the Corps to bypass my entrance exam," I say, "why didn't your uncle do the same for you?"

"The only reason he didn't make you take it yourself was because you missed the deadline. You have no history of disappointing him. You're a gamble he's willing to make." He averts his gaze with a scowl, neck muscles feathering. "Uncle can't stand inadequacy. He would never bribe anyone for my passage if he already knew I failed."

My brows knit together.

This is why Walter was so eager to take me in. Ansel had just ruined his only chance of becoming a Chaser, and he wanted to pass the torch to me —the godson of Noriko Teshima, who will be more loyal to him than any stranger like Tern ever could be. If I screw him over like Tern did, he already made it clear he'd do something worse to the Cut in return.

But this is backwards. I'm not supposed to be a long-term plant like Walter wanted Ansel to be. Like he wants *me* to be. I'm going to pass the final test, be out in the field for a few weeks, and fake my death as soon as I have enough information for this to be worth the trouble. That's it. None of this Viper bullshit.

"But I don't want to be an Agent," I mutter.

"Oh, that doesn't matter." Ansel chuckles tiredly. "He'll make you think you do. If the Corps doesn't get around to it first, that is."

His words make me pause, giving him time to maneuver out of my grip. I'm too taken aback to fight it. He points a finger in my face.

"You've disrespected me one too many times, Becky. And one day, when I've obtained power your minuscule mind can't even imagine, you'll regret your decision to speak out of line. You *will* respect me."

With that, he storms off, throwing the orange behind him.

I continue walking down the hall and gasp when I see Lily. *How long has she been standing there?*

She glares. "That was cruel."

Now I'm glaring too. "You're not seriously defending that prick, are you?"

"He's my brother," she snaps, then looks away. "You shouldn't have said those things."

We stand in silence for a long time. My jaw clenches. "You have no idea the kind of day I've had, alright? My feet hurt, I'm exhausted, I'm angry, and I don't have the patience to sit here and listen to you tell me how hard his life's been or whatever excuse you have. I just wanna get to bed."

"Well it's true, okay?" Lily looks at me again. "I know we have privileges other people don't. But that doesn't mean we're happy."

I don't know what to say to that.

"You should know better than to let what he says get to you. You're clearly the bigger person. Trying to fight fire with fire is stupid." She sighs. "You really don't want to be on his bad side, alright?"

"*He* shouldn't get on mine either."

"He'll be in charge someday whether we like it or not. And if an alliance is made with the Cut, he'll have some control over you too. Just like my father controls the other Unseen under his wing."

I avert my gaze and shove my hands in my pockets. I know she's probably right, but I'm too pissed off to admit it.

"You said your feet hurt."

I nod.

"Why is that?"

Slowly, I sit down against the wall and take off my shoes. Her eyes widen at the sight of blood soaking through my socks.

"They gave me medicine for it." I retrieve the jar from my pocket. The thought of putting more ointment on my open wounds makes me feel sick. "Corps healers work miracles, apparently."

That's because they put things in their *medicine* that Dad never would. Quick-fix chemicals and engineered ingredients with a laundry list of side effects that keep your body from working the way it should. They have the money, research, and tech to do it.

I scoff. It's all funded by Immunity—by culling society of those who use more resources than they return. I wonder how many lives paid for this jar in my hands.

I lean my head against the wall. "It'll all be scabs by morning."

Lily kneels in front of me, taking the jar. "Let me help you with that." She does.

"I'm sorry," I say when she's done. *For her. Not for him.*

She nods. "I know."

She goes off to bed. I sit there and stare at the snake sconces on the wall for a long time before doing the same. I fall asleep dreading the moment I'll open my eyes again.

Wednesday, July 13

I'm starting to understand why no one else made it through training.

It's not the physical conditioning, even though it aches. It's not running on hot coals either even though I get sent to that room more than anyone else and have never felt a greater pain. It's not learning to wield Nightjade weapons used for murder, or learning about the operations of each twisted division in the Corps, or hearing people talk about the Pick like it's nothing.

It's what they tell you.

Every day, you are reminded of your own insignificance. Your worthlessness is drilled into you until it feels like you might crack. You are told that you are nothing, over and over again, until you start believing it's true.

The only part I somewhat enjoy is combat training. We learn how to use weapons that don't involve Nightjade. Knives. Bow and arrows. Swords. Our bare hands.

For a while I hide my skills with the blade on purpose. If it's obvious I have previous experience, people will start to ask questions. But after practicing my throwing for hours on end, day after day, week after week, it's gotten difficult not to hit every bullseye.

Sometimes—just for a moment—I catch myself being dumb enough to believe Dad would be proud. But I don't think that's true.

I'm becoming the very thing he's dedicated his entire life to fighting.

Still, there are moments when I like this. Moments when I feel exhilarated, or good at something for once in my life.

And it disgusts me.

Friday, July 29

Every night I go home, drop off my uniform, walk into the woods, and dive into the swimming hole.

I found it after my first week of training, when I couldn't sleep and decided to go on a walk. The nightmares started after Ansel and I put Tern in that furnace. They only get worse with every day of training I complete.

The swimming hole is a deep blue pit of water that looks endless. A cold sanctuary in a world that burns. The only place where I feel truly weightless.

I'm floating on my back, staring at the sky through the gaps in the canopy of evergreens above me. It reminds me of the pond back at the Cut, where Beau and I spent so many sticky summer days, catching frogs and swimming until our fingertips became raisins. I close my eyes, tasting the pine and algae in the air. Letting myself breathe.

A twig snaps. I scramble upright, treading water. Lily waves from a few yards away.

"You scared me," I say.

"You woke me on your way out."

"Sorry."

She sits on a boulder and pulls a tiny sketchpad from her pocket. I watch her pen scratch the paper in effortless sweeps. We stay in our own little worlds for a long time—me on my back in the water, her on that rock. It's nice not to talk about what's clearly on both our minds.

My last day of training is tomorrow. That means I'll have to face whatever killed our past Doubles before they could become real Chasers.

I sigh, watching my breath solidify in the cold moonlight. I know I won't find any this close to the city, but I try to locate stars through breaks in the trees. I wonder if this will be my last time seeing the night sky.

My fingers get wrinkly after a while, so I step out and dry off. I take a seat beside Lily, breathing in the serenity of the woods. Everything is drenched in the dark blue of night. Crickets harmonize. Bullfrogs croak. *It sounds like home.*

I glance at Lily's sketchpad. She's drawing a twisting rattlesnake with unrealistically round and empty white eyes. It looks like it's emerging from another snake's mouth. *It's shedding.*

"You like snakes too?" I ask, thinking of Walter.

She nods.

"Must run in the family."

"They're my favorite animal."

"Why's that?"

"They have admirable qualities."

"Admirable?" I raise a brow. "I thought a *snake* meant a traitor or something. Deception. Manipulation."

"Not like that." She circles over the eyes again, making them bolder with messy line work. "I like the way they shed their skin."

"You don't think that's creepy?"

"It's like they're constantly being born. Always letting go of old versions of themselves to make room for new ones. They welcome change. It's refreshing, really. The idea that we can always be renewed." She smiles to herself, still focused on the drawing. "I like to think we're the same."

"We?"

"Humans and snakes."

"You've lost me a bit."

"We're reborn a thousand times over in one lifetime. Every second, really. Our bodies are always shedding old cells, generating new ones. We think new thoughts while our brains file away memories we won't even know we've forgotten. We're never static."

I shake my head. "I don't understand you."

She shrugs. "That's okay. I'm used to it."

"Doesn't that get lonely?"

"Not anymore." When she looks at me, her eyes are smiling. "I understand me."

I let out a soft chuckle. "I wish I could relate."

"Don't worry. I understand you."

I look at the treetops again. "I don't think you do."

More quiet. Crickets. Bullfrogs. Reminders of a home I may never see again.

"Don't feel guilty, Aaron," she continues. "You're helping the Cut. Your family."

My throat tightens. I stare at my hands. "It doesn't always feel that way."

"I know you're worried. But... after all this is over, you'll shed too."

She gives me a friendly pat on the shoulder before pocketing her sketchbook and walking away.

I jump in the water again. I wash my skin until it's raw and there are lines in my fingertips.

When I head back inside, I'm surprised to see Ruth waiting for me.

"Walter wants to see you in his office."

"But it's midnight."

"He knows."

Sure enough, he's there behind his desk, the smell of old cigar smoke and cloves lingering in the air. He grabs an orange from a bowl on his desk and starts scraping it with a peeler.

"Tomorrow is your last day," he says, eyes glued to the fruit.

I sink into the chair across from him. "Yup."

"Sit up straight. Slouching is a sign of weakness."

I straighten without arguing.

Walter eyes me, amused. "I see your jaw twitching. What's the plan—threaten me with this orange peeler?"

My eyes widen, thinking back to that confrontation in the hallway. "Ansel told you about that?"

"No. I see everything here at Whitestag. You know how tight my security is. I assumed you already knew about the cameras."

Security cameras? I've walked that corridor every day for weeks, and I haven't noticed any. Just those creepy snake sconces.

Then it clicks.

"The sconces," I say.

"Very clever." He chuckles again and continues peeling. "I see many things—both here at Whitestag and beyond. I have contacts in every neighborhood, every tier of status. I've spent my life studying more subjects than you can imagine. But there's one thing I don't know."

He pops an orange slice into his mouth. "I have no idea what happens at training."

I blink. "What do you mean?"

"We've never had a *true* Viper in the Corps. Every piece of intel we have comes from one-off bribes and drunken chatter at our clubs. Tern was once our most trusted source, but the final test never came up in conversation before his tragic passing."

I bite back a scoff. *Tragic.*

"I do not know what the exam entails or what they will ask of you," he says, "but I do know you'll be watched. Every choice you make will be dissected. If you're not useful, you will be tossed aside. Just another scrapped card in the deadwood pile. You understand this, yes?"

"I do."

Walter chews another slice. "And let's say you do prove yourself valuable. Do you know what happens next?"

"I'll be sorted into a division."

"And?"

"I'll do what they tell me until I've gathered enough intel to go home."

The Serpent shrugs. "Or you could stay."

My shoulders tense. "What?"

"You heard me." Another slice disappears into his mouth. "If you've already put your foot in the door, why not step through? See where that path takes you? I could expand your sponsorship. Make this arrangement more permanent."

"I can't do that."

"Why not?"

"Because they're Chasers," I snap—then catch myself, softening my tone. "They're murderers."

"And the Unseen haven't killed anyone?"

"That's different."

"How come?"

"We're not mindless about it. We only defend ourselves when we have to."

"Remember what I told you, Aaron. Meat is meat." He drops another piece into his mouth. "Death is death is death."

"I'm not staying."

"You understand that if you want to play the part long enough to be a decent spy, you will need to do what they do eventually, yes?"

A chill runs through me.

I haven't thought that far ahead.

I've always known what this job would entail, but thinking about it always felt like too much. Too sickening. I drifted through training on the burning fumes of desperation and denial. I told myself Chasers mainly exterminate criminals. That I wouldn't be hurting anyone innocent. But does that even matter?

They're still people.

Ideally, I'll get sorted into the NOT division, and I won't have to hurt anyone. That's probably where I'll land, given how much Gilbert hates my guts.

You're doing this for the Cut, I remind myself. We need an advantage if we want to propel this rebellion forward. If we want to put an end to Chasing and the Presidency and the Nightjade Order, we have to know how to think like our enemies.

At least I won't be here long enough to see the Pick.

"What if the Cut ends up needing another Double farther down the line?" Walter asks. "Would it really be worth it to risk the life of another one of your rebels when you could be doing the job for them?"

"That's a stretch."

"Then consider the lasting benefits you can provide for the Unseen by extending your stay. The higher you climb, the more you will know. Think about how useful it would be to have a long-term Double in the *Agency*. If they ever discover anything revealing about the Unseen, you could warn your friends and family and give them time to escape. You wouldn't want another Harebell Hill now, would you?"

Harebell Hill. The mention makes me pause. Dad never talked about it much. I think it pained him to think about. It pains me too, knowing that Chasers massacred one of our sister compounds, and we couldn't do a damn thing about it. It holds the record for the largest Unseen encampment raided by the Corps in history—but that title would be passed to the Cut if we were ever discovered.

My throat tightens. I shake my head.

Walter extends an orange slice. "Want one?"

I study the fruit in his palm, like I'm staring at that rattlesnake all over again. Like there's a weight to this seemingly harmless offer that I can't detect.

I don't want to repay this favor.

I look the Serpent dead in the eye. "No."

He shrugs. "Suit yourself."

He finishes the last of his orange, wipes his hands on a napkin, and levels his gaze with me. "The choice is yours, Aaron. I just hope you keep the future in mind when you face the final exam tomorrow."

I nod, uncertain.

"I've taught you sharpness of mind. Fulfilled every promise I made to your parents. From now on, it is your job to use that head on your shoulders and refrain from doing anything reckless, because you are completely on your own." He looks me straight in the eye. "No one is coming to save you."

His words are cold enough to reach my bones, but I don't let it show. "I know."

He waves me off. "You may go now."

I do.

And I fall asleep wondering if I ever will again.

17

Saturday, July 30

♪ FALLING MAN - BLONDE REDHEAD ♪

I'm suspicious of my breakfast.

I sit in the dining room with the Schneiders, staring at my smoked salmon Eggs Benedict. There's nothing unusual about the meal itself. It's the fact that everyone else is eating French toast that freaks me out.

Walter's newspaper blocks me from his view, so I lean in and sniff the plate. Nothing unusual. *What does snake venom smell like?*

"That's insulting, Cedar," he says from behind his paper. "You really think I'd poison you with something you could detect?"

I scowl. He really meant it when he said he sees everything.

"If I'd been planning to kill you all along, I would have done so sooner. No point in wasting perfectly good food on you for four months." He pauses. "I thought Eggs Benedict was your favorite breakfast."

"It is."

He says nothing more.

My appetite's grown stronger after weeks of conditioning and larger portions, but right now, the food looks less like breakfast and more like bait.

This could be my last meal.

I'm being fattened up for slaughter.

Walter doesn't say goodbye when he leaves the table. Lily hesitates at the doorway. We meet eyes, but we can't bring ourselves to speak. She offers a faint smile before walking away, leaving me with Ansel.

He studies me while sipping his coffee. "Your final day?"

"Yeah."

He chuckles. I glare.

"Ready to go?" Ruth's voice cuts in from behind. She's by the door, dressed in her usual green suit. I glance down at my plate. I didn't even get to finish my food.

"Yeah." I stand up and grab the white cube tucked beneath my chair—my uniform, compacted for transport. I'm halfway to the door when Ansel speaks again.

"Goodbye, Aaron. If we meet again..." He smirks. "Then I was very wrong about you."

He lifts his cup in a mock salute.

Ruth leads me outside. I pause by the car to look at Whitestag one last time.

Funny. I used to think this house would eat me alive.

It doesn't feel so big anymore.

I don't know what I'm waiting for.

For the past half hour, an elevator has been swallowing cadets with *A* names. They disappear one by one. Some don't come back.

My leg shakes up and down as I stand in line, staring at my reflection in the perfectly polished floor beneath me. I look ridiculous in this uniform. When I see Cedar Beck staring back at me, clad in a suit of blinding white armor, I wonder how the other trainees don't see it too. That I'm a fraud, existing right under their noses.

I think about the Doubles who came before me. I wonder if any of them made it this far. If they too stood in line, scrutinizing their reflections and wondering how they got here. Not knowing what they would face beyond the hungry jaws of that elevator—or why some of the cadets haven't returned.

Whatever I'm facing today is the one thing our Double Agents couldn't overcome. And there's a very good chance I might disappear too.

My name is called too soon.

For a moment, I swear the world stops spinning. I feel its jarring pause, like the invisible hands of gravity are playing tug of war with my limbs. I think back to the moment after I saw that deer's eyes, when the car skidded to a halt right before everything went numb.

I'd stand still forever if I could. But there is no going back now, and if I don't move, there will be no going forward, either.

I'm here for a reason. I'm here to put my life on the line for the people I care about. To survive this final test and return home with all the information I've gathered, so we can finally put real change in motion. So we can finally get the upper hand.

And maybe someday, I can live a normal life again. No more separation. Just Mom and Dad and Lori and I, together as we should be.

And maybe—just maybe—I can prove myself, too.

I'm not stupid. *I am Unseen.*

I step forward.

The elevator spits me out into a dark hallway.

Unlike the blinding white decor upstairs, the ceiling and walls are covered with polished black tiles. I keep moving forward. I just want to get this whole thing over with.

I hear a chirping sound—like the little *beep* the scanners let out when you walk inside the building. I look down. A blue ring of light appears on the floor, spinning like a loading signal on a computer.

A robotic voice materializes out of thin air.

Subject identified: Beck, Cedar.

I keep walking, eager to get away—right as the voice speaks again.

Please walk forward and wait at the end of the hall. You
will be tested shortly. We thank you for playing your part.

I sigh in annoyance. I was already doing that.

I walk at a normal pace while looking around, studying every surface for signs of a trap. I can't help but feel like I'm back at Whitestag, being watched by bronze snake sconces or tested by Walter. I expect to stumble across something weird—like a pressure plate that triggers a bunch of darts laced in Nightjade, or a pitfall filled with snakes, or maybe some poisonous gas—

Stop being paranoid and focus.

To my surprise, I reach the end of the hallway without encountering any hidden traps. There's a door. I wait for it to open, but it doesn't. I knock. "Hello?"

Nothing.

"Can I come in?"

Still, not a sound.

I shoulder it open. My eyes squint to adjust to the light. It's a small white room with seamless walls and floors. No windows. The door shuts automatically behind me.

No escape.

I nearly jump back when I realize someone else is here too.

There's a white chair with a kid my age strapped to it. Sweat plasters strands of red hair to his forehead. His eyes are peeled so wide I wonder how they don't pop out.

"Uh... hi." I give him a small wave.

He doesn't say anything. Doesn't even blink. His entire body trembles as he stares at me like I'm something to fear.

I think about the uniform I'm wearing, suddenly a bit nauseous. *Maybe I am.*

"Are you... okay?" I ask.

No answer. The silence is filled by that robotic voice from earlier.

Subject: Beck, Cedar.

My brows crease. I glance up, searching for the source of the voice, but the ceiling is blank. Still—I know they're watching me. I think back to Walter's warning from last night. *I'll be discarded if I'm not useful.* My mouth suddenly feels dry.

The voice continues.

Life is a gift. It is a gift allowed by the Presidency, but gifts can be taken away when it is deserved.

This citizen has knowingly abused that gift. They have been accused of: Treason.

My hands clench into fists.

Treason. I almost laugh. We all know who the real traitors are. They're the ones watching me right now, feeding off this system like parasites. They betray their own species every time they choose wealth and power over life.

This citizen is now your Assignment. In accordance with the Nightjade Order, by the authority of the Presidency, you have been given clearance to exterminate the subject.

My stomach lurches.

Exterminate?

A panel in the wall slides open. A robotic arm extends, holding a metal tray. I squint to make out the object resting upon it.

A syringe, filled with dark purple serum.

Nightjade.

I stagger back and hit the door.

No. This can't be right. This isn't how it's supposed to go. Exterminations happen *after* training. *After* the final test. *After* I'm long gone, safe back home with the information I needed.

All at once, the air depletes from the room. From me.

The final test is extermination.

I close my eyes, exhaling shakily. *Of course it is.* How could I have been so stupid? Why didn't I see this coming? Of course this is what they really want to know. Not how we fight, run, or track.

They want to see what we do when we're ordered to kill another human being.

This is why none of our other candidates have made it through training. This is the mistake that killed them.

No one passed, because the kid in that chair is a traitor just like us.

Just like me.

How will you proceed, Cedar Beck? Will you play your part?

I open my eyes. A single tear glides down the kid's cheek. Something about him reminds me of Beau. Maybe it's the color of his hair. The freckles on his nose. The flicker of pure-hearted innocence clinging to his gaze.

My heart slams against my ribs like it's trying to kick its way out, over and over again until my head throbs and my ears ring. It's like the ticking of some incessant clock.

I've always hated clocks. They never shut the hell up. Their entire purpose is to pester you—to annoy you into remembering that time is fleeting, and it's passing you by, and there's nothing you can do about it but watch it slip through your fingers like sand. They are the epitome of lost control. A reminder of how helpless I really feel.

When I was six, I took down every clock in our cabin and smashed them with a hammer. I was taking back control. Freeing myself from the prison of feeling so goddamn helpless.

But here I am, counting down again. Trapped in another cage. Every breath is just another tick, because time is running out, and if I don't do something—right here, right now—we are both going to die. *They're watching me.*

I glance at the syringe.

I could do it.

Just one jab. Quick. Painless. *Clean.*

He wouldn't even feel a thing.

I'd walk out of here alive. I'd go back through that hallway and get spat out by the elevator again. Ruth would pick me up and take me to Whitestag, where I'd tell Walter that it's over. I'm not doing this anymore. I've already seen enough. *I can't be a Chaser.*

I could go home.

But that would be playing their game. That would mean accepting what they're trying to tell me—that this boy's life is a disposable resource. That law and wealth and order surpass the intricate value of a human heartbeat.

If I got any closer, I'd hear it. His clock is ticking just like mine.

Death is death is death.

I think back to Lily's goldfish and the boy who made sure it was returned to her. I remember the promise I made to myself that night.

I will never stand idly by and let an innocent person get hurt again.

Even if it's stupid.

Even if it gets me killed.

I step forward, raise my chin, and cup my hands around my mouth. "Like hell I will."

"What are you doing?" the boy hisses.

"Definitely not putting *this* through your neck, that's what." I pluck the syringe from the tray, turning it over in my hands. Dad would kill to get his hands on a sample of this stuff.

Dad will kill *me* for what I'm about to do.

"They'll kill you if you don't cooperate!" the boy whispers, frantic.

I kneel in front of him. He's my age—maybe a year or two older. But strapped in this chair, shaking and small and so damn afraid, could be a child.

This is innocence.

This is what the Unseen protects.

"They'll definitely try," I say.

"This is stupid." His eyes brim with tears. "There's nothing you can do."

I start unscrewing the needle cap. "What's your name?"

"Max."

"Listen, Max." I keep my voice low, fidgeting with the syringe as I talk. "I've already failed. They'll dispatch Officers to handle the situation. And when they get here—"

The door behind me hisses open.

I don't have the chance to turn before a voice speaks. "Stand up slowly and drop the syringe."

I rise and raise my hands, still gripping the needle. Two Officers stand in the doorway, Nightjade guns ready.

"I said, drop the syringe," the one on the left growls.

"Drop the gun," I reply calmly.

"What?" His brows twitch. "No. You have five seconds to drop the syringe, or we'll shoot."

"Alright. Don't say I didn't warn you."

"Five—"

I throw the syringe.

It lodges into the Chaser's neck.

He blinks in disbelief, then chuckles. "If you're this dense, you would've failed training anyway." He removes the syringe with a smirk. "You need to *plunge* the Nightjade to—"

His voice cuts out. The smirk vanishes.

He crumples.

His partner gapes at me. "You..."

"Laced the needle? Yeah."

I don't give him time to react. I rush over and slam my boot into his hand, sending the gun flying. He calls out in pain, bringing the knuckles I probably crushed close to his chest. I've gone through enough combat training over these past few weeks to know that must've hurt—even with armored gloves.

While I catch the gun, he dives for his fallen partner's. He's quick to shoot at me, but I'm quick to dodge. Nightjade pellets splatter on the wall.

Now we're both standing upright, circling each other, guns drawn.

I don't have time to get into a stand-off with this guy. Whoever's monitoring the test will probably dispatch more Officers for backup. *There's no time to waste.*

I reach down and pluck the syringe from the fallen Chaser's neck. By the time the living one shoots, I'm already standing, and the bullet hits my chest instead of my head. It rebounds off my armor, then the wall. He dodges the ricochets just in time.

While he's bent forward, I kick him in the face. He falls back with a scream, clutching the nose I cracked with both hands. The gun falls to the ground. Blood trickles from behind his gloves, staining the front of his uniform red.

I sprint to Max and undo his bonds. "Up."

I help him to his feet. He can't peel his eyes from the dead Officer. "You killed him..."

I grab the spare gun and hand it to Max. "No time for that. Come on."

The surviving Officer is still crying about his broken nose by the time I pull him up. He brings the screen on his wrist to his mouth, but I graze the needle to his neck before he gets the chance to call for backup. "I'd think twice about that if I were you."

"Help!" he calls out.

I press the needle firmer against his throat with a low chuckle. "Like that'll stop me from doing what I did to *him*. Now walk."

The trip down the corridor is less intimidating with a hostage to call my own. Max trails close behind as we hurry into the elevator.

"I don't have clearance to operate this thing," I seethe into the Chaser's ear. "So you're going to program it to go to the lobby."

"I—I can't—"

"You *will*. And if you so much as hover over the wrong button, you're dead."

Frantically, he taps the screen on his wrist. The elevator shuts and starts moving.

Max's foot won't stop tapping as we wait. Ten seconds last years, until finally, the elevator opens.

The lobby is empty, save for the Sitter at the front desk. She drops her tablet with a gasp when she sees the syringe and the gun in my other hand. She grabs a phone and brings it to her ears. "Requesting backup in the lobby. We've got a combative trainee."

Something about the shaking of her hands and the worry in her voice tells me this has never happened before.

I turn to Max and lower my voice. "Run."

"What?"

"Run to the woods," I whisper, so no one else can hear but him. "Find the river. Go south. Someone will meet you there. I'll hold these guys off as long as I can."

He stares at me, stunned. "But what about you?"

"Max." I look him dead in the eye. "Go."

He stares at me for a moment, no longer trembling. I know that look too well—the shattering realization that the life you once had will never be yours again. That every truth you once knew will only exist as fragments in your memory.

"Thank you," he mutters.

And he runs.

The elevator opens as Max bolts across the lobby. A dozen Officers pour out, guns drawn. They encircle me. I yank my hostage closer, holding the needle to his neck and my own stolen gun outward. No one moves. No one fires.

What are they waiting for? Why aren't they chasing after him?

I spin back, eyes locked on Max as he finally approaches the scanners in the distance. My pulse hammers. Every step he takes feels like a miracle.

Maybe they think he won't survive out there. Maybe they think I'm the bigger threat. Maybe they'll send someone for him later.

He's so close to reaching those doors. So close to freedom.

The scanner lights up.

Red.

Max freezes within it, but he's not still. His body convulses.

His clothing burns first.

He can't even scream as something invisible courses through him. His shirt catches on fire, then the skin beneath it. His hair.

By the time he falls, there is no inch of him that isn't charred.

All at once, the world slows to a stop. I don't blink. I can't breathe. There is no sound. No feeling. Only the smell of something burning and flesh that still smokes, bright red against the floor's blinding canvas.

Electrocution.

No.

No no no no.

This can't be happening.

But I know that smell. I've tasted it before, under Eden. Felt it seep from my own flesh.

That boy is dead, and it's all my fault.

I don't know why the Chasers don't shoot me. For a moment, I almost wish they would—until two of them approach, yanking the gun and syringe from my hands. That snaps me out of it.

I reel my fist back, but an Officer catches it before I get the chance to punch him in the face. Two others yank my hostage free while two more restrain me, each one gripping either of my arms. I elbow, knee, and kick, but when a third Officer puts me in a headlock, I'm outnumbered.

They shove me down so I'm on my knees, arms pulled behind me while one Officer grips my hair. He yanks my head back so I'm staring forward, locking his arm firmly around my throat. I'm about to break his nose with a headbutt when someone walks through the front doors.

The lobby stills.

He doesn't rush, doesn't even flinch. Just strolls right in like it's any other Saturday. A long black jacket drapes over his suit, hands buried casually in his pockets. He walks with an air of confidence, like he doesn't care that his tie is slightly crooked, or that the sandy, chin-length waves of hair on his head are a mess. A pair of jet black sunglasses shields his eyes.

This is an Agent.

The scanner doesn't light up when he passes through. He steps over Max's body with a wrinkled nose, barely sparing him a glance. His focus is on me. He stops just two feet away.

The Chaser holding my hair makes me stare up at the Agent. The other Officers tighten their grips on my arms.

"Agent Finch." One of the Officers manages an awkward half-bow. "Apologies if this interrupted your schedule, sir. We have the situation under control. You really didn't need to come all this way for a mere—"

Finch lifts his hand. The Officer falls silent.

"When I got the alert," Finch says, voice low and gravelly, "I didn't believe it. No one's ever pulled a stunt like this." He chuckles, removing his sunglasses to hang them from his collar. "Had to see it myself."

The Officer shrinks back.

Finch turns to me. His face is unreadable, but there's a glint in his eye, something like amusement. If I had it my way, I'd wipe the look off his face with my fist.

He crouches in front of me. "Didn't know the scanners double as electric fences, huh?"

I spit at his feet.

A sharp gasp escapes the receptionist behind the desk. The Chasers stiffen like someone just pulled a trigger.

Instead of giving me the injection I deserve, he tilts his head. "You don't think things through, do you?"

I bite my tongue hard enough to taste blood, but it's not enough to keep me quiet. "You killed him."

"That kid?" Finch glances back casually. "I thought you did."

I lurch forward, but the Chasers pull me back.

Finch chuckles. "So this is how it's gonna be, huh?" He lifts my chin with one finger. "You'll bite if I get too close?"

I grit my teeth. "Count on it, you bastard."

He stands and slides his hands back into his coat pockets. "They were going to assign you to the Agency, you know. Officer Gilbert recommended you to me personally. Said you were sharp."

My brow furrows. *This guy's the one who makes Agency assignments?*

A shudder courses through me. His rank must be higher than I realized if he can make decisions like that.

"I take on two fresh trainees each year, sometimes less. The Agency Division is mostly made of promoted Officers. But you..." He grins, crooked and cruel. "You've been on my radar, Cedar Beck."

I don't know whether to feel flattered or sick.

"I just have one question for you," he says. "Why did you do it?"

"I'm not a killer."

Finch lifts a brow. "But you are." He thumbs toward the scanners. "Look at him."

The elevator parts. Two Officers drag out the poisoned one I left upstairs.

"And him." Finch gestures toward my former hostage. "You've clearly got the guts for it. The disposition. Skill. It's just... misdirected."

"I could direct it elsewhere."

"I see." That earns me a thoughtful squint, then a chuckle. "Sharp tongue, no real bite."

I'll show him bite.

My head cracks into the face of the Chaser behind me. There's a crunch and a howl of pain as he stumbles, clutching his nose. I twist, break free, and elbow my way toward the nearest Nightjade gun. I hold the weapon high over my head, aiming at Agent Finch as the other Officers try to yank it from my grip. Someone shoves their gun to the back of my skull.

Then everything halts.

Finch has drawn his own gun—but it's not pointed at me.

While I aim at Finch, he aims at the Chaser behind me, gun night black to match his suit and shades.

The Agent's voice is iron. "Shoot him, I shoot you. You're useless anyway if you let an unarmed *child* overpower you."

For a moment, all is still. Like everyone is stuck floating in honey until the Officer blinks, retreating slowly. The other Officers watch in quiet, curious fear as the Agent finally directs his gun toward my neck.

"Are you going to shoot me, Beck?"

His amusement makes my blood boil. How can he act so casually after what he saw on his way in here? After what—*who* he stepped over?

There is no soul in his shell.

"Yeah. I'd like to."

"Why's that?" He tilts his head, slipping one hand in his pocket. "You can't say you're not a killer. Not anymore. You can't claim you're trying to save that boy. He's long gone. And if you're trying to save yourself, shooting me would be a death sentence."

My grip around the gun tightens. It trembles in my hands.

"So what is it then? Something I said?" Finch steps closer. "Have I really given you a reason to hate me that much in just..." He lowers the gun and checks an expensive-looking watch on his wrist. "Five minutes?"

"You're an Agent," I seethe, holding the gun with both hands now. "That's what."

"Ah," he says. "So it's Agents you hate."

He holsters his weapon without a second glance. The gesture makes me want to scream.

Why doesn't he think I'll shoot?

Sweat beads at my temples. I try to still my shaking arms, flexing my fingers. Every nerve in my body screams that he is my enemy. This man— this Agent, this *monster*—is everything the Unseen stands against, wrapped in a fancy suit and tie. I should shoot him for everything he's done.

So why haven't I pulled the trigger?

And why hasn't he?

"If that's your reason," Finch continues, "then *I* might have reason to believe you're a traitor. Is that true?"

My blood goes cold. All at once, the reality of the situation hits me like a truck.

This is the mistake Dad knew I'd make.

If the Corps believes I'm Unseen, they will dissect me for information. I'd give them what they want eventually, even if I don't want to. The Cut would fall because of me.

Dad was right. He was right all along, and I was too stubborn to listen.

I'm stupid. Reckless. Not strong enough for this.

I messed everything up, just as he predicted.

"No," I mutter.

"You hate Agents, but you're not a traitor." Finch rubs a thumb across his unshaven chin. "Something's not adding up."

The words taste foul even before I say them. "I'm loyal to the Chaser Corps and the Presidency. No one else. Why else would I have gone through training? It's hell."

"Then why didn't you kill that prisoner?"

My arms drop slightly. I lower the gun, eyes flicking away. "He reminded me of my brother."

"Should we go find your brother, then? Have you kill *him* instead, to prove your loyalty and make up for what you've done?"

I pull the trigger.

Nightjade guns make little noise. Just a soft whoosh, quiet like the wind. Finch clutches his abdomen, eyes bulging out of his sockets as he studies his purple-stained shirt, then me.

I step back. The gun slips through my fingers, clattering on the floor. My hand flies to my mouth.

What have I done?

Then he lifts the bottom of his shirt, revealing a thick black vest. His look of terror melts into another crooked grin. "Gotcha."

A bulletproof vest.

He throws his head back and laughs. I'm still frozen when an Officer swoops in to confiscate the gun I dropped.

"Now I get it." Finch releases an amused sigh. "You hate Agents because we're assholes."

He turns to the cluster of Chasers still crowding the lobby, dismissing them with a wave. "You can go now."

One of the Officers furrows her brow. "Are you sure?"

Finch's smile vanishes. "I'm never uncertain."

"But... he shot you, sir. Protocol says—"

His gaze snaps to her like a switchblade flicking open. "Do you know who I am?"

She swallows. "O-Of course, sir. You're Agent Finch, Head of House."

Head of House? My eyes widen.

This Agent is in charge of every Chaser in the entire Pacific Region.

And I just shot him.

Finch raises his chin. "I *am* protocol."

Every shoulder in the lobby tenses.

"But your higher-ups—"

"If my higher-ups have a problem with how I run my region, or how I choose to deal with this kid, they can bring it up with me. They've got more problems to deal with than one trigger-happy cadet."

My fists clench at my sides. By *problems*, I know he means rebels. Runners.

The Unseen.

"Now go, before I exterminate *you* for questioning protocol," Finch orders.

The Officer nods, eyes downcast. "Yes, sir."

The Chasers file back into the elevator. I stand motionless, the silence wrapping around me like a noose.

It's just the two of us now.

"You screwed up, kid. Big time."

I don't answer. I can't peel my eyes from Max, whose body still smokes.

"Do you know why Gilbert sent me that letter of recommendation?"

I say nothing.

"Because you were damn good at running coals."

My brows crease.

"Out of every trainee this year, you were sent to firewalk the most. Eleven times. I'm sure that broke a few records.

"I went back and checked Gilbert's notes. Security footage. You were never sent for anything substantial. You rarely spoke out of turn. Always followed orders. Didn't complain, didn't crack."

I feel like one of the goats at the fair. A prized animal in a corral.

"To be honest," he continues, circling me slowly, "it almost seemed like Gilbert was making up reasons to send you to that room on purpose. Manufacturing excuses. And I get it now. He was... *curious*. The same curiosity a child harbors when they toss a toy into a fire. They want to see what melts. What breaks. How it will change and evolve."

My jaw feathers. *If I ever see that man again, I swear to God, I'll kill him.*

"You see, the other cadets let fear control them. Once they made one mistake, they grew paranoid. Never made another. Not because they wanted to be better, but because they were scared of getting sent back. They displayed many signs of weakness. Got spooked into mediocrity. Most of them got sorted into desk jobs."

He pauses in front of me.

"But you, Cedar..." He grins. "You may have been sent to the coals the most, but you grew stronger every time. It conditioned you to run for much longer before collapsing. And eventually, you stopped crying at the end.

You fell to your knees with grace. No resistance. *Perfectly.*"

I taste bile in the back of my throat. I remember what it felt like to collapse. To cry quietly so the cameras wouldn't catch it. To hope Gilbert wouldn't send me again, because I was so tired of the smell of burning flesh.

He starts circling me again. "Gilbert tried the same thing on another cadet. Jimmy Dellucci. Do you remember Jimmy?"

"No."

"That's because he didn't make it. Got sent to the coals one too many times and had a nervous breakdown."

A chill trails down my spin.

"But you, Cedar... you adapted. You *used* the pain to become more resistant to it, and that's what we're looking for. That's the sign of a good machine."

He stops pacing. "Let's cut to the chase here, shall we?"

"Fine."

"If you weren't already under my radar, I would've killed you. Hell, if you were one of the Sitter types, the Officers dispatched to your exam room would've killed you. But you were rather resourceful with that needle. Bold. Self-preserving. And now, here we are.

"The simple answer is this: you were lucky to make that shot. Lucky the eye I already had on you made me hesitate when I walked through these doors. Lucky that, as Head of House, I am the one who determines your fate. *That's* why you're not already dead."

"If you're going to kill me," I seethe, "just get on with it."

"It would be a shame to let a darkness so raw and untamed become wasted potential. You've already shown you can kill. You hardly seem fazed by what you've done. In fact, out of all your other peers, you had the quickest reaction time. Truly record-breaking, actually. But again, your aim could use a bit of work."

My hands curl into fists.

"With conditioning, I believe you'll be an incredibly useful tool for the Corps. Sure, you're a little rusty. We'll just have to... invest a little more into your return. But that's the lovely thing about knives, Cedar." He leans closer. "They can be sharpened until they're ready to get the job done."

I shudder. He laughs.

"I have a special assignment for you, Rusty. One that will show you the true value of being on the winning side. *Our* side." He smirks. "A very special assignment indeed."

PART THREE
JAGGED

Monday, August 1

♪ ALABASTER - ALL THEM WITCHES ♪

I've never ridden a prison bus before.

At least I *think* it's a prison bus. I've never taken any bus, actually. I've seen them in Yesterday movies, read about them in stories—but I never expected them to smell this strongly of sweat and exhaust.

My leg stopped bouncing a while ago. I'm not sure how many hours I've spent in here, but it's definitely been long enough to drain most of my energy. I rest my head against the window and stare past streaks of dried rain and dust, watching the world smear by in shades of beige.

Motion sickness. Driving anxiety. The constant weight in my gut like I've swallowed a boulder. It all fades a little, beneath a layer of awe I feel guilty for having. After a life spent surrounded by towering cedars and misted coasts, this endless sea of sand may as well be another planet. I've never seen so much *nothing*.

There's something eerie about the emptiness. The absence of clouds. It makes me feel exposed—like at any moment, we might be swallowed whole.

We're definitely not in Washington anymore.

I lean my head back against my cracked leather seat. The bus is thick with syrupy heat. Sweat clings to my skin like glue. God, what I'd give for a good shower right now. I think about Whitestag's rainfall shower heads, expensive soaps, and soft towels. The Aaron of yesterday would call me an imposter if he heard me missing the place.

Cedar, I correct myself. *I'm still living a lie.*

Funny how everything can flip upside down in less than twenty-four hours.

I pause. Actually, I don't know what day it is. After the Chasers locked me in that empty room at the training center for hours—no clocks or explanations—they shoved me onto this bus. We stopped at one rest area where I pretended to get some sleep in this very same seat. There's a bathroom in the back. I've puked in it at least three times. I haven't eaten anything since I left Whitestag for the final exam. Not that I could stomach anything, anyway.

I've gotten good at avoiding eye contact with the other passengers. There are maybe a dozen of us. A few are handcuffed. Others bear faces I swear I recognize from training. They don't have bonds, but we all share the same tight-wound tension behind our eyes.

I wonder if they know where we're going.

I certainly don't.

I jolt awake when the bus stops.

The engine dies down, leaving behind a stale, empty silence. I grimace and rub the knot in my neck. My head pounds. My mouth is cracked and dry like the leather seat my clothes stick to. I can't remember the last time I had water.

I frown at my black long sleeve shirt and pants. If I'm already soaked in sweat here, I'll be miserable out *there*.

Beyond my window, there's a stretch of rocky sand with a few scarce tufts of brittle wild grass. The sun sinks beneath the purple silhouette of a low, rocky mountain in the distance, drowning everything in a wash of warm violet.

I think it's the most beautiful sunset I've ever seen.

Apricot orange. Smoky rose. Periwinkle blue. Streaks of vibrant watermelon. All the colors melt together into something that should be an oil painting—not my view from a dingy bus that reeks of feet. If I weren't on the verge of collapse, I'd probably laugh at how something so beautiful could exist in an ugly desert.

My eyes widen. I'm in the desert.

No.

No no no no no.

I run my hands through my hair, trying to squeeze a breath through my tightening lungs. This can't be right.

There is only one destination the Chaser Corps would send a bus like this. Only one destination surrounded by so much sand.

I stare ahead through the windshield of the bus—and the pillars of smoke in the distance tell me everything I need to know.

My heart turns to lead and sinks. It feels like the air is solidifying around me, the way melted wax might.

I thought they never sent ex-Chasers to the Tombs. Hell, there isn't even such a thing as an ex-Chaser. They know too much. But I was never a *real* Chaser, was I?

I study my hands. *Why am I not handcuffed like the others?*

Before I can address the thousand other questions racing through my head, a loud hiss at the front of the bus grabs my attention. The doors open.

Two people step inside the vehicle, wearing high-necked uniforms made of stiff gray fabric. I notice a bright white Nightjade gun in a holster at both their sides. One of them—a blue-eyed young man with a head of messy light brown hair, a few years my senior—folds his arms. "All of you, up. Now."

Slowly, the passengers rise to their feet.

"My name is Officer Holden Saylor. This is my associate, Officer Elena Fantaine."

He nods to the young woman standing to his left. Her curly black hair is tied back into a neat ponytail. A mole rests above her upper lip, which remains unsmiling like Saylor's.

"I won't waste time telling you where we are or what you're doing here. And if you haven't already figured it out, good luck lasting a day beyond that fence." Saylor jabs a thumb over his shoulder. "Prisoners out first."

The handcuffed passengers file out one by one.

"Now the rest of you."

I look behind me. The remaining passengers look just as confused as I am.

"*Now,*" Saylor barks.

We listen.

Stepping out of the bus feels like walking into an oven. Even as it sets, the sun's enduring glare blankets my skin, drawing out more sticky sweat. My head throbs with exhaustion and dehydration. My eyes feel drier than the sand crunching beneath my feet as I join the cluster of other passengers.

"Line up. Prisoners in the middle, newbies at the ends."

Newbies? My brows knit together. *What the hell is he talking about?*

We comply, filing up behind the two Officers. If they're calling themselves Officers, are they Chasers? And if so, what happened to their real uniforms? Why are they wearing gray, not white?

They turn around and start walking, beckoning for us to follow without another word.

An engine sounds behind us. Only when I watch the white bus drive away do I realize how easy it would have been to steal. Dread courses through me as it grows smaller and smaller—then finally disappears.

"We're alone out here, aren't we?" one of the prisoners mutters.

No one replies.

Twenty minutes of hiking through sand, rocks, and rigid wild grass in this heat is enough to make me wish for death.

I don't think I've ever craved water so badly. *Needed it* to an ache like this. I can taste iron in the cracks of my dry lips. It doesn't help that the air is thick with dissipating smoke. Something smells like a campfire.

We stop in front of a towering fence made of thin, intricate wires. Every post is shaped like a *Y*. The top wires run horizontally in a string of large coils. It must be at least a dozen feet tall. When I look left and right, I'm convinced the fence continues endlessly in either direction.

I squint to make out the buildings beyond. We're losing light, so I can't see much, but I make out wooden cabin-like structures, large brick buildings, and a water tower in the distance.

I run my tongue along the dry roof of my mouth. *Water.*

Officer Fantaine walks up to a double-door gate. Two more people wearing the same uniform stand behind it. After pressing a few buttons, the gate slides open with a rattle. Then the realization hits.

These aren't Chasers. They're Guards.

This must be the Tombs.

Panic floods through me as I remember everything Ansel told me in the tunnels—about how Chips handle death. At the Cut, we have a small grave-yard on the hill, with tombstones Dad carves himself. We mourn like they did in the Yesterdays. But Chips today are too numb—too desperate for their own survival that they would rather spend funeral funds on personal needs. Like Immunity, if they can afford it. And there's simply too much death to handle. With so many exterminations, processing corpses became about efficiency, not respect.

That's why the Tombs exists.

And they make prisoners do the work. People like the Unseen.

People like me.

I learned about the Guard position during training, but Gilbert's lesson was brief and vague. It isn't even regarded as a real division in the Corps. This is where they send failures. Trainees who don't quite meet the mark, yet still retain enough value to render their extermination wasteful. The ones who don't listen, the ones who need to learn to pull their weight—or the ones who enjoy what they do a little too much.

This is where dull knives get sharpened.

And for civilians, this is where criminals who don't get injections work themselves to death.

I've read about prisons from the Yesterdays. We don't have institutions like that anymore. The laws of the Nightjade Order deem rehabilitation too expensive. Wasteful. Apparently, the Tombs are modeled after those prisons—except no one leaves. Every prisoner gets a life sentence. A slow, painful execution of withering away, dedicating every last drop of your life to the Corps until you have nothing left to give.

A bearded man with handcuffs must be realizing the same thing. He steps backward, nearly stumbling as he studies the Tombs with wide eyes. He trembles.

And he bolts.

We watch as the man runs away, struggling to maintain his balance with his bonds and the shifting sand.

"Poor guy," Fantaine mutters. "He seemed sensible."

"Traitor scum." Saylor watches him run away, shaking his head. "Heat like this can boil the brains out of anyone."

"You're just... letting him go?" I ask.

Saylor shrugs. "Vultures gotta eat too."

I shudder. *Of course.* I watch the runner turn into a small silhouette before disappearing completely.

He's not getting anywhere without water.

We follow the Guards through the gate. Only when it closes and locks behind us do we pass through a second one, also guarded. I glare when an older man dressed in even darker gray pats me down. His brows furrow. "What's in your pocket?"

"Nothing."

"Oh really?" He reaches in and retrieves Lily's tooth with a glower. "Then what's this?" He turns it over in his hand, nose crinkles in disgust. "What the..."

"It's a tooth, genius." I take it back and try to put it away, but the Guard grabs my wrist.

"Being smart now, are we?"

"I wouldn't call knowing what a tooth is *smart*, but thanks for the compliment." I jerk free and shove it in my pocket. If I'm not in handcuffs, Finch sent me here for something else, and I highly doubt this guy is in charge. I'm tired and hungry and I just want something to drink. Or a decent night's sleep.

"Listen, punk." The Guard points a finger in my face. "You better straighten out your tone before someone else does it for you. And you *really* don't want it to be me."

"Cute threat, old man." I pat him on the shoulder and step forward, disinterested.

Before the Guard can yank me back and follow through with his threat, Saylor steps between us. "Is there a problem?"

The Guard grits his teeth. "Someone oughta teach this kid some manners."

"I appreciate the concern, but he'll learn to shut his mouth soon enough." Saylor pushes me forward. "The smart ones always do."

The second gate closes behind us with another haunting rattle.

Fantaine takes the prisoners in one direction, while Saylor stays with me and the five other unbound passengers. It's eerily quiet as he observes each of us carefully. There is no wind, no rustling of leaves—only an endless expanse of emptiness in every direction.

"This way, newbies," he finally says, walking forward and beckoning for us to follow. "Keep up. Dinner's starting soon. No one's coming to find you if you get lost."

Sand crunches beneath our feet as Saylor leads us through an alley sided by brick buildings at our left and dusty wood cabins at our right. I see something move from the corner of my eye and glance upward to find a large black bird circling high above our heads. *Turkey vulture.*

We reach a cluster of small buildings made of gray bricks. It reminds me of the Block back home, with narrow dirt alleyways and stray tumbleweeds.

"Guards' quarters," Saylor mutters, pointing in different directions. "Two of you in that one, one of you in that one, one of you in that one. See you at dinner."

He walks away. The other *newbies* divert, leaving me to figure out where to go on my own.

I pause for a moment, looking around. It's uncomfortably quiet. There is no birdsong, no rushing water, no pine on my tongue. Just a dry mineral taste and a burning in my nose.

I'm completely alone.

I study the fence, which stands a few yards away. It's tall, but not un-manageable. I've climbed higher trees back home.

Home. The word hits like a fist to the stomach. I stare through the gaps in the fence wires, trying to make out the shadow of that mountain in the distance. Beyond it, the Schneiders are eating dinner without me. They know what it means when someone doesn't return from training. They will not come looking for me.

Somewhere farther, Asa and my father will begin their trip to the cabin to retrieve me. It will be empty. And even farther than that, when Dad knocks on their door, Mom and Lori will hear the news.

Everyone will think I'm dead.

All at once, the desperation that's been stifled by exhaustion and denial in the pit of my stomach comes back to life, writhing and twisting itself into knots. My legs shake. I think I might be sick.

This is the assignment Finch prepared for me. *They want me to be a Guard.*

This is where they send their failures. Not Cedar—Aaron. The criminals who aren't allowed to take up space unless they serve a purpose. The people who believe in life and true liberty—not wealth and power.

I run my hands through my hair. I can't be a Guard. If anything, I should be a prisoner. *But that would make this a lot more difficult for me, wouldn't it?*

My eyes adjust so I'm not staring through the fence, but at the wires themselves. The mountain blurs behind it. *I can climb this*, I tell myself. *As soon as I find some water, I'm going to climb this fence, and I'll find my way back home.*

I spin and study my surroundings. If these are the Guards' quarters, there must be a bathroom. Bathrooms have water.

I hurry to the building Saylor pointed to earlier, which says *CABIN 12* in big blocky letters. I step inside. It's an open room with dusty wood floors and six rusty bunk beds arranged against the walls. The only windows are narrow and close to the ceiling, barely letting in any light. A flickering lamp with a chain hangs from a slow, creaking ceiling fan.

I'm the only one in here; everyone else must be at dinner like Saylor said.

A few of the bunk beds are unmade, strewn with scratchy-looking blankets that their occupants were too lazy to fold this morning. There are night-stands between each bed with miscellaneous objects. A few toothbrushes. Some soap bars. Dirty socks. Tattered notebooks. *No one's making them clean up after themselves?*

I get the feeling there might be worse things to worry about within this fence.

Only one bed is neatly made—a top bunk perfectly smoothed out. Beneath it is an empty mattress with a folded blanket, a pillow, and what appears to be a fresh uniform. This one is white, not gray like the others I've seen.

This must be my bed.

A round canteen on the nightstand snags my attention. I pick it up and shake it around, hoping to hear the sound of water sloshing inside. My shoulders slump. Nothing.

I scour the room for some sort of door, something to lead me to a faucet. All I can think about is water. Running my hands through it. My face. My hair. I could drink a whole gallon if I could find any, but there isn't a bathroom door in sight.

"You must be the new guy."

I spin around, startled by the voice. A Guard with deep brown skin and a light gray uniform stands in the doorway, smiling at me. His black hair is cut short and his eyes are youthfully round, almost like an owl's. He seems too young to be in a place like this.

I realize I'm an imposter for more reasons than one. Most cadets at training were already eighteen. Cedar is, but Aaron's birthday isn't until November.

Maybe we're both too young for this.

"Uh, yeah. I guess so." I shove my hands in my pockets and walk toward him, trying to conceal my shaking arms. "Do you know where I can find some water?"

"There's water in the cafeteria if you want me to show you the way." He coughs and points over his shoulder. His breathing sounds raspy, almost frantic. "Let me just grab something real quick."

He coughs again into his elbow and walks to the bunk bed, then retrieves something from beneath the pillow on the top bunk. Using the post to steady himself, he turns his back to me and brings the object to his mouth, inhaling sharply.

"Huh, that's weird." He puts the object back in its hiding place and turns around with a nervous chuckle. His breathing has returned to a steady pace. "Can't find it. Oh well."

He's about to walk away, but freezes when I speak. "Was that an inhaler?"

"Is it really that obvious?"

"You were trying to hide it?"

He rubs his face tiredly with both hands. "I'm a terrible liar." He sighs. "Please don't tell anyone."

"Okay..."

"If people found out I had one, they'd steal it." He chews on his lip for a moment. "Look. I'll let you use it if you keep it between us, alright? If the Captain knew I took this from the infirmary, I'd be in real trouble."

"Chill out, alright? I don't want your inhaler."

He blinks. "You don't?"

"No."

He makes a face like he doesn't believe me. "You will soon."

I feel the warmth drain from my skin. I need to get the hell out of here. Yesterday. *Now.*

"Peppermint tea," I say a little too suddenly. "If you're having respiratory issues, menthol is a good decongestant. It'll loosen up the mucus in your lungs and clear your airways. Add a bit of honey to soothe your throat too."

He blinks. "Thanks. I'll... see if we have some in the cafeteria. We probably don't though."

"Great. I helped you, now you help me."

"Oh." His eyes grow wide. "Well, I'm flattered, and you're not a bad-looking guy, but I prefer forming a genuine emotional connection with someone before—"

"God, what? No. I want *water.*"

"Oh yeah. That." He chuckles nervously and points to the door. "Get dressed and I'll take you to the cafeteria."

I stare at the folded uniform on my bed.

If I put it on, does that make me like them?

This is only temporary, I tell myself. You're playing pretend. *Just wear it for now and take it off when you find a way out of here.*

I throw off my sweaty training clothes and slip into the uniform, making sure to grab Lily's tooth. The fabric is stiff and cheap. Itchy. I don't like the way it touches my neck. It makes me feel confined.

Where the folded uniform used to be, there's a lanyard with a key card. I put it on. I grab the empty canteen from the nightstand and attach it to my belt loop. *I'll need this where I'm going.*

"Oh, and these are for you." The Guard reaches under the bed and throws me a pair of worn brown boots. They're covered in dust, but they look sturdier than the shoes I have on now.

"These aren't new," I note, putting them on.

"Neither is the uniform."

"They just... gave me someone else's?"

He nods.

"What if they didn't fit?"

"Then you'd be stuck with some very uncomfortable shoes."

I don't know why that gives me goosebumps. I glance at the bed again, wondering why it's empty in the first place. "What happened to the last guy?"

He averts his gaze. "Lung sickness."

I shudder, staring through one of the thin, dirty windows. Even the Guards aren't safe from all this smoke. "I thought Corps healers could fix anything."

"We've got one in the infirmary, but you can't exactly operate without good tech. Aside from him, we're on our own."

We exit the cabin. It's dusk now, with only a few streaks of purple remaining in the sky. *This is good*, I tell myself. Once I fill this canteen and climb that fence, I can make most of the trip in the dark while it's cool. Then I'll find a road and hitchhike my way back to Whitestag. I just got here. No one will even notice I'm gone. And if Saylor meant it, no one would care.

This could work.

I'm still studying the fence when something moves, nearly making me jump. I freeze and squint to make out the shape. Another turkey vulture.

It circles above, watching closely. I watch too. I watch it circle one last time. I watch it veer toward the fence.

When it lands, I hear a hum—and I watch it twitch to death.

The bird falls. Smoke curls upward like desperate fingers, clawing for help that will never arrive. Suddenly I'm back in the lobby, watching the boy I sent to his death meet the same fate.

"An electric fence," I mutter.

My head spins. This can't be true. It can't be, because if it is, that means I'm really stuck here. There is no climbing the fence, no journeying to a road beyond it. I'm trapped.

It doesn't matter that they want me to be a Guard.

I'm still a prisoner too.

"I don't know why you newbies would expect anything different from the Corps." The Guard studies the fallen bird with a sigh, shaking his head. "Just be glad you weren't someone else's teaching moment."

The Guard keeps walking. And as I follow him, already melting beneath a desert sun I just met, the Serpent's words echo in my head.

"No one is coming to save you."

19

Monday, August 1

♪ GODLESS - THE DANDY WARHOLS ♪

The Guard's name is Marty Dawson.

He's seventeen, like me—skipped a grade in elementary school because he taught himself how to read at a young age. He has an affinity for board games, piano, and a video game from the Yesterdays that he's technically not supposed to have back home, let alone talk about, but there are no mics out here, so he says it doesn't matter.

I'm not sure if I should feel relieved or sickened by the lack of surveillance.

Marty tells me all this as we walk through camp, compacted dust crunching beneath our boots. I zone out while he babbles about the video games he played back home. My attention is glued to the people who walk past us wearing dark orange clothes. The fabric looks like rust. They shoot us dirty looks. Others seem too tired to look over at all. Maybe even scared.

These must be the prisoners.

Don't be afraid of me, I want to scream. *I'm like you.*

My uniform says otherwise.

We pass a large building, one of the tallest I can see. Its bricks are dark gray, clearly stained by the smoke curling from its cylindrical chimneys. I stare at the sky, thinking about the smoke clouds I saw from afar back on that bus. This must be what's polluting the place. I can already feel the smell burning into my skin and hair. My lungs.

"What's this place?" I ask.

"Don't worry about it for now."

"You promised me a real tour."

He sighs, averting his gaze. "That's the cremation facility."

I swallow dryly. "Cremation?"

"If your family can afford it, they'll buy you a nice tombstone close to home. If not, which is usually the case, your body's shipped out here to get processed. No charge." He points to the facility.

Just the mention of burning corpses sends images of Tern flashing in my mind. Of Max in the training center. My throat burns.

Don't go there. Not now.

"What's that?" I point a shaking finger to the empty field of sand occupying the camp's northwest corner. It stretches so far that I can't see where the fence ends beyond it. But I *can* see that it's dotted with people in rust jumpsuits, holding shovels and digging holes. My face pales. "Are those..."

"Graves?"

I nod.

"Yeah."

My heartbeat hammers, every tick buzzing in my jaw. I'm trembling, but I try to keep my voice steady. "What's the point of graves if you have a furnace? Isn't fire more... efficient?"

Marty sighs. "Thousands of people die every day, Beck. There are multiple facilities just like this spread throughout the country, but... we still get a lot of bodies. You can only fit so many in a furnace at a time."

"So it's random, then," I clarify. "Who gets burned and who gets buried."

He nods. "The graves are also where the prisoners' bodies go when they finally... you know."

My hands flex at my sides. *When they work themselves to death.*

They make the prisoners bury their own.

That must be another way to keep them in check. Reminding them of the fate they avoided by getting sent to the Tombs alive—and where they will end up if they step out of line.

I feel sick.

I stop walking. Beyond the fence, I watch a pair of Guards drive a truck out into the desert. A dump trailer folds back to release its cargo.

Ashes.

A soft wind spreads them across the sand, which is grayer than I noticed before. There's so much of it, discarded like it's nothing. It's becoming a part of the desert. A part of my lungs.

I can't breathe.

My hands shake. Suddenly I'm back in those tunnels with Ansel, watching a fire distort a man I had dinner with no less than an hour before. A man who so quickly became the very substance that now coats my nose and throat.

I want to spit it out, but my mouth is so dry. I don't even have food in my stomach to throw up—only the gut-punch feeling that something is so terribly wrong I can't even stomach it. Like my body is rejecting every thought racing through my mind.

"You okay?" Marty asks.

I nod, forcing myself to breathe even though it feels impossible. Even though the air scrapes my throat like sand. "I'm fine."

The cafeteria is a square building made of stone bricks. Marty shoulders open the door to let me inside.

It's a large open room filled with plastic tables and chairs. LED light bars cast everything in a stale, greenish haze. An industrial fan hangs from the center, spinning slowly, creaking like the one in our cabin. It doesn't do a thing to combat the heat glazing over me. The smell of something cooking and the salty stench of about fifty Guards makes everything feel so much hotter than it did outside. Everyone coughs. They don't even cover their mouths.

Dad would lose his shit.

My stomach knots. *Don't think about him. Not yet. Not now.*

I notice all Guards wear varying shades of gray. I wonder if it means something.

Marty leads me down an aisle of tables. It looks like dinner's ending soon; everyone's focused on halfheartedly picking at the remnants of suspicious looking meals on metal trays. We collect more eyes the further we walk. Aside from the other newbies I spot here and there, I'm the only one wearing blinding white fabric. That's when it hits me.

We're wearing the same clothes. My uniform is just free of soot.

I wonder how long it will take for mine to turn gray like theirs.

The curiosity fades quickly. They return to their meals. No one talks either. They seem too tired to care.

Marty leads me to the food counter. An older man wearing rust-colored clothes stands behind it, holding a big spoon. He piles greenish mashed potatoes onto our trays.

I frown at the mush. "Solanine."

Marty's brows crease. "Who?"

"The toxic stuff in potatoes gone green? Makes you sick?"

"I don't think the potatoes are what you should be worrying about."

The next helping is a pile of what I think are canned green beans, but they're closer to yellow, so I'm not entirely sure. The prisoner then scoops a slimy-looking slice of mystery meat on my tray.

I crinkle my nose. Ansel would piss himself if he saw this.

"Believe it or not, you arrived on a good day," Marty mutters as we walk away. "I can't remember the last time I've seen anything green."

We fill our canteens at a crusty fountain in the corner, then take a seat at an empty table. I down enough water to feel ten pounds heavier. Marty doesn't hesitate to shovel food into his mouth—almost *too* quickly. Like it'll disappear if he doesn't eat fast enough. I wonder if that makes it taste less like feet.

My stomach can't handle food yet, so I take the opportunity to observe my surroundings. I don't see anything particularly useful as far as makeshift weapons go, aside from a fire extinguisher on the far wall. I'm sure I could hit someone with that. Our utensils are reusable, but plastic and flimsy.

In a pinch I could smack someone in the face with one of these trays. Or force feed them this God-awful food.

Not that I'd accomplish much by attacking a few Guards, anyway. I've already seen enough of what that kind of recklessness can cost you. If I'm going to escape, I need a real plan.

One that won't cause collateral damage.

My attention snags on a broom I hadn't noticed before. I'm about to start brainstorming ways to use it for violence when I notice the girl attached to it. She sweeps the floor one table away, wearing the same dark orange jumpsuit as the man serving the food. They're the only prisoners in here.

She's my age, with deep olive skin and inky black bangs that remind me of the obsidian Lily's showed me. Jagged and sharp-edged, like she cut them herself. But her hair is sleek too, woven in a loose braid with a red velvet ribbon at the end. I can't help but wonder how she ended up in a place like this. She's so young.

I am too.

"Why aren't you eating?" Marty asks through a mouthful of mashed potatoes, pulling me out of my thoughts.

"Not hungry."

"You really should—"

Before he gets the chance to finish, someone approaches our table. "Hey. You're one of the new guys, right?"

I stare up at the Guard, recognizing him as Saylor from earlier. I nod.

"Can I borrow this?" I don't have time to react before he reaches over and steals my water—knocking my food tray to the ground. "Oh. My bad."

It takes me a few blinks to realize what just happened. And when I do, I can feel a different kind of heat crawl over my skin. I clench my jaw. *I'm really not in the mood for this.*

Saylor tilts his head, sipping *my* water like it's been his all along. "Is there a problem?"

I shoot to my feet, but Marty yanks me back down and whispers in my ear. "He's just testing you. Trust me—it's not worth it." He flashes Saylor a quick smile. "No problem here."

I stand up again. "You bet I've got a problem."

The cafeteria goes quiet, save for the sweeping of a broom. All Guards glue their eyes to me.

Saylor raises a brow. "Oh?"

"Cedar..." Marty warns under his breath.

Saylor folds his arms, pretending to care. "By all means, tell me about this *problem* of yours."

I step closer. "You dropped something."

"Did I?" He glances down at the food, then brings a hand to his hair. "Shit. I'm such a klutz." He sighs. "Well, it's a good thing these filthy rats are at our every beck and call."

My fists tighten at my sides. The Guard nods over in the sweeping girl's direction. "You."

She freezes.

"Yeah, you. Get over here."

Slowly, she approaches. Now that she's closer, I notice the faded bruise encircling her eye.

"Actually, I was hoping *you* could pick it up for me," I say, nodding toward Saylor.

Someone gasps in the far corner of the cafeteria. Marty's gaze widens. Even the prisoner seems surprised, brows lifting in shock.

Saylor narrows his eyes. "Now why would I do that when we have *them* around? That's what they're here for. To work."

She flinches when he gestures at her. I notice her knuckles wrap tighter around the broom, trembling like she's fighting the urge to hit him with it.

"Now why would *she* do that when we have you around?" I say. "You're the one who dropped it. Weren't you also sent here to work? After... you know... failing to become a *real* Chaser?"

The cafeteria is filled with statues. It's like everyone stopped breathing. For a moment I swear the fan stops spinning. Saylor doesn't say a word.

Remember how you dealt with Ansel at Whitestag? I remind myself. *Just make this guy feel incompetent, show him he doesn't get to you, and he'll leave you alone to bother someone else. Then you can focus all your energy on finding a way out.*

I chuckle at his silence. "Looks like I've hit quite the sore spot." I step closer. "I heard they only send screwups here."

Saylor grabs my hair and slams my head onto the table.

The impact rings through my skull. It burns my nose, salts my tongue. White light sears my vision. My ears ring and my head already feels like it's on fire, but I can't get up because Saylor's holding me down.

"You're forgetting something, Officer... What was it again? Beck?"

I try to jerk free, but Saylor shoves my head back down, turning it so my cheek is pressed against the table. He folds over to look me in the eye.

"This hell hole is a catch-all. Sure, they send the failures here—the ones who weren't skilled or obedient enough to be out on the field. Your arrival proves that. But you're forgetting about the Officers who are too competent to get rid of..." He leans closer. "The ones who enjoy what they do, just a little too much."

My blood boils. A sharp exhale puffs through my nose. I want to move. Punch. Headbutt him. But I still feel so weak from the trip here—so empty without food.

I'm stuck.

"So let me make one thing clear, Officer Beck. The next time you think about disrespecting the wrong kind of Guard..." He gets so close I can smell dinner on his breath. "Keep that mouth shut or lose your tongue."

Saylor gives me one last shove as he lets go. I peel myself off the table, rubbing my forehead.

He glares at the girl. "What are you just standing around for? Waiting for *your* turn?"

She leaves. Saylor walks away. Other Guards start filing out of the cafeteria, uninterested in being picked on next.

The girl returns with a cleaning cart and a trash can. She crouches by the spilled food. My head is killing me, but I crouch too. "Here. Let me help."

Her brows draw together. I can't tell if she's surprised or scared. Maybe both. She ignores me and starts scooping not-green beans off the floor. I reach out, but she flinches. My hand stays suspended in midair.

"I'm fine," she mutters. "I've got it handled."

"But—"

"I said I'm fine," she snaps.

I'm stunned for a moment—then nod.

I return to the table with Marty and hold my head in my hands. My vision feels swirly and my neck is stiff.

"You alright?" he asks.

"Feels like the lights are drilling holes in my head, but yeah, I'm alive."

"Are your ears ringing?"

I nod, but even that hurts and I wince. My neck pinches.

"Let me see." Marty swings his leg over the bench to face me. He removes my hands from my face, studying my eyes.

Shit. I can't remember the last time I checked my reflection in the mirror to see how the makeup covering my scar is holding up. Hope he doesn't notice. *At least my contact is still in my left eye.*

"Your pupils are dilated. I think you have a concussion. It's a pretty common welcome gift around here." Marty slides his tray over. "You should eat something."

"I'm not hungry."

"Trust me, you need every bit of food you can get. Delivery trucks only come every three months." He scoops up a spoonful of mashed potatoes. "And Cleancoats are easy targets. Saylor will steal your food or water until he gets bored of you and moves on to the next batch of newcomers. If you don't put up a fight, that is."

"Cleancoats?"

"Your uniform. It's still clean."

He's right. His clothes are much grayer than mine. I stare back at the girl, still scrubbing away at Saylor's mess. "What's the point?"

"What?"

"Saylor picking on Cleancoats. We're on the same side, aren't we?"

I hope he doesn't hear the lie straining my voice.

Marty shrugs. "Most Guards who've been here long enough know better than to do what you did. They're scared of him. As long as it stays that way, he and his buddies can get all the extra rations and privileges they want." He extends the spoon in my direction. "Open."

"Dude, I don't wanna be spoon-fed—"

The second I open my mouth, he feeds me the spoonful.

I nearly spit it out. It's cold and bland and unsalted, and I think I'd rather eat glue. But the weight of substance on my tongue suddenly makes me aware of how empty my stomach feels.

I swallow the bite down. And when Marty hands me his spoon, reluctantly, I take another one. We sit in silence for a while as the others finish their food. Pretty soon we're one of the few remaining Guards left.

"Can I ask you something?" I say between bites.

"Alright."

"Why are you being nice to me?"

He pauses. "Because if someone hadn't done the same thing to me, I'd probably be dead by now." He forces a brief grin. "And then I wouldn't be here to be nice to you."

If I weren't on the verge of vomiting, fighting to keep my eyes open and my mind from falling completely apart, maybe I would have smiled back. "Tell them I say thanks."

He averts his gaze. "I wish I could."

I don't question him further.

I just eat my beans and think about how green they would have been at the Cut.

We return to our cabin after dinner. The Guards in Cabin 12 aren't nearly as talkative as Marty. Other bunkmates seem to have formed bonds already, so they don't pay us attention.

Communal bathrooms are located a short walk away from the cabin. They're mostly empty since Marty and I were so late to dinner. It's fully dark now. Desert roaches scurry past our feet. I'm surprised to hear and spot a few buzzing crickets too. I'm not sure how anything can survive in this heat.

I wash up with a bar of soap in front of a sink with a broken mirror, careful not to touch my face. I'd love to scrub every inch of my skin ten times over to get the soot and sweat off, but I don't want to ruin my remaining makeup until I find a better solution to hide my scar. I'm not sure if anyone will even think anything of it. Still—I want to be careful.

At least I have this contact covering my left eye. Brown to match my right. Ruth told me it's safe for sleeping, so I don't need to take it out. Dad helped with the design.

If any one of these Guards finds out who I really am, they'd either kill me on the spot or put me in a rust jumpsuit. Then there'd really be no escaping.

I change into sleepwear—a white shirt and gray sweats. I lie down on the bottom bunk and stare at the metal bars above.

I go over everything Dad told me about concussions. I don't think I'm supposed to fall asleep, but it's hard to resist the beckoning of slumber. My eyelids are heavy. My head throbs, stomach churning. All I want is to close my eyes.

The other Guards are fast asleep while I'm still tossing and turning. I feel feverish. Nauseous. I can't tell if it's from the heat, the concussion, the questionable green beans, or the smoke—maybe even a combination of everything. But eventually, it's too much to bear.

I drag myself out of bed and over to the communal bathrooms. I choose a sink and throw up everything. I hurl so many times it feels like I'm scraping out the contents of my gut with a spoon. Like my abdomen is covered in bruises.

I grip the side of the sink with pale knuckles, arms trembling, head low. My knees shake too. My mind spins and I can hardly stand straight.

I don't care about this damn concussion. I need sleep.

I begin the hike back to the cabin, but I don't make it far before falling to the dirt and throwing up again. And when I do reach it, I'm so worn out I can't even step inside without taking a break first. I lean against the wall and slide down, throat tight as I sit in the dirt.

Don't cry, I tell myself, breathing in shakily. *Don't cry don't cry don't cry.*

I lean my head back and close my eyes. Everything is too quiet out here. The desert is so vast. Empty. Maybe it swallows all the sound, like how it swallows all the smoke.

I wonder what everyone back home is doing right now. At Whitestag too. I wonder if they think I'm dead. I wonder if it even matters. Maybe this place will kill me after all. *It's just a slower Nightjade injection, isn't it?*

I don't have the strength to fight it anymore.

I bury my head in my hands—and I sob.

I can't decide what I'm crying for. Maybe I cry for Max. Maybe I miss the home I never thought I would. Maybe I'm scared of what wearing a Guard's uniform will do to me. It could be the smoke in my lungs. The churning in my gut. The ache in my head. Maybe I don't want to become a part of that endless sea of gray sand. Agent Finch said I'd sharpen in here —but how am I supposed to survive long enough to see that happen? This place will chew me up and spit me out as dust.

I'll disappear, and the world will forget me.

Because I haven't done a single goddamn thing to earn a name worth remembering.

I hear the soft crunch of shoes against dirt. I lift my head up. *Who could possibly be out at this hour?*

And then I see her—the girl from the cafeteria.

She walks from that direction, toward the prisoner cabins, carrying what looks like a jug of cleaning solution. I recognize it from the cart. She freezes when she sees me, eyes wide at first. Maybe she thinks I'll turn her in. Then they narrow, brows creased. Like she's surprised to see me cry.

In our silence, we agree to keep each other's secrets.

She looks away and disappears into the night.

Tuesday, August 2

♪ HAMMER SONG
- THE SENSATIONAL ALEX HARVEY BAND ♪

I wake up wishing I hadn't. Wishing I'd stop aching. Wishing I'd eaten more last night. But when I meet our breakfast of cold, soggy oatmeal —no honey or cinnamon, head still throbbing—I take back the wish for more food. But it is still food, and I force myself to eat it because I'm too proud to let someone else take it from me.

That doesn't stop Saylor from hitting the back of my head with the heel of his palm as he walks by. He doesn't even spare me a look. Fantaine does —one of disgust. She walks with her shoulder pressed to his, followed by a shorter Guard with dark brown hair slicked back behind his ears. He gives me a look too.

"Ignore them. You don't want trouble," Marty warns. "I heard Fantaine got herself sent here on purpose. Don't know how, but I'm guessing it was something bad. Just to follow Saylor."

"And their friend?"

"Cota screwed up an assignment—he got in a fight with his partner."

Marty shovels oat sludge into his mouth like it's a delicacy. "Saylor's the only one who can really get away with telling him what to do."

I wonder what Marty did to get sent here.

And Saylor.

"I want yesterday's newcomers to follow me," a voice shouts, snagging my attention. A bearded man in his late twenties with cropped, straw-colored hair stands in the center of the cafeteria, cupping his mouth. "It's orientation time."

The other Cleancoats and I line up outside. The Guard stands a few feet in front of us, next to an older man with a slender face, thick eyebrows, and graying hair. His mouth seems like it's been permanently sewn into an overturned arc.

"My name is Officer Casey Stokes," the younger Guard says. "I'm a Supervisor here. I report directly to Captain Ron Valdez, who's in charge of this faction of the Tombs."

He jabs his thumb toward the older man, who flashes a perfect set of glistening teeth. "Welcome, Officers."

Valdez shakes our hands before returning to Stokes's side. His palms are soft. Not like mine.

"We've got work to do today, so I'll keep this short." Valdez checks an expensive-looking watch before placing his hands behind his back. "I'm sure you've all heard of this establishment before, but I'm obligated to confirm a few facts. First, no one enjoys being here. It will do you some good to let that soak in and spare the rest of us from your complaints."

He pauses. I hear a hawk's shrill cry in the distance before he goes on.

"The Tombs are a necessary cog in our greater societal machine. As the Nightjade Order strategically and fairly culls our population for the betterment of our planet and future, we support this purpose by processing the results of extermination."

Burning and burying people your Presidency murdered, I correct silently, tightening my jaw. *Not extermination.*

"Before overpopulation soiled the Earth we are trying to restore, in the vast arctic tundras far north, wolves once roamed as noble creatures—not the skeletal captives they are in today's conservation programs. These predators were the epitome of authority and fairness, cunning and wisdom. They were gods. They preyed upon diseased caribou who could not run for themselves, and this kept the herd healthy. Without the wolves—hunted to near extinction by man—the caribou were left untouched. Herds grew to anomalous sizes. If their diseases hadn't killed them off, unchecked by the wolves, they would have starved to death in competition with each other for resources.

"The food chain is nature and it is law. And in our law, we are the decomposers. Our only purpose is to support the efforts of the Nightjade Order and the Pick by disposing of society's waste—so those above our ranks can keep doing their jobs. And we do it out here, where our smoke doesn't poison those who still serve a productive purpose.

"I don't give a damn why you're here. I don't care what you did or didn't do." He stops pacing. "Just keep these bloody prisoners in line, so we can all do our collective job."

Silence.

I hear that hawk again, so far out of reach. So far from our smoke.

Far from me.

"Is that clear?" Valdez barks.

"Yes, sir!" We chant in unison.

Valdez leaves, then Stokes goes over formalities. Rise at 6:00, off at 6:00. Breakfast and dinner are at both times. Curfew's at midnight, enforced by Corrective measures. Prisoners stay in their cabins, we stay in ours. Anyone might be randomly searched at any time—pockets or rooms. We must only speak to prisoners when absolutely necessary.

No one is safe from the threat of Correction.

Guards work rotating shifts for different tasks. We make sure the prisoners do their jobs.

As a Supervisor, Stokes has some authority over the rest of us. There are six others like him. As for Valdez, *Captain* isn't even a real position in the Corps; he's just the Chaser someone assigned to be in charge of this hellhole.

Apparently, there are other Tombs *factions* like this one here in New Mexico. There's one in Texas. Nevada. The oil fields of North Dakota. The rural plains of Kansas. This one is the largest. It's also the most secure.

Stokes goes over what our different shifts entail.

Dig supervision means watching prisoners shovel graves in the scorching desert sun. The furnace involves a similar heat, but it's covered, so there's shade. In the Archives we organize files and do simple data entry tasks to update the Corps database—clerical work the Captain doesn't want to do himself. Transport means hauling ashes and disposing them out in the desert, using trucks that will automatically lock up and send out an alert if you drive too far.

Guards need to supervise prisoner mealtimes too. A few NOTs are stationed on site to serve as techs for the electric fence and anything else that needs fixing. They wear rubber boots and gloves to avoid getting shocked.

I think about how nice it would've been if I got assigned to the NOT instead—the Nightjade Operations and Technology Division. I bet that would've been more useful for the Cut than whatever the hell this is.

Failure, I remind myself.

That's what this is.

Then there's the Correction building, where a handful of Guards are stationed during working hours, just in case any issues come up. They usually don't, Stokes says. The prisoners' work is punishing enough.

"And remember," Stokes continues, "our annual Evaluation is October 24th. An Agent and a representative from the Officer Division will be here to observe. They'll talk to Captain Valdez and each of us Supervisors to assess whether any of you need reassigning. Be on your best behavior until then, and maybe you'll get a good word from me.

"After that, the next delivery truck will be here November 14th with food and supplies. We get shipments on a quarterly basis. Those are all the dates you need to remember for now."

After a half-hearted tour, Stokes assigns us new recruits to our respective Supervisors. There are seven units total of about fifty Guards each. Stokes is in charge of Unit 3, which happens to be my group.

He walks me over to the front of the Archives building, where Unit 3 usually meets after breakfast. The rest of the unit is already lined up in rows. I'm the only Cleancoat in the group. I spot Marty in the crowd, frowning when I notice that Saylor and his buddies are here too.

"Thanks for waiting. Everyone, this is Officer Beck." Stokes gives me a pat on the back. "Now let's get started."

I stand beside Marty as Stokes pulls out his tablet and begins announcing today's assignments. It's not even noon and the sun is already a kiln. My head still aches from yesterday.

"How are you feeling?" Marty whispers.

"Like shit."

"The first few days will do that to you." He gives me a small smile. "It gets more bearable, I promise."

He doesn't sound very certain.

One by one, Guards walk up to Stokes to receive their assignments, until Marty and I are next. Without looking, Stokes points his thumb toward the building behind him. "You two are on Archive duty today."

"This one's not so bad," Marty whispers. "Boring, but the only room besides the Captain's quarters with decent climate control."

"He's right," Stokes mutters, still looking at his tablet. I didn't realize he was listening.

"Oh," I say. "Thanks."

Don't be fooled, I warn myself. *He's just being easy on the new guy. He's still a Guard.*

They all are.

"Saylor, Fantaine—you're on Dig," Stokes announces.

Marty and I are about to walk away when Saylor speaks behind us. He crosses his arms, head tilted. "Are you sure?"

"I'm positive," Stokes says.

"I think you should double-check." Saylor glances at Marty and me, then back at Stokes.

The Supervisor flexes his jaw, clenching the tablet tighter. He keeps his glare fixed to Saylor. "My apologies, Officer. I read the chart wrong." He clears his throat and pretends to read it again. "You're on Archive duty, Dawson's on Dig."

"And Fantaine?"

Stokes sighs. "Fantaine's on Archive. Cota can join you. Beck, you're on Dig."

My brows crease. *How come he lets Saylor walk all over him like that? Isn't he supposed to be our Supervisor?*

I peer over to catch a glimpse of Stokes' chart. Marty and I are listed under Archives, just like he originally said. My fists clench. I feel like absolute garbage, I'm in a mood, and I *really* don't want to stand in the sun all day.

"Actually..." I tilt my head, pretending to read the tablet.

Marty tugs at my sleeve, urging me to leave it alone. I swat his hand away.

"It *does* say Dawson and I are on Archive duty." I turn to shrug at Saylor. "Sorry, pal. Looks like you're on Dig after all."

Cota shoots me a frigid glare. Fantaine looks like her head might explode. Saylor just stares at me for what feels like ages until he finally sighs. "Sorry, Stokes. Just double-checking, that's all."

Cota and Fantaine turn to walk away. I'm about to do the same, but Saylor grabs my arm and whispers in my ear. "I thought I warned you, Beck."

That's all he says before taking his leave.

Marty and I start walking toward the Archives. He looks over his shoulder in disbelief before giving me a wide-eyed stare. "Dude... what the hell did you just do?"

"You're welcome."

"You really don't get it, do you?"

"Get what?"

We walk up a few creaky wooden steps and into a brick building. The air conditioning hits like a wave of ice water. Marty closes the door behind us, and I pause to take in the brief moment of almost-comfort.

"Look, man. There's a strict food chain around here, alright? There's the Guards like us, and the Guards like them. You and I aren't here for the same reasons they are. *They're* here because they did some screwed up stuff. You really, *really* don't wanna mess with him."

"I've dealt with guys like him before," I say, leaning against the door and thinking of Ansel. "The best way to handle entitled people is to remind them they have nothing to feel entitled about."

"That's not always true. You'll just provoke them and make everything worse. You don't want to turn yourself into a target."

"Look. I get why you're apprehensive about him, but trust me, I've got this handled." I sigh. "I hate letting people get away with acting like that. It goes against everything we—"

I stop myself. *Careful.*

"Everything *I* stand for," I go on. "It just pisses me the hell off."

"I know it's unfair, and I know he's a real piece of work, but you've just gotta go along with it and hope he eventually leaves you alone."

"Go along with it? Go *along* with it?" I chuckle cynically. "Going along with shit like that is exactly why—"

Keep it together. No one can know who you really are.

"Why what?" Marty asks.

"Nothing." I pause. "So what is it, then? Some kind of deal with Stokes?"

"Saylor?"

I nod.

Marty sighs. "Something like that. No one knows what it is, exactly, but... there's definitely some unspoken agreement going on."

"Blackmail?"

"Who knows?" He shrugs. "He's got a few prisoners wrapped up in deals too."

"Deals?"

"He bribes them. Messes with them. Orchestrates problems so *he* can be the one to solve them and earn brownie points with our Supervisors."

We walk farther into the room. Dull light filters in through dusty windows. It's a small building, with creaky wooden floors to match the front steps and white walls of peeling plaster. There are a few desks with computers. They seem out of place with the rundown decor and the worn file boxes stacked in various places. There's a back door, and I'm sure more boxes are stored behind it. Apparently they've been working on digitizing old death records for years. Most of them are from the Yesterdays, before the Corps database was established—their cloud of information, statistics, public surveillance.

Marty says you can't think too hard about what you're doing on this shift. Otherwise you'll notice how pointless it feels, and then you'll realize there's more to it than looking good on paper or proving our productivity to the Corps. This job exists so we don't drive ourselves mad. So we can catch a brief break from the other stuff, like watching prisoners man the morgue or load corpses into the crematorium.

It's just like digging, he says. It keeps the prisoners too discouraged to rally up and rock the boat. Everything here has a greater purpose. A balanced ecosystem, Marty calls it.

So we sit in our air-conditioned room, sorting through names of people burned long ago, who are forgotten now in a way I fear more than anything. I wonder if their names will show up in the fountain at the training center. The one without water—just a stream of blue holograms, names belonging to those exterminated by the Corps. People who were sacrificed for this *greater good* Marty speaks of.

I don't want to become a part of that fountain.

My back starts aching after a few hours, and my canteen is empty, so I get up for a refill and some fresh air. The drinking fountain is on the front porch. It's surprisingly high-tech. The water's filtered, too. No wonder this shift is so coveted.

I fill my canteen—then hear something shuffle behind me.

I spin around to see someone emerge from the building across from ours. The crematorium. We're separated by a packed dirt road, a few yards wide. I squint, then realize it's the girl with the braid and the ribbon.

She stops by the prisoner's rusty water fountain, which stands by the entrance. It sputters a bit and stops. She kicks it with a scowl. The water starts up for a brief second before stopping again. She presses the button over and over, cursing at it.

I glance around me. No Guards. Only us.

I walk over and extend my canteen. "Here."

She jumps back at the sound of my voice, eyes wide. Then she recognizes me and glares. "I'm fine."

"You're thirsty. It's hot as hell. Have some."

"I said I'm fine," she snaps.

I eye the crusty fountain and lift a brow. "Are you sure?"

"Look, Officer. I don't know what you're up to, but I promise I'm not interested in your *help,* or the strings that I'm certain are attached to it.

So stop trying to play nice, because I'm not an idiot, and I'm *not* going to be your little charity project."

I blink at her for a moment. She covers her mouth with both hands, like she's only just realized what she's said. Like she's worried she'll get in trouble.

Strings? My face warms.

I study the fading bruise around her eye. I've seen other prisoners wearing similar marks, and I understand why she's so afraid of me. *She doesn't know I'm like her.*

I think back to everything Ansel said at the carnival. His tips.

Maybe if I joke with her, she'll trust me.

"I hate to break it to you, but if you think this is flirting, your bar is too low."

Something in her relaxes a bit, but she's still glaring. "I wish I had a bar so I could *hit you* with it."

I lean against a post and cross my arms. "I'm insulted, quite frankly. If I were interested, you'd know. I've got better game than *this*." I raise the canteen.

"And *I've* got work to do."

"So you don't want my water?"

"No."

I shrug. "Alright then."

I uncap the canteen and start pouring it out in the dirt.

"What the hell are you doing, wasting that?" She falls to her knees, cupping it in her hands. "Are you stupid?"

I stop pouring. "I wasn't going to drink it anyway."

She's glaring again as she rises to her feet, still holding the water. "Do you know where this came from?"

"The sky?"

"You really think it rains out here?"

"Isn't all water recycled dinosaur piss or something?"

"It comes from over *there*, genius." She gestures toward the old water tower in the distance. "They pump groundwater into that tank, and when you turn on your tap, that's what comes out. It doesn't just come from thin air, alright? We need that tank full for fire safety, because we're all alone out here, and if something goes wrong in the furnace and we get a fire going, the water in that tower's the only thing that'll keep us from burning. So don't go around wasting it."

"Alright, fine."

Now her attention is glued to the water in her cupped hands. Her lips are chapped. Her palms are dry and cracked and calloused. She can't stop staring at it.

"Have some," I say, no humor this time.

"You first."

I take a sip from my canteen. "See? Not poisoned."

She hesitates for a moment—then drinks from her hands. Quickly. Desperately. When that's gone, she grabs my canteen and gulps the entire thing, down to the very last drop.

She wipes her lip and returns it to me with a nod. I walk back to my drinking fountain and fill it up again. She watches for a moment before disappearing into the steaming crematorium.

I return to the Archive room, which is air-conditioned and comfortable.

Archive work could have been a lot worse, but my back hurts, my head throbs, and the mystery meat we had for lunch and dinner is disagreeing with my stomach. The second I got off my shift, I curled up in bed, trying to nap the pain away. It didn't work. Now it's almost curfew and I still haven't washed up.

The communal bathrooms are across from the Guards' quarters. I trudge there slowly. They're empty now. It's dark. No one's out but me.

My stomach is still twisting as I splash water on my face. I'm reminded of Beau and the junk food we devoured on our adventures. Whitestag was different; the Schneiders ate the best because they could afford the best. This food is cheap. Artificial.

I think about the Cut and living off the land—only eating food we grew ourselves. Once, I would have done anything to escape that life. I thought I was missing out on the wonders of junk food and sugar. I blamed Dad for robbing me of chipped life. Now I'd do anything to go back home. I miss clean, real food grown by our own hands and soil. Hell, I even miss Whitestag. Ansel feels more like an annoying mosquito compared to the creeps here.

If I make it out of this alive, I'll never eat meat again.

In a life beyond this fence, I don't even think I'd be able to stomach it. Not without returning here, to this sickness.

It's only been one day.

I finish washing up and walk back to the cabin, mentally preparing myself for another night of tossing and turning in a hot room that smells like armpit. I can't see very well. It's dark and I left my glasses on my nightstand.

Before I reach the door, someone yanks the back of my collar.

I'm pulled into the alley between Cabin 12 and the one next door. Someone pushes me against the wall. My eyes widen, but I can't call out because a hand is over my mouth.

As my vision adjusts to the dark, I make out Saylor's smirk. "I warned you, didn't I?"

The hands that grab my shoulders and push me forward feel soft. Untouched by things like shovels, but still strong enough to maintain a grip I can't fight in my weakened state. I try anyway, elbowing and shouldering against the Guards who hold me.

"Back the *hell* off," I shout, elbowing someone in the stomach. They don't like it very much and soon both my arms are grabbed.

"*Shh*, people are sleeping," Saylor whispers in my ear. "Let's go somewhere a little more quiet, shall we?"

Someone shoves a balled up sock in my mouth so I can't shout. They tie my hands with scratchy rope.

Saylor, Fantaine, and Cota drag me northeast, weaving between alleys and shadows to take me to the Graves. Over the hard sand and desert grass, over mounds of dirt both old and new, until we reach the rows of empty graves waiting to be filled.

They let me go and I spit out the sock. We're so far from the cabins it wouldn't even matter if I screamed. I save my breath.

"I watched them dig this grave earlier today, you know," Saylor says. "The poor girl's blisters cracked. There was blood all over the shovel."

Saylor forces me to my knees, inches away from the nearest empty grave. He crouches behind me, clutching my hair and making me look down into the pit. It's shallow for a grave—maybe four feet.

"So what do you think about this one? Was her blood worth the result?" He shoves my face forward. If he lets go, I'll fall in. "Take a good look, Beck. You'll be in it for a *very* long time."

I chuckle tiredly, too sick to be scared or angry. "All this because I got the shift you wanted? I think you're overreacting."

Saylor yanks me away from the grave. Fantaine and Cota pull me up and spin me around to face him, holding my arms.

"Slow learner, are you?" He seethes.

"I could be better at math."

He punches me in the stomach so hard I'd probably vomit if it weren't empty. The other Guards' bruising grips are the only things keeping me upright.

He clutches the collar of my shirt, forcing me to look at him. "We've been in this shithole *much* longer than you have. You can't just waltz in here and act like you own the place. Like you're above our rules."

"A Guard like you, threatened by one rookie Cleancoat? Now that's surprising." I chuckle. "If I scare you this much, you must be weaker than I thought."

That's the sentence that gets me beaten to a bloody mess.

Fantaine and Cota don't even help him. All it takes is one Guard, one boot to kick me so hard I swear I see the stars. No—I do see them. I'm on my back. My face is swollen and my eyes are barely open, but I see it—an endless expanse of nothingness above me. Empty like the desert. Empty like me.

I close my eyes. Only then does Saylor stop kicking my abdomen. Then I hear something. A crunch, like footsteps. No. Not footsteps.

A shovel's blade in the sand.

My heart races. Before I can spring upright, Cota and Saylor grab my arms and legs. They lift me up.

"What are you doing?" is all I can mutter. I know the answer, but I don't want to believe it.

They lower me into the grave.

My eyes flutter open again. This time it's not the stars I see, but Saylor's smiling face. A cruel half-moon grin that blocks out the real crescent behind him.

"You can call for help all you want, but no one will hear you. Guards' quarters are on the far end of the facility."

My head spins. Something falls on my legs. *Sand.*

"The prisoners might hear your screams, if you've even got it in you to cry. But getting one of them to help *you*? A Guard? Now that's another story." He laughs. The humor dissipates. "You're all on your own."

I feel myself weaving in and out of consciousness. More sand falls. I hear the chorus of two shovels now as his Guards bury me. By the time my face is covered, I can't even fight it. There is no strength left in me. Only sand in my nose. My mouth. My throat.

I'm suffocating. I'm losing air, and I don't even have the energy to panic as I feel it slipping out of me. The shoveling stops. As I hear three pairs of footsteps grow quieter and disappear, I think back to choking on Lily's tooth—how trapped I felt when I couldn't breathe. I feel that way now.

The tooth is still in my pocket. So much for luck.

What a shitty way to die.

Scratching. Clawing. Brushing. A cold wave of air, like water washing over me. It brings me back to life but not to Earth. Somewhere in the dark I am floating—mind suspended, not really here. Empty.

Dragging. Across the desert, over a threshold. And I'm not even awake to see who saves me.

Wednesday, August 3

♪ DESERT RAVEN - JONATHAN WILSON ♪

"Wow. That's one ugly scar."

The voice wrenches me into consciousness. I spring forward —only for my forehead to crack into another one.

My eyes clamp shut as I rub the collision site. When I open them, my observer is doing the same, glaring. "What gives, dude?"

I'm in the bottom half of a bunk bed beneath a thin, scratchy blanket. A boy my age with shoulder-length black hair and pale, almost sickly skin sits at the edge of it with a hand over his face. He looks a year or two younger than I am.

"Jelly, I'm done babysitting now," he calls over his shoulder. He stands with a glare. "This guy could take on anyone with that big head alone. He's just fine by himself."

"Oh, stop that. He has a perfectly nice head," a woman's voice responds from another part of the room I can't see. She gasps. "He's awake?"

"You're right. His head can't be *that* big if his brain is so damn small. Making the enemies he did is one stupid move."

"Lockley, a bad attitude harms yourself just as much as it—"

"Alright, alright, *fine*. I'll shut up now." Lockley coughs into his elbow, giving me one last scowl before walking away. He occupies a chair in the far corner of the room, watching with his arms folded.

I sit up slowly, taking in my surroundings. My head throbs. I'm in a small room that reminds me of Cabin 12, but everything is older and made of wood. There are cracks in the floor and cobwebs in the corners. There's one half-open window on the wall across from me, which is lined with more bunk beds like the one I'm resting within. They're all empty. A warm violet glow emits from the window's dusty glass. Patchwork curtains billow in a soft breeze. It must be early morning now.

A younger woman with long, wavy auburn hair walks into view, holding a damp cloth. She sits at the edge of the bed. I blink, still waking up. She has green eyes and a light dusting of freckles across her nose and cheeks. She's a few years older. Her hands are covered in bloody bandages. Her fingertips are calloused. This must be the *Jelly* that Lockley was talking to.

She starts patting my forehead with the cloth. "What were you thinking, making enemies with Saylor? People like him are dangerous, you know."

My face warms. I'm suddenly very aware of the fact that I'm shirtless, covered in bruises, and probably don't smell very pleasant. I glance down at my chest. I'm wrapped in bandages.

Who undressed me? I look up at the woman again. *Was it her?*

Wait—where am I?

"You're lucky Raven found you when she did," Jelly says. "She saw them drag you out there. Dug you up and brought you back here."

"She saved your sorry ass from becoming worm food," Lockley adds from his chair.

I'm about to ask about Raven but pause, clicking my tongue. My mouth is dry and my throat feels scratchy, like I've spent the last few days eating cotton. Talking would burn.

"I'll get you some water," Jelly says with a small smile.

Only when she stands up and walks away do I notice her rust-colored clothing—and her stomach. *She's pregnant.*

The realization makes my heart sink. Being in a place like this can't be good for her. The smoke. The food. The work. The heat. It all makes me want to punch a wall, but I can barely hold my neck up.

Jelly returns and hands me a canteen. I take one gulp, only because it seems like she wants me to. She needs it more than I do.

She urges me to drink the rest. I comply, because I get the feeling that despite her kind demeanor, she might force it down my throat if I refuse.

"Raven and Doc will be here soon. He's coming back to check on you again," she says.

"Raven? With the ribbon?"

Lockley nods.

"I'm Evangeline," the woman says. "You can call me Jelly."

"A—" I clear my throat. "Cedar."

I almost feel guilty lying to them. But I still have a cover to maintain.

The door opens and shuts with a creak. I hear two sets of footsteps, and I sit up straighter to see who they belong to. A shorter man with white hair and a bushy mustache enters, carrying a brown leather case. The girl with the ribbon walks in too.

Raven.

"He's awake," the man says with a grin. He pulls a chair up to my bedside. "How are you feeling?"

I glance at the bruises covering my skin. The bandages. "Fine." Another lie.

"I've been meaning to take a better look at this." He scoots the chair closer, squinting to study my scar—which I realize must now be visible since they washed me clean of all that sand and blood. He looks into my eye too. My breathing stops when I see his coat.

Embroidered on the front is the cross of a Corps Healer.

My breathing falters. This guy isn't a prisoner like the rest of them. He's a Guard too. *Then why is he here? Did Raven and the others alert the infirmary?*

But why would they do that? Hell—why help me at all? They don't know what I really am. As far as they know, I'm a Guard like the rest of them.

There's nothing I can do to hide my scar now. All I can do is sit still with my breath held and let this guy take a look.

"You're wearing a contact in your left eye," he mutters, then lets his gaze trail back up and down my scar. "Interesting."

Raven busies herself at a run-down sink in the kitchenette at the far corner of the room. A kettle whistles over a fireplace I hadn't noticed before. Jelly smiles before rising to fetch it. She returns with another warm washcloth for my forehead, patting my cut skin and stroking my hair. It makes me miss my mom.

"We've made enough water for you too," she says. "I'm sure Doc can give you one of his teas."

Raven walks over with two mugs of steaming water. Doc retrieves two tea bags from his case and places them in the cups before giving one to Jelly and the other to me. I smell it.

"Where'd you find dandelion tea in a place like this?" I take another sniff. "Fennel? Elderflower?"

"I have my contacts. Pay the delivery drivers a little extra to bring me back supplies. We'll get even more with the next shipment in November."

My forehead creases. That doesn't sound very legal.

Why tell me any of this?

I glance around the room. *Why is he being so nice to the others? To me?*

I nearly jump when something buzzes loudly. On the wall, an alarm bell rings to announce the start of the prisoners' first shift.

"We've gotta go," Raven mutters. "See you around, Doc."

She and Lockley exit without another word. It breaks my heart a little to see Evangeline follow them, tea unfinished—leaving Doc and me alone.

He studies me in silence for a long time, arms folded, eyes narrowed. I wonder if he might interrogate me.

"That's an old wound," he finally says, nodding toward my scar. "Must've been young when you were debugged."

My eyes widen. *What?*

Panic kick-starts my pulse. All at once, the heat drains from my body and flushes into my face. "I don't know what you're talking about."

"I've been here a long time, boy. I've seen all kinds of Underground folk come and go. I know the signs of debugging when I see one."

Shit.

My heart slams against my ribcage. This is bad. This is *really* bad.

He's going to turn me in, isn't he?

He'll turn me in, and if they don't inject me right then, they'll put me in a jumpsuit, and I'll spend the rest of my life working myself to death. In the end, I'll join the others in that sea of gray sand. No one will even know what happened to me.

No one will remember my name.

Doc chuckles. "You should see the look on your face."

My brows crease.

"Don't worry. I'm not turning you in."

A small taste of relief relaxes my shoulders. "You're... not?"

"So you know a thing or two about plants, huh?" He strokes his chin. "Most Chips these days couldn't even tell you what elderflower is, let alone isolate the smell like that."

Chips?

I keep my mouth shut. I still don't know who this guy is. He could be pretending, luring me in until I trust him enough to reveal something I shouldn't.

"The good news about this whole situation is that you've been beaten quite badly. The other Guards won't question any new scars showing up on your person. That means at least one of your secrets is safe, for now. No more makeup required. Though I'm not sure how you'd find any out here, anyway."

I don't say anything.

He leans back, sipping Jelly's unfinished tea. "So where are you from, *Cedar Beck*?"

I glance around the room.

"No mics out here. Not worth the operational cost, I suppose. No use spying on people already sentenced to death. The Guards keep them in check. This is where they send those who say the wrong things, anyway." He sets the cup down and folds his arms. "People like us."

I resist the urge to pinch myself when he winks. *Us?*

My lips part. "You're..."

"An Undergrounder? A traitor? An *Opticultist*? Unseen?" He smirks.

"Take your pick."

My eyes widen. "No freaking way..."

This can't be possible. There's no way this old man is a *Double*.

I've never even seen him before. And by the looks of it, he's had this job for a long time. He can't be from the Cut. I would recognize him. And Noriko's in contact with every group in the Pacific; we've never had a real Double in this Region before me.

He must be from somewhere else.

The room spins. I rub my forehead. Technically, it would be possible for Doubles from other places around the country to exist. Unseen certainly do. They're everywhere. The Cut doesn't have any official alliances with anyone aside from End Harbor, and the Regions aren't unified by any means, but there is some thin chain of contact.

We all call ourselves Unseen, don't we?

If that's true for every rebel, there must be *some* thread holding us together. But who the hell is this guy?

The man chuckles. "Believe it, Cedar. In here, we need all the allies we can get."

My head spins. I glance at the empty beds. "What about the others?"

"The Tombs don't hold as many Unseen as you'd think. Most prisoners end up adopting our beliefs eventually, mostly in silence. But for a true rebel to be sentenced here... now that's a rarity." Doc leans back in his chair. "Treason is the ultimate crime. Anyone who openly defies the system gets an automatic death sentence. The productivity of a Tombs sentence isn't enough to outweigh the risk of even the smallest rebellious spark—and you know how the Corps feels about efficiency."

"So there are... *Undergrounders* here? In the Tombs?"

I'm careful with my word choice. Only people with an inside look call us Unseen.

Don't reveal anything incriminating to him yet. He could still be lying.
"You've met a few," he says.

I rub my temples. I feel like shit, I'm hungry, and I don't want to be here —let alone digest all of *this*. "I thought treason gets the death penalty."

"Occasionally, some Unseen who haven't yet uncovered the truth about the trackers get caught for other crimes and shipped out here. If they can keep their true allegiance a secret from the Guards, they won't get exterminated."

"Some Guards call all prisoners traitors."

"That's merely an insult. Most Corps loyalists view any crime against the system as a betrayal. Even something as small as shoplifting a candy bar. Or getting caught with harmless Yesterday contraband, like books."

I nod, letting it all sink in.

"She's... one of them, isn't she?" I swallow. "One of the *few* I've met?"

He doesn't require elaboration to know who I'm talking about. His silent smile gives me my answer.

Is that why the girl with the ribbon saved me? Does she somehow know my secret?

What gave me away?

"Where are you from?" I ask. If he gives a real answer—the name of a camp I've heard of, something only one of us would know—maybe I can trust him.

"Out east. Fort Swanford."

I frown. I *have* heard of that place before. I've seen them mentioned on Cecil's maps. "Vermont?"

"You still haven't answered my question."

I bite my cheek. *I really do need allies, don't I?*

"West Washington. Olympic Peninsula."

"The Cut, I presume?"

I nod.

"Now I *really* think you know a thing or two about healing. Your folks are big on herbal medicine over there, yes?"

"That's how we get by, so yeah."

"You trade with sympathetic Chips who need healing, yes?"

I nod again.

"Never visited, but I've heard of your group, alright. Most of us have." He sips his tea. "You should be proud of the name the Cut has made for itself over the years. Not many of us are as organized as you are."

"How'd you get stationed all the way out here, anyway?"

"I'm sure we've both made similar mistakes." He stares at his wrinkled hands. "I couldn't be who they wanted me to be."

I stare at my hands too.

"Corps healers are similar to Guards, in a sense. We're technically part of the Sitter Division—those who work for the Corps at desks, in labs—you get the gist. As you know, doctors are a thing of the Yesterdays. The only purpose of a Corps healer is to serve Chasers. If we're caught giving aid to anyone outside of the Corps—even the Immune—we are reprimanded. Killed, if the patient is a traitor of any kind. Because nature must do its job, they say. We cannot interfere by preserving the weak. To do so would hinder the rest of society."

He leans back in his chair, eyes glued to the wall. "Magnolia was a blessing not meant for this world."

"Magnolia?"

"My daughter."

Was. It's almost unbelievable how three letters can hold so much meaning. So much pain.

"One day, she got sick. I started bringing medicine home under the table. Anything to bring her comfort. But... I was caught. So was she. But I'm a skilled surgeon, and she was..." He chokes on the words. "A *parasite.*"

My throat tightens. I want to tell him how sorry I am, but I don't. Sorry can't bring people back.

"Sometime between Magnolia's illness and my failure, I stumbled across the folks at Fort Swanford. Started helping them smuggle medicine for others. Treating them in secret. I was never debugged as you were and I never got caught for my crimes, but I still consider myself Unseen... through and through."

I think of Asa and smile weakly. My mom. "We have a few contacts like that."

"But, the Corps learned my... *other* secret eventually. My daughter was chronically ill, and I failed to report it to them. Even with the Immunity I provided as a Corps employee, withholding that information was enough to..." He clears his throat. "It wasn't treason, but it was still a crime. Not to mention my thievery. If I weren't skilled at what I do... if I wasn't *productive* and valuable to them... they would not have been so merciful."

"The Immunity didn't save her?"

"Immunity spares the chronically ill a death sentence. They are allowed to exist with the right protection. That doesn't mean the Presidency allows them to be *treated*."

"That was the crime that got you sent here?" I ask, voice quiet. "Stealing medicine for your daughter?"

Doc nods.

There is a field of vast, aching silence until he clears his throat. "Well, I'm here now, and have been for quite some time." He forces a fleeting, empty smile. "Seeing life behind this fence opened my eyes, Cedar. It opened my eyes to the truth. We worship the Presidency like gods who will never do anything but take and take. And I will not stand for it.

"I made a vow, long ago. To honor Magnolia's name and use these hands that were spared so cruelly for something good. I am a healer, and it is my duty to heal all—no matter who they are. I don't give a damn if it kills me."

I should say something. But all I can think about is my dad. Not sure why I feel like crying. I avert my gaze so Doc can't see. *They'd probably get along.*

But I'm not like them. I don't have that kind of drive, or loyalty, or whatever it is Dad thought I lacked before I volunteered for this. I'm here because I was selfish. I wanted to prove myself and experience the outside world I dreamed of knowing for so long. I wanted to become someone worth remembering—*do* something more than hide in the woods until I'm forgotten, just like my old name.

I wanted a taste of what life might be like if I wasn't Unseen.

I'm weak. *Just like he said.*

"I could use some help around here," Doc continues. "I'm getting older, and one man can only do so much. I make most of my rounds at night, but I still need rest to stay sharp. If I had someone to share the load with, we could provide more prisoners with access to—"

"I'm not sure I'd be much help," I interject.

I'll be escaping soon, anyway. *As soon as I figure out how.*

"But you know about healing."

"My dad's the healer, alright? Not me."

"I could teach you what I know."

"Why not teach one of them?" I nod toward the empty bunks.

"Because the prisoners are exactly who need us the most," Doc says. "They work themselves to the bone out there. All day, they bake in the heat and dust with little food or water, subjected to the temper of the Guards. They are exhausted and grieve the lives they once had, so far from their loved ones. They view life behind this fence as a means to an end, and that *has* to change.

"You and I—our roles, our status—it gives us a rare opportunity to help behind the Guards' backs. We're not sick like they are. And you're willing to let that advantage go to waste? To sit by and do nothing while *our people* waste away?"

I look away again.

"I can't offer you anything for your time—only knowledge and the comfort of helping your own. We're alone out here. Everyone beyond these walls thinks these prisoners are dead. Escape is impossible and no one is coming to save them, or you. If we don't build each other up, we will all fall. Isn't that what the Unseen is all about?"

Is it? I almost ask. I still haven't figured it out.

"Without one, there is no many," Doc continues. "Without many, there is no one."

I let his words sink in, fidgeting with my thumbs, staring at my reflection in the tea I haven't yet touched. I think about the sand, of how terrified I am of fading to nothing—of being nothing while I'm alive.

To *be* something, don't I have to *do* something first? *Why am I even here in the first place?*

Training alone gave me enough valuable information to bring back to the Cut. We'll have an inside perspective we've never had before, and it'll finally help us take a step toward making a difference. To put real action behind my parents' vague dreams for a better tomorrow.

I know everything there is to know about the Corp's divisions, technologies, resources—the seemingly endless advantages they have over us. I also know what training *really* holds. I could teach the next generation of Doubles to do this better than I did.

But what's the point? This *rebellion* the Cut dreams of starting... why do any of this at all?

The many, I realize.

Helping those who can't help themselves. Creating a better world for everyone. For my children, and their children—every person after that. For the unborn human Evangeline will meet someday.

I don't want that kid to grow up in a place like this.

I thought I took this job to prove something to my dad—that I *am* Unseen. But he's not here to see me prove anything. Hell, he probably thinks I'm dead.

Now I wonder if it was ever really about him at all.

Maybe I need to prove something to myself. That I can still do good. That I *am* good, despite everything I've done. That I have a purpose.

I refuse to become another pile of gray sand.

I am Unseen.

I look Doc in the eye and nod. "I'll help."

Until I find a way back home, I'll do what I can. And it's like he said. We're alone out here. I *will* find a way to escape—but I probably won't get far by pissing this guy off. If I can get a few prisoners on my good side, even better. *I need all the allies I can get.*

Doc nods, concealing a smile.

He checks me out to make sure I'm not dying or anything like that. Then he leaves. He tells me he'll let Stokes know I'm out sick for the day. He says not to worry; it can take a while for Cleancoats to fully adjust to the conditions here.

I weave in and out of sleep, wondering if I should tell someone the real reason for my absence once I get back to work. But if I rat out Saylor and he gets reprimanded, I have a feeling he might respond with something even worse.

For now, I let myself not care. I hide in this cabin, in a bed that is not my own, in an unfamiliar place where my head won't stop aching.

I assume it's noon when Raven returns, covered in soot and reeking of smoke. Her jaw is clenched, shoulders rigid. She walks over to the sink and washes her face, coughing into it. The water is cloudy and brown and doesn't look good enough to drink. She puts it in a kettle and hangs it to boil in front of the fireplace. *She was working the furnace again*, I realize.

"You shouldn't stare," she says, startling me a bit. "It's creepy."

She sits in front of the fire and pins her gaze to the kettle.

"Sorry."

She shrugs.

Slowly, I peel myself off the bed's sweat-stained sheets. Every bone and joint in my body creaks like a sinking ship. I limp over to Raven and sit cross-legged on the floor.

We're silent for a while, listening to the crackling flames. She glances at me and my bandages, then back at the fire.

"Why'd you do it?" I ask.

"Do what?"

"Save me."

The kettle screams. She pours the water in a mug. No tea. *She's just sterilizing it*, I realize. The thought makes me sick. *Of course the Guards would get better filters.*

And I'm one of them.

"So no thank you?" she asks.

"Sorry." I pause. "Thank you."

"You should stop doing that. Saying sorry so much." She sips her water. "It's weak."

"You didn't answer my question."

She studies me for a moment, then shrugs. "You gave me water."

I nod. More quiet.

"I'm not supposed to be here, you know," I say.

"That's what every Guard claims."

"I didn't—" I sigh. "I didn't *choose* this."

"Cut the bullshit, alright? We make a thousand choices every day. You wouldn't be wearing that uniform if you didn't decide to put it on in the first place." She stares at the fire again. "We're all here because we chose something."

"I don't think you understand." I scoot closer, looking her dead in the eye. "I'm *really* not supposed to be here. Just ask Doc. He knows what I mean."

"You're no prisoner."

"And I'm no Guard." I lean back on my palms, thinking of what Doc told me. "But you're no ordinary prisoner either, are you?"

She stands, looking away. "I don't know what you're talking about."

I stand too. "Who's spitting bullshit now?"

"*Excuse* me?"

"You see my scar. You know what I am. And I know what you are."

Her eyes widen. "Doc told you?"

I nod.

"You're..."

"A Double Agent."

She glares. "You really expect me to believe you were sent here on purpose?"

"Yes."

"No one plants Doubles here. There's no point. It's a lost investment."

"Look. I was supposed to finish training, gather a bit of info out in the field, and take it back home. Getting sent out here wasn't exactly part of the plan."

"So you screwed up." She studies me like all the pieces are coming together.

I avert my gaze, jaw tight. "Yeah. I screwed up."

It's quiet again as Raven absorbs it all, brows still creased.

"You've gotta help me get out of here," I say.

She laughs bitterly. "That's cute."

"I'm serious, alright? This place is a shithole, I don't know what I'm doing, and I *need* to get back home."

"You think I'd still be here if there was a way out?"

I frown. She makes a good point, but I don't tell her that and sigh instead. "We're both on the same side here, alright? Maybe the reason why you haven't found a way out yet is because you haven't had a Guard to team up with."

"Escaping is a death wish. Is that really something you want to pursue?" She pauses. "Do you really want to go home that badly?"

I stop to think.

If I weren't Unseen—if I grew up chipped like everyone else—I'd be considered lucky. The right Agent showed up at the right time. Agent Finch, Head of House, king of the entire Pacific Region. He's the only one with enough sway to get away with a pardon.

He showed up partly because no one had ever pulled anything that stupid before, and it was an emergency situation that called for the Head of House's oversight. Having Gilbert's recommendation certainly aided my case.

Somehow, every mistake I'd made lined up so perfectly that Agent Finch and the Corps spared me and offered me a chance to fix my mistake. A chance for rehabilitation, so that one day, I can leave this place and serve them as the real Chaser they want me to be. Any Chip would be grateful for this opportunity to lead a successful career with wealth and Immunity.

That's why there are annual Evaluations here at the Tombs. We are studied by Supervisors and the Captain, who take notes on how we work. They send an Agent out here once a year to evaluate our standings and move us around to other assignments as needed. Marty told me about it. Some Guards do go home.

But a prisoner can never go back.

I think about that for a moment. I have a false tracker—this identity as Cedar Beck, a distant relative to the Schneiders. In theory, I *could* go back to chipped life. I could accept Walter's offer and live at Whitestag, working as one of his Vipers, feeding him information from inside the Corps. It'd be a life brimming with the chipped pleasures and comforts I dreamed of knowing for so long.

But that life would betray the Unseen.

Death is the scaffolding this system stands upon. While the wealthy are safe on their raft of privilege, the rest of us are drowning beneath them— and there is no room for the lesser where they stand. To enjoy the security of Immunity would be agreeing with the way things are.

I would be safe with Immunity. Comfortable. I'd have access to anything I could possibly want. I'd die well-fed and swimming in dopamine. Another oblivious goat, so fat and happy.

But I'd never be Aaron again.

My family is Unseen and the Unseen is my family. If I want to see them again—if I want to be on the closest thing this country has to a good side —I *need* to go back home.

I don't care about the risk. I don't care if I get caught and imprisoned or turned into sand. *At least I'd die doing something meaningful.*

Another version of myself would have given anything to leave home. Now I'd give anything to go back to it.

I am still Unseen.

I look Raven in the eye. "Yes."

She nods, still uncertain.

"Look, you seem smart, okay?" I say. "I haven't even been here a week, and I've got it much easier than you. If I'm already desperate to get out, I can't even imagine how eager you are."

"Yeah, you can't," she snaps.

"You're familiar with this place. I hardly know anything about it, but I've got advantages you don't. We could help each other. Don't you see that?"

She thinks about that for a second. "Lockley and the girls are like family to me. I could never leave them here."

The girls? I think of Jelly—but who else?

"I understand," I say.

"The more people we try to get out, the bigger the risk."

"I get that."

She pauses. "Why should I trust you?"

"Because this place sucks."

"Doesn't mean you won't turn me in. They'd reward you, you know. Extra rations. Smuggled comforts. Maybe even promote you."

"I know."

"You're really willing to give that up? To risk something no one's done before?"

"Yes."

She chews on her lip in thought. "What if I turned *you* in?"

My pulse falters. "What?"

"The Guards are cruel when they realize there are real traitors among the prisoners. But they're even crueler when they find a traitor amongst themselves." She steps closer, arms crossed. "If I reported you, they'd reward me for my loyalty. Some Guards like having spies. I've seen prisoners report others for extra rations. Water. Forbidden infirmary visits." She tilts her head. "A Guard gone bad? That's gold."

I step closer too. "Is that a threat?"

"I'm just making it clear that your uniform gives you no power over me."

"So you don't trust me."

"No."

"Well after your little *threat*, I'm not sure I trust you either."

"Great. Then we both agree on something."

"Agreement is a great start."

We glare at each other for a moment until she finally speaks. "You really want to earn my trust?"

"I wanna get the hell out of here."

She pauses. "Then you're going to help me out with something."

"Anything."

"We're going to steal from the Guards."

"Easy. What do you need?"

She smirks. "Gasoline."

Thursday, August 4

♪ CALL IT A RITUAL - WOLF PARADE ♪

I'm unsure if Raven's plan is genius or incredibly stupid.

I don't know what she needs gasoline for. It can't be for setting fires —she told me about that water tower herself. The Guards could put out any flame in an instant. We'd just get ourselves killed.

But if she's planning to steal one of those delivery trucks that Marty and Doc told me about, stockpiling fuel would be the smart thing to do. Though I'm not sure how plausible that idea is either.

According to Raven, security for prisoners is much stricter at night. They expect more suspicious activity in the dark. But during the day, both prisoners and Guards are busy with their shifts. This is when we'll strike.

I ask her why she doesn't want me to steal the gasoline myself and bring it to her. She says we need to get as much as possible in one trip. And apparently, I don't know where or how to obtain it.

Which is true. The Serpent didn't exactly cover gas siphoning in our lessons.

It's my first time on dig duty—which the other Guards just call Dig.

Standing under this unforgiving sun with no shade is a misery I'd only wish upon my worst enemy. My skin is cracked, my nose and throat dry. Sweat tickles the back of my neck and plasters my clothes to my arms and legs. It makes me feel trapped. A prison all on its own.

I feel like soup in a slow cooker. The longer I stand out here, the stronger my headache grows. One day off wasn't nearly enough to recover from Saylor's torment, which only slowed my adjustment to this routine.

I'm just glad I'm not wielding a shovel.

Watching the prisoners work is the worst part of it all. It's hard not to imagine what they might be feeling—a habit Dad drilled into me at a young age. I study their blistered palms and poor posture, the way they pause to stretch and clutch their heads and lower backs with hidden grimaces. I'm already brainstorming a dozen tincture blends and stretching regimens in my head.

Of all the prisoners on Dig today, Lockley and Raven seem to be the best at hiding their pain. I'm not sure if it's a teenage pride thing, or if they're just used to the discomfort.

I think the latter is true for Lockley, judging by the sound of his cough. All the prisoners and Guards have one, but Lockley's is nearly constant. His hands don't bleed either, unlike Raven's. Her calluses are not as hardened. Her cough is hardly noticeable. I don't think she's been here as long as the others. She hides discomfort well—face blank, set in a deep state of focus. That sort of resilience is almost always learned.

I can't help but wonder who taught it to her.

Marty makes the job slightly less miserable. We're partnered again. I think Stokes paired us on purpose after he saw my bruises, like some silent apology or something. I get the feeling Saylor's behavior is common knowledge around here.

I like Marty's stories. He talks a lot, so I don't have to. It's nice to just nod and let him do the heavy conversational lifting. I've never been good at talking to people. Marty, on the other hand, talks like he needs it to breathe. His mind jumps in zig-zags like mine, always getting distracted by something else before finishing his previous train of thought. That small commonality between us brings me some comfort, at least.

He tells me about his parents, who always wanted him to be a Chaser so he could provide Immunity for himself and his younger siblings. From what he says, they might be good, honest people. Maybe they don't understand the true cost of that goal. If anyone saw the world behind this fence, I doubt they'd be so adamant about such a dream for their son. Or maybe I'm wrong.

People don't usually care about suffering unless it applies to them.

You still can't trust him, I remind myself. *Just because he's being friendly now doesn't mean he's any less Chaser. Don't let your guard down.*

"What the hell is your problem?"

Raven's voice snags my attention. She stands next to her half-dug grave, pointing inside and glaring at Lockley.

He folds his arms. "*My* problem? *You're* the one yelling at me for no reason."

"You just dumped all that sand in my grave!"

"Aw, how awful."

"Look, I work out here all day, and I'm exhausted. I don't want *your* carelessness slowing me down."

"It's just a bit of sand."

"And it's making more work for me," she snaps. "Just watch where you're going, alright?"

The other prisoners pause. They glance at Marty and me, then Raven and Lockley, waiting for something to happen.

"Those two bicker all the time, but they're friends," Marty whispers under his breath. "Just ignore—"

"I'm sick of you acting like this," Lockley interrupts, fists clenched.

Raven scoffs. "Like what?"

"Like you're above the rest of us somehow. I do just as much work as you do. You're entitled and it's annoying."

"Annoying?" Raven laughs in disbelief. "You're one to talk."

"What's that supposed to mean?"

"You're whiney and grumpy and all you ever do is complain. It's weak. *You're* the one who never shuts up about how miserable you are. News flash, Lock—we're *all* miserable. And don't get me started on your coughing.

Would it kill you to cover your damn mouth for once in your life?"

"You have *no right* to talk to me about misery." Lockley's voice grows colder, deeper. It sends a shiver down my spine.

I almost buy it.

He steps closer to Raven. Marty and I exchange uncertain glances.

"I've been here longer than any of you," Lockley continues. "I've spent my entire life rotting away behind this fence. I've seen things that'd make you piss yourself, *Princess*."

"Watch it," Raven hisses, gripping her shovel tighter.

"What, don't like the nickname? That's what you are though, right?" Lockley tilts his head with a chuckle. "Just because your dad ratted you out doesn't change the fact that you grew up living the cushy life of an Agent's daughter, while I've known nothing else but this. So sorry if I complain, or *cough a little* now and then."

My brows furrow. *Lockley grew up here?*

And Raven's dad is an Agent?

Raven steps closer. "I thought I told you to watch it."

Lockley moves forward too, coughing obnoxiously in her face. "Does that annoy you?" He coughs again. "What about that?"

"Yeah, it does."

"And what are you gonna do about it, *Princess*?"

That's when she punches him in the face.

I conceal laughter as the brawl begins. It doesn't take long until they're both rolling in the sand, punching each other like fed-up siblings. Neither of them hold back.

That's my cue.

I step forward and pry them apart. "Alright, that's enough."

I yank them up by their collars. Lockley spits blood at Raven's feet. She lurches forward, but I hold her back.

"Nice touch," I whisper in her ear, nodding toward the very real bruises forming on Lockley's face.

"Thanks," she mutters, wiping blood from her nose. "He deserved it."

She doesn't waste a second before attempting to jerk free from my grip with a shout. "Get off me!"

She elbows me in the gut—also very real.

I pull her arms behind her back and tie her wrists with the bit of rope I'd saved from my burial. "You'll regret that in Correction," I say loud enough for everyone to hear, deepening my voice for effect. I whisper in her ear again. "Now *that* wasn't so nice."

"Neither am I, Beck."

"I just got the chills."

I spin her around and nod at Marty. "I'm taking these two to Correction."

Marty lowers his voice so the other prisoners can't hear. "Just leave it alone."

"Why?"

"You don't wanna get involved in this."

"They just got in a fight. They disrupted work for everyone, and they should be punished for it."

"It was just a fight. No other Guards saw, and they're friends. They'll get over it."

"How do you know?"

"I see them together all the time. They'll resolve it on their own," he says between clenched teeth.

I open my mouth to reply, then pause. He's trying to save them from Correction.

But why?

I clear my throat. "They broke the rules. I'm following them."

Marty glares. He looks over his shoulder—the prisoners have gone back to work—then at me. "I thought you were better than this, Cedar."

Raven gives me a look. I ignore it and lean closer to whisper to Marty. "I won't let them get hurt, alright? Please trust me on that. I'm just following protocol. Better me than Saylor."

Marty's brows furrow. He looks at me, then Lockley, then me again. He nods. "I don't know what you're doing, but hurry back. Shift ends in an hour."

Once my prisoners and I are far enough from the Graves, Lockley bursts out in laughter. "Oh man. You should've seen the look on your face. I thought you were gonna kill me."

"Keep that up and you'll get another shiner," Raven says.

Lockley coughs in her face again. She rolls her eyes.

Correction is carried out in the warehouse, which I open with my ID card. It's usually pretty empty, save for the rows of industrial shelves filled with Nightjade, food storage, and other supplies—and the dump trucks that aren't in use at the moment.

Raven maneuvers out of my faulty knot and gives me back the rope. She surveys our surroundings, then nods. "Coast is clear."

We wait as she hurries out of the building, then returns with three empty jugs of cleaning solution. "Hid these out by the front."

"You steal these often?" I ask as she hands me one.

"No one ever misses them," she says.

Lockley takes his own jug and hurries to one of the trucks, leaving Raven and me alone with ours.

"We never take too much from one truck, otherwise they'll notice." She points to the four parked vehicles. "We'll fill the jugs halfway and split it evenly between them."

"And what exactly do you need gasoline for, again?"

"No such thing as free lunch, Beck." She pats my shoulder before crouching beside the truck. I join her. "You still haven't earned my trust."

Raven reaches into her jumpsuit and pulls out two clear tubes, maybe hoses of some sort. She opens a panel on the side of the vehicle. "Watch and learn."

I don't know anything about trucks or whatever it is she's doing, but Lockley's already tackling the same thing at his own truck. Raven hands me the end of one of the tubes. "Suck on this. Stop before the gasoline reaches your mouth. You don't want to ingest it."

Reluctantly, I obey. No fuel makes contact with my tongue, but the taste is still foul. I spit out the tube and try not to gag. "Now I see why you brought me along."

She shrugs. "If you want in, you've gotta pull your weight."

Gasoline flows through one of the tubes and into the empty jug. We wait.

"So..." I clear my throat. "What exactly happens in Correction, anyway?"

"They didn't train you?"

I shake my head.

"Of course." She sighs. "Use your imagination, Beck. A prisoner *misbehaves*, a Guard takes them in here to teach them a lesson." She averts her gaze. "You're not the only one Saylor and his buddies like to kick around."

I pin my gaze to her bruise. My jaw tightens. "Saylor did this to you?"

"Fantaine."

"And they get away with it?"

"They're *encouraged*." She shakes her head. "They can't hurt us too bad. Otherwise we'd be dead weight. The Captain would have their heads. But they're supposed to scare us. It keeps us in check."

"So you've been here before?"

"We all have." She stops the siphon. We move to the next truck. "Which is why we all stay in line, for the most part."

"You sound unhappy about that."

"Of course I am." She prepares the siphon again. "We could easily *do* something if we all got organized. But the other prisoners are too scared to think big. Too scared to fight back."

She hands me the tube. I get the fuel going again and she directs it into one of the jugs.

"It's the same out there too," she continues. "Past the fence. Deep down we're all unhappy about the way things are, but no one does a damn thing about it."

"I don't think it's that simple."

"It is that simple. It's just not that easy."

I pause. "So... what are you going to do about it?"

"More than what the other Unseen have done, that's for sure. Groups like yours at the Cut do a whole lot of talk and doomsday prep, but not much else."

"That's not true." I try not to glare as we move to the next truck. "We smuggle medicine now and then. Help people seeking refuge."

"And what about weapons? Training people to fight back? Taking *action*?"

I blink, unsure of what to say. "You really think that's worthwhile?

Starting a war we can't win?"

"That old-school pessimism is exactly the problem." She continues fiddling with the siphon. "People who are too scared of losing their life never risk it for anything meaningful."

"There are more peaceful ways of bringing change," I say, thinking of my dad's lectures. "Without unnecessary sacrifices."

"I'm talking about comfort zones. Most people get so used to the way things are that they never try to bring that change, let alone permit themselves to hope for something better. *Your* idea of change will take years. Decades, even." She stops the siphon. "We can't afford a single more death by their hands."

We stare at each other for a moment. I try to read her.

I've lived my whole life Unseen, and somehow, I've never given any of this more thought than I've had to. I'm not sure how I feel about it. I didn't exactly choose this way of life; I was forced into it.

If I was raised in the system like everyone else, would I choose this? Being Unseen? Or would I remain passive like other Chips, blindly following leaders I don't believe in just to get by? *Would I have chosen resistance on my own?*

Before I can say anything, the warehouse door creaks open.

Raven scrambles to stop the siphon as a pair of footsteps approach. Whoever it is can't see us behind the trucks—yet. Lockley rolls under one to hide.

The footsteps grow louder. Closer. I glance over my shoulder, then back at Raven. "Hurry up with that, would you?"

"I'm trying."

"They're getting closer," I hiss.

"No shit!"

"I swear to God, if I get imprisoned because of you—"

"*Dammit.*" She drops the tube, spilling the gasoline left inside all over both our shoes. "Nice going, Beck. *Real* nice."

"How is this my fault?"

"You're distracting me!"

My whispers are quick and frantic. "I can't help being devilishly handsome."

She shakes out the tube and unzips the top of her jumpsuit to hide it. "The second we get out of here I'm kicking you for that."

The footsteps are louder and closer than ever. My leg shakes. She shoves the rest of the tube inside her jumpsuit, just as the footsteps halt behind me. I turn around.

"Well what do we have here?" Saylor tilts his head, arms folded. Raven zips up her jumpsuit. "The living dead fraternizing with a prisoner? Now that's quite the sight to behold."

Fantaine stands next to him, leaning against the truck with a snicker. Cota's here too.

"We're just about to load this bad boy up and take it for a ride out to the dump field." Saylor pats the side of the truck like it's hauling ice cream, not ashes. "And you are..."

"Correction." I clear my throat, pointing my thumb back in Raven's direction. "This prisoner got in a fight. I was sent here to uh... reprimand her."

"Uh-huh." Saylor studies the gasoline on our shoes, smiling emptily. "You know, I'm having a hard time believing that."

"It's the truth."

"She doesn't look very reprimanded to me."

I swallow the nervous lump growing in my throat. "I gave her a good talking to. She won't be causing any more trouble."

"I'm sure you did. Though I'm having a hard time believing that too. If corporal punishment hasn't worked on her yet, I highly doubt a *talk* will make a dent. Can't teach an old dog new tricks and all that."

"Maybe she just never had a good teacher."

Saylor goes quiet. For a moment I worry I've screwed up again—that I should brace myself for another concussion—but to my surprise, he laughs. He places a hand on my shoulder. "You know what? I think you're right."

I blink. "You do?"

He pulls away and starts pacing casually, arms folded. "She's got quite the track record, this one. A real knack for theft. That's why she was put behind this fence, you know. I saw her file in the Archives. It's made her quite the pest. First it was the cafeteria—stealing *our* food, *our* resources.

She certainly didn't learn her lesson then either, because next it was our rooms. *Our rooms*, Beck." He stops pacing. "I think it's about time this traitor gets taught a proper lesson—by a proper teacher."

A shiver courses through me. "Next time, then."

"No. No no no." He shakes his head with a hollow chuckle. "You see, there won't be a next time. Isn't that the point of a proper lesson?"

"Hey, would you look at the time? Her shift's ending soon. We'd better get back." I grab Raven's shoulder and guide her forward, but Saylor steps in front of us.

"Not so fast."

I look him in the eye, jaw feathering as I fight the urge to hit him. *You can't afford another incident*, I tell myself. It's a miracle I'm standing upright after what he did to me. If I provoke him even more than I already have, I can only imagine what other lessons he has up his sleeve.

And this time, it's not just me I have to worry about. *I don't want to drag Raven and the others into this.*

It takes strength I barely have to force the words out. "What lesson do you have in mind?"

The smirk tugging at the corner of his lips reminds me of a snake's rattle. A warning. He steps over to the jug of gasoline, disguised in its cleaning solution vessel. He picks it up and inspects it. "Why is there fuel in here?"

"Not sure. That was already here when we arrived."

Saylor nods toward our feet. "Seems like you had a spill."

"I tripped over it."

Saylor narrows his eyes at me. He knows I'm lying about something—he just doesn't know what.

He turns to Raven. "You started a fight?"

"I did."

"Sir," he corrects.

Raven's fists clench. "I did, sir."

"You disrupted work for the others."

"That's right, sir."

"Time is money, and you wasted it with your holdup. You are aware of this, correct?" He steps closer to her. I force my legs to remain firmly planted.

"That's thievery, *traitor*. You stole from the Corps, from the Presidency—who so generously pardoned you from extermination and offered you an honorable death here, serving your country. And *this* is how you repay them for their magnanimity?"

Raven doesn't say anything.

"You'll be punished for your actions. Do you understand?"

"Yes, sir."

The smirk returns. "That's what I like to hear."

It takes everything I have not to beat this guy to a pulp.

Raven steps forward, unafraid. There's not an ounce of fear in her eyes, even as her face is mere inches away from his. They're the same height. Now that she's close, they're both realizing it—and I don't think Saylor likes it very much.

"And what would you have me do?" Her lip twitches, a brief flicker of a defiant grin. "Sir?"

Saylor's smile is chilling. He extends the jug of gasoline. "Drink this."

My eyes widen. A wave of dread washes over me, pricking my skin. Even Fantaine and Cota exchange unsure glances.

He can't be serious.

Before I can stop it, Raven snatches the jug and looks Saylor dead in the eye. "Tell me when, *sir*."

She drinks.

All I can do is watch in horror as amber liquid dribbles down her chin. I can smell it. My throat burns from the stench alone, but her face doesn't shift. Even as her eyes begin to water, she keeps her glare pinned to Saylor.

This is her rebellion. Defying the Guards—defying everything—by showing they cannot get to her.

This will kill her.

I snap out of it and move to intervene, but Saylor grabs me before I can. He pulls me against his chest, pointing at her.

"You see this, Beck? This is her lesson. And she's teaching it to herself." He chuckles. "Marvelous, isn't it? What people will do within the invisible reins of authority?"

"You're killing her," I seethe.

She pauses to cough, spitting out mouthfuls of the liquid before bringing the jug to her lips again.

"No. She's doing that to herself."

Fantaine steps forward. "Holden, this is a bad idea—"

"I haven't said *when*," he snaps.

Cota nudges him. "Come on, man. *We'll* get Corrected for this. She's one of the stronger ones. Does good work. Higher-ups won't like it. I don't want them pissed at *me* for your mistake."

"Stokes knows our agreement."

"*The Captain* won't like it," Fantaine hisses. "Let's just go."

"Saylor, come on!" I shout.

Raven drops the jug and falls to her knees. A lake of gasoline spills around her, pungent and golden. She throws up into it, her vomit the same color. She retches again and again until she can hardly hold her head up.

That's when she collapses.

Saylor chuckles. "When."

Thursday, August 4

The Guards drive away, closing the dock door behind them.

We hurry to Raven's side, kneeling in fuel. I set the jug upright before more of it can spill. The smell makes Lockley cough, but he doesn't seem to care.

"Raven." He pats her face. "Raven, wake up."

She groans in discomfort, half-conscious and already drenched with sweat. Her skin is pale and clammy.

"How much did you drink?" I ask. She can't answer.

Lockley shakes her gently. "Hey. Stay awake, will you?"

I study the gasoline pooling around us, then glance inside the jug. Even after what she drank and what spilled, it's fuller than I expected.

"I think she was pretending to drink it," I realize aloud.

"Bull *shit*, man! Look at her!"

"No, look at this." I try to show him the jug, but he swats it away.

"Does it matter? She obviously ingested *some*!"

"I'm just trying to figure out how to help her, alright? Be thankful she didn't drink more." I rise to my feet. "She'll be okay if we act quick."

Genius, I think to myself. Stupid, but genius. I'm guessing she kept a small amount in her mouth while pretending to chug the rest. Even that would be enough to make her this sick—and she still swallowed some.

Lockley is too frail to carry her, so I'm the one who scoops her up and rushes her to the cabin. It's dinner now. No one sees us. Lockley sprints out the door to fetch Doc.

"You're gonna be okay, alright?" I tell her, though I'm not sure she can hear. I lay her down on the bed. "Doc will be here soon."

I unzip her jumpsuit. The ragged shirt and sweats beneath it seem unaffected by the gasoline spill. I toss the stained clothes in the farthest corner of the room where the fumes won't reach. I take off her shoes too. Mine are just as drenched as hers are. I'll need new ones once this is all over.

I sit on the bed and hold her upper torso in my arms. I don't want her to choke if she starts vomiting again. She's not awake, but her face seems clenched. Tense. She doesn't cry. *Even unconscious, she's still trying to hide her pain.*

It's in this moment that I realize I wish I knew more about this sort of thing—that I paid closer attention to everything my father taught me over the years. Then I would know what to do.

I hate sitting and waiting. I hate being useless. Pathetic.

How should I position her? Does she need to be propped up in a certain way? Should I give her water?

"Dad..." I lean my head back and stare at the slats above me. "What do I do?"

For now, all I can manage is sitting here, holding this strange girl I know nothing about, wishing I could do something to stop the pain. The minutes drip by like molasses, slow and dense. She's awfully still.

I realize I've never been this close to a girl my age before. And I don't mean a girl like my sister, or Lily, who felt like the cousin she pretended to be. But her...

Now that she's not glaring at me or making me commit crimes against society, I tilt my head and study Raven's face. Curiously, like how I observed plants back home. I note the fullness of her eyelashes. The silkiness of her hair.

She's beautiful, I think. I've never thought that about a person before.

Aside from the Yesterday actresses I've seen on TV, or that girl on the Ferris wheel. But I've never... *held* a girl like this.

I can't remember the last time I was this close to someone.

My face warms. *Get it together, Aaron.*

I don't know why I suddenly feel the need to stand, but I do. I take an extra pillow from one of the other beds and lay her back down, making sure her head is propped up. I'm kneeling by her side when Doc and Lockley burst through the door, breathless.

"What happened?" Doc joins me, already pulling a stethoscope from his case.

"She drank gasoline."

"Why the hell would she do that?"

"Saylor made her do it," Lockley says, pacing back and forth. "I swear to God, the next time I see that prick I'm—"

"You will do nothing," Doc commands. "Retaliation will only make it worse." He presses the chest piece over her heart. "How much did she drink?"

"I'm not sure. Not more than a few mouthfuls. She threw up a bunch after. I think it was more of a gag reflex thing."

We pause, waiting for a heartbeat. Then he listens to her lungs. Doc sighs in relief and puts the stethoscope away.

"She's still breathing. Her heartbeat isn't slowing yet, which is a good sign. She is wheezing quite a bit, so we'll want to keep an eye on that. I don't think the gasoline entered her lungs directly, but the fumes may be irritating her airways. They seem to be constricting slightly, which is expected, given our collective predisposition to respiratory issues around here."

"Is that a bad thing?"

"Only if her wheezing worsens." He exhales heavily through his nose. "That could indicate contamination in the lungs."

"Would an inhaler help?"

"It would relax the muscles around her airways, so perhaps. Shallow breathing may deplete her blood oxygen levels, which won't benefit her recovery."

"So… open airways, good."

"Yes. But the only inhaler I had on hand at the infirmary disappeared." My eyes widen. *Marty.*

"What about vomiting?" I ask. "Should we make her throw up what she swallowed?"

"Inducing vomiting can worsen lung exposure or spread the toxins further throughout her body," Doc says. "Forcing it may do more harm than good. From what you've told me, she's already thrown up most of it."

"What about water?"

"Same goes for fluids. We shouldn't force her to drink." He sighs heavily. "I'm afraid there's not much else I can do at the moment."

A wave of frustrated heat spreads across my neck. "What do you mean, there's nothing you can do?"

"We have to wait for her body to flush it out of her system. We'll monitor her vitals and breathing to make sure her lungs are okay, but too much interference could irritate her further. What she needs is rest, and hydration when she's ready to drink on her own. I'll prepare her some teas tomorrow."

Lockley glares. "*Tomorrow?*"

"I thought Corps healers could fix anything," I say.

"Out there? Maybe. In here, I don't have a fraction of the tools and medicines I'd have access to otherwise." Doc shakes his head. "It's all up to Raven now, I'm afraid. Lady Luck, too."

"No." I rise to my feet. "I'll be back."

I run out of the cabin and through camp. Everyone's still at dinner. The sun is already setting. I barge into our quarters, breathless by the time I reach mine and Marty's bunk bed. I climb up to his and rummage through his bedding, frantically. "Come on… where is it?"

Lady Luck must have a sense of humor, because Marty walks in.

"Shift's over, Cedar—" He pauses when he sees me on his bed. "What are you doing?"

"Where's your inhaler?"

"What?"

"Your *inhaler*," I snap, a little harsher than I meant it. I soften my voice. "Where is it?"

"Why? Are you feeling okay?"

I climb down from the bunk, hoping to get a better angle from the outside as I continue my search. "It's not for me."

Marty's eyes peel wider. "Lockley."

I freeze, turning around slowly. *He knows his name?*

"It's for him, isn't it?"

I don't say anything.

Marty's voice quickens. "Did something happen during Correction? I know he has trouble breathing sometimes." He hurries to my side and reaches under the mattress to retrieve the red tube, handing it to me. "Here."

I don't have time to question this further. I start walking toward the door. "Thanks."

"Is he okay?" he calls after me.

"He will be."

"Cedar?"

I stop walking. "What?"

"Tell him..." Marty pauses. "Nevermind. Just hurry. Before the others get back."

I'm about to take my leave, but I look over my shoulder first. "Marty?"

"Yeah?"

"Don't tell anyone about this."

Marty gives me a salute. "Consider it a thank you for keeping my secret."

I nod, and I leave.

I run back to Raven and Lockley's cabin unnoticed. Doc shows me how to administer the medicine through the inhaler. She's still out of it, but just enough there to breathe in when we tell her to. Then we let her sleep. Lockley has a coughing fit, and Doc makes him take a puff too.

"I should get going," Lockley says after a while, standing. "Gotta finish mine and Raven's work for the day." He hands the inhaler to me. "Give this back to him, will you?"

"Who?"

"Marty."

My brows crease. *He knows his name?*

Lockley shakes his head. "And tell him to stop bothering me. He needs it more than I do. My lungs are too far gone to be worth saving."

Before I can tell him that's a stupid thing to say, he opens the door and exits.

I shove the inhaler in my pocket and turn back to Raven.

"I'll stay with her," Doc says. "You must go to dinner, unless you want the other Guards to be suspicious."

"I can't just leave her."

"She'll be alright."

"You're not supposed to be healing prisoners, anyway. What if someone finds out?"

"And you're not supposed to be making friends with traitors, Cedar."

I clench my jaw and fists, averting my gaze.

"I'll look after her until the others return," he says. "You've done enough. You need to be with the other Guards. They'll find it strange if you keep going missing so frequently."

I sigh. I know he's right, but I can't help feeling guilty. I could have done more to stop this from happening.

I look at Raven, then nod. I reach into my pocket and extend my hand to Doc. "Give this to her when she wakes up."

He holds out his hand. I drop the object into his palm. His brows furrow. "Is this…"

"A deer tooth. For good luck."

Doc smiles. "I will."

While the other Guards in our quarters are washing up after dinner, I return Marty's inhaler. He thanks me and puts it back in its hiding spot.

"Can I ask you something?" I say.

He climbs down from the bunk with a grin. "Sure."

"Why did you steal that from the infirmary?"

He pauses, biting his lip. "I'm keeping your secret."

"You have. And I'm grateful for it."

"Will you keep another one of mine?"

I nod. "Alright."

Marty sighs, taking a seat on the bottom bunk. "I stole it for him."

"Who?"

"Lockley."

My brows crease. I take a seat next to him.

"I just... I heard some of the other Guards and prisoners talking. He was born here. That means this world—inside the perimeter of our fence—is all he's ever known."

That's why his coughing must be so bad, I realize.

"Sometimes he coughs up blood." Marty stares at his hands. "I went to the infirmary one time. For an asthma attack, actually. Never had one of those before I got here. These rooms have built-in air purifiers, but the smoke still affects us Guards too, you know."

I nod.

"The healer gave me a puff of his, and the medicine felt *great*. It opened up my lungs and I could breathe so much better. But..." He sighs. "I just felt so guilty for breathing in easily while *he* wasn't."

"So you took it."

Marty nods.

"And why didn't Doc..." I clear my throat and correct myself. "Why didn't the healer try to get it back? Surely he knew you were the one who stole it."

"I think he wanted me to get away with it. I know that sounds ridiculous, but he's a nice man. He really is."

I give him a small smile.

"Anyway, I tried offering it to Lockley. Several times, actually. And he never let me help. I think it offended him. He thought I pitied him or something. But it's just the opposite, really.

"I see him laughing with that girl sometimes. *Laughing*, in a place like this. None of the Guards ever laugh, not truly. But *they* do. That's why I..." He pauses, unsure of how to form the words. "That's why I stole the inhaler."

It's quiet for a moment. I glance at him. "He's a prisoner."

"I know."

"So why do you care?"

Marty glances at me, then at his hands. He shrugs. Something tells me there are words he's too afraid to say.

For a moment, I wonder if he's just as not-supposed-to-be-here as I am.

Not in an Unseen way. He just seems too... *kind* for a place like this. I still don't know him very well, but he might be the only Guard in this entire facility that I'd hesitate to stick with a Nightjade syringe. Because he seems like the only one who'd hesitate to do the same to someone else.

Maybe that's why he was sent here.

"Your secret's safe with me," I finally say.

"Thank you."

"I still don't know why he refuses the inhaler when he *needs* it." Marty traces the back of his hand with his thumb. "Maybe he just hates us. For being what we are. I can't really blame him for that."

"I don't think he hates you."

Marty lifts his head to meet my gaze, almost hopeful. "What makes you say that?"

"Because he told me to thank you."

He blinks in confusion as my words settle in. "Oh. Tell him..." He strokes his chin to think about it, then lets his hands fall to his lap in defeat. "I don't know. I'm not good at this sort of thing."

"Me neither."

"Oh, come on." Marty chuckles, nudging me playfully. "With those killer looks? You could charm your way through anything."

"Stop that." I swat him away, but I'm laughing with him. It dies down, then I turn to him. "Hey."

"What?"

"We're laughing."

Marty grins from ear to ear. "We are, aren't we?"

This is rebellion, I think to myself. Another flicker of light in the dark. Another swig of gasoline.

Tuesday, August 9

"Slippery elm," Doc says, dropping a tea bag into Raven's mug of steaming water.

I observe from a chair at her bedside. Thick wafts of heat and warm light drift in from the windows, signaling midday.

"Contains *mucilage*," Doc continues. "It's a gluey substance. A demulcent filled with powerful antioxidants that can reduce inflammation. It forms a soothing and protective film over the gastrointestinal tract. Mouth, throat, stomach, intestines. Your throat is still bothering you, yes?"

Raven nods. She doesn't speak much lately. And when she does, her voice is thin and raspy. She's been coughing a lot too.

I've been spending my lunch breaks here instead of eating with the others. I pop in to make an appearance, grab a quick bite, find a talking point, and then leave. So far, no one but Marty seems to notice.

I take mental notes in my head as Doc informs me of all the teas he's been preparing for Raven over the past few days. I know my dad's rambled to me about slippery elm before. It doesn't grow well in Washington; he has to organize trades with healers from other Regions to get it. But this is the first time I've actually *wanted* to pay attention to a lecture about it.

I don't know why it took me so long to realize that healing is pretty damn cool.

"Ginger." Doc plops in another bag. "Aids with nausea and vomiting. Reduces pain. *Also* contains powerful antioxidants that reduce inflammation and support the immune system."

"Remember those ginger candies with the little ginger man on them? That your parents would give you so you wouldn't get carsick?" Raven croaks. "That guy freaked me out. I had nightmares about him."

"No," I say. "We didn't have cars. Or candy."

She frowns. "You're no fun."

I glare. "It's not *my* fault I grew up the way I did, alright?"

She leans back against her pillows, arms under her head, staring at the slats above her. "You mean sheltered."

My jaw tightens. She's like this a lot. Disagreeable.

"Peppermint," Doc interrupts loudly, putting the last bag in the mug. "The menthol will soothe a sore throat."

I nod. "Easy."

"And honey." He opens a small packet and drizzles the golden substance into the tea. "Soothing, antimicrobial, and also provides a protective coating for the throat."

Doc hands the cup to Raven. She sniffs it and makes a face. "Smells weird."

"Be glad you can still smell anything at all, after what you did."

She rolls her eyes and drinks.

A beeping sound emits from Doc's wrist. He checks his watch. "Well, that's all the time I can spare. I'm heading back to the infirmary. You know where to find me in the event of an emergency." He stands and collects his things. "You'll watch her until Jelly returns?"

I give him a salute. He winks and takes his leave.

Raven and I sit in silence for a while. The others have been working out rotations to cover her shift and have someone check in on her every now and then—when the Guards don't notice, that is. As long as headcount remains the same and someone shouts *here* during roll call, they usually don't.

Her breathing has improved since the incident, but she isn't ready to return. Her throat and stomach are still inflamed.

I hear a fly buzz. I focus on that instead of Raven. She and I aren't exactly friends; we don't talk much.

I crinkle my nose. The insect makes me think of the dead vulture I passed on my way here—the one that got electrocuted. It's already decomposing and swarming with flies, its belly full of maggots. No coyotes or other scavengers live inside the fence. It'll be left to bugs alone. It'll take a while for the bones to show.

Surprisingly, the other turkey vultures avoid the corpse like the plague. There's food right there and they continue circling in search of something else, anything but their own kin.

I let out a one-note chuckle. They're better to their kind than we are.

"What's so funny?" Raven asks, annoyed.

"Decomposition."

"Lovely." She sips her tea, not questioning it further. "You don't have to stay."

"I know."

"Then why are you here?"

"Because Doc asked me to keep an eye on you."

"If he asked you to lick the fence, would you?"

"Probably not."

"Because you wouldn't want to lick an electric fence."

"Depends on how good it'd taste."

A pause. "So you want to be here." She gestures around the room. "In this dump, with no air conditioning." She sits upright a bit and brings her knees closer, taking another sip. Her eyes pin to mine. "With me."

I shrug, leaning back in my chair. "I guess so."

It's quiet again.

"Here." Her voice startles me. She reaches into her pocket and pulls out the tooth. "Looks like your good luck worked after all."

"Keep it."

I give her a once-over. She seems okay. I glance at the window. I should be heading back. *She doesn't need me here.*

I rise to my feet and turn to the door.

"Wait."

I stop, arching a brow.

She gives me a small smirk. "I wanna show you something."

I help her out of bed. She leads me to the center of the room and pulls aside a worn brown rug. I watch her remove a few loose floorboards until there's an opening barely big enough for one person to squeeze through. She lowers into it and descends a ladder.

I peer down from above. It leads to a crawlspace beneath the cabin, under the porch.

I go down too, kicking up dust when I land on a dirt floor. I cough through the cloud and follow Raven to the better-lit half of the area, where thin rays of light stream through the cracks in the porch above us. They illuminate the dust until it dissipates.

My mouth falls open when I realize what I'm looking at.

The entire room is filled with containers. Tin cans. *Bigger* tins for bulk food storage. Rusty water canteens, like the standard ones they issue Guards.

Jerrycans of gasoline.

"Holy shit." My eyes widen. I spin around, taking it all in. "This is…"

"Impressive?" She holds her hands behind her back and takes a playful step toward me. "Exhilarating?"

"I was going to say a fire hazard, but yeah, that too."

She walks back to the stockpile, tracing one of the cans in admiration.

"How long have you been doing this?"

"Since I got here."

"Which was… how long ago, exactly?"

She glances at me, then back at the gasoline. "Two years."

My heart sinks. I've barely been here a week and I'm already approaching my breaking point. "Two years?"

"Two years is nothing. Lock's been here all his life." She starts pacing around the room, fingers gliding across dirt walls. "His mom was a prisoner.

Died during childbirth. His dad didn't last long after that, so Doc took him in. He's the closest thing Lock's had to a father. And Jelly to a mother."

A heavy knot forms in my chest. The atmosphere shifts. I can't shake the feeling that similar tragedies have occurred before.

Of course they have. No one deserves to withstand the conditions here. Even the Guards go home changed, never fully able to cough up the smoke. The stench of burning flesh. They live short, mediocre lives in the Corps until their lungs or hearts fail. Sometimes their livers. A fuse gone out prematurely. It's either sickness or grief that gets you in the end, they say. Mostly the bottle. And the prisoners have it worse than we do.

Evangeline. Her name strikes like lightning.

"Jelly…" I begin, unsure of how to form the words.

Raven nods. She stares at the gasoline distantly, something like desperation glossed over her gaze. "We need to get out of here before that baby is born."

"How long do we have?"

"Five months."

"That can't be enough time to come up with a plan."

"It'll have to be." She turns and picks up a small tin can, sloshing it around. Like she's trying to look at anything but me. "Gasoline can go bad, you know. It'll lose its combustibility in six months or so. Can't keep it in plastic either. It'll break down over time."

"The jugs we used were plastic."

"I use those for transport. It's easier to carry around one inconspicuous container of *cleaning solution* than a bunch of tin cans. The Guards expect us to be cleaning up after them, anyway." She walks over to the larger tins —the kind we used for storing beans and flour back at the Cut. "I use the cleaning jugs to carry the gas back here, then I store it in these. Stolen from the kitchen."

"If you've been doing this for two years, shouldn't some of the gas be bad by now?"

Raven shakes her head. "The containers have taken the longest time to collect. The fuel is a more recent project of mine."

"You still haven't told me what all this is for." I walk closer, hands in my pockets. "Something tells me you've already had a plan this entire time."

She views me carefully, maybe deciding whether to trust me. Like she's scouring my eyes for some kind of flaw, some crack she hadn't noticed before. Her gaze lingers over the bruises on my face. The scar cutting down my cheek. She's more somber than I've ever heard her when she finally speaks.

"We're burning this place to the ground."

It takes a moment for the words to sink in. "What?"

She doesn't say anything.

I laugh in disbelief. "You can't be serious."

"I'm dead serious."

"That's... impossible." My smile fades. "You told me about the water tower yourself. They could put out a fire easily."

"With enough accelerant we could be strategic about it. Make it *not* easy for them."

"And what about the fence? You'd just trap everyone else inside."

She shrugs.

"You've gotta be kidding." The amused denial seeps out of my voice, leaving it more bitter than I intend. "There are other people here, you know. Prisoners who can't defend themselves. Guards."

"Guards?" she scoffs. "They can burn for all I care."

"I just don't think we should view them the same way they view us. That's stooping to their level. Gives the other side more fuel to use against us."

And they're still people, a small voice inside me adds. Barely, but people nonetheless. If I didn't remember that, wouldn't I be just like them?

Does that make me human or ignorant?

"In case you've forgotten, Saylor tried to kill you, Beck. He and his friends *buried you alive*. Did any of the other Guards notice you were gone? And before that, did anyone care that you were sick with food poisoning? Or sobbing outside your cabin?"

The last part makes me flinch. I forgot she saw that.

"They shipped you out here with no training or support, just to get rid of you." Her voice is louder now. Sharper. "To either make your disposal as productive as possible, or to make you snap. So you'll harden your shell and turn into another one of their monsters. Another obedient military dog ready to do their bidding and catch every bone they throw at you, drool and tongue out and all."

I glare. "I'm not like them."

"Then remember that next time you pretend to give a damn about them."

A muscle in my neck twitches. I walk away and lean against the wall, arms crossed. We don't say anything for a while.

"You can't start a fire," I finally say. "It's stupid. It'll hurt people."

I try not to think of Max. The weight of the irrational mistake I made in the name of what I thought was right. But I can't help it. My knuckles tighten.

We don't have rebels like this at the Cut—people who channel their anger into violence instead of organized strategies. People who let their broken hearts break their rationality too.

I've never had a conversation like this before.

I'm not the son my father wants me to be, but we've always agreed on one thing—hatred is a dangerous path to tread. The kind that chews you up and swallows you down into a dark place you'll never see the end of. A road that only gets easier to follow until it's too late to turn back.

Rage like this will consume her.

"I was kidding about the fire, by the way. You're right. It would be stupid." She leans against the wall across from me, unable to look me in the eye. "But if you think I was kidding about the Guards, you're severely mistaken."

I sigh heavily through my nose. It's hard to be mad at her for what she said, given everything she's gone through. I'm not fond of the Guards either. Definitely not Chasers. *But I don't want to be like them.*

"Then what's all of this for?" I ask, softening my voice. "Stealing one of the trucks?"

"Those lock up, remember?"

"You couldn't just... drive one through the fence and go the rest of the way by foot?"

"Not without disabling it first. Unless you want to get electrocuted."

I think about it for a moment. "The delivery truck."

She nods, waiting to see how I'll react.

I can't help but grin. "Now we're talking."

She smirks—just as Lockley climbs down the ladder.

Raven seems startled until she realizes it's him and frowns. "What are you doing down here?"

"Heard you guys talking." He leans against the ladder with his arms folded. "So you showed him the stash?"

"I'm assuming you knew about this too," I say.

"I filled him in on the plan," Raven intervenes. "Told him about the delivery truck."

Lockley's brows crease in confusion for a moment, then sharpen into a glare. "You *told him*?"

"The others already know. It's about time he does too."

"Are you crazy?"

"Lockley," she warns. "He's helping us, remember?"

"He's still a Guard!"

"And he's still on our side."

Lockley clenches his jaw.

"So... *who* knows what, exactly?" I ask. "Just so I know when to shut my mouth."

"Lockley and I, Fern, and Jelly. Now you."

"Fern?"

"Jelly's younger sister," Lockley clarifies.

"Sister?" My shoulders slump. "How did that happen?"

Raven sighs. "Their whole camp was infiltrated earlier this year. Their parents... didn't make it."

"Harebell Hill," I mutter. *The Unseen encampment that the Corps massacred.*

She nods.

"Wouldn't that make them..." I glance up the ladder, just to make sure we're really alone. "Traitors? Unseen?"

"The Agent in charge of the operation managed to convince the Head of House to ship them here instead of exterminating them. Those who could dig were spared an injection, if they verbally denounced the Unseen.

Those who couldn't, or tried to fight back..." Raven fidgets with her hands. "We don't know much about the whole story."

"It's still a death sentence," Lockley mutters. "Just a slower one."

"They're so young," I say, throat tight. "You all are."

"Jelly's twenty-four." Raven gazes at the floor. "Fern's only thirteen."

My stomach churns. If I'd eaten a decent lunch, I'm sure I'd be retching it up.

Guilt snakes around my throat when I sigh with relief. Even if I'm here—even if I never make it out—at least the Cut is safe.

And if I want to keep it that way, I'll have to be careful about who I trust.

If I'm caught trying to escape, and my higher-ups believe I have a connection to the Unseen, they'll interrogate me for information, just like Dad said they would. There's no telling what they'll do or what I'd give up.

I won't let them be another Harebell Hill.

I stare at the sky through the thin cracks in the porch above us. I never thought I'd miss home like this before.

Now, there's nowhere else I'd rather be.

Thursday, August 11

♪ FURNACES - ED HARCOURT ♪

I t was different with Tern.

I knew him while he was alive, at least for a bit. Ansel and I took care of him in the dark. He just felt... asleep. He didn't feel like a *corpse*. Not until the weight of what we'd done finally settled later that night. And with Max's death, I only saw a glimpse of him from a distance. He was unrecognizable.

For the most part, I'd gone my whole life without seeing a dead body.

Until I entered the furnace.

I was originally given a shift at the Archives. Saylor made our Supervisor Stokes swap things around again, so he could get the comfortable job. Now I stand here, staring at my shoes when I'm supposed to be overseeing prisoners. The Guard I'm partnered with does the same, and his coat is as gray as charcoal. *I don't think anyone could get used to this.*

Cement floors. Brick ovens. Prisoners in dark orange clothes, transporting bodies in carts from the morgue—where the corpses are stored and processed before their final cremation. They are delivered in refrigerated trucks.

The prisoners manage everything. All I have to do is watch.

I think about the lives these people must have held. Most of them were ordinary people who did everyday things. People whose family either couldn't afford a tombstone in an overcrowded graveyard, or simply didn't care.

Sweat coats every inch of my skin. I can't look at anything. Not the prisoners. Not the fires. Only my shoes. I grip my Nightjade gun like I'm supposed to and focus on every breath, forcing them to be slow. Forcing myself not to think about what I'm breathing in through the face covering they issued me. Forcing myself to breathe at all.

I did end up getting new shoes after the gasoline incident. They aren't *new*, though. I wonder who they belonged to. *A Guard or a prisoner?*

And I wonder if—just maybe—there was something to be learned in the Serpent's lessons after all.

Because if I hadn't already seen what he showed me, I would have given up here.

I'm not sure if I should feel relieved or ashamed.

In this moment, drenched in sweat, choking on the surrounding air, I decide I hate Walter Schneider. I hate his brother, Francis. I hate Ansel. I hate their wine and rainfall showerheads and fancy meats.

Because while they're perched on their Immune thrones at Whitestag, dining on dry goose and mediocre crème brûlée, we are here.

These prisoners are the ones cleaning up the Presidency's mess, so everyone else can benefit from the resources preserved by slow, painful deaths. Shovels. Bleeding palms. Girls with gasoline stuck in their throats. Boys who can't take a full breath without coughing up blood, simply because they were born in the wrong place.

The Immune already spend money to bend the rules in their favor. They just refuse to use it to help anyone. *The well-fed keep the world hungry.*

I think about what could be accomplished if every citizen who can afford Immunity sacrificed a *fraction* of what they had for someone else. Maybe then, our world wouldn't need Immunity at all. Maybe then, the Nightjade order wouldn't exist. And I wouldn't be here, wondering when we stopped caring about each other.

"I'm a vegetarian," I mutter, testing the words. I've never said them before.

The other Guard's brows pinch. "Huh?"

"I'm a vegetarian," I repeat. Louder this time. Certain.

"Good for you, kid." He shakes his head and stares at his shoes again.

Sometime near the end of my shift, a girl with a long braid of fiery red hair collapses.

She can't be any older than thirteen. She falls to her knees in the center of the room, palms planted on the ground, throwing up what little she had to eat today. Two of the other prisoners move to help her, but she swats them away.

"I'm fine," she croaks—just before vomiting again.

The other Guard doesn't seem to care.

I run to her side, dropping down in front of her. "You alright?"

"I said I'm *fine*," she snaps. She wipes her mouth with the back of her hand, eyes widening when she realizes I'm no prisoner. Her posture straightens. "Sorry, I didn't—"

"It's alright." I extend the back of my knuckles to her forehead, pausing. "May I?"

Slowly, she nods. I feel her skin. Clammy. It's pale and much cooler than it should be in a room like this. *Heat exhaustion.*

"What's your name?" I rise to my feet, helping her do the same. "I'll talk to my Supervisor. You shouldn't be working."

"They won't care," she says.

"I'll make them care," I say a little too loudly. A few prisoners shoot confused looks in my direction.

Keep your cover, I remind myself. *Guards don't care about prisoners.*

I lower my voice. "Look. My higher-ups prioritize productivity over anything else. The most efficient option would be to let you rest so you can get back to work."

Her jaw tightens. "Will you let me get back to work, then?"

"Name?"

"Fern Goodwin."

My eyes widen. *So this is Jelly's younger sister.*

I walk over to the entrance, studying the tablet embedded in the wall that displays the prisoners' shift information. I squint to read the chart. Her name isn't on the list—but her sister's is. *She's covering for Jelly.* I swipe to check where she's really supposed to be, then walk back to her.

"You're in the wrong place," I say. "You're on Dig."

"Oh. I-I must have misheard—"

I lower my voice so no one else hears. "I know you're covering for someone."

"I-I'm sorry. As soon as I finish up here I'm going straight over to the Graves. I'll dig through dinner and everything. Ten graves, just like we're supposed to. Three feet deep."

"That'll take you what, eight hours? More in your condition." I sigh. "You need rest."

"Please." Her eyes water. "Just let me stay."

"I can't do that."

She nods, pressing her lips together. My stomach drops when I realize a tear is streaming down her cheek. *Shit. I made her cry.*

"You're taking me to Correction, aren't you?" she asks quietly.

My heart sinks. *They punish the kids too?*

I nod. She closes her eyes.

"I'll be back," I shout over my shoulder—but the other Guard is napping upright against the wall. I roll my eyes.

Once we exit the building, I glance around to check that we're really alone, then turn to her. "I'm not taking you to Correction."

Fern exhales in relief. "Good, because I've never been before, and I don't know what goes on in there, and I *really* don't want to find out—"

"Hey, hey." I bend over so I'm at her height, softening my voice. "It's okay. You don't have to worry about that, alright?"

Her forehead wrinkles in confusion. "Why are you—"

"I'm taking you to see Doc." I gesture her forward, surveying our surroundings one more time. "Hurry. Before someone sees."

Her jaw drops as we walk forward. "It's you."

I raise a brow.

"You're the Guard Raven told me about, aren't you? The one with the scar."

I hold back a smirk. "So she talks about me?"

Fern stops to cough, bending over with both hands on her knees. She clutches her stomach like she might vomit again.

"Here." I kneel. "Piggy back?"

Now that she knows who I am, she doesn't hesitate to climb on. I carry her so we can get back to the cabin quickly. I set her on a bed. Raven is fast asleep in hers. Jelly, who'd been napping in her own bunk, wakes with a start, rushing over to Fern's bedside.

"What's wrong?" Jelly presses a hand to her sister's face, feeling her temperature. "Are you hurt?"

"Heat exhaustion. She's overworked."

"I'm fine," Fern snaps, then glares in my direction. "*He* insisted on bringing me here, so I had to leave my shift."

"Your shift?" Jelly whips her head around to check the alarm bell on the wall, where a small digital clock displays the time. "You didn't wake me?"

"Jel, just calm down." Fern pulls her sister back. "I covered for you."

Her shoulders slump. "You didn't have to do that."

"It's not like you can do it! You were on Furnace today. You can't go in there."

"You should have woken me."

"You need your rest, Jel," Fern insists. "And so do they."

She points to Jelly's stomach.

"If you covered for me, then who will take care of your shift?" Jelly asks.

"I will. As soon as *he* stops taking me hostage."

"*You're* not going anywhere for the rest of the day," I say, rolling my eyes. "I'm getting Doc."

Doc rubs his forehead with a sigh. "You picked up one of her shifts again."

Fern glares. "I can handle it."

"We discussed this."

"What else am I supposed to do? Jelly can't do it!"

Her sister averts her gaze.

"I want you to ask for help when you need it," Doc says. Fern fidgets with her thumbs. He sighs. "You're not in trouble, okay? I understand you're only thinking of what's best for your sister."

"It's not like Lock can do it either," Fern argues. "And you know what happened to Raven last time she was caught covering for Jelly."

Correction, I answer in silence. I think about Raven's bruises—her flinching. Between stealing supplies and covering for Jelly, it's no wonder the Guards have a problem with her.

My hands flex. Why is she getting punished for trying to survive in the situation *they* put her in? The thought alone makes me want to punch the wall. Or a Guard's face. Anything.

"I'll do it," I say. "I'll help cover the shifts."

They blink at me in silence.

"Most Guards are too jaded to give a damn what I do. I'll be sly about it. The one back there fell asleep, anyway."

Doc suppresses a grin. "That's kind of you, Cedar."

"Thank you." Jelly wraps me into a tight hug, taking me by surprise. My face warms.

Doc and I step outside to let the others rest. We stand on the porch for a while, watching the sun go down. He checks his watch. "Your shift's over now. It's dinner."

Down the road, I study the stream of Guards filing into the cafeteria. "I should head over to the Graves."

The Guards won't think anything of it. Not every prisoner finishes before the dinner bell; some of them work well into the evening to meet their quota before Supervisors count the finished graves the next morning.

I've come to realize this is a place for bending the rules. As long as the work is done and prisoners obey, the Supervisors are happy. The Captain is happy. The Corps is happy.

"I might head over myself," Doc says.

I raise a brow. "You? Picking up a shovel?"

He frowns. "I could say the same about you, with all those bruises."

I sigh. He has a point. I extend a hand. "Five and five?"

He shakes it with a smirk. "We'll make a good ten, you and I."

"We'll see about that."

Digging graves is nothing like turning garden compost.

The Graves are empty tonight; no stragglers. There's a small shed out near the dig site, far from the busier parts of the facility. This is where they keep the shovels. They're rusty things, with unfinished and splintery wood handles. They remind me of what Officer Gilbert said at training. *Sharpen or rust.*

It takes two hours for my palms to crack open.

Doc and I talk to distract ourselves from the aching in our backs. The tremors in our arms. The burning in our hands.

He asks me more about my dad. How I learned healing. How *he* learned healing. I tell him that when they were younger, Dad and Asa started collecting old Yesterday books in secret. It was their first real taste of rebellion —and once they started, they couldn't stop.

That's how Dad discovered his love for herbalism. He consumed everything he could, until that wasn't enough. He had to perform his own studies, write his own books. Eventually he started creating his encyclopedias, so he could distribute them to people who needed access to herbal medicine, and educate them about the value of naturopathic healing.

When that wasn't enough, he started smuggling bottled medication for those who needed a different kind of intervention. He partnered with the Syndicate to do it—until a job went south, and he had no choice but to abandon his old life for one at the Cut.

I almost laugh at the familiarity of it.

He got in over his head and screwed up, just like I did. Maybe that's why he never wanted me to do this in the first place.

Like father, like son.

"The Syndicate..." Doc shakes his head. "Messy business."

"Tell me about it," I mutter, cutting my shovel into the ground. "They stopped smuggling with them after that. Got too risky, I guess."

Doc scoops a shovelful of sand over his shoulder. "Smart move."

We dig in silence for a bit. It's dark now. The moon is our only source of illumination, until something flashes in the corner of my eye.

I squint at the horizon. Silver webs crack the night like glowing fault lines before flickering out. Another fracture appears and fades just as quickly. Something rumbles—a sighing thunder.

My brows furrow. "Is that... lightning?"

"Yep." Doc doesn't look up from his shoveling.

"But there's no rain."

"There is, actually." He digs again. "You just can't see it."

"That makes no sense."

"The storms out here form at high altitudes and in low humidity levels. Most of the precipitation evaporates before it hits the ground."

"Dry lightning..." I study it for a moment, watching it bloom and fade, bruising the sky with deep violets and stale golds. "It's raining and we can't even feel it."

"Don't act so surprised. Most of the world behaves that way."

"How so?"

"You can't feel the Earth turning. You can't feel the pain of another; you can't hold it in your hands. But it exists, doesn't it?" He digs. "Hunger. Laughter. Love. The product of rebellion, grown from the seeds we plant today." Another dig. "A father's love we don't yet understand."

I avert my gaze and jam my shovel into the sand.

"I've never met this Simon you speak of. But from what you've told me, he sounds a great deal like my own father."

I scoff. "Sure."

"He was hard on me too—always wanting me to help him with work. He was an arborist, you know. When I was your age, I spent most of my time up in canopies. Cabling and bracing trees. Pruning them. Monitoring their health."

"A tree doctor?"

He chuckles. "I suppose you could call it that."

I grin. "Apples don't fall far, after all."

"I loved trees and learning new things. But I never applied myself in that field, because it was always *his* idea, not mine." He digs. "Only after he was gone, and I began healing for the Corps, did I truly learn to appreciate what he taught me."

"I *do* appreciate it," I argue. "I just... don't remember much of it now."

I grip the shovel tighter, thinking of Raven unconscious in my arms. Fern's exhaustion. Lockley's coughing. Jelly. *I wish I did.*

"Once you start joining me on my rounds, you'll remember. And what you don't, I'll teach you. How to not die—should be simple enough. By the end, maybe you'll know enough to write your *own* book."

"I can see it clearly." I spread my palms out in the air. "*How to Not Die.* Bestseller."

Doc chuckles. "A superlative idea indeed."

I fight a weak smile.

It's quiet again, nothing but the soft hiss of metal against sand until I speak. "Why are you doing this?"

"Hm?"

"Helping me." I dig. "Teaching me."

He pauses to lean against his shovel. "Apples, Cedar."

"I don't get it."

"I believe in goodness, son, and I believe in spreading it. I believe in planting seeds for a future we cannot feel yet. I believe in the children of today and the change they will bring tomorrow." He smiles at me. "I believe in you."

I'm not sure why a lump forms in my throat, or why I suddenly feel warm despite the rapidly cooling desert night. I fixate on the grave I'm digging. "Not sure that's the smartest move."

"Most young men in your situation would be worried about themselves —not helping the prisoners they're supposed to be suppressing. After being exposed to the reality of this place, in *your* shoes, even some Unseen would rather convert their loyalty and work their way toward a promotion than pick up a shovel." Doc tosses a scoop of sand to the side. "With your help, Raven and the others may have a real chance of leaving this place behind.

Do you understand how valuable that is?"

I don't feel very useful.

"I don't think this tree grows apples, Doc." I chuckle half-heartedly. "I'm more of a magnolia myself."

"Oh?"

The greenhouse had a few magnolias back home. They're nice trees, but their leaves fall frequently, and they're real thick and painful to step on. And what's with those damn seed pods? Beau used to throw those at my head. They felt like rocks.

"Messy," I reply. "Hard to manage."

When I drop my next scoop onto the mound, a bit of sand falls, trickling back into the grave. My knuckles tighten. "A pain in the ass."

Doc chuckles. "You're forgetting about something, Cedar."

"Yeah?"

"When they bloom, their flowers are beautiful." He looks at the sky. "With your neck turned up like that, the leaves fallen at your feet don't matter much at all, do they?"

I plant my shovel in the ground and look up too. I pretend every star is a white magnolia blossom—that I'm in a place where trees fill in the empty spaces. That there is no sand beneath my stolen shoes. No graves.

Magnolia, I remember. That was his daughter's name.

"Maybe," I say.

I keep digging. I don't realize my next scoop is my last until I add the sand to the mound and notice there's a full grave at my feet. I lean back on my heel, wiping sweat from my forehead. "I think I'm done."

Doc shovels his last scoop with a relieved sigh. He extends a bloody hand, just as blistered as mine. "We did a good ten after all, didn't we?"

I'm angry at the world and my arms feel ready to fall off, but I take it. "A good ten indeed."

We return our shovels to the shed and walk back toward camp. Thunder rolls behind me. I peer over my shoulder, just as the lightning fades. I think of the rain I can't see, evaporating before it ever touches the ground.

Dad would love this, I think to myself.

I'll tell him all about it when I get home.

Saturday, September 3

♪ KINGDOM OF RUST - DOVES ♪

I'm doing a lot of things I probably shouldn't be doing.

I spend most of my breaks with the Gamblers. I don't know why they call themselves that—Raven and the others. I just know they really like stealing gasoline, which I continue helping them with. Sometimes we steal from cans stocked throughout the warehouse, if we have the time and opportunities to search for them and transport them unnoticed.

When curfew arrives and the Guards shut their eyes, if I'm not working on the escape plan with Raven, I go on rounds with Doc. It reminds me of life at the Cut. Delivering teas, extra rations, and other favors to people who need them. Sometimes the prisoners we check up on don't need anything tangible. We just sit and talk and make sure they're as okay as they can be in a place like this.

Sometimes they're very sick.

It makes sense. No human is designed to live behind an electric fence— breathing in poison, eating cheap artificial food, drinking water that's probably filled with all sorts of bacteria and heavy metals. Even the food we get as Guards is preferable to what they give the prisoners.

Heat exhaustion. Food poisoning. Fatigue. Infected blisters. Injuries. There is no shortage of ailments for Doc and me to treat. And even though it keeps the prisoners able to work, we are still committing crimes in the eyes of the Corps.

The wolves eat the weak, as the Captain said.

We won't let that happen.

I'm learning lots of things I've probably been lectured on before, but it's different out here. Life at the Cut was peaceful; I wasn't *needed* like I am behind this fence. I sew stitches for a man who sliced his stomach open when he fell on a shovel. I make salves to soothe sore muscles and treat infections. I pop dislocated shoulders and kneecaps back into place. I'm not just watching my dad handle everything. Under Doc's instruction, I'm actually *doing* things myself, because he trusts that I can handle it.

Back home, I never believed I could live up to my father's legacy. Now, trying to make him proud is the only thing holding me together.

But then I go to sleep in a room full of Guards. I wake with them, dine with them, work with them. I watch Saylor and his friends beat a man to near unconsciousness for an offense so simple I can't even remember it. The next day, another Guard does the exact same thing. Saylor is no anomaly. All Guards are cruel, and they remind me of it every single day.

If the fate of the Unseen and our secrets didn't rest on my tongue, maybe I would have stopped it. But I didn't.

There is no pride in that kind of silence.

So, I work with Doc instead of getting a full night's sleep. At least it makes it easier to pretend my father wouldn't despise the person I've become. Easier to believe he'll want me back.

Doc's lessons are distracting enough. Even though we're stranded in a sea of sand, he teaches me about trees. He talks about people the same way.

"There's always a root," he likes to tell me. "Always a reason why one acts the way they do—why they make the choices they make. A reason why the body displays certain sets of symptoms. The roots determine the way everything else stands; they must always come first."

Before, his ramblings would have made me zone out. Now I drink them like water, absorbing everything so I'll never forget again.

"It's hot as piss tonight," I grumble as we walk through the prison. The night air weighs heavy on my skin, a dark purple blanket.

"A charming visual," Doc says, wiping sweat from his brow. "It'll cool down soon enough. Always does. Even the desert can't stay warm forever."

"Yeah, well, soon isn't now."

"You're an impatient boy."

"Whatever."

We walk past the dead vulture. It's mostly bones now, save for a few stray feathers. No one has bothered to clean it up. It's a cruel reminder of how long I've been here—that I too risk a similar fate.

A cry cuts through the silence.

Doc and I freeze, exchanging glances. Another one rings out even louder.

We hurry toward the source of the sound—a prisoner's cabin. We burst through the door. The occupants crowd around one bottom bunk, where a young man lies with his eyes squeezed shut. His skin is clammy and beaded with sweat. He's only a few years older than I am. A blonde woman his age kneels by his side, patting his forehead with a damp cloth.

"Thank God you're here, Doc." A wide-eyed man hurries to meet us. He has dark brown hair and a beard, like the younger man in bed. *His father, maybe?*

"Mark." Doc nods in greeting and beelines to the bed. "What happened?"

"It's Ron," Mark says. "His foot."

The other prisoners give Doc some space. He kneels next to the blonde woman, opening his briefcase. She keeps patting Ron's forehead. Mark and I follow.

"It's bad, Doc. Real bad." Mark's breathing is fast, voice wavering. "Infected blisters, I think. But he didn't say anything about them—just let them fester. And now..." He swallows. "Take a look."

When Doc removes the blanket, we both gasp.

Ron's foot is a mottled, angry red. What must have been large blisters have long since ruptured. The skin is raw and oozing, with blotches of dark purple spreading down to his toes. The entire foot is swollen and puffy. Some areas seem pale and ashen. The others seem... dead.

"Necrosis," Doc mutters, eyeing Ron's toes. They look like they've been dipped in ink. "I see significant tissue death. The infection could spread into his bloodstream, if it hasn't already. We must act quickly to avoid sepsis."

"Sepsis?" The girl's eyes glisten. "What are you saying?"

"We need to amputate the foot."

"Amputation?" Mark exclaims. "Are you mad?"

"Out here, it'll be his only chance for survival. We have to keep the infection under control."

"I won't allow it. *They* won't allow it." Mark's voice cracks. "He can't work without a foot."

"And he can't live with this one." Doc removes the lanyard from his neck. "Now run to the infirmary. Use my ID card to get in. We'll need alcohol—and lots of it."

Mark opens his mouth to argue, then looks back to his son who's writhing in pain. His eyes gloss over. He nods and obeys.

I help Doc check Ron's vitals. His pulse is quick and faint. Although his forehead is hot and glazed with sweat, he shivers. He's cold, which is all he can say in his disoriented state. The only other thing he seems to be aware of is the girl's hand, which he holds like a lifeline. Her name is Meghan. She loves him, she says.

We don't have much time.

"Ankle disarticulation," Doc says. "We're removing the foot at the ankle joint."

The infirmary here may not contain the cutting-edge equipment and technology most Corps healers use, but Doc does have a surgical saw. It's a large, toothy thing with a wide blade and a serrated edge. It reminds me of the hand saw I have back home.

I've only ever used one to cut through wood. Not a person.

Doc walks over to the fireplace to sterilize the blade—or at least get it as close to sterile as possible in a place like this. He borrows a belt from one of the other prisoners and secures it tightly around Ron's lower leg. To minimize blood loss, he says.

Mark returns with an unlabeled bottle of clear liquid. Doc helps Ron down as much of it as possible. Even Beau would have a hard time handling that much alcohol at once. I can only imagine the bitterness, the burning in his nose. Doc says we need to keep him subdued to prevent involuntary movements. To keep the cut as clean as possible.

We spread a sheet over the floor and transport Ron on top of it. Meghan tries to calm him down, stroking his hair, whispering sweet things in his ear that I can't hear over the crying as we wait for the alcohol to take effect.

It does soon enough.

Doc instructs Mark and the other prisoners to each take a limb. Gently, but firmly—just enough to keep him secure without causing any more stress than necessary. Meghan holds a stick in his mouth so he'll have something to bite down on. Doc uses a pen to outline where the cut will go.

"Amputation through the joint is preferable to avoid cutting through bone," Doc says. "We must use the sharpest and cleanest tool we have for the skin and soft tissue layer." He sterilizes a scalpel in the fire before handing it to me. "Downward force, steady movements."

"Why are you giving this to me?"

"Downward force," Doc repeats, slower this time. "Steady movements."

My face pales. "No."

"Cedar—"

"I can't do this! I can't amputate a foot!"

"Cedar, please."

He holds up his hand. It tremors. He lowers it with a sigh.

"My dexterity is not what it used to be. I will guide you through every step, but if you leave this operation to me, there is no guarantee that I won't cause more harm than good. A procedure like this requires preciseness, otherwise we risk accidentally nicking an artery and causing more bleeding. You are the only trained individual in this entire facility who can do this, Cedar. You have a steadier hand than you believe."

"Please," Meghan begs. She's been trying not to cry all evening, but her eyes still water. "He needs you."

Her words slice like a scalpel.

He needs me.

The room spins and blurs—then slows to a pause. I feel like I'm back in my greenhouse with Cecil. *"You've got a steady hand,"* he said.

But this is a blade, not a pen. Cutting through flesh is far more permanent than ink.

If I don't do this perfectly, I could kill him. Hell, it could kill *me* if the Guards find out I operated on a prisoner.

But if I don't do this, he will die.

No more standing still. No more staying silent.

I'm trying, Dad. I close my eyes. *I want to make you proud.*

When I open them, I don't feel afraid anymore. "Tell me what to do."

Doc and I sit on the porch with sweat on our backs and blood on our shirts.

"You did well, Cedar," he says. "You should be very proud. He'll be alright, I'm sure of it."

My hands won't stop shaking. "I hope so."

Ron is asleep inside with his father and friends. Even with the alcohol we gave him, the pain is what knocked him out eventually. We'll return to change his dressings as frequently as we can to reduce the risk of infection. He'll be in pain for a while, but at least we avoided sepsis, if it hadn't already begun before our arrival.

I lean my head against the wooden post behind me. "How do you do it?"

"I ask myself the same question more than you'd think. I have yet to find the answer, but I know my why, and that keeps me going." He sighs. "Even on nights like these."

My why... I turn the word over in my mind. I think of my father, dedicating his life to healing others. I think of Lockley and Jelly. I think of Meghan, pleading for me to help the man she loves.

For the first time in my life, it feels like I finally know my *why*.

Maybe this is what I'm meant to do—to help those who can't help themselves. People who need me.

"Does it get easier?" I ask quietly, still too tired to look him in the eye.

"I wish I could say it does, but I don't think anyone in their right mind enjoys cutting through tendons." He gives me a small smile. "There is some good in the right kinds of sacrifice. Selflessness. And I will gladly give up my own comfort if it means helping those who need it more."

I nod. Maybe Raven was right about comfort zones after all.

Doc pulls something from his pocket and sticks it in his mouth. Only when he lights it do I realize it's a cigar.

I glare and scoot over. "Really, man? You're a doctor."

"We're already dying out here, son. Might as well indulge." He takes a long drag. "I never said we should give up *all* comforts. Can't pour from an empty glass, you know."

He extends the cigar.

I crinkle my nose. "Dad says those kill you."

"Over time, absolutely. But how much money would you bet on tomorrow's sunrise?"

"I don't know. A little, I think."

"But it's never guaranteed, is it?"

My shoulders relax a bit. It doesn't smell as terrible as I thought. Certainly not as bad as cigarettes.

Doc chuckles and lowers the cigar. "Don't worry, boy. I'm only teasing. Your old man would kill me if I—"

I take the cigar from his hands, and I breathe it in.

I close my eyes, inhaling the earthy taste of chocolate and campfire smoke and something like cracked pepper. It's different from what comes out of the furnace. Warmer—until it burns my throat and lungs. I cough violently. "God. That's not pleasant."

Doc snatches it back. "Foolish boy. They're vile things, I know. And you're not supposed to *inhale it* like that. You'll get sick."

I'm still coughing. "Sorry."

He gives me a mischievous side glance. "But... it was pleasant for a moment, wasn't it?"

I fight a smile. "For a moment."

He points a finger in my face. "Never again. Unlike me, *you've* still got your whole life ahead of you."

I salute. "I'll bet my money on tomorrow morning, sir."

He rolls his eyes.

We're silent for a while. He puts out the cigar in the dirt. "Do you know what deadwooding is?"

"Like in cards?"

He shrugs. "Sure. Explain it to me."

"Burning the deadwood," I say. "People say that when they get rid of cards they no longer need..."

Something in my chest aches for home. I spent so many late nights playing cards with Dad and Beau. And now, I'm here. Imprisoned with all the other *deadwood* discarded by the Presidency.

I wonder if I'll ever play a game with them again.

Doc nods. "It's a term my father talked about quite often. A common form of strategic pruning performed by tree surgeons. A branch may die due to pests, disease, lack of sunlight—anything. Regardless of the cause, once a limb loses life, it will never grow again. It becomes dead weight and no longer serves any purpose to the tree. Theoretically, removing these branches improves the tree's overall balance and minimizes the risk of future infections. But do you know what I find rather humorous?"

I shake my head.

"Deadwooding is a human thing. Before we came along and messed everything up, trees survived on their own for millions of years. No other animals do it."

"That is weird."

"Isn't it?" Doc sighs. "Some say the concept of deadwood stretches beyond that. It could be a habit or perspective weighing you down. An old version of yourself you must kill off to make room for new growth. An infected foot. The sickest caribou in the herd. Unproductive citizens who must be eliminated to make sure the system only feeds resources to those the Presidency deems worthy."

The thought makes my stomach ache.

"We outgrow old sweaters, old ways of thinking, people and places who no longer serve our purpose. But this world... this country... they go about it all wrong. The Corps believes they are the surgeons—that they are removing inefficiencies from the world to prune the ideal tomorrow. They do not realize that *they* are the pests. The Nightjade Order is an infection, and it must be eradicated if we intend to heal the wounds we have all suffered for so long."

I nod. There is a long stretch of silence. I still taste cigar smoke on my tongue.

"If there is anything you learn from me, Cedar, let it be this." He shifts to face me. "Do you know the vaccine?"

I shake my head.

"Compassion, son. Wearing shoes that are not your own. Wielding shovels that belong to someone else. Thinking beyond your own circle of comfort. Do you understand the potency of that kind of medicine? How profound of an impact you can have on the world by simply being *good* to those who share it with you?"

I pause to think about it, but the answer is already there. "I do."

"Good." He puts a proud arm around my shoulder, patting my back. "Another good ten, my boy."

His smile makes me ache for my father.

"A very good ten indeed."

Sunday, September 4

♪ OH LIGHTNING - VALLEY MAKER ♪

On my thirty-fifth day at the Tombs, I learn about Cobra.

It's Sunday night, almost curfew. I sit in a circle with the other Gamblers as Raven deals us seven cards each.

"Scientists hail the king cobra as the most intelligent snake," she says, voice comically formal.

Lockley's eyes roll. "Do we really have to do the speech every time?"

"Yes. It's part of the game," Jelly says, already inspecting her hand.

"Dealer says the speech," Fern tells me. "It's customary."

Raven frowns. "Everyone shush."

She clears her throat, straightens her posture, and starts over.

"Scientists hail the king cobra as the most intelligent snake. This cunning predator can strategically adapt its hunting tactics to suit any situation thrown its way.

"Female king cobras are the only snakes known to humankind that build nests and guard their eggs." She gives me a concerningly vicious smirk. "They will defend their own to the death."

I realize very quickly just how much she means it.

The objective is to earn the most points by strategically managing your cards and stealing from opponents' *nests*—a pile of face-down cards each player accumulates during the game.

To *hunt* is to attempt to steal a card from an opponent's nest, which you can *defend* by playing the first card in your hand. If it's higher in value, the nest is defended, and both cards are discarded.

On your turn, you can draw, hunt, or implement *tactics*, which are special actions like stealing, swapping cards, and other obnoxious moves.

In other words, Cobra is all about pissing people off.

It's fast-paced and confusing and brings out the worst in all of us. Even Jelly yells and curses anyone who steals her cards. It's hard to believe she's the same girl who lectures Lockley for squishing spiders and shooing away mice.

And despite the threats and ruthless acts of vengeance, we can't stop laughing. Even as we sit here—sailor-mouthed and cross-legged on a dirty floor, in a building that's falling apart, trapped behind a fence that will kill us if we so much as touch it, imprisoned by those who believe we are worth less—we laugh. We are so unapologetically loud in a world that demands our silence.

We have unburied joy in the bleakest place this system has to offer.

There's something addictive to this defiance, this disobedience. And I lose myself in it. Game after game, defeat after defeat. I could play this forever and never get bored.

This is rebellion—and it's exhilarating.

Until a knock on the door freezes us.

I swear my heart drops to my stomach. We exchange nervous glances, holding our breaths as another knock rings through the air.

"Stay here," Raven says. She walks to the door, opening it just a crack. Her shoulders stiffen.

"Is Cedar here?"

My eyes widen. *Marty.*

"I'm sorry, I'm not sure if I know—"

"You know who I'm talking about," Marty interrupts.

Raven sighs. "I haven't seen him. Sorry."

"Do you know where he could be?" Marty's voice sounds different now. Worried. "If you've seen where he's gone, you *need* to tell me."

"Raven," I say. "It's okay. Let him in."

Marty pushes through the door. Raven closes it behind him. He puts a hand to his chest when he sees me. "Thank God."

"What's wrong?"

"What's *wrong*?" He laughs cynically. "I thought you were in trouble with Saylor again. It's 2:00 in the morning, dude. I woke up to take a piss, and you were gone, and I *broke curfew* to look for you, thinking you were dead in a grave somewhere." He scoffs, gesturing to the hand I hold. "And you're playing cards. With prisoners."

My shoulders slump with a bit of relief. "Oh. Thanks, man. I uh... I really appreciate that."

Marty shakes his head.

"I'm sorry, okay? I didn't mean to freak you out, but you can't tell anyone about this, alright?"

He doesn't say anything.

"Marty," I hiss.

"Look—I don't care that you're friends with them, alright? You all seem very nice."

Jelly smiles. Raven glares.

"I won't say a word." Marty turns toward the door, pausing with his hand on the knob. "Just... tell me next time you disappear, alright?"

I nod. He moves to open the door, but Lockley speaks before he can. "I know what you did."

Marty freezes. "What?"

"I heard you trying to save us from Correction. After the fight."

Realization softens the furrow in Marty's brow. "No one deserves that."

"So you won't turn us in, then?" Raven nods toward me. "Or him?"

Marty glances around the room. He knows I'm not supposed to be here. He knows they're not supposed to have stolen cards. We could all get in trouble for this. We could all get *killed* for this.

"No."

Raven returns to her seat next to me. She pats the ground to her right. "Don't just stand there. We're dealing you in."

Marty can't hide his grin.

He sits between Raven and Lockley, careful not to touch his shoulder, very clearly nervous as Raven deals him his cards. Lockley leans closer. "Boo."

That makes Marty jump a bit. Lockley finds it hilarious.

We play Cobra until we can't anymore. Until Jelly is asleep on Fern's shoulder, and our faces are sore from laughter.

It's late by the time Marty and I return to our own beds, but I can't sleep.

I know it's risky to be out past curfew, but I can't help my restlessness. There are too many things to think and worry about. Too many things to haunt my dreams.

I've started having nightmares. Worse ones, I should say. They've been around ever since I was a kid, but I could never really remember the details. Now they're hard to forget. Even after I wake up and realize I'm not *really* suffocating beneath sand, drowning in gasoline, or coughing until my lungs glide up through my throat and fall into my hands, it's still hard to shake the bitter aftertaste they leave behind.

Sometimes tiring myself out until my body has no choice but to sleep restfully is the only way to avoid those dreams.

Doc was right. It does get cold at night. I shiver with my hands in my pockets. I don't realize I've walked all the way to the water tower until I notice something move from the corner of my eye.

Climbing down the ladder is a girl with a messy black braid, and a red ribbon in her hair.

What the hell is she doing?

I walk over, just as she lands on the ground.

"That's dangerous," I say.

She jumps at the sound of my voice, sighing when she realizes it's me. "What are you doing here?"

"I could ask you the same question."

"You first."

I shrug. "Can't sleep."

She leans against the ladder. "You too, huh?"

I nod. She nods. Then it's painfully quiet.

I'm just about to turn back around when she smirks. "Follow me."

Raven leads me up the ladder. I force myself not to look down until we reach the platform at the top. It's just wide enough to walk through, with simple wood railings that I could still fall through easily.

I look over the edge with a shiver. There's no way anyone would survive a fall from this high. Too bad we can't just jump over the fence from up here.

"It's wood," I say, patting the railing.

"Cedar, actually."

"Doesn't it rot, then?"

"It'll last about thirty years or so. Cedar's antimicrobial. It contains oils and resins that make it resistant to decay. Insects too." She places a hand on the side of the tank. "I'm guessing this one's just about ready to topple over."

"Your water tower knowledge never ceases to amaze me," I tease.

She shrugs. "Back home, I read up on civil engineering from time to time. It's interesting stuff."

She takes a seat, leaning against the tank's wall. I do the same. We hang our feet over the edge through the gaps in the railing.

"Is that what you wanted to do?" I ask. "Before becoming Unseen?"

"Engineering is interesting, but... I think *this* was always what I was meant to do." She traces the post in front of her and winces. "That was corny, wasn't it?"

"Not really."

She smiles.

I lean back, using my palms as a pillow. "So how did you get mixed up in the Unseen, anyway?" I give her a brief side glance. "From what I've gathered, your dad's an Agent."

She shrugs. "Hated my life. Hated my mom for leaving after I was born.

Hated my dad for who he was when he was around. Hated the world." She runs her finger along the post again. "Hated the Corps, because they took someone from me."

"Who?"

She forces a pained smile. "The boy I loved."

A weight burrows into my chest. "Raven..."

She shrugs, still smiling. Her eyes glisten. I never thought I'd see her cry, and I realize now how little I want to.

"We don't have to talk about it if you don't want to," I say.

"The day I stop talking about it will be the day I stop breathing. They want us quiet. They want us to submit—to move on in silence, without resistance. To worship the people who take and take and never give a damn thing back to anyone who can't afford their protection."

I nod. "What was his name?"

She exhales shakily, leaning her head back to stare at the sky. "Harley."

"What was he like?"

"Summer." She grins again. "Pulling over to buy strawberries at farm stands. Picking me up and spinning me for no reason. Ice cream parlors and walks around the block and the berry pies his mom made every weekend." The smile fades. "They killed my best friend for the Yesterday book my father found in his bag."

I want to tell her I'm sorry, but I don't think that'll do any good. I never know what to say in situations like this. Instinctively, my hand reaches out toward her shoulder, then stills in midair. I bring it back to my side.

She doesn't need me to tell her how abominably she has been robbed.

"Something in me... I think it died that day," she says softly. "But it awakened something too. That's when I found the Gamblers."

My brows crease. "The Gamblers?"

"Not the others here." She shakes her head. "The real ones, out there."

"I don't know what you mean."

"They're Unseen. Just... differently. A branch of people who are willing to take the right risks for the greater good."

My eyes widen. *The Gamblers.* I realize I've heard that name before. Dad's mentioned them a few times, but I never put two and two together until now.

"The others here agree with the Gambler ideology. When we get out, they'll join me. Lockley, Jelly, Fern, Doc—all of us. We won't just sit around. We'll fight like hell. We'll find other people just like us and get organized." She stares at her hands. "People with nothing left to lose."

Something about that saddens me.

There's another long stretch of silence. We stare at the sky, until she speaks. "I heard what happened with the amputation yesterday."

I take a long, sighing blink. *This is the last thing I want to talk about right now.*

"Are you okay?" She asks.

I shrug.

"You did everything you could." A pause. "Doing all we can with what we're given—that's what this is all about, isn't it?"

"Doing all I can doesn't exactly translate into saving him. He still hasn't woken up." My throat tightens. "Can we talk about something else?"

"What do you wanna talk about?"

I turn my head to face her. She does the same. "Tell me something about you."

"What do you want to know?"

I pause to think about it. "Where'd you learn how to play Cobra?"

She looks away.

"I've heard of it before, but I never played it until I got here," I say.

Walter played Cobra with his associates regularly. According to Lily, it's usually the game of choice at Prairie Pit too. Any Syndicate gathering, really.

Raven sighs. "My father was a gambling man. Sometimes he'd take my sister and me with him."

My brows crease. From what I've heard, places like Prairie Pit don't sound like a safe place for kids.

"Were you close?" I ask.

Her jaw twitches. "We used to be."

I nod.

"He liked me more when I was younger, I think. When I was compliant. Controllable. Ignorant to the man he really was." She fidgets with a loose string hanging from her shirt. "But when Jade started outperforming me in school, and I started getting in trouble—talking back and sticking up for myself—that seemed to go away."

"Jade?"

"My sister."

Quiet.

"Do you remember the day you realized your parents were only human? That they make mistakes and don't know everything like you always thought they did?" She averts her gaze. "That they can only do so much to protect you?"

"I do."

She traces the grains in the wood beneath us. "Sometimes I wonder if that was the day he stopped loving me."

There it is again—the weight fixing into my ribcage. Making it harder to breathe.

I don't know this girl very well, and I can still feel the hurt she must be feeling. The pain she swallows down so no one else can see it.

But here, beneath a smokey sky, on this rotting water tower so separate from the rest of camp, I *can* see it. And it makes me ache.

"Eventually he realized I didn't have the potential to become an Agent like him, so he started feeding all his attention to Jade. It makes sense, really. She's perfect, Cedar. Beautiful and smart. Careful. Obedient. My polar opposite."

"Were you close with her?"

"Yeah." Raven smiles sadly, shaking her head. "I miss her like hell."

"I know what you mean."

She raises a brow. "You have siblings?"

"Lori's my little sister. Beau's my foster brother. He's... something else, that's for sure."

Just mentioning their names plants a pain in my chest.

"And what about Lori?"

"Smartest person I know. Hilarious too, if she lets you get close to her." I chuckle sadly. "I don't think I've met a kinder person in all my life."

"Sounds like Jade."

I look at her. She looks at me. And I realize she knows just as well as I do what it feels like to be separated from people you love.

"We'll see them again," she says.

I hold out a pinky. "Promise?"

She loops her finger around mine. "Promise."

Her pinky is soft. Calloused from work, but smooth.

"Your hands are cold," I note.

"Clever observation."

She doesn't pull away. I study her, the way I did when she was sick. But now her eyes are open, and I look at those too. I still think she's beautiful.

Not because it means anything. Just another observation.

She's shivering. I enclose her hand in both of mine and bring it close to my chest. I blow air into my palms.

She laughs. "What are you doing?"

"Warming your hands."

"Yours aren't much warmer." She brings mine closer to her now, blowing on them instead. Her breath tickles my skin.

"How's that?" she asks.

It's quiet. I'm looking at her. She's looking at me.

Slowly, her fingers lace between mine.

Not because it means anything. It's just cold up here, and my hands are all she has to hold.

Soft rays of sunlight pry my eyes open.

I wince, sitting up to rub my neck. I glance down at my side. Raven is asleep on my shoulder, hand still in mine. A warmth spreads over the bridge of my nose.

Wait a minute.

It's morning.

"Raven," I whisper frantically. "Get up."

"What?" she groans, eyes still closed.

"It's *morning*."

She folds forward. "What?"

We hurry down the ladder. It's still pretty dark, and the sun is only just now peeking above the horizon. No one should be up yet, thankfully.

My feet hit the dirt. Raven is still climbing behind me when I see something move in the distance. I squint to make out the shape—and my stomach cartwheels.

Officer Stokes gently shuts the door of a prisoner's cabin behind him, with a cardboard box in hand. It looks empty.

He freezes when he sees me staring.

Raven hops off the ladder behind me, wiping dust on her pants. Stokes and I are still locked in place, eyeing each other from yards away.

What's with that box? And what could he possibly be doing in a prisoner's cabin? Even Supervisors aren't allowed to break that rule. He could get Corrected for what I'm seeing. *Or worse.*

We're in the same boat.

I expect him to walk over and reprimand us. I expect this to be my final mistake—the one that will get me questioned and killed. Because I'm standing here at dawn, hair a mess, side by side with a prisoner as though she is my equal. That alone would give any Guard reason to question my loyalty, or at least my obedience. So why isn't he saying anything? *Why won't he move?*

Without a word, he disappears into the dark.

"What's wrong?" Raven asks. *She didn't notice him.*

I shake my head. "Nothing."

28

Tuesday, October 11

Marty slaps my index finger with two of his own. "Shit."

"Haha." I retaliate with my last three fingers. "I win."

Marty drops his hands into his lap with a defeated sigh. "Usually I'm great at Chopsticks. I don't know what's with me today."

"Maybe I'm just extraordinarily talented."

Marty shakes his head, picking at his breakfast of cold oatmeal. "That game doesn't need talent. You're just lucky."

"Luck is a *theory* humans constructed in a futile attempt to explain coincidence and overlook privilege. It's not real." I shovel a spoonful of oatmeal into my mouth. It's disgusting, but it's better than mystery meat. "It's a comforting lie."

"Dude, it's like 7:00 in the morning."

"Well aware."

"Pessimism at breakfast? Now that's bad luck."

"Sometimes shitty things happen and there's no good reason for it." I stab my spoon into my bowl. "Sometimes life just sucks."

"Okay, fine." He raises his hands in innocence. "Someone's in a mood."

"If I were *lucky*, I wouldn't be here. And if you were lucky, *you* wouldn't be either."

"Maybe you just can't see the luck playing out yet."

I rest my head in my hand. "Whatever."

Marty's right—I am in a mood.

I should be exhilarated. Ron's making steady progress. His scars are healing without signs of further infection. Doc says he's doing really well. I visited last night and saw it myself. He's been hiding out in his cabin for a while while others pick up his shifts. We don't know how long it'll be until someone notices, but at least he's recovering quickly.

Beyond the overwhelming relief, I can't help but feel proud too. I saved him—or at least played a part in doing so. I did something worthwhile. Something my dad would praise me for, if he were here to see it. The thought is comforting.

But that doesn't change the fact that I'm here, the prisoners are still suffering, and not a single Chip beyond this fence gives a damn about it.

Some days it feels like there's nothing I can do.

Once you escape, you can come back for them, I remind myself. *One thing at a time, Aaron.*

"May I have your attention, please?"

The voice of Captain Valdez rings through the cafeteria. I sit upright. Everyone goes silent.

He never shows up at breakfast. As Captain, he gets a cushy cabin all to himself, where he can enjoy his meals in peaceful solitude. Funny how he's supposed to be running this place, but we hardly see his face at all.

So what the hell is he doing here?

"It has recently come to our attention that, in a tragic turn of events, one of our workers lost his foot."

I choke on my oatmeal. A few heads turn to give me dirty looks.

As soon as I'm done coughing, Valdez continues.

"This is not uncommon here at the Tombs. Accidents happen, but the world keeps spinning. That is the reality of our ecosystem here.

"However, this is not a common case." He pauses to scan the room, a vulture searching for carrion. "He lost his foot, because someone with medical training amputated the limb as an act of intervention. To save the man's life from an infection that threatened to take it."

The Guards exchange uncertain glances.

"As you all know, treating prisoners is a crime in the eyes of the Corps. They are sentenced here to work their way to a peaceful, efficient death. This act of intervention defies not only the way we operate around here, but the very Nightjade Order itself."

My pulse quickens. Beneath the table, my leg shakes violently. I fight the urge to tap my fingers, tightening a fist around my spoon.

"The amputation was flawless. Every cut was deliberate and precise. This is why we believe this crime was committed by a Guard, not another prisoner. They do not have the training and sophistication seen in Corps professionals."

I fight a scoff. I know an Unseen surgeon who could cut him up just fine.

"Several Guards and Corps officials at this facility have backgrounds as Healers. Or Sitters, conducting autopsies and forensic studies at our labs. A few Chasers were sent here for cutting up Assignments out of curiosity. Enjoyment, even. So there are plenty of worthy suspects."

I feel like I'm going to be sick.

The Captain folds his arms behind his back, pacing the room. "The prisoner is no longer with us. May his soul rest in peace, wherever it is. Before his death, we questioned him for information he refused to give. We also questioned several of this man's bunkmates with no productive results. May their souls rest in peace.

"My Supervisors and I will be conducting an investigation to find the root of this mystery, ideally before Evaluation on the 24th. To fast-forward results, we're offering a reward to anyone who steps forward with information about this forbidden procedure. A pardon for a Supervisor, and a promotion for a Guard."

Gasps and whispers fill the air.

"The Chaser Corps thanks you for your cooperation. May we all continue to play our part in the advancement of humankind."

With a bow, Valdez exits.

I can't breathe. My eyes cement to the table, lungs pinching shut as the room spins.

This can't be happening. I was just there. Ron was awake. His father cried tears of joy. Meghan grinned from ear to ear. He played cards with his friends and won a stolen ranch dressing packet. He was alive and happy. *They all were.*

Now, they're gone. All of them.

And it's entirely my fault.

After everyone is assigned jobs for the day, I walk up to Stokes. "I need to talk to you."

He's too busy typing something into his tablet to look up. "Not now, Beck. We both have work to do."

"I know you saw me."

His hands freeze.

"And I saw you too," I add.

That gets him to look up.

His eyes are wide with concern, which I understand. Sympathizing with a criminal who sinned against the Presidency is in itself a sin—a direct defiance of the Nightjade Order and its rules.

"What were you doing in that cabin?" I ask quietly, even though no one is around to hear.

Stokes glares. "I don't know what you're talking about."

I cross my arms. "I keep your secret, you keep mine. But I wanna know what's going on."

Stokes sighs in frustration, glancing over his shoulder to make sure no one's listening. He leans forward. "Look, it's not that big of a deal, alright?" He rubs his forehead. "Sometimes I'll distribute extra food and supplies to the prisoners. But it's always mine and for the good of the Corps. I'm *not* a sympathizer. They need more than what we've been giving them to stay productive. I had nothing to do with that amputation."

"Alright, alright." I raise my hands in innocence. "I get it."

He nods, then gives me a knowing look. "Do you want me to ask what you were doing?"

My face warms. "No."

"Then I won't."

"Thank you."

"You'll stay quiet, won't you?" He sighs again. "Hell knows what they'll do to me if they find out."

My brows furrow. *Wait a minute...*

"Saylor knows," I say. "That's what he's holding over you."

Stokes looks away with a shrug.

I sit cross-legged on the ground beside him. "I hate that guy."

Stokes sits next to me. "Me too."

"See? You get it." I shake my head. "I mean—why does he act like that? What's his motive? I've been racking my brain for the answer and I just don't get it. Being that angry... I don't know. It seems like such a miserable way to live."

My shoulders relax a bit. Only now do I realize how much frustration I've been keeping to myself, and how good it feels to let it out. It's nice to vent to someone who gets it. Someone who won't get me in trouble.

I hope.

"People who feel out of control will do anything to find solid footing again, whether they realize it or not." Stokes sighs. "He wasn't always like this, you know."

"What do you mean?"

"He used to be more like you."

My eyes widen. "You're shitting me."

"It took him much longer to get used to the way things are around here. You toughened up quick, but Saylor was unwell for a long time."

Used to it? My jaw feathers. *I'm not used to any of this.*

Am I?

I think about what Agent Finch said at the training center, before I was trapped within this fence. Before *he* put me on that bus. The damn Head of House called me rusty. Said I needed to *sharpen*. Officer Gilbert said something similar during training.

What does rusty even mean? Am I too reckless? Sensitive? Stupid? What is it that the Corps is trying to wring out of me? My humanity?

A lump forms in my throat. I stare at my hands.

If that's their definition of sharp, then I sure as hell hope I haven't gotten to that point.

Stokes stretches out his legs, leaning back on his palms as he continues his story. "Saylor couldn't adjust to the food. Got sick with nearly every meal. Broke down crying for no reason. Some Supervisors worried he'd turn into a sympathizer, if you can believe it. He even got Corrected a few times for chatting too much with the prisoners."

My lips part. "No way."

"He had his own Saylor. An older Guard called Garth. He had a thing for picking on Cleancoats, but he loved messing with prisoners even more. They'd go missing sometimes, you know." Stokes swallows, averting his gaze. "Graves filled a lot quicker when Garth was around."

A shiver worms through me. "What happened to him?"

"Saylor killed him."

I clench my hand into a fist so it doesn't fly to my mouth. "And he got away with it?"

"Leadership was starting to view Garth as a nuisance. If anything, Saylor running that fork through his neck in the cafeteria did them a favor. It also showed he finally earned the resolve the Tombs is supposed to carve into you. As for the other cadets, they were probably glad he was gone. And too scared of Saylor to say a word about it. Everyone just... kept on eating."

I try not to shudder at the imagery. "He killed another Guard in front of everybody, and no one did a thing?"

"The Captain did let Saylor off with a warning. If he so much as *attempts* to take someone's life again—prisoner or Guard—he'll get the injection."

So that's why he hasn't killed me yet, I realize. Back when he tried burying me alive, I was too new to be noticed or memorable. Not every Cleancoat lives to see their clothes turn gray. If Saylor succeeded, no one would have missed me. I doubt they'd think to check the Graves either. The crime would never be linked back to him.

He would have gotten away with it, if Raven hadn't saved me.

"What about the other Guards? You're telling me they all just... sat there? And *ate*? After a man was killed right in front of them?"

"Minding your own business is part of staying alive out here. Taking initiative does earn you some brownie points where promotions are concerned, but most don't think far beyond making it another day."

I swallow. *And to think I'm on his bad side.*

"I watched this place change him," Stokes continues. "Over time, Saylor realized just what he could get away with behind this fence. Under the Presidency's protection and privilege. I think the old him died with Garth."

"I had no idea."

"Power in any form—it's like a drug, Beck. And it's one Saylor can't stop taking every chance he can get. Showing others he's in control... establishing these unspoken rules over the other Guards... I think it's therapeutic for him. It's how he deals with the consequences of his failure." He looks at me. "Comfort. That's the motive."

"So you're saying all the shit he pulls is okay?"

"I'm just warning you to be careful around him, alright? You're a good kid, Beck. You work hard. You don't complain. They were right about you." He gives me a small grin. "I think you'll make a fine Chaser someday."

I open my mouth to thank him, then stop myself. Guilt tightens my throat. *That shouldn't be a compliment.*

"You just gotta keep your head down for a while," Stokes says. "Don't cause any more trouble than you need to."

"But Saylor's an asshole. I hate letting him get away with shit."

"Sometimes going along with things keeps you safe. And the people around you." Stokes sighs. "It won't be this way forever. Just... do what he says, for now. Try to avoid him and stay out of trouble. Keep the peace, survive another day."

I rise to my feet, rolling my eyes, "Alright."

"Who knows?" He stands too. "Maybe Evaluation will bring you good news."

I don't know what to say. Stokes winks before walking away.

I stand there for a while, trying to make sense of what I just heard. *Would he really put in a good word for me?*

When I realize what this means, I swear my heart stops beating entirely.

If Stokes meant what he said... and I stay on my best behavior... does this mean I have a chance of getting reassigned? A chance of going home?

My hands tremble. I stand still, unblinking. Vultures circle above me, casting shadows on the dirt. I feel like I'm sinking into it, melting into the ground that slowly grows unsteady beneath me.

Getting reassigned would be a pardon. It would be my chance to show that I've sharpened here, and that I'll be able to serve the Corps as they want me to. Resiliently. No questions. No resistance.

It would be a second chance to continue my mission. I could work in the field as a real Officer and gather the first-hand insight I was sent out to retrieve in the first place, just like Walter suggested. I could live safely at Whitestag until my job is done, and I'd go home alive and well-fed. *This could be my escape.*

But I can't deny the fear I feel too.

What if I get too comfortable in that life? What if I never want to leave Whitestag or the safety of the Corps? If I fall too deep in that lie, making it a truth will only become more tempting. Stokes was right about power being addictive, and the comforts that come with it.

The longer I stay, the harder it will be to leave.

If I'm reassigned, and I follow through with that reassignment, I'd be doing more than betraying the Unseen and everything we stand for. I'd be leaving Marty and the Gamblers behind too.

But if I really am faced with this choice... will it matter?

I want nothing more than to go home. To see my parents and Lori and Beau again. To finally play that game of pool Cecil promised me.

One thing at a time, Aaron, I tell myself. *One thing at a time.*

I walk to the Graves and watch the prisoners dig.

The day drips by like molasses. By the time sunset arrives and the dinner bell rings, my head is pounding. I can't tell if it's from tension or baking in the sun all day. Maybe a bit of both.

Marty and I walk into the cafeteria. I'm surprised to see Lockley on a cleaning shift today, mopping the floor. I wiggle my eyebrows at him from across the room when no one's looking. He blows me a kiss. I catch it and pretend to eat it.

Only when Lockley returns to his task do I notice who's standing in the dinner line behind him.

Saylor doesn't do anything out of the ordinary. He bosses around the prisoner on serving duty, complaining about the quality of our food again. I scoff. Like it's somehow in her control. It's nothing new, though after my conversation with Stokes, I can't help but look at Saylor differently. All I can picture is a bloody fork in his hands. I try not to imagine what one would feel like lodged in my throat.

The Guards standing behind him abandon the line. I've seen this happen. We all know his tantrum will last a few minutes longer than anyone this exhausted is willing to stand. They'll return to the line once Saylor is gone. And with what Stokes told me, I'm sure most of them are also trying to avoid getting caught in the crossfire.

My hands clench into fists at my sides. Is everyone really so afraid of him that they're willing to let him get away with acting like this?

No one cares how prisoners are treated around here, I remind myself.

No one will do a thing.

I'm about to get in line behind him when I see the prisoner's arm move.

It's subtle, just a flicker. Her hand darts to slide something under Saylor's tray. She glances over her shoulder to make sure no one saw. Saylor does the same. *Was that a piece of paper?*

My eyes widen when I remember what Marty told me when I first got here. What Raven said about Guards having spies.

"I've seen prisoners report others for extra rations," she said. *"Water. Forbidden infirmary visits."*

This must be one of Saylor's.

But I don't see him as one of the rewarding types. I think back to his blackmail situation with Stokes and wonder what Saylor must be holding over this woman's head.

I walk up behind him just as he's picking up his tray, and whatever the prisoner slid underneath it. I set my tray down and pin my eyes to Saylor as she piles food on top of it. He flashes me a fake smile and turns away. I grab my food and hurry after him.

"What was that about?" I mutter, walking by his side.

He keeps his voice steady. "I don't know what you're talking about, Beck."

I grip my tray harder. I can either follow Stokes' advice and keep my head low, or leave it alone. Stay safe... or keep eating.

Screw that.

I made a promise to myself back at Whitestag that I won't stand by and watch innocent people get hurt again. I've made it this far. No use turning back on it now.

If Saylor keeps thinking he can get away with shady shit, he will. He needs to know he's not invincible.

"I saw you talking to that prisoner," I say.

He gives me another fake and fleeting grin. "I was telling her how to do her damn job correctly. That's what we're here for, isn't it?"

"I saw the piece of paper."

His gaze darts to mine, nostrils flaring, but he composes himself quickly. "What paper?"

I reach under his tray to grab it, feeling only aluminum. I pat around for the note I *know* I saw—and I find nothing. I retract my hand. *What the hell?*

He must have slipped it into his pocket already.

"Get ahold of yourself," Saylor seethes. "I don't know what you're talking about, but touch my tray again and you're *dead*. You hear me? And you keep your nose *out* of my business, Beck."

I bite back a scoff. He can't *really* kill me. Not without anyone noticing.

He shoves his way past me to track down Fantaine and Coda.

While he's occupied with them—likely complaining about me—I study the prisoner serving the food. Everyone has their meals now. She's all alone behind the counter. Now that I'm taking a closer look, I recognize her. I helped treat her friend's heat exhaustion with Doc the other day. I think her name is Gina.

I hurry over to where she stands, glancing over my shoulder to make sure no one's paying attention. Then I lean in, speaking low. "What was that note about?"

Her brows crease. "What?"

"The note," I hiss. "We both know you know what I'm talking about. Now tell me, what was on that piece of paper?"

Gina opens her mouth, ready to deny it—until her eyes settle on my scar. *She recognizes me too.*

She sighs. "A lie."

Now my brows do the furrowing.

"Look. I'm only telling you this because you helped Jennifer." She bites her lip, craning her neck to make sure Saylor's still occupied. "He was asking about you."

The words draw the air from my lungs. I swallow. "Me?"

"Not *you* directly, but... he's heard the rumors. That someone's going around and helping prisoners. He believes whoever must be doing this is the person who carried out the amputation."

Well, he's not wrong.

"What exactly did he ask?"

"If I've ever seen a Guard walk out of one of our cabins. Or act too friendly with the prisoners. Said I'd be subjected to Correction if he found out I was lying."

Shit.

Gina checks Saylor's table again, then shakes her head. "That healer of yours has been sympathetic for years. But now with all this scrutiny... your Captain might be catching on."

It feels like I've swallowed a river rock. A weight settles in my chest, stomach cartwheeling.

This is bad. This is *really* bad.

If Doc and I are caught, we're done for. The *Cut* is done for. *Who knows what I'll give up under interrogation?*

"If they had evidence, they would've killed the both of you already. But they don't. We've been throwing him off your trail. The doctor's too. I told Officer Saylor I haven't seen anything."

My throat tightens. "Thank you."

"Keep your thanks, *Officer*," she seethes. "It's not you I'm protecting. We need your medicine. Don't mistake my rationality for generosity. We all know what you really are."

I open my mouth to argue, but decide against it. I can't blame her for hating me—nor can I tell her where my loyalties truly lie. I nod, pick up my tray, and turn around to walk away.

And when I do, Saylor is staring right at me.

My face pales. Well, shit.

I expect him to stand up and march at me—but all he does is point to his nose with a smirk.

I sure as hell didn't heed his warning.

I avert my gaze and beeline toward the table where Marty sits. Dinner is a rubbery slice of gray mystery meat, an expired can of shriveled sardines, and a slice of bread so stale I worry I might lose a tooth. I trade my meat and fish for Marty's bread. I'll toss and turn with hunger pains all night, but I'm committed to my new identity as a vegetarian. I'm almost done eating and ready to sneak over to Raven's cabin when a loud crack echoes through the cafeteria.

I scour the room for the source of the noise, settling on Lockley, the fallen mop on the ground, and the spilled cup of water staining Saylor's shirt.

Everyone falls silent. Lockley coughs violently, clutching his chest, eyes squeezed shut as he brings an elbow to his mouth.

He's having another episode.

"What the hell is wrong with you?" Saylor rises to his feet, shaking excess drops off his hands. He glares at Lockley. "Care to explain why I'm wearing my drink?"

Lockley grabs the edge of the table and hunches over, still coughing.

"What, too busy hacking up a lung to say sorry?" Saylor scoffs. "Disgusting."

Lockley can't answer.

"You got water in your ears too?" Saylor grits his teeth. "Get up and clean this mess. I don't have all day here."

Lockley holds up a hand. He's on his knees now, still fighting to breathe.

Shit. This is bad. I haven't seen him cough like this before.

"He needs help," Marty whispers.

He stands up, but I yank him back down. "Don't."

"But—"

"If he tries anything, I'll handle it."

A ring of curious Guards forms around the scene, waiting to see it play out. We join. Lockley's wheezing heavily now, eyes tight as he tries to inhale.

"Get up before I lose my patience. And trust me..." Saylor crouches down, arms balanced on his knees. "You *really* don't wanna see that."

"Give me a damn minute, *asshole*," Lockley hisses between coughs.

The Guards flinch. Saylor freezes.

Lockley finally manages to catch a breath, rubbing his throat in discomfort —just as Saylor kicks him backward.

He digs his knee into Lockley's chest. He swings an arm back, but I grab it before the punch can land. "That's enough."

Saylor snaps his head back. "What did you just say?"

"I said that's *enough*. He can't do his job if you keep pestering him."

"This prisoner disrespected me, Beck." Saylor rises to his feet, arms crossed. "If we let them get away with that kind of behavior, they'll keep stepping out of line. Causing problems for the rest of us. And now..." Saylor walks closer. "Seems like you're doing just that."

"You're no Supervisor. I don't have to listen to you."

He grabs my collar and pushes me against the wall. "Say that again, Beck. I dare you."

I chuckle, slowing down each word. "I don't have to listen to you."

I ready myself for another brawl, but to my surprise, Saylor doesn't hit me. He *laughs*. "I know what this is all about."

I blink.

"You've got a soft spot for Wheezy over there, don't you? Not to mention his little friend. The girl with the ribbon."

It feels like my blood is freezing over.

"Don't think I haven't noticed you and Dawson talking to them." Saylor glances at Marty and lowers his voice. "You're not supposed to have soft spots for prisoners, Beck."

"I don't."

"Why else would you intervene? You're not a sympathizer, are you?" He leans in. "That would make you a filthy traitor, just like the rest of them."

I swallow the knot forming in my throat.

This is why he's picking on Lockley. Because I put my damn nose where it doesn't belong, and he's regaining the upper hand. He's already seen me interact with the Gamblers. With Raven. *He's suspicious of me.*

It's like Gina said. If he had real evidence about where my sympathies lie, I'd already be turned in. And dead. But if I crack under his pressure— if I confirm his suspicions—he's killing two birds with one stone. He'll get me out of his way, *and* he'll be able to turn in a traitor.

Lucky him.

"I'm not a sympathizer," I hiss.

"Oh really?" Saylor tilts his head. "So you wouldn't care if anything... unfortunate happened to him?"

Marty's eyes widen. It takes strength I barely have to keep mine from doing the same.

"You know what? I would."

His brows furrow.

"Because every time you harass one of *them*, you're making it harder to do *my* job. All we're here to do is make sure these prisoners work, but you insist on throwing your little tantrums and holding up the dinner line. And I'm sick of it. So cut it the hell out."

"Or what? Complain about it to our Supervisors, and they'll think you're a sympathizer." He leans even closer, pressing his arm firmer against my neck. "Especially with that little girlfriend of yours."

My jaw flexes. "I don't know what you're talking about."

He lowers his voice so the others can't hear. "I know you helped her after that *accident*. We saw you carrying her back to her cabin."

A heat boils in my gut. *Keep the peace. Keep the peace.*

"It'd be a real shame if another accident were to happen. Wouldn't it, Beck?"

My teeth knit together. "Stay away from her, or I swear to God I'll kill you."

Saylor laughs. "Is that a threat?"

"It's a promise."

"That's adorable."

"I'll tell Valdez about the gasoline."

Saylor flinches. "What did you just say?"

"Your friends were right. I doubt the Captain would be happy to hear you cost him a week of labor from one of his most capable prisoners. Especially given your unique... *arrangement*."

His eye twitches. "Excuse me?"

"Forcing a prisoner to drink gasoline? That sounds like another murder attempt to me. Rumor has it you're already on thin ice with the Captain." My grin fades. "Can't get that promotion you're after if you're dead, can you?"

Saylor's jaw tightens. I smirk. *Two can play the blackmail game, Saylor.*

I expect another beating. Maybe I'll be the next Guard to get a fork in the throat. But all I get is one last push before he storms out of the cafeteria.

I'm still rubbing my neck when Marty wraps me in a tight hug. "Thanks, man."

My shoulders stiffen. *Thanks?* I almost question it, but then I realize what he means. *He's thanking me for protecting Lockley.*

I pat his arm. "Don't mention it."

"You're a good friend, Cedar."

Friend. My shoulders relax. *Am I really friends with a Guard?*

Guilt tightens my chest. *Am I really a good friend?*

Marty wants to be here as little as I do, and I've been planning an escape behind his back. If I leave him here, he'll be alone with Saylor. Maybe his new bunkmate will be even worse.

He's still a Guard, I remind myself. *You shouldn't care.*

But he's not like the others.

I hug him back. "You too."

Our nightly Cobra game is just as ruthless as ever.

Marty and Lockley get along surprisingly well, considering their opposite attitudes. The girls seem to like him too. Even Raven cracks a smile with him from time to time.

"Alright." Marty stands up after we finish our latest round. "I've gotta take a leak. I'll be back."

As soon as he's gone, I clear my throat. "I think we should tell him."

"Tell him what?" Lockley asks, gathering cards scattered about the floor.

"About the plan."

Everyone freezes.

Raven's voice is stern when she breaks the silence. "He's a Guard."

"He's just as desperate to get out as any of us. And he knows more about the way things work around here than I do. He'd have useful insight."

"No."

"He's a nice guy."

"Just because he's fun to play cards with every now and then doesn't mean he's any less Chaser."

"Guard."

"What's the difference?"

That hurts more than I want it to.

"I think Cedar has a point," Lockley says.

Raven lifts a brow. "What makes you say that?"

"We're committing treason just by playing stolen cards without Immunity. He could've easily turned us in for a reward by now for *several* broken rules, but he hasn't. And he's always trying to give me that damn inhaler of his." He looks down at his cards with a shrug. "I think it's worth considering."

"I like him," Jelly says. "He's a kind boy. Good manners."

"And he's good at Cobra," Fern adds.

"We've been stealing gasoline just fine, but it's about time we actually come up with a solid plan," I say. "We need something with dates and steps. And I think Marty could be the key to getting us on that delivery truck in November."

The Gamblers exchange glances, speaking silently with looks I can't read. Fern averts her gaze. Lockley scratches the back of his neck.

Jelly's brows slope downward a bit, almost pleading. "Don't you think it's time we—"

"Fine." Raven sighs. "We'll tell Marty."

Jelly sighs, giving me an apologetic smile.

Before I have time to question it, Marty returns, rubbing his hands together. "What'd I miss?"

I walk over to the old rug with a smirk. "There's something we need to show you."

Sometime past midnight, I'm washing my face at a communal bathroom sink when I realize I'm not alone.

The faucet next to me turns on with a creak. I jump back with a start.

Saylor splashes water over his face with a chuckle. "Don't worry, Beck. No need to be frightened. Just washing up."

Past curfew? I want to add, but that'd incriminate me too.

"By the way..." He brings more water to his face. "I told Captain Valdez about the gasoline incident myself."

A chill runs through me.

"Risky business, I know. But I didn't want you to have a hold over me or anything like that. And thank God I did."

He shuts off the water and turns to face me, like we're friends chatting about the weather.

"He gave me a pat on the back. Said if I keep up the good work—honoring the Nightjade Order with integrity—he'll put me in line to get bumped up to Supervisor. *Supervisor*, Beck." He dries his face on a towel. "One more display of loyalty, and I'll be in charge of you. All of you, really."

My face pales. Saylor whispers in my ear as he walks past. "You'll regret getting in my way, Beck. You should have listened."

With that, he walks back to his cabin, whistling cheerfully all the way.

Thursday, October 20

♪ SWEET HEAT LIGHTNING - GREGORY ALAN ISAKOV ♪

You start to lose your sense of smell after a while.

All I know is smoke. It's in my hair. My mouth. My clothes. My lungs. Breathing feels less automatic than it used to. I miss not having to think about it. Now every inhalation has a weight to it.

I spend most of my time with Doc in secret. We've been more careful since Valdez announced the investigation. Until that dies down, our rounds are strictly reserved for necessary visits. I've also started taking over Jelly's shifts when I'm stationed on Dig to give Fern and the others a break. Luckily, Saylor's rarely out by the Graves, since he's still blackmailing Stokes to give him the good shifts. He's not around to see me work.

They don't tell you that generosity can be just as addictive as control. It's annoying, really, because I feel guilty covering Jelly's shifts without helping the other prisoners too.

An older woman named Claire, who's too frail to meet her daily quota when she's assigned to dig. To help her avoid extermination, I finish up her shifts when she gets tired.

A young boy named Wilbur who coughs almost as bad as Lockley. He gets tired too.

A man named Albert who gets migraines.

Prisoners faint. They get sick. They break down crying, because they miss their families and the lives they left behind, and every day they watch another friend collapse. They can't take it anymore.

So I pick up their shovels with little more than a nod.

I hardly get any sleep. All my time is spent with Doc, working on the escape plan, or digging late into the night.

Raven says I obsess over it—digging. Sometimes I think it's the only thing keeping me sane here. Saylor is proof of what happens when you don't have a purpose in a place like this.

Some of the other Guards have commented on my digging. I tell them it's my strategy for earning brownie points with the Supervisors. If the prisoners can't work, it's more efficient for me to pick up the slack and let them recover. They usually shrug and move on. They don't care enough to think too hard about it.

It's exhausting, but it gives me time to think—and a way to stall my sleep. The nightmares get worse every day. Wearing myself out is the only thing that helps, at least a bit.

All this digging makes me thankful my dad taught me to use a shovel early on. I know how to work hard and ration my energy. The hardened calluses on my palms protect me from daily blisters. They are my armor.

I never thought I'd yearn for my chores back home. I'd turn compost forever if it meant getting away from this sand. This heat. This emptiness. I miss being in the garden, surrounded by so many green things. Sunflowers and snapdragons. Blueberry bushes and tomato plants. Twirling vines of squash with sweet-smelling blossoms. The ripe, wine-like stench of compost that used to make me dizzy. Even that's better than the reek of ash and burning bodies and rotting flesh.

Now, there is no green. There is only desert as far as the eye can see.

This is not the endlessness I wished for.

Sometimes I pretend my dad is behind me as I work, watching me with his arms crossed. When I start to feel myself slouching, I hear him tell me to fix my posture and save myself the back pain later. When I notice I'm holding my breath while caught in long stretches of thought, I hear him tell me to breathe so I don't get lightheaded.

He tells me to do better. To stop slacking and focus, because I have things to do.

One thing at a time, Aaron.

It's the Friday before Evaluation. October in New Mexico without shade is cruelty. It's torrid and thick and it feels like wading through half-melted candle wax. I feel that way too. Like I'm melting. My brain is viscous. I wonder if it's seeping into the dry pores of my skull. I can hardly think straight through the ache.

All the prisoners of today's group were able to get work done on their own, but I still helped anyway. Our quota is almost met. Then I can lie down and take a quick nap before dinner.

Almost there, I tell myself, shouting over the screaming in my joints and muscles. *Just a few more digs.*

Someone faints.

The prisoners gasp. A few drop their shovels and rush to the man's side. I do the same.

I crouch and feel for a pulse. It's fast and he's sweating pools. I lean back on my heels with a sigh. "Heatstroke."

"Will he be alright?" A young woman asks.

"With lots of water and a cool place to rest, he will be."

"You're not going to Correct him, are you?" a young boy asks. He could be Fern's age, maybe thirteen. I've seen him around. I think the man who fainted is his dad.

"Why would I Correct him?" I ask.

"He won't be able to finish his work," the boy says.

I exhale shakily, trying to stay calm. I lower my voice. "Do you know Raven?"

"Everyone knows Raven."

"Listen carefully. You're gonna take your dad back to your cabin and get him comfortable in his bed. Then you're going to find Raven and ask for Doc."

"How do you—"

"Don't worry about it."

He nods, and he listens.

My muscles feel like someone shredded them with a fork. My spine burns. My bones feel malleable. A deep throb pounds my head and the back of my neck. My throat is dry and it's only a matter of time before I throw up the cold oatmeal I had for lunch.

I pick up a shovel anyway.

It's dark by the time I'm done.

I don't care that I missed dinner. All I can think about is falling into bed, but I can't make it that far. I can barely walk. I nearly vomit twice on the way to Raven's cabin. It's closer than mine. I haven't been eating enough lately to do anything but dry heave.

I knock on her door and collapse on the porch.

I'm barely awake when Raven helps me inside.

I'm delirious and so numb to the pain that all I can think about is how nice it feels to touch something that isn't the handle of a shovel or gritty sand. The rust-colored fabric of the baggy shirt she wears as she brings my arm around her shoulder. The softness of her fingertips wrapped around my wrist. Her other hand on my waist.

The light is off. Her hair is down. She must have been sleeping.

"Where's Doc?" I manage.

She eases me into her bed. "Helping your friend from earlier."

"And everyone else?"

"Playing cards in another cabin. Allegedly."

Her words are quicker than usual. Sharper. I can't tell if she's tired or angry.

She lights a fire and gets some water boiling. "You're an idiot, Beck."

"Thank you."

She returns to my side, feeling my forehead with her knuckles. "You're hot."

"I know."

"I'm serious." She takes off my shoes. My eyes flutter in a fight to stay open. "This is so incredibly stupid."

I don't have the energy to glare. My words come out slurred. "I was just trying to help, alright?"

"And you'll get yourself killed, pushing your limits like this." She sighs. "You can't help others if you never help yourself either. It's impossible to be entirely selfless. Some selfishness is a good thing."

The kettle whistles. She pours water into a mug and sets it on the counter to cool, then returns to the bed. She starts taking off my socks. "Now *I'm* going to have to pick up Jelly's shift tomorrow."

"I can do it if I'm on Dig—"

"You're not doing anything tomorrow," she interrupts. "You should go to the infirmary. Your Supervisor will let you off the hook tomorrow if you've got a note."

"No." I shake my head and regret it instantly. I bring a hand to my forehead in a futile attempt to stabilize the pounding. "They'd lose their shit if they learned I got sick from covering for prisoners."

"Plenty of Guards get heat exhaustion just from standing around alone. The desert's brutal to everyone."

"No."

"Cedar—"

"Please." I exhale painfully. "Just let me stay."

She opens her mouth to argue, then shuts it with a sigh. "Fine."

She walks over to a cabinet and retrieves a jar of something orange. "Doc has this famous beeswax and olive oil salve. An old family recipe dating back to the Yesterdays, actually. He can't make it without bribing the delivery drivers to bring him spices. Cloves, cinnamon, nutmeg, ginger. Some other stuff I can't remember." She sits down on the bed again and opens the jar. "Take off your shirt."

"So soon? At least take me to dinner first."

She frowns. "Just do it."

"Alright, alright." Slowly, I force myself upright with a grimace. I do as she says.

She pauses. I look down to see what she's staring at, worried I have dried vomit on my neck or something. I don't.

She clears her throat and maneuvers behind me, sitting cross-legged to apply the salve on my back. Her hands have been calloused by her time here, but they're still soft. It feels nice. I let my head hang low and close my eyes. My breathing slows. The salve really does smell good. Like cinnamon.

It burns a little, but not like a desert sun or the fires of a furnace. It's just... warm.

"It burns," I note, surprised I manage to get any words out at all with the way my head is spinning. I can feel myself drifting closer and closer to unconsciousness.

"Sorry."

"It's... a good burn."

Raven nods. "Sometimes I forget about that."

"Hm?"

"That there are good burns." She moves to kneel in front of me now, massaging my wrist instead. "Sunbathing by the pool. Dry lightning. Wildfires clearing out forests for new growth. Hot tea." She pauses, staring at my arms. She lifts up the jar of salve. "Cinnamon."

We stare at each other. The fire cracks across the room, casting flickering shadows across her face. I break the silence with a smirk. "I can't imagine you by a pool."

She glares. "Well don't."

"Not like that. I mean... elsewhere."

She closes the salve and sets it aside. The water is cool now, so she helps me take a few sips. "I did have a pool. At my old house."

I nod, falling back so my head is on the pillow again. The Cut has a pool. It was there when Noriko found it. But I could never really swim in it. It wasn't maintained. It was filled with mosquito larvae and we didn't see the point in cleaning it out when there was a beautiful pond a short walk away from our cabin.

I look up at Raven. "I had a pond."

She sits next to me, leaning against the wall with her knees tucked into her chest. "Were there frogs?"

"A whole army of them."

She leans her head in her hand. "Tell me more about this pond."

"The duckweed looked like butter. Like when you leave a dirty pot to soak and all the cooking grease floats to the top."

"Butter?" She chuckles. "Did it taste like butter too?"

"No." I close my eyes. I can see the pond so clearly in my head. "The water tasted like death."

Not this death. Lily's death, I want to say. But I'm too tired to explain what it means, so I don't.

It tasted like sugar and life and mud. Like tadpoles hatching and growing legs and dying as old, croaking bullfrogs, over and over again. It was a fountain of youth.

And I'll probably never see it again.

I can feel my throat burning—not a good burn. Like I might start crying if I say another word. So I turn on my side and stop fighting sleep.

"You don't have to stay," I mutter, barely awake. I'm boiling, but I still feel so cold.

"You're in my bed, Beck."

"Kick me out."

"I'm not going to do that."

My teeth are chattering now. *Chills*. "Take Lockley's. He doesn't need one."

"You're cold."

"*You're* cold."

"Okay, you're clearly losing it." She climbs under the blanket with me. "Is this warmer?"

I nod.

"Raven?"

"Hm?"

"Can I imagine you by a pool now?"

I can practically feel her trying not to grin behind me. "Alright."

"Thanks."

"Anytime."

I don't, though it's nice to know I can.

Every cell in my body feels heavy. Sleep doesn't come as easy as I thought it would. I'm still in so much pain. Hot and shivering all at once. Miserable.

But she wraps her arms around me, and things feel less not-okay.

Just another observation.

I think back to what Officer Gilbert said about being sharp. About everything Finch said this place would help me become.

I don't feel sharp.

I just feel jagged.

I dream of catching on fire from the lungs out. I wake in the middle of the night, plastered in sweat and curled around Raven.

I head out to the back porch and sit on the steps. It's cool out here in the dark. There's just enough moonlight for me to see the desert through the fence. If I focus on the mountain, the thin wires blur to the point where I can't even see them. Only the taunting shadow of a rock in the distance, so far out of reach.

From here, even the desert looks beautiful in comparison to the bleak, boot-worn pathways of dust that encircle every building. Beyond the fence, there are rocks and tufts of dead grass and brittle shrubs. The night is flavored purple. The stars are flecks of paint, like someone ran their finger across the bristles of a giant brush.

A crack of dry lightning.

It paints the landscape in blinding radiance before dissipating as quickly as it arrived. For a moment, it almost felt like day. It leaves behind a slowly fading violet glow, like a new sunset I get to watch all over again.

"There's a tragedy to dry lightning, I think."

I don't realize Raven's standing behind me until she takes a seat at my right. I turn back to watch another flash, followed by a soft roll of thunder.

She sighs. "How can something so beautiful be so fleeting?"

"Most beautiful things are," I say. "Cactus blossoms. Spots on a fawn's coat. Autumn leaves." I watch another strike paint the sky pink. "Sunsets."

"I've always loved the sunsets out here. I almost feel guilty for finding them beautiful. Like I should hate them." She smiles tiredly. "I love the dry lightning even more. It's like a second sunset, you know?"

There's a long but comfortable silence as we watch the sky shift, as though it can't decide between night and daybreak.

"Cedar?"

"Hm?"

"I've been meaning to ask you something."

"Go for it."

"That's not your real name, is it?"

I shrug, tracing circles in the dirt coating the porch planks. "What makes you say that?"

"If you grew up Unseen, you were debugged when you were small. There's no way you'd get through training without some sort of new tracker. A false identity."

I puff out a sigh with my bottom lip, shaking my head. She's annoyingly smart.

"What is it, then?" she asks. "Your real name?"

"I can't tell you that."

"Do you trust me?"

I try to read her. It's not easy in this darkness—let alone during the day. But in another flash of dry lightning, I catch a glimpse of her eyes. They hold on to mine long after the light fades away. "I think so."

She nods. "Good."

"Do you trust me?"

She waits for another flash to illuminate my features. "I think so."

My voice lowers. "I can tell you my middle name, if you'd like."

She's closer than I thought she was. I don't know why it makes me nervous, but I clear my throat and stare back at the lightning instead, placing a hand on my chest. "I too was named after a bird."

She smirks. "Oh really?"

"Lark."

"It's nice."

"My dad advocated for that one."

"Why'd he like it?"

"*A lark is a songbird, son. A symbol of daybreak,*" I say in Dad's voice. "*Bring the morning with you. Always bring the morning with you.*"

"Bring the morning with you?" Raven snickers. "What does that mean?"

"That's just my dad. Cryptic. Often poetic. Obsessed with books. Aggressively educational."

I omit some truth in that sentence. I know exactly what it means. It just hurts too much to talk about it.

I can hear his voice so clearly in my head. *"It's never too late to start over and be good."*

My chest aches. Like someone's scooped out parts of me with a spoon, leaving a cavity where my lungs should be. I never thought I'd want to hear those words again so badly.

And to think I hated them, once.

If he saw the person I've become—if he realized how terribly I've failed him—I don't think it'd be so easy for him to say them again.

"He sounds lovely," Raven says.

"He is." I lean my head back to stare through the slats in the awning, propped up on my elbows. *Some apples fall around the goddamn world.*

"For the record, I *wasn't* named after a bird."

I lift a brow. "You weren't?"

"Well—yes and no." She sighs. "Nevermind. It's stupid."

"Now I'm curious."

"I'll have you know it wasn't my idea."

"A given."

"It was my father's." She lets out a tired, one-note chuckle. "We were named after Nightjade."

Of course. Her dad is an Agent, after all.

"Well, Jade came first. I was a surprise, I think. My name was meant to compliment hers. We were supposed to be two halves of the same, perfect whole." She shakes her head, staring at her palms. "We both know how that turned out."

"I don't think you were named after Nightjade, then."

She raises a brow.

"*You* were named a beautiful bird with wings like night." I grin, but it fades when I lower my voice. "You are not your father, Raven."

"And you are lovely."

Heat flurries in my chest. No one's ever called me that before.

She thinks about it for a while, narrowing her eyes at the horizon. "Nightfall and daybreak." She smiles at the lightning. "We make an interesting pair."

I look to the sky. "We do indeed."

We sit in comfortable quiet, watching the distant storm make night feel like day. After a while, despite the beauty of the horizon beyond the fence, I discover how much I prefer to look at her instead.

I realize I might like to kiss her.

I've never felt like kissing someone before. Maybe it wouldn't be so terrible to lean closer and discover what that kind of nearness feels like. A small comfort in a world of discomfort. Something sublimely brief in a place of slowly rotting vultures. One beautiful, fleeting moment.

Not because it means anything. *Just another observation.*

"Ooh, lightning!"

Fern's voice shatters the silence. We turn our heads with a start. I'm not sure why Raven moves an inch away from me as Jelly and her younger sister join us on the porch.

Fern sits between us while Jelly takes the spot on my left with a sigh. "I love nights like these."

"There's 300 million volts of electricity in a single flash of lightning. *Nights like these* could kill you if they wanted to." Lockley walks out too. To my surprise, Marty is with him. He gives me a wave.

Jelly sighs. "What did I tell you about attitude, Lock?"

"I'm just saying." He raises his hands in innocence. "That's exactly 375 times worse than that fence right there. Makes 8,000 volts seem like nothing."

Jelly gives him a look.

"Alright, fine. It's pretty." Lockley nudges my shoulder. "Glad to see you're not dead. This guy came to check in on you a while back."

Marty pats my back as he and Lockley take a seat behind us. "Glad you're okay, man."

I give him a smile.

"If you two keep breaking curfew like this, someone will notice." Jelly shakes her head. "It's dangerous. Especially with the investigation."

I lean closer. "But you love our company, don't you?"

She rubs my hair.

"How do you know it's 8,000 volts, anyway?" I ask Lockley.

"I've been here a long time, buddy." He leans back against his elbows. "I've talked with a tech or two. As an annoying and inquisitive child, I'll admit. But they told me some good stuff."

"Hush," Jelly says. "You're ruining the ambiance."

"Ambiance?"

She swats his knee. He laughs.

The quiet is music. The thunder is gentle. The lightning feels like medicine, and we take it all in together. Sunset after sunset after sunset.

This is rebellion.

Saturday, October 22

There is something ruthless about today's sun.

I've felt brutal heat before. Hell, I haven't known a day without it for months. But today on Dig, we may as well be working in the furnace.

My mouth is dry and tastes like rocks. I down the last few drops of water from my canteen, but they do little to quench my thirst. A waste. I should have rationed it out better, but the desert makes anyone desperate. It brings out the fool in all of us.

I try to remain steady as I stand with my hand as a visor, watching the prisoners work. The nameless Guard to my side does the same, but we observe for different reasons. Where he's scoping for trouble, I'm keeping an eye out for exhaustion.

Today, I find it in her.

I don't think I've ever seen Raven look so worn down. Dirt sticks to her glistening skin, slick with sweat. I watch her close her eyes, wiping the back of her hand across her forehead with a deep, trembling sigh. She swallows dryly. She pulls out her canteen and tries downing some water. It's empty.

All she can do is stare at it, unblinking. Her knees buckle. She looks like she might pass out.

I glance to my side. The Guard stationed with me is zoning out, staring in the other direction. I can tell the heat is getting to him too. He doesn't notice when I jog up to Raven's side.

"Hey." I place my hands on her waist to steady her. She grabs my arms like a lifeline. Her lips are cracked with lines of red. "You okay?"

She nods. "I'm fine."

I grit my teeth. "Raven..."

She closes her eyes. Her head moves like she's trying to shake it, but all she can do is let it fall into my chest. She clutches the fabric of my shirt to stay upright. "I'm gonna be sick."

My heart sinks. She's been picking up too many of Jelly's shifts. *She needs water.*

Instinctively, I reach for my canteen, only to remember it's just as empty as hers.

"Can you stand on your own?" I whisper.

"Yes," she mutters.

I step back and fold my arms, clearing my throat and raising my voice so everyone can hear. "What did you just say to me?"

The prisoners pause. The other Guard lifts his head up.

"What the hell are you doing?" Raven hisses under her breath.

I tilt my head. "Being defiant again, I see?"

She studies me for a moment, then sighs, speaking louder to play along. "I'm not being *defiant*, Officer. I'm asking for water."

"Water?" I scoff. "You filled your canteen this morning, didn't you?"

"Yes."

"Then what's the problem?"

She takes the container and turns it over. "It's *empty.*"

"We've still got another hour until lunch. Not my problem you didn't ration it out properly."

"It hasn't been this hot in weeks, and you know it. If you want us to keep working, we need a refill break. Unless you'd rather see us die of heatstroke."

"A refill break?" I force a bitter chuckle. "I think it's time we have a little chat with the *Captain* about your attitude."

I grab her arm and steer her away from her grave. Her shoulders relax a little. What I disguise as firmness is a desperate attempt to keep her upright.

"I'll be back," I say to the other Guard.

He salutes without giving me so much as a glance. He's too tired to give a shit.

The other prisoners roll their eyes. Some nod. Others glare. They know I've done this before with a few of them when they need a break. It's my way of sneaking them to the good water fountains, when Guards are too busy with their shifts to notice.

We make it to the fountain outside the Archives. I check to make sure the coast is clear—and she falls onto it. She gulps the water down like she's been digging for days without it, not hours. I stand guard as she drinks her fill.

She steps away with a sigh, wiping her mouth with the back of her hand. "God, that's nice."

"Feeling better?"

She takes a deep, shaking breath. "My muscles are still on fire, but yeah. Better."

She fills up her canteen. I do the same, then lean against the fountain, gesturing toward her shirt. The front of it is stained with water. "You've got a little…"

"What?" She looks down.

I take the opportunity to flick her nose.

She gawks at me, but she's grinning from ear to ear. "You asshole!"

I sip from my canteen, laughing when she hits my shoulder playfully. Water dribbles onto my shirt. I frown at it. "Now look what you've done."

Then it's *my* nose getting flicked. She crosses her arms. "Now we're even."

There it is again. That smile. God, I like that smile. It's like a knife to the chest. A rare sip of water in a desert so far from any river or lake. Wound and medicine, wrapped into one.

I'm afraid to think about the things I'd do to keep it on her face.

I wonder if she knows that. *I hope she knows that.*

"You could have come out here to fill your canteen by yourself, you know," she says. "We didn't have to pull that stunt."

"The others would have seen me giving you water."

"You've come up with distractions before. I'm sure you could have managed."

"Probably. But I assumed you could use a break too."

She suppresses a grin. "If I didn't know any better, I'd think you *wanted* to be alone with me, Officer Beck."

"And what if I do?"

Raven was teasing, but I'm dead serious.

She doesn't know what to say.

We stare at each other for a while, neither of us wanting to move. We'll have to go back eventually, but no one's out here. What's the harm in just one more minute? In inching just a bit closer?

She looks down at my arm. Her finger traces the scar cutting through it, a river in my skin. "Thank you."

I hide my own grin. "For what?"

She looks up again. "For being here."

Her smile fades, but I can't bring myself to mind. Because she's looking right at me, and I like her eyes just as much. Then it's her mouth I'm staring at.

Until something moves from the corner of my eye.

I straighten my posture. She jumps away from me like I'm on fire, standing with her arms behind her back as two prisoners approach with buckets and sponges. My brows crease. *What are they doing?*

One of them nods toward me. "Morning, Officer. Mind if we get by?"

I nod and step aside to let the pair walk up the porch. They dip their sponges in soapy water and start scrubbing the walls.

My eyes widen when I realize what this is about. Evaluation is on the 24th. *That's two days away.*

Agents are coming.

I look around as more prisoners on cleaning duty walk out of the cafeteria and down the main dirt path, buckets and sponges in hand. Now that they're done handling the aftermath of breakfast, they'll probably be polishing up as many of the important buildings as they can before lunch. I have no idea when the Agents are getting here, but this tells me it's sometime soon.

My hands curl into fists. It's almost humorous. Like they can somehow scrub away the horrors that take place here. The truth is, if the Agents dug around and upturned this prison's stones, I don't think they'd give a damn about what they'd uncover.

They can clean the walls all they want—but no amount of soap will scrape the ashes from our lungs.

"We should go back soon," I mutter. "If they're having all these prisoners come out to clean, more Guards are sure to follow."

Raven nods.

We start walking back. I grab her arm again to solidify our act, though my grip is gentle. Sure enough, the Guards who'd been supervising cleaning duty in the cafeteria file out with the last of the prisoners, ready to watch them out here instead. They don't pay us any mind.

A shadow passes over us.

I glance upward, expecting a turkey vulture—but what I see instead makes me stop in my tracks.

It's small, no bigger than a leaf. Bright orange and striped black like the tigers I saw in our wildlife encyclopedias back home. It flutters like paper bending in the wind, dancing and curling in figure eights.

A damn monarch butterfly.

My lips part. *What the hell is that doing all the way out here?*

Another one follows close behind.

Then another.

And another.

Before I can blink, there's ten of them. Dozens. *Hundreds* of monarchs, swarming together as one cloud of orange and black. But this cloud is alive, and it's unlike anything I've ever seen.

No—that's a lie. The memory floods back to me. I've seen them migrate like this before, once when I was younger. Right after my dad took me to the Cut, when I was still too afraid of him to speak. He took me out to that pond in the woods, slick with duckweed, where he told me to watch and wait.

He crouched behind a boulder with me, just as silent as I was.

And then the kaleidoscope arrived.

It was like they came out of nowhere. That's what I thought, back then. That the orange leaves breathing and dancing on the trees were some kind of magic, and the man smiling next to me must have been the one to cast the spell. I thought he brought them there just for me.

For the first time since he took me from my mother, I smiled—and I laughed.

I stretched out my arms and spun in circles and giggled until my belly ached. Dad did just the same. He scooped me up and lifted me on his shoulders so I could reach for them. One landed on my finger. Another on my nose. Dad called it a sign of good luck.

But that was back home. In Washington, not New Mexico. A forest. Not a desert.

These monarchs don't stop. There are no trees to land on, no nectar to eat, no water to quench their thirst. This isn't their final destination.

Everyone around us stops what they're doing. Even the Guards pause to study the kaleidoscope in awe, pointing with their eyes wide. The insects are silent, but their audience erupts with sound. Most of the prisoners gasp. Some of them laugh. A few fall to their knees and sob.

"I haven't seen a butterfly in ten years," an older woman cries—but she's grinning from ear to ear.

"This is..." Raven shouts over the gasps.

"Impossible?"

She nods.

I almost agree, but then I remember what Dad told me about monarchs so long ago. They migrate south in the fall and north in the spring. It's October. It's not uncommon for them to travel through New Mexico this time of year, even out here. They are simply passing through on their way to greener places.

But they tend to follow riparian zones. They can't fly over a truly barren desert for long stretches of time. They need food and water to stay alive and travel such long distances, especially out here.

There has to be water somewhere.

Beyond the fence, farther than the eye can see, there has to be a river.

I can't help but wonder where they came from. Their story. Their path. Maybe they've known the milkweed that took Gooseberry. That's the only plant they deem acceptable for laying eggs and feeding their young.

And maybe people are just the same. We all come and go and change and grow into different versions of ourselves. Lily was right. *Dad* was right. Every day we are something new. Every moment shapes us into something else, down to the very second.

I'm not sure why I feel like crying when I stare up at the cloud of breathing fire above us, but I'm smiling at the same time.

I think about how impossible it seems that one tiny worm can morph into something entirely different. That a mere insect can travel across an entire continent with wings it wasn't even born with.

What a beautiful way to bring the morning with you.

"This has never happened before," an older Guard mutters. His uniform is gray like stone. He's been here a long time.

My grin only grows.

They call the Tombs inescapable. They say no prisoner has ventured beyond this fence alive. But no one's tried what the Gamblers and I are planning, either.

If this can happen, maybe something else can, too.

Something flutters in my chest. Like I've swallowed one of the monarchs above me and it's trying to get out.

Hope. For the first time in a long time, I feel it.

I scan the crowd for Raven. She stands in the center, staring up at the butterflies like they're magic. The shadows falling over her face bend like a river, and she is smiling. While everyone is busy screaming and laughing and crying and pointing at the monarchs, I run up to her and cup her face in my hands. "Raven."

"Are you seeing this?" She laughs, meeting my hands with her own.

"There's water nearby. There has to be." I can hardly hear myself over the commotion, but her eyes widen. "Out there, where we can't see it. Somewhere close."

"They can't survive without water..."

I whisper in her ear. "If there's a river nearby... we can get more people out."

She smiles up at me like she already knows what I'm thinking. Beyond those hills, close to the mountains where the vegetation begins to cluster nearer together, and the tufts of grass turn from brown to green, there must be a source we can use. The delivery trucks can only fit a few of us. But with a river, we don't have to worry about getting back to civilization so fast. We can go farther than we thought and keep more people hydrated and fed.

"Maybe we can think beyond the delivery truck," I mutter. "Do something bigger."

Behind her eyes, I see those gears turning. She knows exactly what I'm thinking.

And there it is again. The urge to move closer.

My hands are still on her face. Her fingers still clutch mine. In the center of this chaos, everyone is too busy looking up to see how close we are.

God, I want to kiss her.

But then the look on her face shifts. Whatever trance the realization put us in sputters out. The glint of hope in her eyes is exchanged for something different—something like guilt.

"Cedar?"

"Yeah?"

"I need to—"

"What's the meaning of this?"

The Captain's bark cuts through the excitement. We pull apart. The crowd of onlookers stills. Everyone goes silent.

He walks down the dirt path, approaching in slow, rigid footsteps. We part around him as he paces to the center, rotating to scorch each of us with his scowl. A few Supervisors trail behind him.

"How long have you all been standing out here!"

The last straggler from the cloud flutters around the Captain's face. He shoos the butterfly away. No one says a word.

"Someone answer me," he snaps.

A Guard clears their throat. "Only about ten minutes or so, sir."

"And there's... what, twenty of you?"

The Guard nods.

"Multiply ten minutes by twenty, and it doesn't seem so small anymore, does it?" Valdez growls. "And all to observe a few insects? You should be ashamed of yourselves."

A shudder bleeds through me. The Supervisors shake their heads.

"Correction is the only fair treatment I see for your wastefulness," the Captain spits at the prisoners. "None of you may leave until your lesson is learned."

My stomach lurches. I turn to Raven, who can't look me in the eye. Her hands shake.

She's already been Corrected before.

And because of me, she'll go through it again.

Valdez whispers his command into the ear of a Supervisor. She nods, gesturing for the first prisoner to follow her into the warehouse, where Saylor nearly killed Raven with that gasoline.

When the prisoner emerges, there are tears streaming down his cheeks and bandages on his hands. At least he's walking upright.

I am just like them, but I'm spared.

When it's Raven's turn, it takes every ounce of strength I have to stay still. My muscles scream to move forward. To do something to intervene or volunteer to take her place. But I can't do any of that without putting our operation in danger. Putting the entire Unseen in danger.

I have to stand here and do nothing while they hurt her for my mistake.

I could have gone back for water myself. I could have stepped away to fill my own canteen and figured out some distraction to give her sips in secret. But I was selfish. I wanted those moments alone with her.

I wanted to see her smile.

And when she walks out of the building, palms wrapped in bandages stained red, I have to pretend that I don't care. That I don't see the gashes peeking out, so clearly carved into her skin by a blade. That I don't want to plunge a Nightjade syringe into the neck of every Guard who played a part in doing this to her. To all of them.

But that would make me worthy of an injection too.

I walk by her side and escort her back to our station. I clench and uncurl my fists so many times there are lines in my own palms, crescents of tension. I can't bring myself to look her in the eye.

I force my voice to remain steady. "What did they do to you?"

"Ten minutes wasted." She keeps her gaze straight ahead. "We paid for each one."

And when we get back to the Graves, she wields her shovel anyway.

The vulture is all bones now.

I walk past it on my way to the cafeteria, every sunrise, every sunset. Its decay used to track my time here. Now that the rot has stopped, time moves slower than it used to. Maybe faster. I can't tell anymore.

I wonder how long it will be before the wind buries it in sand.

If I'm still around by then, I doubt I'll ever make it out of here.

I clutch my stomach as I walk to dinner in a futile attempt to soothe the growling. The hunger aches have only worsened since I cut out meat. I don't let it go to waste, though. I always bring my leftovers to Jelly.

Maybe I'll be bones soon too.

I make out the infirmary in the distance and think about paying Doc a quick visit before dinner. It's been a while since our last lesson. I'm getting restless, and I need to let him know what happened with those damn monarchs. We'll have plenty of new wounds to monitor. Raven's included.

But when I get closer, I freeze.

A crowd has formed around the building. Doc stands in the center with Saylor, Valdez, and the boy whose father I helped the other day. Bobby, I think his name was. Trembling, he hides behind Saylor with his gaze fixed to the dirt. His face is paler than the gray-white bricks of the infirmary.

I weave my way through the ring of onlooking Guards and prisoners, standing next to Marty when I find him. His eyes lock to the scene, unblinking.

"What's going on?" I whisper.

He doesn't say anything.

"Dr. Shelton," Valdez announces, hands folded behind his back. "It has come to our attention that you recently treated a prisoner for heatstroke. Is this true?"

My heart plummets.

What?

"I'm afraid I don't know what you are referring to, Captain." Doc's voice is eerily calm.

"Officer Saylor noticed some suspicious activity around the prisoner cabins. After conducting his own investigation, he stumbled across this young man, whose claims contrast deeply with your own."

A shiver snakes around my spine. *Was Saylor spying on me?*

"Officer Saylor gathered that you treated this young prisoner's father," Valdez continues. "Now if this boy is lying for the reward of extra rations he will receive, we will have to arrange Correction, of course. We will conduct a search of your person and the infirmary regardless, for caution's sake."

Doc's jaw feathers, but his voice remains unwavering. "I thought we didn't Correct children."

Valdez shrugs. "Only when necessary."

My hand flexes. *Keep the peace. Keep the peace.*

Saylor steps forward. "This prisoner claims you gave his father an elixir of water, ginger, salt, and... honey, was it?"

The boy nods, still shaking.

"I wasn't aware that we had ginger at this facility." Saylor says, pretending to be oblivious. "Were any of you?"

The crowd shakes their heads.

"From my knowledge, not even Captain Valdez has clearance to request special orders from quarterly deliveries. For security purposes, of course. But if this prisoner's claims are true, then clearly *someone* managed to breach these security measures. That's criminal enough—but to break this policy for the sake of comforting one tired prisoner?" Saylor shakes his head. "The Corps would find that unforgivable."

"Officer Saylor is correct," Valdez continues. "These offenses are unfor-givable."

My heartbeat falters. I can feel my lungs constrict, like some invisible serpent is coiling around them. *Unforgivable?*

"For the sake of a timely dinner, let's cut to the chase," Valdez says. "Our witness claims you have been treating prisoners under the table for years now. With supplies either taken from *our* infirmary, or smuggled through our fence by means of bribery. Do you have any idea how severely insulting these crimes are? To me? Your fellow Guards? The very Corps itself?"

"*Claims.*" Doc keeps his eyes pinned to the Captain's. "You have no evidence."

"Then we will find some." Valdez nods toward Saylor. "Search him."

Instinct nearly urges me forward when Saylor approaches Doc, but I force myself to stay put. Shoulders stiff, jaw set. *No one can know about your apprenticeship—for both your sakes.*

Saylor isn't gentle when he pats Doc down. He makes him remove his coat, and Saylor turns out his pockets. Miscellaneous first aid tools fall to the dirt. He checks the pockets of Doc's trousers with no luck.

"Take off your boots," Saylor demands.

With his stare unwavering, Doc removes one boot. Two.

Out tumbles a little glass vial the color of gold.

The crowd stills. Nothing moves but the shadows of circling vultures as Saylor slowly retrieves the vial. He holds it up against the sunset to inspect it, then offers it to Valdez. The Captain accepts the bottle and gives it a sniff. "Ginger."

A few Guards gasp. Some prisoners start crying. I can't let myself do either.

"It appears our witness is telling the truth after all." Valdez hands the vial back to Saylor. "You conducted that amputation, didn't you?"

Doc doesn't say a word.

"If you don't confess, we will have no choice but to interrogate your associates as well."

A murmur spreads through the crowd. Prisoners trade worried glances.

"We know you're quite fond of taking in wounded prisoners like strays," Saylor says. "Who knows? Maybe you even have a few *Guards* under your wing."

His eyes dart to mine.

A pallor washes over me. It takes all I have to remain upright—to take full breaths, even as the air feels like it's solidifying. I weave to the front of the crowd, trying to catch Doc's gaze, but he refuses to look at me. It's like I don't even exist.

His stare is cemented to Valdez when he finally speaks. "I am responsible for the amputation, and I work alone."

The captain's nose crinkles in disgust. "That's what I thought."

What are you doing? I want to scream. *Tell them it was me. All me.*

Why can't I say anything? Why can't I move? I want to do something—to rush forward and shout the truth until everyone knows that I'm the real one to blame. But my legs won't move. My mouth seals shut. Even my lungs are perfectly still as Valdez reaches into his pocket, pulling out a small white case. He opens it.

The Nightjade syringe glints like a diamond in the fading sunlight.

"Officer Saylor, would you mind doing the honors?"

A cruel half moon crawls up Saylor's face. He accepts the syringe without a word.

The world spins. My knees buckle. This can't be happening. *It can't be.*

The seconds take years. Every footstep echoes like the fire of a gun as Saylor walks closer, and closer, and closer.

"Wallace Avery Shelton, in accordance with the Nightjade Order and our honorable Presidency, you are hereby sentenced to extermination."

Please, I beg in silence. *Look at me.*

Doc closes his eyes.

The needle enters his neck, and he falls to the ground.

Someone wails. Guards clap. Saylor takes a bow. For his noble deed, he is rewarded a pat on the back and a vague promise of something better on his horizon.

All at once, the sounds melt together and drip to a stop. There is no hearing. No seeing. Only blurs of colors and shapes and textures as two prisoners carry his limp body away.

I want to cry. Scream. Tear my hair out. Fall to my knees and never get up again.

But I have a uniform to wear, and I cannot cry for a traitor.

In the middle of a sleep I thought would never arrive, a hand clamps over my mouth.

I smell the cigarette stench first. It's different from the smoke here.

My eyes open. It's too dark to see who's standing over my bed, or the shadowy figure accompanying them. But when I hear the gravel of his voice, I know.

"Rise and shine, Rusty."

Monday, October 23

♪ HAMMER SONG
- THE SENSATIONAL ALEX HARVEY BAND ♪

gent Finch and Officer Gilbert escort me out of my room and into the Archive building by the back of my shirt.

I thought I could have been dreaming, at first. Another nightmare, haunted by the Chaser who supervised my training and the Agent who sent me away. But when they yanked me out into the sticky night air, there was no mistaking it. *I'm still trapped in this damn desert.*

So what the hell are they doing here?

It's past midnight. They put me in a chair and turn on a sad, flickering excuse for a lamp. They lean against the desk, staring at me in silence until Finch finally speaks. "You never told me you were the Serpent's *nephew*."

I blink as the words sink in. *How does the Head of House know Walter?*

I glare. "It never came up."

He peels away from the desk, picking up a glass paperweight and tossing it back and forth. Confident business. It'd shatter with one fumble. He's dressed in the same black suit and long, unfittingly tattered coat he wore last time I saw him. His sunglasses hang from his collar.

"You're not supposed to know this, but I'm a gambling man. I play a mean game of Cobra and I spend more nights at Prairie Pit than in my own bed. I try not to get involved in your family's business. I drink. I play. I indulge. I go home richer and fatter and don't question the *who* or the *what* behind my vices. But I'm no fool, kid."

As he says this, the paperweight slips. He catches it with a chuckle, like he enjoyed the thrill of it.

"No Agent is invincible to the influence of the Syndicate. We keep our noses out of each other's business. As long as they pay for their Immunity and there's no treasonous activity involved, we let them get away with more than we should, and in exchange, they give us everything we're Immune for in the first place. All the goodies and pleasures little baby Chasers like you dream of during your pathetic scramble to the top.

"But you already know this." He stops pacing. "*Nephew.*"

I glance at Gilbert. He stares at me in cold, unreadable silence.

"Why are you here?" I ask.

"I'm getting to that." Finch swats the air and continues tossing the paperweight. "Long story short, the barrier I keep between me and them is officially broken. All because of you."

"I don't get it."

Finch sighs. "You disappeared, but Walter didn't believe you died in training. Insisted that he prepared you for the final test. So he contacted Gilly over here to find out what happened, who tracked *me* down in the Pit, ruined a perfectly good game of Cobra, and said if I didn't reveal where the hell I sent you, the goddamn *Serpent* would skin us both. I've seen it happen, so of course I believe it."

Gilbert nods.

"Naturally, I have connections of my own, given my position," Finch continues. "But if I were to send someone after Walter to save my own skin, I'd be asking for war. Man's got a tighter rein on the Syndicate than his brother. You catch my drift?"

I nod.

"Of course, he's no animal. He did offer generous compensation for our efforts. And what can I say?" Finch shrugs with a grin. "I'm a greedy old bastard."

I realize he's missing a tooth. It doesn't surprise me. I'd punch him too if I wouldn't get killed for it.

"So..." He tosses the paperweight in my direction. I barely catch it in time to keep it from hitting me in the face. "We're reassigning you."

My eyes go round when I remember what day it is. *Of course they're here. Evaluation is tomorrow.*

"Reassigning me?" I question.

"Yep."

I blink, still unsure I heard him right at all. "You mean..."

"You're going home."

Home.

The word sounds strange in my mind now. Uncanny, almost—like the way a desert sun warps faraway things with buzzing heat.

Home has become a mirage, a dream I gave up believing in long ago. I've forgotten the taste of pine and coastal salt on the wind. The smell of log cabin walls and lupine meadows after rain and the herbs Dad smoked on the porch when he couldn't sleep. Wormwood for pain, St. John's wort for thoughts that don't leave. I miss Beau's ascending laugh and owl eyes. Noriko's steady voice and grounding advice. Cecil's constancy and understanding. Viv and Hugo and Asa and Mom and Lori.

Dad.

Stronger than hurt, stronger than the exhaustion, is the way I miss all the people and places I've called home.

I'm going home.

Finch chuckles. "Jesus, kid. I thought you'd be more thrilled than that."

"I'm going home?" I ask, just to make sure I'm not dreaming.

"That's what I said."

I turn the paperweight over in my hands, observing my reflection. There's a playing card trapped inside—a 2 of Spades, like the one on my wrist. A distorted version of my face floats above it, almost unrecognizable.

I wonder if they'll see me the same way when I get back. Will they even want me to return when they learn what I've done? The mistakes I've made?

The lives I could have saved?

"We'll reassign you to a cushy job as a Sitter for our local Agency HQ. Answering phone calls, scheduling, you get the gist. Walter's offered you room and board, though I'm sure there'd be strings attached. With that kinda job, you wouldn't even need his help. Financially, at least.

"Speaking of money, don't forget you *are* getting paid for living in this shithole. Not much, since you're technically not a real Chaser yet, but enough to get you a car or something. All Guards' earnings are held by the Corps until they're released. So you'll walk out of this place with a nice chunk of cash, a secure career, and a head attached to your shoulders.

"Most importantly..." He bends down to meet my stare, placing his palms on his knees. "Freedom to do whatever the hell you want with your life." He chuckles. "And of course, the Serpent won't skin me alive. Maybe I'll pay off a bit of my gambling debt too. Win-win."

Freedom. *Whatever I want?* I stare at the paperweight again.

Isn't this what I've spent my whole life dreaming of? An opportunity to experience life outside of the Cut? Freedom to choose what *I* want to do with *my* life?

I take a slow, shaky breath and close my eyes. I think about what it would mean to say yes.

I'd never have to step foot here again. I'd get money. Immunity. Probably a nice car, a house of my own. I'd work a desk job as Cedar Warren Beck for the rest of my life. I'd have weekly three-course meals at Whitestag, overflowing with tender meats and buttery vegetables and rich desserts. Expensive wine. Spicy cigars. Dry goose and cotton candy and the best crème brûlée.

Maybe I'd find a girl—one who doesn't like setting things on fire. Someone I'd live a bland but comfortable life with, far away from debugging surgeries and talks of the rebellion on our horizon. We'd exist in blissful, comfortable ignorance, without dying prematurely for the cause we were born into. There would be no *cause* at all—only survival in its easiest format.

Fat and happy like the rest of them.

I open my eyes.

That sounds like misery.

"What about the others?" I ask. "Can we take them too?"

Finch makes a face. "The others?"

"I have friends here."

He sighs, rubbing his temples. "Fine. Whatever. We'll reassign them too. Nothing fancy, though."

"That's not what I mean."

He looks at me, brows pinched in confusion. "Surely you don't mean prisoners?"

I don't say anything.

It's quiet for a moment. I worry I've made another mistake—that he'll see this as disloyalty to the Corps, to the country.

I'm not sure how I expected him to respond, but laughter certainly wasn't a part of it.

Finch leans his head back and cackles so loudly Gilbert shushes him with a glare. He wipes his eyes as it dies down. "Oh, kid. You're hilarious. I can't get enough of your sense of humor. I can see why the Serpent's so fond of you."

"I'm serious."

The grin fades. "What?"

"I think he means it, Finch," Gilbert mutters.

Finch's face shifts. The humor drains from his voice and expression. "Look, kid—I'm risking a lot just to *offer* this. You do realize who you're talking to, right?"

I shrug.

"The Head of House has an image to uphold. Order to maintain. And if my higher-ups realize I'm pulling favors for the Syndicate, they'd question my ability to keep that order in place." He retrieves a cigarette from his pocket and lights it frantically. He takes a long drag, slowing his voice.

I hate the smell. It's not like Doc's cigars.

"They like to think their leaders are incorruptible. *Perfect.* No one is, really. But I can't let them know I take the occasional bribe." He takes another drag. "Get what I'm saying?"

I nod.

"If this ever gets out, it'll piss people off, up and down the ladder. It could stir up old grievances, inspire strikes, all that bullshit. Complaints do add up, you know. *Especially* if I'm pardoning criminals. God, kid. That's like asking for an insurrection. I'm not risking *my* ass or *my* corner of the Agency to let a few grimy prisoners tag along."

"Then I'm not going."

Finch chuckles. I don't budge.

His smile fades. "You're still not joking."

"I'm not."

Accepting his offer would mean more than betraying my home. My family. My cause. I can't abandon Raven and the Gamblers either. I can't leave Marty. I can't let Jelly have that baby here.

Especially with Doc gone.

"There won't be another Evaluation for months," Finch says, voice low. "A *year*, actually, unless an incident requires emergency Agent attention. You'll be stranded."

"I know."

"Come with me, we'll reinstate you in the Corps, I'll get brownie points with the big man's little brother. Win-win all around." He takes another drag. "Or you can stay imprisoned. It's up to you."

Quiet.

"You know, just the few months you've spent out here have already taken years off your life. Shit air quality. Malnutrition. Overexertion. Chronic stress. The compounding effects of all four. Add a few months more and you'll be a decade closer to death."

"I know."

"What are you gonna do then, huh? Rot in here for the rest of your life? You've gotta leave eventually."

I don't say anything.

"So what's it gonna be, kid?" He snuffs out the cigarette in an ashtray. "Freedom, or captivity?"

I look him dead in the eye. "I'm staying."

"Is that what you want me to tell Walter? That you're refusing his favor?"

I shrug. "I'm saving it for a rainy day."

He studies me for a moment, then chuckles in disbelief. Maybe even frustration. "Fine. Your choice." He walks toward the door. Gilbert follows.

"Have fun dying at my age, then."

Finch pauses with his hand on the doorknob, giving me one last look. "If you last that long."

Monday, October 24

The next morning we are evaluated like livestock awaiting a blue ribbon at the fair.

The Chasers watch us eat. They watch us work. They don't say anything. Gilbert just takes notes using the screen on his uniform's wrist. Finch wears his sunglasses now and pretends to be serious. The other Guards are scared shitless.

I'm not.

At sunset, just before dinner, we line up outside the cafeteria in perfect rows.

The Chasers have been briefed about each of us. They studied us carefully all day. They even inspected the electric fence to make sure it's still working. Everyone holds their breath, waiting for an answer as Finch and Gilbert stand in stern silence at the head of the crowd. Waiting for a chance to get home.

Not a single person gets reassigned.

"Come on, Officer Gilbert. Nothing new to see here," Finch finally says. They walk away in the direction of the gate.

He gives me one last look. "This year's crop is rather dull, isn't it?"

32

Monday, October 31

On Halloween night, Raven and I steal jars of water from the cafeteria. The good kind—clear and cold instead of lukewarm. We hike to the Graves and sneak into the shed where we are far from everyone and everything else. We sip it like fine wine and sit on the ground, surrounded by walls lined with rusting shovels. We don't care about the dust and splinters and cobwebs. We just need quiet.

Raven says Chips don't celebrate Halloween anymore. The Corps doesn't like the idea of community and large gatherings and handing things out for free. There's nothing to dress up as anymore either; most of the good Yesterday books and movies are banned. It's not like anyone can legally walk around with weapons—even if they're fake.

I was the only kid for a while, but we still celebrated at the Cut. Dad would take me around to visit the other cabins and portables and people would give me trinkets and honey candies and tell me I looked adorable in whatever costume I managed to put together.

I got old for it quickly. By then, more small children started calling the Cut home. It became my job to take them around camp and keep them from hitting each other with the wooden swords I made them.

I tell this to Raven. She laughs. She can't picture me keeping my temper in check around kids. I tell her they're the hardest to get mad at and the easiest to forgive.

They don't deserve to grow up in a world like this.

"Is Bates fully settled in now?" Raven asks, sipping her water.

"I gave the infirmary a visit. Just to have a look around." I sip too, staring at the wooden planks by my feet. "She took down the old anatomy posters. The ones from the Yesterdays that Doc loved. Said she preferred empty walls for *focus*."

"Cardboard has more personality than that woman." She shakes her head. "Focus on what? Getting a soul, I hope."

"You dream too big."

Dr. Larrissa Bates was transferred here the day after Evaluation. She's an older woman who keeps her graying hair in a tight bun at the top of her head and her lips sewn into a permanent frown. She has no interest in *criminals*. She walks past prisoners with her nose crinkled and upturned in disgust. Like they don't exist.

Last Thursday, a young man who hadn't heard the news knocked on the infirmary door past curfew, seeking help for a friend's concussion. Doc didn't answer—but Bates did. He hasn't been seen since.

That's what happens when you get caught breaking curfew, the Guards are saying.

We get a slap on the wrist for that.

Prisoners get exterminated.

The disappearance spread the news about Doc. Now it's me the prisoners come to for help. I don't have any tea, medicine, or access to Doc's supplies. His bag was confiscated. But I have enough knowledge to explain what's going on in most cases, which brings them comfort, I think—even when there's nothing I can do.

Raven reaches into her pocket. She pulls out the deer tooth. I forgot about that. She inspects it under the moonlight seeping in through the broken ceiling boards. "I still carry this with me, you know."

I hide a grin. "Really?"

She nods and hands it to me. I turn it over in little circles, rolling it between my fingertips. Feels like it's been years since it was in my own pocket.

The tooth looks pale in comparison to my uniform. The fabric is light gray now, stained by the smoke in the air. No matter how many times it's washed, the gray never goes away. I think it's changed for good.

Maybe I am the same way.

I hand the tooth back to Raven. She pockets it and sips the last of her water. She sets the jar aside and looks me up and down. "You look like shit."

I frown. "Thanks."

"No, I mean... something's eating at you."

I shrug, staring at my hands.

Her voice softens. "It's Doc, isn't it?"

I don't say anything.

It's quiet for a long time. I lie back, using my palms for a pillow. She joins me.

We stare at the sky through the gaps in the roof. I puff out a slow breath. "Life is meaningless."

"Beck..."

"But that's the beauty of it, isn't it?" I hold a hand out, tracing my thoughts in the air. "It's like Doc's posters. We're just... goo and tendons propped up by bones and held together in bags of skin."

"That's disgusting."

"All of that? It rots away. We're sand and dirt in the making, but I don't think that's such a bad thing."

"I'm lost."

"Don't you get it? It's *meaningless*." I turn over to face her. She does the same, propping her head up with her hand. "We get to give it meaning."

"You should have existential epiphanies more often." A smile tugs the corners of her lips. "It's adorable."

My face warms. I turn on my back again. She's still watching me.

"Doc... he's not here, but he's *here*." I point to my head.

"In what he left behind. Beyond his flesh."

"Exactly." A flicker of dry lightning flashes through the roof. "And I think that's something he'd be proud of."

She watches me watch pieces of the sky for a while until she turns on her back again. Our silence is extensive, but comfortable. Meaningful. I stare at a spiderweb in the far corner of the shed. I see the shell of a beetle trapped within it, long forgotten.

Maybe we all die. But there is rebirth too. We are reborn in the beauty of our bones, and the vultures who will bake us off their feathers, beneath a sun that rises and falls and comes back up again.

Maybe Lily's reasoning makes sense after all.

Raven sighs, breaking the silence. "I'm so tired, Cedar."

"We can head back if you want."

"No. I mean... *tired.*" She closes her eyes. "I'm exhausted, and my head always hurts, and no amount of extra rations or shitty water is going to do a damn thing to fix it."

She keeps her words soft, but they weigh heavy on her breath. I know better than to think I can do anything to make that go away. We both know escape is the only real answer.

She sits up and removes the red ribbon from her braid. Her hair spills out in inky waves. She lies back down, spinning the ribbon in her hands. I know who she must be thinking about.

"Remember our promise?" I ask quietly.

She nods.

"We'll find a way out." I extend my pinky. "Soon."

She ties the ribbon around her wrist and takes my pinky in hers. We hold our hands like that for a long time. She looks at them, then my arm. My jaw. My eyes. "Can't we just be here for a little while?"

I realize how close she is. I study her hair. It looks soft, like silk. I almost reach out to touch it, but I stop myself. I look at her lips instead. A mistake.

I observe that I desire to kiss her again.

"I'm here," I say. "Are you?"

Slowly, she takes my face in her hands. She brushes a thumb across my cheek.

And she presses her lips against mine.

It's barely a kiss at all—a touch so light I hardly feel it before she pulls back an inch, eyes locking to mine. "I'm here."

I pull her closer and kiss her back.

This one is firmer. I close my eyes. Her lips taste like salt and dust. Soft, but chapped by the dry air, which suddenly gets harder to breathe in when I realize I'd rather taste more of her instead. She loops her arms around my neck. My hand finds the back of her hair. It is silk.

I could go longer without breathing, but she pauses. "Can I ask you something?"

"Anything."

"What's your real name?"

My hands are still in her hair. I comb my fingers through it. "Aaron."

She turns on her back. "Aaron." She tries my name on her tongue like a new sweater, brows furrowed. Her face softens. She says it again, this time a whisper. Like the sweater fits. "Aaron."

I grin like an idiot. "You kissed me."

"Don't let it get to your head."

"I won't."

"I don't love you."

I coil a strand of her hair around my finger. "I know."

"I can't love you."

"That's okay."

She cups my face in her hands and kisses me again.

This time, it feels like it means something.

Saturday, November 5

Fern slams her cards down with a frown. "Screw you guys. I'm done."

After winning for the fifth time tonight, Lockley gathers everyone's cards with a smirk. "Come on. Just one more round?"

"Yeah, one more round," Marty insists, helping Lockley. "We can't let him win *again*. We need all hands on deck if we wanna take his ego down a notch. If that's even possible."

Lockley glares. Marty winks.

"Alright, *fine*," Fern says. "But only because I wanna see Lock cry."

He gasps, placing a hand over his chest in mock offense. "I'm insulted."

Fern sticks out her tongue. "Good."

"Does anyone know where Raven went off to?" I ask. "She left on that walk like an hour ago."

Lockley speed-recites Cobra's intro speech under his breath while shuffling. "Just let her be. She likes her alone time."

"Yeah, but..." I glance at the clock. "It's past curfew."

He starts dealing out the cards. "She'll be alright."

I pick up my hand and look through it with a sigh. Shit luck.

"I think *someone's* got a crush," Fern says. My face heats up.

Lockley rolls his eyes. "Don't be annoying, Fern."

I clear my throat. "I'm just worried, that's all."

"Maybe she's wherever you lovebirds ran off to the other night," Lockley says plainly, observing his cards. "Waiting for *you* to join her."

Marty grins. "Oooh..."

I glare. "Who's being annoying now?"

Lockley raises a brow. "So you don't deny it."

"Oh, stop it you guys. You're making him blush," Jelly says.

"They kissed," Fern announces.

"We didn't kiss."

"His face *is* turning red."

Now I'm the one slamming my cards down. "I'm going for a walk. By *myself*."

I rise to my feet, but before I turn to the door, Jelly gasps. Her eyes clamp shut. She rubs her stomach with a grimace.

My eyes widen. I place a hand on her shoulder. "You alright?"

"I'm fine." She forces a grin. "An especially violent kick, I think. Must take after their aunt."

Fern glowers.

"Are you sure?" I ask.

She nods. "Go on your walk."

I do.

I stay close to the shadows, boots crunching softly against dirt as I shove my hands in my pockets. Something tells me that wasn't a kick back there.

I don't know much about this sort of thing. But from what Raven told me months ago, Jelly's due date should be soon. Very soon, by the looks of it.

And that's terrifying.

We've been so caught up in what happened with Doc and stealing gasoline and simply trying to survive each day that the logistics of our plan have gone under the rug. Like dirty clothes you shove in your closet so you don't have to deal with them until some other day far in the future.

We can't procrastinate anymore. We need dates and numbers and a sequence of designated tasks. Something solid. But every time Marty and I try to bring up that delivery truck, the subject gets changed. Raven brushes it aside and says it's handled. Lockley averts his gaze and says we'll cross that bridge when we get to it.

I think back to Jelly as I walk, the way her face contorted with pain. That baby will be here any day now, and we need to leave before that happens. Quietly. Safely. I'll debug them, have Raven handle mine, and we'll find our way back to the Cut. Dad will deal with the baby. Not me.

Back home, I only ever helped with livestock births, not human ones. I've had lessons about it, but I didn't pay much attention.

In other words, I'd have no idea what I'm doing.

I sigh, staring at the sky. That baby better hold on until the 14th. Just another week, and we'll be on that delivery truck.

We'll be going home.

I approach the water tower, studying its shadow from my distance. I feel a flicker of warmth in my chest when I think back to climbing it with Raven. Holding her hand. Waking with her head on my shoulder.

As I grow closer, something moves beneath the tower. I narrow my eyes to make out the shape in the dark.

It's her.

I fight a smile. *Of course.* I stay close to the walls of the closest prisoner cabin, hoping to give her a good jump scare. I pause.

She's crouched by one of the tower's legs. I hear a scratching sound, like a saw against wood. *What is she doing?*

I shove my hands in my pockets and walk closer. "Hey."

Raven jumps up with a start. She hides something behind her back, eyes saucers until she realizes it's me. She brings a hand to her chest. "God, Aaron. You scared me."

Aaron. I'm still not used to the sound of my name on her tongue, but it doesn't give me butterflies like it usually does. "What are you doing?"

"I just... needed some fresh air. That's all."

I nod. "What's behind your back?"

Her smile fades. She clears her throat. "Nothing."

"Raven."

Her lips part, then shut. She lets out a shaky, drawn-out sigh.

Then she shows me the knife.

It's long and serrated and it glints in the moonlight. A bread knife, likely stolen from the kitchen on one of her cleaning shifts. It's covered in wood dust.

Slowly, I walk over to the post and crouch to inspect it. My heart falls into my stomach.

An entire chunk of wood is missing.

It's triangular and not enough to make the tower lose its balance. Each post is connected with intersecting beams, and the pipe in the center that sprouts up from the ground helps hold the tank above in place. It won't fall—yet.

I look at the next post. A chunk is missing from that one too.

This couldn't have been done in an hour. This is the result of days, stealing minutes under the cover of darkness to cut away at the posts unnoticed.

"Aaron..."

I walk to the other two posts. No saw marks there. I return to the first one, flexing and unflexing my fists.

"Aaron—"

I hold up a hand, staring at the sawed post in front of me. I try to keep my voice steady. "You're trying to control where it falls, right?"

She doesn't say anything.

My heartbeats grow louder. Sporadic. My throat tightens.

Why hide this? What's the point?

I stand up slowly. "If something were to hit this tower with enough force from there..." I point to the side with the untouched posts. "It would fall in this direction and land..." My finger moves in the air—then freezes. "On the fence?"

I whip my head around. "Raven, are you out of your mind?"

"Aaron..."

"The fence? The *fence*?" I scoff in disbelief. "Do you have any idea what will happen if a thousand gallons of water meet 8,000 volts of electricity? When the fence short-circuits, all that water's gonna *carry* the electricity. If anyone comes over here, they could get electrocuted. Hell, there's a cabin *right there*. Multiple, actually."

"I know."

"You know?" I laugh bitterly. "Have you ever seen a human body get electrocuted? Because I have."

I step closer.

"Your hair and clothes catch fire first. That's what makes the rest of you burn, until you can't tell where the fabric ends and the skin begins, because none of it looks like either of those things anymore. It's all burnt blood and smoke and flesh so charred you wouldn't even recognize who you just killed."

"I have it handled."

"You have it handled?" I shake my head in disbelief. "So what, you're gonna take out the fence? No one would even be able to get through. This whole area would be a hazard."

"I said I have it handled," she snaps.

My shoulders slump. "You've been planning this, haven't you?"

She doesn't say anything.

None of this makes any sense. There are too many variables, too many risk factors—but the way she looks at me tells me there's more to this than I realize. *She's thought this out.*

"This is ridiculous." I take a step back, running my hands through my hair. "We had a plan. A simple, *feasible* plan. Nothing involving water towers, or electricity, or..." My voice trails off.

If this was her real plan all along, then what does she need that gasoline for?

What is she really planning?

Whatever it is she's up to, it'll only make it harder to escape on that delivery truck. That's the safest option. The *only* option for all six of us to make it out okay.

Raven steps forward. "*You* had a plan. I told you mine months ago, and you said it was crazy. You wouldn't even hear me out."

My stomach churns.

She meant it when she said she wanted to burn this place to the ground.

But what does the water tower have to do with a fire? Is she trying to make it impossible to put one out? Knocking over the tower would take away our only source of water. Anyone who doesn't escape the fence would die of thirst.

Even if we were right about the monarchs following a river, would we really be able to find it? We could get lost and starve to death trying.

I think back to what Agent Finch said. Agents are only sent here for Evaluations or emergencies. A handful of Guards and prisoners quietly disappearing is nothing.

But if that water tower falls, I can't imagine any other outcome besides chaos. This place would be swarmed with Chasers.

"The delivery truck was never a part of this, was it?" I mutter.

"No."

My shoulders go rigid.

Raven sighs. "Look, I know you're upset—"

"Upset? *Upset* doesn't begin to cover it."

She glares. "I don't see why it's such a big deal."

"You've been lying to me for months, just so I'd agree to help you out with the gasoline—which I still don't understand why you need. And this *plan* of yours? Whatever the hell it is, it won't be quiet and it sure as hell won't be safe. For anyone."

"I'm sorry, okay? I know that wasn't fair, but it was the only way I could've gotten you to go along with the gasoline thing. I've been planning this for a long time, alright? It will work. Just trust me on this."

"How you go about *burning this place down* won't make me disagree with it any less." I shake my head. "Trust you. That's funny."

"I said I was sorry."

"You're just sorry I found out."

A muscle in her jaw twitches. She opens her mouth to say something, but never gets the chance.

Behind us, shoes crunch against dirt. A figure runs toward us in the dark, stumbling to a breathless stop. They place their hands on their knees, coughing furiously. *Lockley.*

"It's Jelly," he coughs out. "The baby's coming."

33

November 6, 2024

♪ 6705 - KELLERMENSCH ♪

I deliver a baby.

Well, Jelly does all the work. It's five hours and forty-five minutes of screaming, crying, and a few instances of understandable violence involving a glass of water chucked at my head. I'm lucky I don't have another concussion.

When I run into the cabin with Raven and Lockley, everyone turns to me. I'm the healer here. I'm supposed to know what to do. The only thing is—I don't. I've never done this before. Watching my Dad deliver a sheep is not the same as having experience with a *human*. Just the sight of Jelly, face red and twisted with pain, is enough to make me nauseous. Because this is real life, not one of my dad's textbooks. Not a Yesterday movie. A real human being is about to bring another one into existence.

And I'm the only one who can help.

I close my eyes. *One thing at a time, Aaron.*

In my mind, I scour over every lesson I should have paid more attention to, every passage I should have read more closely. I picture Dad standing in the corner with his arms crossed, nodding in silence. He isn't here. He can't help me.

I'm on my own.

I exhale shakily and open my eyes. "Everybody listen up."

I give Fern, Marty, and Lockley instructions for gathering supplies. Marty's in charge of orchestrating a visit to the infirmary to steal scissors and string for the umbilical cord when the new transfer, Dr. Bates, isn't looking. Fern and Lockley track down as much clean water, soap, and towels as they can find. They return with an older woman and her daughter from another cabin—Martha and Lacey, who are much better at comforting Jelly than I could be.

But I'm still there anyway, talking her through every step, letting her squeeze my hand until it goes numb. I time the contractions until they are strong and close together. And when it's time to guide the baby out, that's when I feel useless. *It's all up to Jelly, now.*

The head. The shoulders. The body. When the screaming ends and the crying begins and I finish cutting the umbilical cord, I'm crying, too.

I did it.

She did it.

The baby is here.

It's nice to know Jelly doesn't *really* want me to burn in hell, among the variety of other strongly worded wishes she announced throughout it all. Because when I hand her that perfect, crying baby girl, Jelly looks at me like I've just given her the key out of this place. Her eyes water. She gives me a kiss on the forehead. "Thank you, Aaron."

I smile, eyes glossy too. I don't even care that Raven told her. I'm just glad Evangeline knows my name.

Raven checks the clock on the wall. "1:01 AM on November 6th." She kneels next to Jelly and wraps an arm around her. She plants a kiss on her head. "A wonderful birthday, don't you think?"

November 6th? I glance at the clock. It's past midnight now.

I hide a grin. I'm eighteen today.

I stare at that mother and her baby, alive and crying and healthy, and I can't think of a better gift.

I lean against the wall and yawn. I can barely keep my eyes open. I fall half asleep and jolt awake about twice every minute.

"Go back to your room," Martha finally insists. "You look exhausted."

I shake my head. "I'm alright."

We still need to monitor Jelly's vitals and watch for excess bleeding, but I don't say that in front of Fern.

"We'll keep an eye on her," Lacey insists. "You've done more than enough. Go get some rest."

"You did a great job, Cedar." Martha grins. "This baby couldn't be healthier."

I swat the air. "I did nothing. It was all *her*."

I watch Jelly cradle the infant. She sings a soft lullaby with words I can hardly make out. I pick up on bits and pieces of it. Meadows and lupine and harebell flowers. Songbirds celebrating a new morning. Purple mountain sunsets.

For a moment, I believe everything will be okay.

I go to bed and dream of a music box. Jelly sits within it, singing her child to sleep.

When I return to the cabin the next morning, Officer Stokes answers the door.

I blink for a moment, unable to believe what I'm seeing. I dig my fingernails into my palm just to make sure I'm not dreaming. I break through the skin and don't wake up.

"You shouldn't be here," Stokes says.

"I could say the same about you."

His stare is stone cold. "You need to leave."

"I'm not leaving."

My brows furrow. *Why are his eyes red?*

I try to look over his shoulder, but he blocks the door. "I mean it, Beck." His stare is unwavering, but his breathing is shaky. "Leave."

"Is something wrong? Where's Jelly?"

"That's none of your concern."

"What happened, Stokes?" I seethe.

He doesn't say anything.

I move forward, but he pushes me back and shuts the door. He lowers his voice. "I know you know about the baby. We all knew this day would come. But if you're here when Valdez arrives, it'll only complicate things. If you want what's best for that child, you'll go to breakfast with everyone else."

"When Valdez arrives?" My heart plummets. "Where is she?"

"Beck—"

"*Where is she?*"

Stokes grabs me by the collar and pushes me forward until we're in the narrow alley between this cabin and the next. "Get a hold of yourself, Cedar. For them."

Every part of me shakes. My lungs pinch together and it's impossible to breathe. "Tell me what's going on."

Dr. Bates is dead on the floor with a Nightjade needle in her neck.

Martha and Lacey are gone. Lockley, Raven, and Fern stand against the wall with their hands at their sides, staring straight ahead. Shaking. Their eyes are red too.

I try to meet Raven's gaze from across the room. She won't look at me.

Then I see the blood staining the floorboards.

The room spins. My eyes dart between the crimson and Bates, back and forth until my knees feel unsteady and I can't take a full breath.

"Who killed Bates?" I manage. I can't look away from the blood.

Stokes can't either. "Evangeline."

A shiver runs through me.

Something went wrong. I know it did. Something wasn't right with Jelly. That's why there's all this blood. Maybe she was losing too much of it. Martha and Lacey must have gone to get Bates as a last resort. *They wouldn't have sought her help if it wasn't a matter of life or death.*

I stare at the needle in the woman's neck.

"Bates wanted to exterminate the baby…" I mutter. "Didn't she?"

Stokes nods.

"Jelly." I clear my throat, swallowing painfully. "Where's Jelly?"

No one says a word. I look at the blood.

And I know there is another body that isn't here.

My eyes blur. Sting. Burn. The room spins. My knees buckle. I slide against the wall until I'm sitting on the ground, clutching my hair with both hands. The walls cave in around me and I can't blink or breathe or see straight.

"Beck, you need to leave. Valdez is coming to investigate."

I think Stokes is speaking, but I can barely hear him. His voice sounds muffled. Underwater.

This can't be happening.

I was just here. Jelly and the baby were perfectly healthy. I *saw* them last night. Jelly kissed my forehead, and she was singing that lullaby, and the baby was wailing, and—

There's a knock on the door. A baby starts crying.

Raven hurries to the center of the room. She yanks away the rug and opens the trapdoor. She pulls me up and pushes me inside. The trapdoor slams shut behind me. A shuffling sound above tells me the rug is back in place.

The crying is louder down here. I walk around the corner, to the part of the crawlspace that sits beneath the porch. Just enough morning light seeps in through the gaps above to illuminate the source of the sound.

There is a pillow on the ground. The baby rests on top of it, swaddled in half of a torn blanket, surrounded by Raven's kingdom of makeshift gasoline cans.

My heart sinks.

Jelly never got to name her.

Another knock sounds above me. *The Captain is here.*

I feel like I'm unraveling. Like someone is pulling on a loose thread, spinning me closer and closer to falling apart. But there is no time for that. I can't cry. I can't unravel. I can't *breathe.*

I hurry to the baby and scoop her up. "Shhh."

That only makes her cry louder. I bounce her gently in my arms.

"It's okay. Shhh."

She wails.

Think, Aaron. Think.

I don't remember the words, but I manage to softly hum the lullaby's melody—just loud enough for the baby to hear it. I'm a terrible singer, but I don't think she cares. The cries stop.

Above us, the cabin door finally opens.

The sound of heavy footsteps illustrates the scene above me. The Captain enters. Someone else does too—another Guard, judging by the boots. Maybe a Supervisor. They walk to the center of the room and pause. They've just seen Bates.

I press the baby against my chest, so I can hum even quieter without giving us away. I hold her head up with my hand. It's soft. So new.

Keep it together, Aaron.

"You really weren't kidding." The Captain's voice is muffled. He sighs. "We'll have to request another Healer, then."

"A Nightjade syringe..." another voice says. "How peculiar."

My eyes widen. *Saylor.*

"It is rather peculiar," Valdez says. His tone ices over. "What happened, Stokes?"

"One of our prisoners has been with child for some time now," Stokes says. "She had the baby last night. Neither of them..." He clears his throat. "Neither of them made it through to morning."

I lean my head back against the wall, closing my eyes. Still humming. *Keep it together. Keep it together.*

"I see," Valdez says. I can picture him staring at Bates's lifeless body. "I'm afraid that still doesn't explain *this*."

"Something wasn't right with the prisoner. Out of desperation, two women who assisted in the birth sought Bates for help. She arrived on scene and realized the mother wasn't going to make it. Thought it best to..." I can hear Stokes swallow from down here, like it's taking physical strength to get the words out. "She thought it best to exterminate the child."

I stop humming. I bring a hand to my mouth. I feel like I'm going to be sick.

The baby coos like she might start crying again.

"What was that?" Saylor asks.

My pulse pounds against my chest. I keep humming.

Lockley coughs. "Sorry."

"So Bates took care of the child," Valdez continues, "and the mother retaliated."

"That is correct, sir," Stokes says.

"If the mother murdered Bates, then how did she die?"

"Lost too much blood. She killed the only person able to save her."

"And where are the other bodies?"

"I already transported them, sir."

My eyes sting. My humming grows shaky and I try to blink back the tears. *Keep. It. Together.*

"Before letting me investigate?"

"I was merely being efficient, sir."

"Then why did you leave *her* here?" Saylor asks. "Seems a little strange to me."

"I thought the Captain would want to see Bates's body for himself, given her status," Stokes says. "Didn't realize you'd care so much about the fates of a few lowly prisoners."

I can practically see Saylor's glare.

"Ah, well—another tragedy, I suppose. Thank God it happened after Agent Finch departed. I'd hate for the Corps to think I don't run a tight ship around here. Clean up this mess, you three. I despise blood."

With that, Valdez and Saylor take their exit.

I slide down to the ground. We wait for them to walk far away. Breathing alone feels like swallowing fire, but I'm still humming. Still keeping this baby quiet.

Above, Stokes speaks softly. "I'll take care of this. You three are free to go to your shift."

Two sets of footsteps exit.

The third set walks to the center of the room. I hear a shuffle. The creak of a trapdoor. The soft landing of two feet against dirt. Fern. I'm still holding the baby when she falls to her knees and wraps her arms around me.

That's when I let it all go.

I press my forehead against hers, and I sob.

I'm not even trying to be quiet anymore. The baby starts to wail. I press the child closer to my chest, but it does nothing to soothe her. It doesn't bring her mother back.

"You did everything you could." Fern's voice cracks. She squeezes me tighter. I feel something hot against my shirt. A tear. "It's the prison's damn fault. That's what did it. She never—" She chokes on the word. "She never would have made it."

"If Doc were here, he could've stopped it." My shoulders convulse. "He could've helped her."

"The Presidency killed her, Aaron." Fern's crying too, but her voice is stern. "Never forget that, okay? *They* killed her. Not you. Not me. It's always them. Always will be until they burn to the ground."

It should be me comforting Fern, not the other way around. She's still a child. She's the one who lost her sister, and I'm the one crying like the baby I still hold in my arms.

Weak.

I think of my mother. Her laugh. Her soft hands, tucking my hair behind my ears. Her arms around me, how they always felt like a shield from everything bad in the world, even after I grew old enough to protect myself. This child will never know what that feels like.

She'll never know her mother's lullaby.

After a while, Fern takes the baby upstairs and leaves me alone. Alone with my thoughts stuck on repeat, digging so deeply into my mind I can feel the ache.

Fern's wrong.

Doc should have been here.

It's my fault he's gone.

I was stupid. Again. Just like Dad said I'd be. If I didn't make enemies with Saylor—if I just kept my damn mouth shut—maybe he wouldn't have spied on me. Maybe the investigation would have fizzled out. Doc would still be here, and he would have helped Jelly better than I did.

This is all my fault.

If I were better, she would still be here.

If Saylor were better, Doc would still be here.

I stop crying. The realization hits like a truck. I stare up at the light shining through the cracks above me.

This is all *his* fault.

PART FOUR
SHARP

34

Monday, November 7

On the morning after my eighteenth birthday, my second gift from the universe is a western diamondback rattlesnake.

It greets me with a percussive hiss when I step outside. If the Serpent hadn't trained me to recognize a rattle, I would have taken another step. I would have died on this porch, barely a day over eighteen, stranded without antivenom. It's sunrise. No one would be awake to help me.

I was taught better than that.

I'm not sure how snakes get through the electric fence. Maybe it came here while it was young and small and grew too big to find a way out. But it's here now, coiled tightly by my feet, ready to strike like a bow drawn taut. One wrong move and I'm dead.

I study its rusty scales, the fangs it flashes like daggers.

This is no warning. It's an opportunity.

"Catching snakes is a mind game, Cedar," the Serpent once said. *"To over-power one is merely a matter of overpowering your own hesitation. Once you*

have mastered deciding exactly what it is you are going to do and acting quickly, all else will fall into place.”

The rattling grows louder.

“It's all in your head.”

Slowly, I crouch down.

I grab the snake at the base of the skull.

The creature writhes and jerks in my grip, but I keep it tight. I grab its body with my other hand to keep it from turning around to bite me.

Everyone else is asleep when I walk to the still-empty infirmary with a four-foot snake and a job to do.

No hesitation.

I follow Walter's steps exactly.

He taught me how to milk a snake once. That's what it's called—getting the venom out.

I set everything up on an empty white table within the empty white walls of the infirmary. It's a small building with small rooms and cabinets full of tools Doc will never use again.

I cover the top of a jar in plastic wrap. I squeeze the snake's jaw and force its mouth open. I let it bite the jar. Its upper jaw is stuck over the wrap. I press its head firmly against it, watching the venom drip into the vessel. Five seconds. Fifteen. Twenty. I give it a gentle massage to get five seconds more. *Just to be sure.*

When there is no more venom left to give, I walk outside and let it go. I just hope it doesn't come back to bite me later.

Breakfast is quiet and bland and gray like our uniforms.

Marty can't eat and neither can I. We'll save our food for the others, if they can manage to get something down. We don't talk.

Halfway through, Saylor stands to refill his water.

I do the same.

I stare at my feet as I beeline toward him, pretending to be surprised when we collide. Water spills all over his shirt. It turns the cloud-gray fabric into a dark charcoal. The rage in his eyes is a cold and quiet fire.

"I—I'm sorry," I mutter. "I'll get you another one. Don't worry."

Charm the snake.

Saylor narrows his eyes, then smirks with a chuckle. He likes my desperation. My submission. He thinks I am defeated. "Alright. But hurry."

He hands me the cup and returns to his seat. I walk over to the water cooler in the far corner of the room. I glance over my shoulder. *No one's looking.*

I pull the vial from my pocket and pour out the entire thing.

The venom is clear like the water and the cup that now holds it. I walk to Saylor's table and set the glass down. He waves me away, mid-conversation with Fantaine and Cota. They ignore me to continue laughing amongst themselves.

I return to my seat, and I wait.

Their conversation lasts a lifetime. I'm too sleep-deprived and angry to keep staring, and I don't want him to suspect anything. If I look at him for too long, I might go over there and wring his neck myself. So I pick at my food and pretend to consider taking a bite.

My stomach feels like it's digesting itself, but I can't bring myself to eat. Not when the woman I always brought my leftovers to is gone. When her baby is hungry because the milk we've stolen from the kitchen is not enough.

Something shatters.

I snap my head up, eyes immediately darting to Saylor. I don't expect for his gaze to catch mine from across the room. He smirks.

It was not Saylor's body that went limp and folded over onto the table. It was the older man next to him.

"Oh my God!" Fantaine jumps to her feet, pointing to the man with his face in his plate. "I think he's having a heart attack!"

All Guards gasp. A few scream. Some run to the man's side, but it's already too late. Marty brings a shaking hand to his mouth.

I'm trembling too.

Someone fetches the Captain eventually. Valdez sighs when he sees the fallen Guard. "Another heart attack? That's our second this year." He shakes his head. "Someone take him away. We'll alert his family."

Throughout the commotion, Saylor doesn't pry his eyes from mine. Not once.

I run to the communal bathrooms and vomit in the sink.

I grip the edges so tightly my knuckles turn pale. I keep my head hung low, scared to see my reflection in the cracked mirror above it. Scared to not recognize my own face staring back at me.

What have I done?

Slowly, I face my fear—and I look up.

The shell in the mirror is a ghost of the boy I used to be. My cheeks have hollowed out. My skin is sallow. There are dark circles under my eyes. I haven't shaved my face in a while. My hair has grown out and hangs flat and greasy against my head.

I look so empty.

I can't bear to see it anymore so I close my eyes, exhaling shakily. I feel guilty for craving an easy breath when I am the reason why that man in the cafeteria took his last.

It was never meant for him. The phrase repeats over and over again in my mind until I'm sick of it.

That doesn't make him any less dead.

And it doesn't change the fact that it was meant for someone else to begin with.

It's Max all over again. The Chaser I killed. Ron and his cabin. Doc. *Jelly.*

So many deaths on my hands—all because of choices I made. All because I think with everything but my head.

I lift my chin and look in the mirror again, just to feel something. To see myself so void and grieve the person I used to be and remember that I am still human, because I still hurt.

So. Damn. Much.

No one is around to hear me mutter to the glass. "You really are useless, aren't you?"

Maybe I would have made a good Chaser after all.

"I knew I'd find you here."

I turn with a start. Saylor stands behind me, arms crossed. "What's the matter? Is something wrong?"

I clear my throat and pretend to wash my hands. "No."

"I thought you knew me better than this, Beck." I feel his breath against the back of my neck and freeze. "I never trust a drink I don't make. I always have someone else test them first."

A shiver coils down my spine.

In the mirror, I feel his smile fade. The facade drops.

"Mark my words, Cedar Beck." He grabs my gaze in the broken glass. "I will never give you a warning again."

He walks away.

There it is again—a whistle like victory.

Monday, November 14

The baby is hungry.

The milk we steal from the kitchen isn't enough. Bates's replacement hasn't been transferred yet, and I manage to find an old jar of powdered infant formula in one of the infirmary storage closets, but we have no bottle and it's hard to get her to drink it. She cries a lot. I would too if I were stuck in that dingy crawlspace all day.

Aside from Stokes, Martha and Lacey are the only ones outside of the cabin who know the truth about Jelly's daughter. Raven and I cover both of their shifts so they can watch over her during the day. They are mothers themselves; they know better than we do.

This can't last.

We need to get out of here. Tonight.

Today is delivery day. Sometime past curfew, a pair of tired Sitters will drive their truck right up to the gates. They will scan their ID cards and the gates will open to let them through. This vehicle doesn't park far away like the bus did; it has too much cargo to unload. They will carry out the food and clothes and supplies for the next three months, all the way over to the warehouse. All perishables are kept frozen in the kitchen.

Marty says this usually takes them all night, sometimes well into the morning, depending on how quickly they unload everything. Curfew doesn't apply to them. It is not unusual to spot someone walking around at night on delivery day.

Valdez supervises the entire unloading process.

To get on that truck, we need to find a way to keep the Captain occupied. Give him something so important to focus on that he will forget about watching the delivery drivers unload frozen bags of milk and peas and mystery meat. That will give us the opportunity to take out the drivers.

It should be easy enough to overpower a few Sitters. They're one of the few Chaser divisions that doesn't require carrying a weapon.

We won't kill them—just knock them out. Marty and I will steal their ID cards and clothes and replace them with our uniforms. We'll tie them up and hide them somewhere. Then all that's left is to file into that truck and drive the hell out of here.

But there's one issue.

Raven didn't return to her bed last night.

No one knows where she is. I've looked for her everywhere. The water tower. The shed. The crawlspace. The cafeteria. Even the warehouse. She must be avoiding us on purpose.

After breakfast, Marty and I are on Dig. We're covering for Martha and Lacey. The sun is just as unforgiving as always. I spend my entire shift before lunch going over my argument with Raven, turning over every line in my head.

All this time, she was just using me to steal the gasoline. Not once did she tell me her real plan, and something tells me that's exactly how things were meant to go. She needed a Guard on her side, and I just happened to be in the right place at the right time. I wonder if she ever even planned on bringing me with her.

I told her my name. I trusted her. We *kissed*.

But what bothers me the most is how little I understand her true plan.

Gasoline, water tower. That's just about where my knowledge ends.

I sigh, slamming my shovel into the dirt. I should have let her explain it to me. At least so I could know the full extent of what she's up to.

I just don't understand what the water tower has to do with any of this. Why cut it down? If she really wanted to topple it over, she could've stolen a dump truck and run into it or something. But I still don't see what that would accomplish, other than short-circuiting a part of the fence that wouldn't even be safe to cross over anyway. *And what about all that gasoline?*

There has to be more to it.

Lockley's on Dig today too. When the lunch bell rings, I whisper in his ear. "We need to talk."

We meet in the cabin and sit in the center of the floor. Martha and Lacey are taking a break in their own cabin, so the three of us are completely alone. Fern is watching Jelly in the crawlspace.

Lockley sighs. "There's an elephant in the room, isn't there?"

"Real big," Marty mutters.

"We can't let Raven carry out her plan," I say.

Lockley nods. "I agree."

I raise a brow.

"Things are different from how they were two years ago." He rubs his forehead in exhaustion. "Raven... she's the closest friend I have. When she first got here, the only thing that kept us going was this plan. Fueling our anger into this *big bang* event. This collapse we dreamed of inciting. Don't get me wrong—I'd give anything to see this place burn to the ground, but... right now, that baby is our top priority."

Marty nods.

"Our original plan was great while it lasted, but it's too risky. But your delivery truck idea?" Lockley sighs again. "It's safe, and it's something we've never been able to consider before, because we never had a Guard on our side. Let alone two."

Marty smiles.

"We need to get out of here on that truck," I say. "Tonight."

"I know, but..."

"What?"

"I think there's something wrong with Raven."

The anger I have for her hasn't left, but worry instinctively writhes in my gut. "What do you mean?"

"She hasn't cried since Jelly. Not once. And I have this feeling she's about to do something really, *really* stupid."

Marty's brows crease. "Stupid like..."

"The original plan."

"And what is that, exactly?" Marty asks.

"The plan?" Lockley leans back on his palms. "Start a revolt, of course."

Marty and I blink in disbelief. The words sink in slowly, like ink bleeding through paper. It takes me a moment to realize I haven't imagined them.

"A *revolt*?" Marty exclaims.

Lockley shushes him. "Keep your voice down."

My eyes are so wide they could pop out. "Are you out of your mind?"

"Maybe a little, alright?" Lockley shakes his head. "It'll never work now with the baby and everything... but we had every detail planned out."

He tells us.

Fire has always been at the root of their desire. They were young, and Raven was newly Unseen, and she hadn't yet learned to tame her rage. They thought about spreading gasoline around the facility and starting one that way, but with the tower and water trailers added to the equation, a fire would never last long enough to do anything meaningful. They'd just get themselves killed and make things worse for the other prisoners.

There's also the issue of the electric fence.

"We needed a way to start a fire that's big and destructive enough to be a serious problem, a way to get rid of the water supply, and a way to take out the electric fence—all in one go," Lockley says. "We wanted to make everything malfunction and go to shit in the most quick and efficient way possible. Something they won't know is happening until it's already too late.

I ask about the tower—if that much water is enough to disable the entire fence, not just part of it.

"Electric fences use parallel circuits," Lockley says. "It's not like a string of lights where one goes out and the rest go out too. It'll only take out a part of the fence."

"So the water tower falls, knocks over that part of the fence, and makes it short-circuit," I say. "That still doesn't account for the ground around it being a hazard. All that water would conduct the electricity."

"How far would the electricity travel?" Marty asks.

"A few meters, a few tens of meters. The current's intensity will decrease the farther it moves away from the source."

"If all these prisoners are running around trying to escape, how would you avoid getting electrocuted?"

"We steal from the fence techs," Lockley says. "They use rubber boots and gloves. Rubber's an insulator, so electricity doesn't pass through it. That's how we'll get prisoners to cross over."

I rub my face with both hands. "This is ridiculous."

"But you're forgetting about one more thing," Lockley says. "The gasoline."

Marty and I swap confused glances.

"Gasoline floats on water because it's less dense. If you put enough of it in that tower before knocking it down, the water will cause the fence to short circuit, and the sparks will be hot enough to make the gasoline ignite. Plus the electrical conductivity of gasoline is very low. So low that it's considered a pretty good insulator."

Marty's eyes widen. "Holy shit."

I furrow my brow and stare at the wall, going over all the details aloud. "So the water tower falls. There'd be no more water to fight the fire. No more water to *drink*, either. The water and gasoline would spread. The fence would malfunction. Gasoline floats, so the sparks would start a fire. *That* would spread however far the water went. The gasoline would insulate the electricity. The fallen tower is wood, so that would catch. There are prisoner cabins nearby, so those would ignite too. The fire would jump from cabin to cabin, all the way down the row. And while Guards are running around like headless chickens trying to figure out which problem to handle first, prisoners are realizing there's an opportunity to escape, possibly fighting back."

"With shovels," Lockley adds.

I can't even blink. "This place would literally fall apart."

"That was the idea."

"All from one fallen tower. Plus slashing a few water trailers."

"Yep."

We sit in silence as Marty and I let the words sink in.

This is madness. Pure, unadulterated madness.

"That wouldn't be an organized revolt," I say. "Everyone on both sides would panic. It'd be every person for themself. People would be too desperate to think straight."

"Not to mention the safety risks," Marty says. "Even if the gasoline dilutes the potency of the electrical charge, it won't eradicate it completely. There'd be fire and electrical hazards everywhere. You can't keep hundreds of people under control in a situation like that. Statistically speaking, *someone* is going to get hurt. People will get themselves killed."

"The Guards would start killing on sight," I mutter. "We have Nightjade guns."

"You'd be surprised what an angry prisoner could do with a shovel, but yeah."

Marty can't even blink. "This is absolute mayhem."

"I know, okay?" Lockley rubs his temples. "A while back, that was the whole point. We weren't just trying to escape on our own, you know? We wanted to destroy this place completely. We wanted to create something people outside would talk about. Something the Presidency would fear. Maybe even inspire other prisoners in other Tombs locations to do something similar if the word got out."

He sighs, staring at the rug beneath us. "But right now, all I care about is getting that baby somewhere safe."

"Quietly," Marty says.

"Unseen," I add.

"And that delivery truck plan of yours? If we go about it right, our escape is practically guaranteed. We *will* make it out okay."

We all nod in agreement.

Lockley sighs. "Now's the hard part."

"And what would that be?" Marty asks.

I lean my head back and stare at the ceiling, answering the question myself.

"Convincing Raven she can't burn this place to the ground."

When the dinner bell rings, we all split up to look for Raven.

She couldn't have gone far. We check the places we've already scoured, just in case she's moving around. We check them again.

By the third time I visit the water tower, the sun is setting, and Raven sits at the bottom of the ladder.

She stands up when she sees me approach, shoulders stiff. They relax when she realizes it's me. She looks away. I duck my head to step through the criss-cross beams and join her in the tank's shadow.

It's quiet for a while. She keeps her arms folded over her chest like armor. I lean against a post and shove my hands in my pockets. "We've been looking for you."

Her eyes are red. There are dark circles under her eyes. Her braid is a mess.

"Have you eaten?" I ask.

A muscle in her jaw flexes. She still won't look at me.

"I saved you some food." I step forward and pull a piece of bread from my pocket, wrapped in a napkin. I extend it to her.

"I'm not hungry." Her voice is hoarse and sharp.

I realize this is a battle I won't win and set the bread on a beam. If it's a pride thing, she'll eat it when I leave.

"You know what day it is, right?" I ask.

"If you have something to say, spit it out or leave," she snaps.

"The delivery truck will be here tonight. Probably within the hour."

"Good for you."

"And you," I say.

"That's funny."

"I mean it, Raven." I step closer. "We have a plan. Marty and Lockley and I talked about it. We'll find some way to keep the Captain occupied, take out those Sitters, steal the truck, and drive as far as we can. That baby is starving, and this is the safest way to get her out."

Raven doesn't say anything.

"When we run out of gas, we'll steal another car, and we'll keep going until we get to Washington. It'll be easy from there. I know the woods."

She averts her gaze.

"We'll all be safe at the Cut." I step closer, softening my voice. She's an inch away. "It's nice there, you know."

She looks up at me. I set a hand on her shoulder. She doesn't pull away. My other hand twitches at my side. Slowly, her pinky finds mine. Just a flicker of a touch.

"It's in Washington, on the coast. A short drive from my mom's place in Northwestern Oregon. Pine trees everywhere. Close to the mountains. We've got gardens to feed us and give us medicine. Bees for honey. Animals. A pool table, if you play."

I swear she almost smiles. *Almost.*

"You said my dad sounds lovely, and he is," I continue. "Maybe we don't always get along and maybe I'll never make him proud, but I'm proud of him. And I think he'll really like you. There's also Beau. He's... Beau, but impossible not to love. Our Commander is a lot like you. She'll have plans for you to work on and jobs for you to do, if you want."

She looks away.

"We can get out of here, Raven." My voice is nearly a whisper now. I tuck a loose strand of hair behind her ear. "We'll leave. We'll get Fern and that baby somewhere safe. We'll find your sister. And someday, we'll come back for everyone."

"I can't go with you."

My hand freezes. Her pinky pulls away from mine.

"We don't exactly have another option here, alright?" I swallow, trying to keep my voice down. "That delivery truck only comes once every three months. If we miss this chance, that baby won't make it. You know that, right?"

She doesn't say anything.

"You know that, *right?*"

"It's not the only option."

I step back. "No."

"Aaron—"

"Lockley told me your plan, okay?"

"Then you know it's feasible."

I chuckle exhaustedly, running a hand through my hair. "Feasible? It's madness!"

"What about everyone else?" Raven steps forward, raising her voice. "We can't just abandon them."

"We don't have a way to get them all out safely right now. Your plan will only cause more harm than good, and you know it. Destruction like that? It'll put more prisoners at risk than Guards. Is that really something you want?"

"You don't know that."

"We can't start a *revolt* with a baby."

"I'll protect her."

"We said the same thing about Jelly, and now look where we are."

Her shoulders go rigid. If a muscle in her neck didn't twitch, I'd swear she was made of stone.

"*Nothing* is guaranteed in this place. Not your survival, not mine, and definitely not that baby's. It's too dangerous. We need to get the hell out of here, as quickly and quietly as we can."

"I already told you." Her voice is colder now. Calmer. "I'm not leaving until I've burned this damn place to the ground."

"You think I haven't thought about burning it down too?"

That makes her pause.

"I know they've wronged us. I know they've wronged you. This place is… so unspeakably *evil*, Raven, and I know that. Hell, I almost killed Saylor the other day." I laugh bitterly. Tiredly. "I tried to *poison him*, because I hate him, and I'm so damn angry all the time. I can't sleep. I can't eat. God, I can hardly breathe because it's *suffocating me*."

Her glare doesn't waver, but I can see her eyes start to water. I feel mine do the same.

"I'd give anything to see Saylor and everyone else burn for what they've done, and I don't care if that makes me a terrible person. Because I hate them, and I swear to God I'll tear this place down someday if you don't get around to it first." My voice cracks. I lower it. "But today can't be that day."

"And why not?" Raven steps forward, fists clenched. "If you're so angry, why don't you do something about it?"

"Because we need to think with our heads about this, alright? Our lives aren't the only ones on the line here, and your plan puts us all at risk. A risk we don't have the means to handle right now."

"It's the best chance we have. The best chance for *everyone.* Not just us."

"It's also the riskiest gamble," another voice says.

Marty and Lockley appear behind us, ducking to join us beneath the tower.

"Even if it works, it'll be chaos," Marty says. "You can't ensure everyone's safety."

"You can't save everyone, Raven," Lockley says. "No one can."

"*Our* plan gives everyone an equal opportunity to escape. What they choose to do with that chance isn't my problem, but it's better than abandoning them."

"You can't guarantee that innocent people won't get caught in the crossfire!" Lockley's close to shouting.

"And maybe that's a gamble we need to make."

Quiet.

"You don't mean that..." I mutter.

"I do."

None of us know what to say.

"Maybe our plan requires more risk, more sacrifice—but it's for the greater good of everyone here. And not just the people trapped in here. People out *there.*" She points to the fence. "No one's ever done anything like this before."

"Because it's impossible," I say.

"You're just worried about saving your own skin."

I blink, letting the words sink to the pit of my stomach.

She can't mean that. *Surely she doesn't mean it.* But when I look her in the eye, her glare is just as firmly grounded as ever.

"I had a way out, and I gave it up for you," I say. "For all of you."

Marty's brows crease. "What do you mean?"

"I was offered a promotion."

A fire ignites behind Raven's gaze. "You were *what*?"

"To Supervisor?" Marty asks.

"They said they'd reinstate me in the Corps."

Lockley glowers. "And you refused?"

I nod.

He scoffs. "That doesn't just *happen*. You can't refuse an official transfer like that. That's not how it works."

"This was different, alright?"

Raven's voice softens, but her glare doesn't waver. "Different how?"

I can't find the words to answer her question.

"You've only been here since August. You're hardly what I'd call a decent Guard. You cause trouble. You don't follow the rules. And you're telling me they want to send you back to the Corps?"

"Yes."

"Who came to you with the offer?" Her brows crease, gears clearly turning behind her eyes. "Surely it wasn't the Captain."

"The same Agent who sent me here." I look away. "Someone I know back home paid him off."

"You can't pay off an *Agent*, Aaron—not with money," she snaps. "It doesn't work like that. What could anyone at the Cut possibly have to make an Agent agree to pull you out of the Tombs?"

I open my mouth to answer, but it falls shut when I have none. The Syndicate's relationship with the Corps is a complicated one, and we don't have time to sit around while I explain it. And what would she think if she learned about my association with Agent Finch?

But her father is an Agent, I remember. *Of course she knows about the Syndicate.*

Before I have the chance to speak, Raven goes still. One word tumbles from her lips. "Cobra."

"What about it?"

"That night on the water tower," she mutters. "You said you've heard of it before. I thought it was strange, but I didn't think much else of it."

My muscles tense. Marty and Lockley swap confused glances.

"How could an Unseen rebel without a tracker possibly make his way back into the system without ties to someone on the inside? Someone chipped?"

"The Cut has connections."

"With who?" She leans back. "With who, Aaron?"

I swallow. "The Syndicate."

"The *Syndicate*?" Her hands curl into fists. "They're almost as bad as the Corps!"

"It's not like we're allies with them, alright?" I argue. "They trade favors with Command every now and then. That's it."

Yet.

"They buddy up with Agents to protect their business. People like my father. They don't care about others unless they profit from it. They *kill people*." Her brows draw together, eyes darting between both of mine. "If you have a Syndicate contact who can bribe an Agent, then what the hell is the Cut giving them in return?"

"I don't know."

"What do you mean, you *don't know*?"

"Keep your voice down," Lockley hisses.

Her eyes go wide. "It's you."

"I don't know what you're freaking out about, okay? We don't have time to—"

"It's you. You're the favor returned."

"You're working for more than just the Cut..." She backs away. "You're a Double Agent for the *Syndicate*."

"I'm just as Unseen as you are."

"You're not denying it."

Now, Lockley's staring at me in just as much confusion as her. Even Marty doesn't know what to say. I doubt they know anything about the Syndicate—but they sure as hell know what it means to be in cahoots with an Agent.

"Look. All our contact did was give me a place to stay and get me ready for training. And when I didn't come home, he sent someone to investigate. *He's* the one who wants me to be a Chaser. *He's* the one who wants me to stay a Double and work for him. I had nothing to do with it."

"Bullshit."

"If I really wanted to save my own skin, then I should have accepted the offer when I had the chance. But I didn't. Because I..." My words falter at the thought of Jelly. Doc. At the look in Raven's eyes, the memory of what it felt like to kiss her in that shed. "I couldn't leave you guys behind."

"Why didn't you tell me?" There are fault lines in Raven's voice that take me by surprise. It softens. "You should have told me."

"I don't owe you anything," I seethe. "In case you've already forgotten, you've been lying to me this whole damn time."

"Look, I don't know what the hell is going on with you two, but we don't have time to argue and point fingers," Lockley interrupts, stepping between us. "Aaron is right. You can't do this. Not now."

Raven looks at Lockley like he's just stabbed her in the back. "Fine. Go ahead, Lock. I get it. Take the truck. Run away. Bring the baby with you." She turns around and climbs through the posts, pausing to look over her shoulder. "I hope you and Marty are happy together. I hope Aaron gets to see his dad, and I hope that baby never has to go hungry again. But I'm not coming with you. I am not leaving unless everyone else has a chance to do the same."

She walks away toward the Graves.

I follow after her, leaving Marty and Lockley behind. "Raven."

"Don't."

"Can you just listen to me for one second?"

She doesn't say anything.

"*Raven.*"

I catch up to her and she spins around. "What?"

"You can't just stay here."

"Why the hell not?"

I don't say anything.

"I'm not stupid, okay?" She steps forward, voice cracking. "I *know* the chances of getting everyone out alive are slim. *God*, Aaron. That's all I know. But if I abandon them, I'd be no better than the people who put us in here in the first place."

"That's not true." I step closer. "Survival isn't selfish. You can't help anyone if you're dead."

She averts her gaze, eyes glossed in anger.

"I know you don't give a damn about me. I know we haven't been entirely truthful. But I..." I take a deep breath and step around to look her in the eye. "I care about you. Not because of what happened in the shed. Not because you're pretty, or smart, or funny as hell—but because you're a human being, and so am I. I want you to be safe." I swallow. "I *need* you to be safe."

"I will be."

"The safest option is leaving on that truck with the others. With me." I pause. "I'm not leaving you behind."

"You're wrong."

"I'm not—"

"I do care about you, okay?"

Quiet. Vultures circle above. Their caws sound so distant from down here.

"If I really didn't give a damn, why would I be upset? Why would I care that the only guy I've felt anything for since—since *him*, would rather run away than stay and fight by my side?"

There it is again. Another punch, like I've swallowed lead.

"*Surviving* is fighting back," I say. "Living to see another day—to laugh and smile and do all the things they never thought you'd get to do again—can't that be enough?" My throat burns. "We'll come back, Raven. Someday, we'll come back and get them all out. I promise. But for now, staying alive has to be enough."

"Somedays and promises don't bring people back from the dead."

"Your friends would never leave you behind. If you don't get on that truck, they won't either."

"This is happening whether you want it to or not." She speaks sternly again. "If you don't want to be a part of it, go ahead and escape while you still can." She turns around. "At least I'm no coward."

I stand still, watching her walk away, far into the sand where she disappears inside the shed.

Marty jogs up to me. "You tried talking her out of it?"

I nod.

"There's no convincing her, is there?"

"No."

It's silent for a while, until Marty speaks. "Then what do we do?"

"We need to find a way to stop her. Make it so her only option is getting on that truck with us."

He studies the shed in the distance. "That door doesn't lock, does it?"

"What prisoner would ever wanna steal a few rusty shovels, Marty? I take one look at them and feel sick to my stomach."

"Fair."

"And we can't just lock her up. She's too smart to stay put for long and it'll only piss her off. We still need her to come with us."

He exhales heavily. "Of course."

I close my eyes, clutching my hair in fistfuls. Every breath feels heavy, taking energy I don't even have. I would give anything to get advice from Dad right now. But he's not here.

Walter's words echo in my head.

"You're all on your own."

Marty's words pull me out of it. "We could turn her in."

My head snaps to face him. "What?"

"It would give the Captain a good distraction *and* detain her while we make a run for it. She's already made it clear she doesn't want to go with us. We could use her as the diversion we've been looking for. *Without* letting her cause mass destruction."

"Like hell that's happening."

"Aaron—"

"Marty, I love you buddy, but I swear to God, if you so much as touch a single hair on her head—"

"Alright, alright. You'll kill me, I get it." He sighs. "So no turning her in."

"No."

He closes his eyes. "I have no idea what to do."

We stand here in silence for a while, watching the sun melt beneath the horizon. The last bits of light are fading. Vultures keep circling above us.

The truck will be here soon. We only have so much time to come up with a diversion for Valdez, a way to stop Raven's plan without pissing her off, and somehow get her to leave with us.

Because I made a choice to stay here, and I'm not leaving her behind.

"I'll turn myself in."

I don't realize I've said the words aloud until Marty glares at me. "Are you out of your *mind*?"

"I'll go straight to the Guards and tell them."

"Tell them *what*?"

"The truth."

My head buzzes with new energy, like I can feel the gears rotating in my head. I turn to Marty with a grin. "I'll tell them her plan. The water trailers, the tower—everything. They'll be so busy monitoring the trailers and the tower that they won't notice you and Lockley handling those delivery truck drivers. There would be no way for Raven to carry out her plan. She'd have no choice but to get on that truck with you guys."

"What about you?"

"I'll figure it out. I'll sneak away and join you once the truck is ready to go and Raven is on it. And then we'll leave. All of us. No unnecessary deaths. With that truck, we wouldn't even need to worry about finding water for everyone out in the desert. We'll follow the road and get supplies in the nearest city. No Chasers on patrol would stop us if we're dressed like the delivery drivers. Hell, I doubt anyone's patrolling out here, anyway."

"The Guards won't believe you without proof," Marty argues. "They'd want you to bring *her* in too."

"I'll show them where her gasoline stash is."

"You've been helping them steal the gasoline, and Stokes saw you with Raven. What if they connect the dots?"

"Stokes won't say anything because I'm keeping a secret of his too. Without him as a witness, they won't know. There aren't any security cameras."

"Are you sure we can trust him?"

"We've kept each other's secrets for this long. If he really wanted to turn me in, he could've done it a long time ago."

"I don't like this, man."

"And even if the Captain thinks I'm in on it, I'll play dumb. I'll tell them I had no idea what they were using gasoline for. I was just interested in…" I scratch the back of my neck. "Raven."

"They'll still call you a sympathizer."

"Not interested in a *sympathizer* way. Just uh…" My face warms. "A sneaking out to the shovel shed kind of way. That warrants Correction, at the very most. Not extermination."

He shakes his head with another sigh. "It feels too risky. There has to be a better way to distract the Captain *and* keep Raven from doing anything stupid."

"There probably is, but we don't have that kind of time. That truck will be here any second."

I look at the last remnants of sunset. The horizon is a dark purple now, almost black. It's strange how the sky can shift so quickly. It could be day one minute and night in a blink. The sun always seems to slip through my fingers.

"I don't want any more death on my hands," I mutter.

"Neither do I."

We stand here for a while, watching a flash of dry lightning in the distance.

"So tonight, then?" he says quietly.

I nod. "Tonight."

"I can't believe we're finally getting out."

"I can't wait to breathe again. See a tree. Touch grass."

"Play a video game. Do a load of laundry."

"Crème brûlée."

His smile is strained, but for a moment, he wears it brightly.

I look him in the eye. "The Corps will figure out we helped them escape eventually. They'll find the real drivers and notice we're missing."

"I know."

"You won't be able to live as you anymore. You and your family won't be safe. You'll all need to be debugged. Marty Dawson will die." I pause.

"Is that really something you want?"

He smiles at me. "I don't think we'd mind being Unseen."

I can't fight a grin.

"Your family will be safe at the Cut. We'll protect you all, I promise." I wrap an arm around him. "You'll be glad to call it home."

Home.

The word doesn't feel so far away anymore.

I knock on the Captain's door.

It's almost curfew. Valdez answers with a frown, gilded in the warm light seeping out behind him. I peer over his shoulder. His cabin looks like it was carved straight from Whitestag and planted here with a crane.

He lifts a bothered brow. "Need something?"

I pause, trying to think of what to say first.

"I advise you not to waste my time, Officer Beck," he says. "I have a long night ahead of me, and you've just woken me up from the nap that was *supposed* to prepare me for it. Unless you have anything meaningful to say, leave."

"The prisoners are planning a revolt."

He blinks.

The world stills. My heart doesn't beat. My lungs stop taking in air as I hold onto my last breath. Like if I let go, all my secrets will fall out with it.

And then he laughs.

The sound booms, bouncing between buildings, lingering in the night air. A few Guards on patrol toss puzzled looks in our direction as they walk by. I even spot a passing prisoner pause to see what's going on.

Wait a minute.

I squint, making out the image in the dark. The slender shape of her shoulders. The long braid trailing over her shoulder, almost blue in the moonlight. The red ribbon tied to its end.

Raven doesn't say a word. How can she in front of the Captain?

How can *I* say anything?

My eyes go wide. She's only yards away, and I scream at her in silence to leave—to trust that it's not what it looks like, and disappear before the Captain sees her.

But the look in her gaze tells me that trust is no longer something we share.

How can she trust me after our argument? After learning about Finch's offer? My ties to the Syndicate, who represents everything she hates about her father?

Can I even trust her anymore, after what she kept from *me*?

I can't back out now. I'm already here on the Captain's doorstep. I've already said what I needed to say. And if I go back on those words—if I lie and tell him I'm only joking—I'll get Corrected in the warehouse for inconveniencing him. And when the Supervisor in charge of my punishment notices the delivery has paused, they'll suspect something is off. They'll find Marty and Lockley dealing with the drivers, and catch on to our plan.

We'll get exterminated immediately.

When Raven finally turns to storm away, I can't run after her.

Monday, November 14

The Captain swipes his finger along his eye, as though wiping a tear. "Oh, Beck. It's terribly funny that you thought I'd actually believe you."

"I'm not joking."

His smile fades. "I don't know what you're up to, Officer, but if you don't go back to your quarters *this instant—*"

"I'm not up to anything. I meant what I said."

"Do not mistake me for a fool, boy," he spits.

"The prisoners, are planning, a *revolt*."

His brows knit together. He stares at me like I've just slapped him. "What?"

"Now are you going to do something about it before it gets out of hand, or let a bunch of traitors overpower you?"

His face pales. "You can't be serious."

"I am."

Valdez steps outside, pointing a finger in my face. "If this is your idea of some sort of sick joke, I will see to it myself that you and whoever else is involved are *thoroughly* Corrected."

"It's no joke."

He stills. He lowers his hand, face paling beneath the moonlight. "A revolt, you say?"

"I have evidence too."

For a moment, I worry he might follow up with his threat and send me off to the warehouse. I've never been Corrected before. I wonder what Supervisor he'd assign to teach my lesson. Maybe it'd be the same one who carved those lines into Raven's palm. Maybe they'd do the same to mine.

Instead, Valdez ushers me inside. He points to a chair. "Sit."

I do.

He grabs a gray coat from the hook by the door and weaves his arms through it. "Do not move until I return."

"From where?"

He gives me one last glare before taking his exit. "I'm summoning my Supervisors."

I sit on a velvet couch in the Captain's living room, surrounded by over a dozen Guards and Supervisors. Stokes is here. He stands in the corner, arms folded tightly over his chest. He hasn't been able to look me in the eye after what happened with Jelly.

Saylor is here too.

And I tell them everything.

I weave the story like my father always does, over-explaining every detail to stall for Marty and Lockley. They'll need as much time as they can to deal with the delivery truck drivers.

It begins with my walk to dinner this evening. I was heading to the cafeteria when I heard shouts coming from one of the prisoner cabins. The words were muffled and I couldn't make them out entirely, but I assumed it was an argument. It sounded serious, so I stood on the porch and eavesdropped.

That's when I heard about their plan.

For months, they've been stealing gasoline from *our* trucks, right under our noses. I tell Valdez and the Supervisors about the water tower—how they plan to knock it down and start the fire. I go over every logistical detail Lockley told me, and judging by the pallor spreading over each Guard's face, they know it's entirely possible.

They know it will be madness.

When the prisoners left for dinner, I searched their cabin.

That's when I found the gasoline.

"I know I broke a rule by entering a prisoner's cabin," I say to Valdez, feigning worry. "However, I was only doing what I thought was right, given the situation. Correct me if you have to, but I will *always* choose what I think is best for the greater good of the Corps, and those we serve to protect."

There it is—the secret I've been keeping since August. The worst of my dirty laundry, left to air in front of Guards who could easily have me exterminated if they discover how I'm bending the truth.

Valdez stares at me for a long time, stroking his chin in thought. I close my eyes and wait for him to call me a liar. My pulse quickens, blood roaring in my ears as he studies my scar. My eyes. It takes all I have not to look away. To swallow down the fear coursing through my veins like ice.

"Where is this gasoline, exactly?" he finally asks.

"I'll have to take you there. It's hidden pretty well."

"I want Stokes, Saylor, Booth, Adkins, and Lucas to come with me." Valdez snaps his fingers. "Let's see what these filthy traitors have been up to."

I lead them across the facility in silence, hoping they don't see me flexing my fists over and over again in the dark. Lockley and Marty should still be dealing with the drivers. Fern is hiding out in Martha and Lacey's cabin with the baby until the truck is ready. The cabin should be empty. *I hope it's empty.*

But if Raven's in there, we're screwed.

We reach the cabin. I knock, just in case she is inside and needs time to hide. None of us knock before entering. She'd know something was up.

"Just open it," Valdez commands.

I do as he says.

We walk inside. Panic blocks my airways as I scan the room for any sign of Raven or the others. I have to hide my sigh of relief. No one's here.

"I'm not sure if any of the other cabins have this too, but... there's a crawlspace. Goes all the way beneath the porch." I walk to the center of the room, crouching to pull the rug away. The trapdoor creaks when I open it. "Follow me."

I lead them down the ladder and into the crawlspace. It's dark, but enough moonlight seeps in through the gaps in the planks to make it navigable. I turn the corner. "It's over here."

I stop dead in my tracks.

The gasoline is gone.

There is nothing but dust and cobwebs. Not a single one of the containers I helped Raven fill remains, save for an empty cleaning jug in the corner. There aren't even marks in the dirt from where they spent months sitting. I see footprints from where Raven must have kicked over the lines.

My chest tightens. "It's gone."

"We can see that," a Supervisor sneers.

"I—I was just here. It was all right here, I swear."

"I suppose it just... miraculously disappeared," Valdez says.

"Yeah. I think someone moved it somewhere else."

I turn around. Valdez rubs his forehead in exhaustion. A few of the Guards snicker behind him. Saylor is one of them.

My shoulders slump. "You don't believe me."

"Officer Beck, you came to me claiming you had evidence that prisoners are starting a *revolt*. I cleared my schedule to follow you all the way out here and gape at an empty room. I should be overseeing the delivery. You realize how frustrating this is, correct?"

"Yes, but—"

"Lying about a matter as serious as this warrants *severe* Correction."

"I'm not lying!"

"Then where is your evidence, hm?"

I don't know what to say.

"Waste of our time," a Guard mutters.

"I know what he's doing," Saylor says. "He's trying to lie his way to a promotion so he can get sent out of here."

Everyone goes silent, waiting for him to continue.

"He's lazy, you know. Does terrible work. Always chatting with the prisoners. Especially that pretty girl with the braid. What's her name again?" He taps his chin, pretending to be in thought. "Raven?"

My face pales.

"Is this true?" Valdez asks.

"Wait a minute..." Saylor feigns surprise. "Doesn't she live *here*? In this very cabin?"

My pulse sputters, tripping over itself as it picks up the pace.

"He's right," Stokes says.

Everyone turns to face him. My stomach lurches.

"I've seen Officer Beck around camp with her," he continues. "Raven."

Valdez lifts a brow. "You have?"

"I didn't think much of it at first. I've always been preoccupied with what I thought were more important tasks."

I try to meet Stokes's stare, but he still won't look me in the eye.

"I think he's been helping them siphon gasoline from our vehicles. I've had my suspicions for a while, though I was never able to confirm it. I've seen that girl walking around with jugs of cleaning solution, but it took me a while to put two and two together. And take a look at this."

Stokes walks over to the empty jug in the corner. It's one of the ones we used to transport fuel down here. He takes a sniff. "Gasoline."

Valdez and the other Guards step forward to confirm. All of them nod.

The Captain pulls a phone from his pocket. "Send a team of Agents our way. *Now*."

My pulse becomes a hammer. A lump forms in my throat, like some invisible snake is wrapped around it. I don't think any air passes through. All I can focus on is the smell of gasoline.

Stokes ratted me out.

I kept his secret, exactly as he agreed to keep mine. And he just gave it away like it was nothing.

"I believe I know what's going on here." Valdez shuts the phone and pockets it. "Two of my Supervisors claim you have some sort of relationship with this Raven girl. Is this correct?"

"I don't know what you're talking about." My voice is shakier than I'd like it to be.

"Don't lie to me, Beck," he seethes. His volume makes me flinch. "I think you've known about this plan for longer than just tonight. You've been helping her, haven't you?"

"I'm not a sympathizer," I hiss.

"You were helping her, until you realized you got in over your head. You came to your senses too little too late. And now you're here, trying to find a way out."

"That's not true."

"It's your word against theirs, Officer." Valdez gestures toward Stokes and Saylor. "Why would my two most trusted Supervisors lie to their Captain?"

My heart sinks. I'm going to be sick. The hairs on my neck stand on end. My mouth is dry, clamped shut. I want to say something—to convince them I'm loyal to the Corps, so they'll send *me* to monitor the water trailers. So I can find my way out of this, convene with Marty and Lockley, and get Raven on that damn truck.

But no words come out. Like so many times before, I'm stuck with so much to say and no way to say it. *Why can't I say anything? Why am I so damn useless?*

Will anything I say even matter, with what Stokes knows?

He's clearly done keeping my secret about Raven. That information alone is enough to strip away my credibility.

This wasn't supposed to happen.

Valdez turns to Stokes. "I want you, Booth, Adkins, and Lucas to guard our water trailers." He spins around. "Saylor, I want you to gather as much information from Officer Beck as you can before the Agents arrive. Make it as easy for them to do their jobs as possible. Now if you'll excuse me, I have a few more phone calls to make."

His phone rings, and he climbs back up the ladder to answer it.

Saylor grabs the collar of my shirt and pushes me forward. Stokes still won't look at me.

"I thought we had a deal," I seethe.

When he finally meets my eye, I see that his own are watering. He shakes his head.

The room spins. My lungs are caving in. I trusted him. I kept his secret because I thought he would keep mine. But now, all he's worried about is saving his own skin. He realized I wouldn't make it out of this without an interrogation and wanted to discredit me before *his* secret got out. So he wouldn't get looped into this mess and get accused of being a sympathizer too.

I close my eyes, exhaling shakily. *This is all my fault.*

How the hell am I supposed to get out of this now?

Saylor pushes me toward the ladder. "Up you go, *traitor*."

I have no choice but to climb.

Valdez and the rest of us Guards file out of the cabin and onto the front porch. The Captain's voice blurs in the background as he barks orders over the phone. Agents will be here soon.

Saylor keeps his grip tight around my shirt, whispering in my ear.

"We're going to have a nice long chat, you and I." He chuckles darkly. "I've had my suspicions about you for a while, Beck. We have a lot of catching up to do.

One of the Guards gasps.

Everyone freezes. Slowly, we turn to see what he's staring at. He doesn't even blink. All he can do is point with one trembling, outstretched finger.

Far in the distance, beneath the glow of a full moon, an ash truck rams into the base of the water tower.

The tower falls.

The fence short-circuits.

And the fire ignites.

37

Monday, November 14

♪ AS BLUE AS INDIGO - TIGERCUB ♪

It is madness, exactly as Raven desired.

Valdez stares at the growing fire in disbelief. The phone falls to the floor, clattering by his feet.

The first row of cabins catches fire. Prisoners flee from them, running in every direction as the flames spread. We're so far away, and I can still feel their screams reverberating in my bones.

There is so much wood and dry vegetation, so little moisture in the air. The fire devours its fuel quickly. Other prisoners run out of the unaffected cabins to gawk at the scene in horror.

"I want all of you manning those water trailers, *now*," Valdez barks.

"They're already slashed!" a Guard shouts as she runs over. "There's nothing we can use to put this out!"

"Then you will all keep these prisoners under control until backup arrives. Use any means necessary, do you hear me? *Any means necessary.*"

Valdez storms toward the commotion. Stokes and the other Guards are quick to follow.

Saylor is too busy gaping at the distant fire to see me run for it.

I sprint. I've never been so thin in my life. My muscles ache and my head spins and my stomach screams with hunger, but I run with every ounce of strength I have left. Like my life depends on it—because in this moment, I know it does.

I reach the prisoner cabins, sticking close to the buildings and staying in the shadows. I turn down an alley and pause to catch my breath, coughing into my fist. I can already feel smoke scraping my throat and lungs as I peer out to study the fire.

I can hear the flames from here. They crack and writhe, twisting like angry serpents rising up into the sky. What's left of the water tower has already gone up in a blaze. I count four cabins already aflame. That number will rise quickly.

The night welcomes a stronger wind than usual. It sends a shiver through me, pricking my skin, tangling my hair. Glowing embers follow its every bend and twist. I can still smell gasoline somewhere within it.

Agents will be here within a few hours. Until then, Valdez and the Guards will be consumed with trying to control these prisoners. Marty and the others should already be readying the delivery truck. We need to leave. *Now.*

But I need to find Raven first.

I stare at the burning ruins of the tower. The Captain and a few Guards are already inspecting the truck, but Raven is nowhere to be seen. *Where the hell did she go?*

I run even closer to the fire, hiding in another alley to cough into my elbow. The air is thickening. This smoke is getting unbearable.

The screaming only continues. Every prisoner has fled their cabin. They stand in the center of everything, studying the chaos in stillness. Some Guards join the onlookers too. For a moment, nobody moves. It's like the monarchs all over again. Children cry. Prisoners clutch the sleeves of friends and family like lifelines. Some pinch themselves, desperate to wake from this nightmare and go back to sleep.

Until one of them shouts.

"The fence is down!"

All heads turn to the source of the noise—a bearded prisoner, pointing toward the part of the fence where the tower fell. Exactly where Raven wanted it to.

"He's right!" Another prisoner yells. "Over there, look! It short-circuited!"

"We can run for it!"

A murmur spreads through the crowd like a wave.

"No one will be going anywhere!"

This voice belongs to someone else.

Valdez stands at the head of the mob, glistening with sweat. Strands of once-perfectly-gelled hair frame his face now, swaying with the wind.

"Anyone who tries to escape will be shot on sight," he shouts over the noise. "Anyone who *moves* will be shot on sight. Agents will be here with backup any moment now, and they will not hesitate to do the same. We will put this fire out and return to work tomorrow morning."

No one says a word.

"*Shot on sight*," he barks. "Do you hear me?"

I stare down at my side. Sometimes I forget I carry this Nightjade gun with me.

The crowd boils over in protest. "Shot on sight?"

"We haven't done anything!"

The prisoners shout in unison, voices weaving into one enraged ball of sound. Their cries drown out the flames.

"Now's our chance!" A prisoner yells. She's grinning. "They can't keep us all in here!"

The sea yells louder.

The Captain pulls out his gun—and he shoots the prisoner in the arm.

Nightjade pellets are not lethal. They are hardly a bullet. It takes her a moment to realize it's buried itself into her flesh. Blood trickles down her skin, thin like a tear.

It's the poison inside it that makes her fall to the ground.

"Does anyone else feel like making an example of themselves?" Valdez shouts.

My heart drops. The crowd erupts. People scream. Cry. A man falls to the dead prisoner's side, sobbing as he cradles her face in his hands. Her eyes are still open. I wonder how long it will take him to realize they will never blink again.

The Captain's glare drills into the crowd. He lifts his gun, making it clear he'll follow through with his threat. Nobody can move. My nails dig into my palms, breaking skin, but my legs are cemented in place.

He's too busy looking for his next example to notice the girl with the red ribbon. She walks up behind him, shovel in hand.

She raises it over her shoulders—and she swings.

Metal cracks against the back of his skull. He falls forward, hitting the dirt with a thud. No one screams. No one does so much as flinch as we all wait for the Captain to move. Even the onlooking Guards are rooted where they stand, ambered in awe.

He never does.

"There are rubber boots and gloves." Raven's shout cuts through the roaring flames behind her. She holds up the stolen items for everyone to see. "They're electrical insulators. Share them and throw them back for those behind you once you've crossed over."

She tosses them into the crowd.

Sound returns all at once. Every prisoner cheers. They holler and whistle, raising their arms in the air like they're watching a game of sports—not here, already surrounded by so much death.

"You see that shed over there?" Raven points to the Graves in the distance behind her. The mob quiets to let her voice carry through. "Every day, we wake up on the same thin mattress, still exhausted from the day before. We wake up with our heads pounding, mouths dry, muscles aching. Our palms are cracked and blistered. Our feet are just the same. They give us unfiltered water that makes us sick, food we wouldn't give our dogs back home. And still, we walk up that hill. We open that shed, grab our shovels, and dig, just like they tell us to do."

No one says a word. Guards swap unsure glances, waiting for something to happen.

"Those shovels are still there." She lifts her chin. "Go hit a Guard where it hurts."

Raven ducks as a Nightjade bullet flies at her. One of the Supervisors clutches his gun in his hands, sending more her way. Another Supervisor follows suit. Raven drops the shovel and sprints off, disappearing between the untouched cabins.

Against the backdrop of smoke and writhing flames, the crowd becomes a blur of rust and gray. A prisoner overpowers a Guard and uses her Nightjade gun against her. Another Guard shoots the culprit in retaliation. That Guard gets his skull cracked open by the shovel Raven left behind.

Nothing is still. Screams drown out the sound of the flames. From my distance, I realize Nightjade guns are only so useful in the hands of inexperienced Guards. We don't have the bulletproof armor of real Chasers.

Against metal and force, fabric does nothing.

A group of prisoners return from the shed carrying more shovels. They start distributing them as another group runs back for more. With a tool like that, they could easily whack a gun from a Guard's hand—as long as they don't get shot first. They are angry and fueled by rage and grief, heartbreak and this newfound, dangerously addictive hope.

It will kill them all.

There are twice as many Guards as prisoners. With every crack of a shovel against bone, there is the silent hiss of a Nightjade gun in multiple directions. Bullets fly and bounce off the metal. Some hit Guards. Most of the ricochets kill prisoners.

I'm not sure how long I stand here, unblinking as the madness unfolds. Smoke crawls into my nose and down my throat, scraping and crawling until I'm coughing again. My eyes water from the fumes. From seeing so many prisoners I knew and helped, fall to the ground—dead.

Don't cry, I warn myself. *Not now.* Even as my throat constricts. Even as I watch another Nightjade bullet lodge into the throat of a young woman I once made tea for. A man I gave stitches to after he fell onto his shovel weeks ago. A boy my age who was only trying to run away.

Don't you dare.

I swallow the lump in my throat.

One thing at a time.

It's hard to hear anything over the screams and the wind, this fire that won't stop spreading. But through the roar, I swear I pick up a familiar voice. I turn around.

Raven stands on a roof, shouting into the night.

It's a small building across from the burning cabins. The tech's quarters, for those who kept the fence in check. I wonder if they met a fate like the Captain's.

She yells at the prisoners. She tells them they have been wronged—that for far too long, the Presidency has ruled our country with terror, and their Nightjade Order is an evil that must be purged. They kill those deemed unworthy of resources and take everything away if we cannot pay for rights we should already have. Only the rich and healthy survive. She says it's about damn time we take back what they have robbed. Those who can manage to shout cheer in agreement. Some who were cowering on the ground in fear pick up a shovel instead.

She's making everything worse.

The prisoners aren't running or using the rubber boots to cross over the fallen part of the fence. They're all staying and fighting. Years of rage fuel every strike, every kick, every scream. Every kill. For so long they have lived without control, and now that it is theirs again, they cannot get enough of it.

They're tearing each other apart.

I have to stop this.

I need to stop Raven—and we need to get the hell out of here. *Now.*

I take a deep breath and run into the crowd.

A prisoner almost hits me with their shovel as I jog, stopping when they recognize my face. I'm the one who helps, the one they can trust. A Guard shoots him for his hesitation.

I swallow the lump in my throat and keep going.

My coughing worsens the closer I get to the fire. Not a single cabin remains untouched by the flames. I weave my way through the chaos, dodging a few more shovels. I unbutton my gray coat and toss it on the ground, hoping I'm less of a threat without my uniform. Nearby, a prisoner punches a Guard in the mouth. His blood splatters on my white undershirt.

I'm close to the building now. Raven's voice grows louder. Nearer. I'm about to reach her when I hear someone crying, and freeze.

A younger prisoner sobs over a fallen man with a Nightjade bullet in his arm.

It's Bobby—the boy who ratted out Doc to Saylor.

He feels my stare and looks up to meet it, face wet with tears. He wipes his nose, going still when he sees the Nightjade gun in my hands. He thinks I'll shoot him for what he did. For a moment, I almost consider it.

I think I would have done the same thing if it meant saving my family from starvation.

I toss him the gun and keep moving forward.

I pretend I am not stepping over bodies and blood and broken bones. Because if I stop and look at them, if I pause to shut their eyes and say goodbye, I'll never get up again. I'll stay on the ground and cry until I meet my end from either a bullet or a shovel.

Keep going.

One thing at a time.

I reach Raven's building and run to the other side of it—the wall facing the western fence, which is untouched by water and fire. It's quieter over here.

I cup my hands and shout, "Raven!"

Her shoulders go rigid. Slowly, she turns around.

A chill snakes around my spine when I see the look in her eyes. There is hatred in her stare, and it is colder than anything I've felt.

She did this.

This isn't what Doc would have wanted. Not Jelly. Not Dad. Not me. This is exactly what the Unseen is trying to avoid in their cautious approach to revolution.

But this is what Raven's idea of rebellion looks like—and I can't be a part of it.

She climbs down, dropping five feet away from me. Her glare feels icier up close.

"What the hell are you doing?" I shout over the wind and screams.

"You're a traitor."

I flinch. *There it is.*

We both know she saw me on the Captain's doorstep. She *heard* me tell him about the revolt. And if she didn't right then, she would have learned the truth eventually—that I was trying to stop her. Stop *this.*

But I never betrayed her. The plan was always to get her to that truck, so we could escape together.

Betrayal would mean leaving her behind. And no matter how she lied to me—no matter what hell she's brought upon these prisoners—I would never forgive myself if I left her here to die.

"You turned us in." Her eyes are watering. "I *trusted you*, and you turned me in to save your own skin."

"I was trying to stop you, okay?" I step forward. "It was just a diversion. Lockley and Marty were going to find you and get you on that truck before I took Valdez to the gasoline. But you were already starting *this*, so they couldn't."

My hands ball into fists at my side. There's a lot I'd like to say to her right now, but I need to focus.

"I know you're pissed at me, but that can't matter right now. Our top priority is getting out of here alive. We can sort this out later. The others are already over there, and we need to—"

"Does that even matter?" Her voice cracks. "You don't care about this!" She gestures to the chaos unfolding behind her. "They've finally found the courage to fight back, and you're acting like it's a bad thing?"

"People are dying, Raven," I seethe.

"At least they're doing something!" She points to the crowd. "I've given them a chance to break free. That fence is down. The Captain is dead. I told them about the boots. What have *you* done aside from arranging your own getaway car?"

"And where will they get water?"

She goes quiet. Wind whistles, whipping her hair. Distant screams fill in the space.

"For the trip," I continue. "Where will they get water? I assume you thought they'd make it by foot, since you *haven't* arranged a getaway car. And how will you debug them without practiced surgeons? Sanitized tools?" I chuckle emptily. "*Water*?"

"The day Doc died? You were the one to come to *me* with your idea about the river. There has to be water out there somewhere."

"Do you know that for certain?"

"You saw those monarchs. There's no way they'd survive a trip out here if there wasn't water nearby."

"And how much time will you waste trying to find it before Agents track you down? You can't hide hundreds of people in a *desert*. And you can't make plans around something you're not even sure exists. Not without risking all of their lives." I jab my finger toward the riot. The flames, which have already doubled in size.

She grits her teeth. "You know I'm right about the monarchs."

"They're just butterflies, Raven!"

My shout echoes. She goes rigid.

"What happened to your logic?" I shake my head. "You can't win this. Agents will be here any minute, and if we don't get the hell out of here while we still can—"

"And what happened to your hope?"

I go still.

"Nothing is certain, Aaron! Nothing!" Her eyes glisten. "If we center our lives around certainty, nothing will ever change. People like us will keep dying, while people like my father and whoever the hell you know in the Syndicate get richer. If we want things to be different, then we need to *do things differently*. There is no gain without sacrifice. Without risk."

"This isn't the right way to bring change! People are dying *now*. What will this accomplish beyond killing your friends? The people you've grown to call family?"

"These people are risking their lives for what they believe in. You're running away."

My jaw tightens.

"I've knocked down that fence." She steps closer. "Maybe we don't have room for everyone on that delivery truck, but until backup arrives, I've given them a way out. At least now they can choose to take it. And if they don't—if they want to give up their lives for their anger, for what they believe is right—that's their choice. You can't make it for them."

I look around us. The fire. The screams. The bodies. So many broken noses. Poisoned blood. Cracked skulls. So much death, and she acts like it doesn't even faze her.

I take a step back. "You don't care who gets caught in your crossfire, do you?"

"This revolt means something, Aaron." She gives me a fleeting smile. A hopeful one. "This is bigger than you and me. Bigger than all of us. Others will learn about what happened here. Unseen, civilians, the Presidency, *everyone*. Our supporters will hear about Guards slaughtering prisoners during this uprising, and they'll be angry. They'll protest. They'll *act* on their anger. This fire will spread far beyond the fence, even after it's gone out."

"No they won't." I laugh cynically, stepping back again. "You really think the Corps will let this become public knowledge? And even if they did, do you really think anyone would give a damn?"

She stays quiet.

"People are scared. They're terrified of acting out because they've seen what happens when we even *mention* trying. This will only make everything worse."

"You don't know that."

"You're putting too much faith in the world to be good!"

"And you put too little in them!"

I shake my head.

"We've made *history* today. Can't you see that?" She chuckles disbelief —like she's proud of what's happening behind her. "History."

My eyes widen. The world slows to a stop. There is only her and me in the center of it. Yesterday, that would have been all I ever wanted. No prisoners. No Guards. No Unseen, no Presidency, no Syndicate, no rebellion. Just a world paused for the two of us. Raven and Aaron. Nightfall and daybreak, caught in a rainless sky where the lightning meets the horizon.

But when I look into her eyes, she is not the same girl I kissed in that shed.

She is rage, and she is not who she pretended to be.

I trusted her.

"You're making a tragedy on purpose." I swallow. "That was the point all along, wasn't it?"

She's quiet.

"You're just going to start all this and leave them to fend for themselves? Run away on your own while they're fighting a battle they can't win? For *history*?"

"I'm making the right sacrifices."

I feel like I'm going to be sick.

All of these prisoners and Guards—dead. Parents and siblings and children and lovers and friends. All of these people meant something to someone else. Even the Guards were children once. No one leaves this world entirely unloved.

No one was supposed to get out, were they?

They were always meant to burn.

I step back. Ever since I arrived at the Tombs, I feared the Guards around me. I worried they would discover my secret and kill me for who I really am.

But it's her I should be afraid of, isn't it?

My eyes water. I can barely breathe through all this smoke. I need to get out of here. I need to gather as many prisoners as we can fit on that delivery truck, and go.

I run to the crowd. The fighting is worse. There are more bodies to step over. More fumes to choke through. I stumble up to the first prisoner I see, coughing so hard I can taste blood.

He's a young man my age. He flinches when I rest my hand on his shoulder, then recognizes me. The Good Guard, they call me. Though now, I feel like anything but.

"The delivery truck is ours," I choke out. "There's room for you."

He glares. "Room for me? I'm not leaving until everyone gets to."

"Just—"

"Pick up a shovel and fight, coward!" He swings at a Guard running toward us.

"You're running away?" a prisoner asks from behind me.

I spin around and lower to her height. She's a young girl, Fern's age. There is blood splattered on her face.

"Come with me," I say. "We can get you out safely."

"He's right." She nods toward the other prisoner. "You are a coward."

I close my eyes, taking in a deep, unsteady breath. I try not to cry. It takes everything I have not to fall to my knees and tear my hair out and give up right here.

"There's a way out!" I shout. "The delivery truck!"

No one can hear me over the fighting.

I pull at my hair, spinning in circles. "*Would everyone just put the shovels down?*"

No one's listening.

"You're just as weak as I thought."

I turn around. This time, it's Raven glaring at me. The fire burns behind her.

"I thought you were better than this, Aaron." She shakes her head. I think she's crying. "I never want to see you again."

A brawl between a prisoner and a Guard separates us. I don't even see where she disappears to.

I stare at the other side of camp, untouched by fire, still protected by the dark. That's where the others are waiting. That's where the delivery truck is. Marty said they wouldn't leave until I showed up, but I can't let them wait forever. Agents will get here any minute.

I stare up at the sky, hoping for a flash of dry lightning. Something to tell me what to do. Wishing Doc was here. Wishing Jelly could sing me to sleep. Wishing I never left home.

I give the battle one last look, then turn around.

"Not so fast."

I freeze. The barrel of a Nightjade gun presses against my head.

I'd recognize Saylor's voice anywhere.

"I still have an interrogation to conduct, *Aaron*." He chuckles. "I always knew you were hiding something."

Tuesday, November 15

I'm tied to a chair.

I expected Saylor to drag me to the warehouse, where Correction usually occurs. He reminded me this is an interrogation, not a punishment.

There is a different place reserved for me.

Attached to the back of the Captain's quarters is what they call the holding cell. It's a dingy room made entirely of splintered wood, like the cabins currently being devoured by the fire outside. There is a table, two chairs, and a flickering lamp with a chain above our heads. I can't even hear the screams from where we are.

The rope keeping me in place is itchy. I've already tried unraveling the knots behind my back, but they won't budge. They dig into my wrists, making my hands go numb. I ditched my coat in the chaos earlier, leaving me in just my white undershirt. I hate having my skin exposed like this. Especially the scar on my arm.

Saylor stands on the other side of the table with his palms planted on top of it. "Agents will be arriving soon." He pulls away from the table.

"And when they do, they'll want to know exactly how this revolt started to prevent it from happening again." He flashes a shark smile in my direction. "That is the task our late Captain assigned to me, and I intend to fulfill his dying wish."

I glance around the room for something I could use as a weapon. I can't find anything. All I notice is one rectangular object in the corner. Something bulky, hidden in the shadows where the lamplight doesn't reach.

"So, before our higher-ups arrive, I'm going to ask you a few... *questions*, if I may. Just to get a good idea of what happened. And your part in it, of course."

Saylor starts pacing around the room. I clench my jaw.

He's not subtle in the slightest. It's obvious he wants an in with the Agents. I could very well be his one-way ticket beyond this fence and back within the ranks of the Corps.

He picks at his nails. "However, I doubt you will have the pleasure of meeting these Agents yourself. Once our little chat is over, I will have no choice but to dispose of you."

"You want to dispose of me?" I force a chuckle. "You really think the Agents will praise you for that? They'll be pissed off. They'll want to take a crack at me themselves."

"I'm not *stupid*. I know that." He rolls his eyes. "But my goal is to become an integral part of the investigation myself. If you're not around to give them information, and our Captain isn't either, I'll be their only source of quality news. Understand?"

"Why tell me any of this? You think I give a shit?"

"Because I want to make something very clear, *Aaron*." He plants his palms on the table again. "You're not getting out of this alive."

I want to crack a joke. I want to piss him off. But when I remember the rope keeping me in place and the odds stacked against me, I can't deny the shiver that runs through me. He's wanted to kill me for a long time.

Now's his chance to get away with it.

I glare at him with everything I have. I think about headbutting him, but I can't even reach him from this angle. And with my legs strapped to the chair too, I can't exactly stand up without toppling over in the process.

I'm completely stuck.

Saylor walks to the shadowy corner and picks up the object. A pallor washes over me when he slams it on the table.

Doc's medicine bag.

"I kept a few souvenirs from your friend's extermination. I hope you don't mind." Saylor reaches inside the bag and pulls out a glinting scalpel. He pricks the tip of the blade with his finger and sucks away a drop of blood. "Mm. Sharp."

He walks to my side of the table and leans against it, crossing his legs. "I'm going to make you do what you do best." He chuckles. "Talk."

I swallow dryly.

"So, Aaron. Where *did* you get that name?" Saylor starts pacing the room, circling me like a vulture. "Cedar Warren Beck. That's what your ID card says, but... I heard your little girlfriend calling you something else. What was that all about?

I don't say anything.

"Are you going to answer my question?"

Still, I keep my mouth shut.

"Giving me the silent treatment now? And that withering look?" He fakes a shiver. "I'm terrified."

I don't even spare him a glare.

"The whole point of an interrogation is to *talk*. And if you don't start talking..." He pauses behind me, tracing the back of my neck with the scalpel. Not enough to draw blood. Just to remind me that he could. "I'll have to cut the answers out of you."

He continues circling me. "Speaking of which, let's cut to the chase here. It's very obvious that you sympathize with more than just prisoners. I'd like to draw special attention to the specific *type* of prisoner you've aligned yourself with." His smile fades. "Rebels."

I look away. "I don't know what you're talking about."

"Oh, so now he speaks. I must have struck a sore spot."

Shit.

"If I were you, I'd cut the bullshit. You know exactly what I'm referring to." He traces the scalpel along my arm now. "That little girlfriend of yours?

Rebel. Her friends? *Rebels.*"

I swallow the growing lump in my throat. I know Raven's allegiance is no secret after what she did tonight. But the others? *How could he possibly know that?*

I can't ask the question without confirming his claims.

"And that old doctor you cried over? After his death, a few Agents did some digging on his background. His friends, family, associates. Public surveillance records. And you know what they found?"

He stops. Goosebumps bite my skin when he chuckles, leaning in close. "They believe he had connections to the Unseen. The *Underground*, Aaron." He straightens his posture. "And I think you do, too."

My pulse races. I know averting my gaze isn't making me look any less guilty, but I can't look him in the eye. I can't let him know that I'm afraid.

These questions are exactly what my dad warned me against all those weeks ago. And if I want to protect the Unseen—protect *him*—I can't answer them.

I can't give anything up.

"You're sweating quite a bit," Saylor notes. "Another sore spot?"

My jaw tightens.

"I'll take that as a yes."

He pulls up the other chair and sits in front of me, twirling the scalpel in his hands like a toy. Just seeing him touching the damn thing makes me want to rip it out of his grip and plunge it into his throat. He has no right to own anything that belonged to Doc. And now here he is, acting like the scalpel was his to begin with.

As soon as I'm out of this damn chair, he'll pay for that.

"You're a spy for the Undergrounders, and Aaron is your real name."

"The Underground?" I force a laugh. When it dies down, it's easy to wipe the humor from my expression. "Aren't you a little too old to believe in fairytales?"

"Don't play the fool with me, Aaron. We both know they're more than ghost stories. In fact, I'd say they're just about as real as *this*." He takes off my glasses and tosses them onto the table. The details of his face blur as he traces my scar with the scalpel—the jagged line snaking through my left eye.

I flinch when the blade gets too close to my waterline. "Where did you get this scar? It's rather peculiar."

My pulse quickens, but I keep my expression blank. "I tripped when I was a kid. Fell on a stick."

He stages a wince. "I'd imagine an injury like that must have affected your eye too, seeing as the line goes *through* it. But... it doesn't seem to be as scarred as your skin. It looks entirely unaffected to me."

What is he getting at?

Does he know I'm wearing a contact in my eye to cover the scarring? But even if he did, why would he care? Only Agents know about the trackers. They're the only Chasers who have that kind of security clearance, while Officers and the other divisions are led to believe they reside in our wrists.

I grit my teeth. "My eye is fine."

"Are you certain?"

"Yes."

"Hm. Well, I don't believe you."

He leans forward, placing a hand over my right eye. Panic floods through me as the world grows dark. Thanks to that botched debugging surgery over a decade ago, I can't see a thing through my left, even without a hand covering it.

"How many fingers am I holding up?"

Shit. I try to open my right lid, but he presses his palm harder against my face, keeping it shut. *I can't see anything.*

"Tell me, Aaron, or I'll give you a scar on your right to match. You don't need your eyes to speak."

"Four."

Saylor pulls his hand away. I blink the room back into place—only to see him holding up three.

"So you really can't see from your left eye. I'm curious. Why lie about something so trivial?"

It feels like someone's injecting my veins with ice water.

He tilts his head. "Unless it's not trivial at all."

I clench my fists and keep my mouth shut as he leans closer, inspecting my eye again. "You're clearly hiding your left eye behind a contact lens.

It's a slightly different shade of brown than the other. And if you got this scar when you were a kid, then why were you also masking it with makeup when you first arrived? I saw no trace of it until after the concealer faded off."

"I don't see why any of this matters."

"Why go through so much effort to hide this scar of yours, unless it *did* matter? And why deny the true state of your left eye?"

I don't know what to say to that. I can't derail his logic without confirming I know about the trackers. And even if he did know the truth, where the hell did he learn it? From an Agent? A prisoner? Someone else?

He stands straight, but remains just as close, crossing his arms over his chest. "If you're not an Undergrounder, tell me how much you love the Corps, *Cedar Beck*. Tell me about the respect you have for us and your methods. Tell me you love the Pick and what it means for the preservation of humanity. Tell me you desire to be a Chaser above all else. Tell me you *despise* the rebels and the filthy traitors we're surrounded by. Tell me, when we catch that girl and carve her into pieces for what she's done, how much you will love us for it."

I spit in his face.

He freezes. My heart plummets into my stomach. *Shit.*

Shit shit shit shit.

"Ha! *Now* we're getting somewhere." Saylor pulls the chair closer, smile fading. "I know what you really are, Aaron." He extends the scalpel, tracing it from my neck to my heart. He twists it just enough to sting. "And I despise you for it."

When I look him in the eye, I know he means it.

"Let's start with the basics, shall we?" He retracts the scalpel, crossing his arms over his chest. "Where are you from?"

I don't say anything.

"Where is your home? Your base?" He tilts his head. "Your files say you hail from the training center in Seattle. I assume your camp must be somewhere in Washington. If you were a Double Agent, they wouldn't send you too far from home, would they?"

I keep my mouth shut. He chuckles darkly. "Still giving me the silent treatment?" I give him the finger—but he can't see it with my hands tied behind my back. He leans closer. "I said, where is your base?"

I smirk. He's not getting shit from me.

That's when he slaps me in the face.

The heel of his palm cracks against my lip, cutting it against my tooth. I spit out blood, hoping to stain his uniform, but it only dribbles down my shirt instead.

"Your silence is making it increasingly clear that you *do* have something to hide. You're just refusing to tell me. And that makes me *very* frustrated. Especially considering how nice I've been up until this point. I could have been carving you up this entire time." Saylor rises, stepping forward to grip the back of my chair, caging me with his arms. "But I'm starting to lose my patience, and I don't think I want to be this merciful anymore."

Saylor leans in, mouth so close to my ear I can feel his breath against it. "You can spare yourself so much pain, simply by having a conversation with me. It would be so easy to get out of this, Aaron." He hisses through clenched teeth. "Just. *Talk.*"

Now, I do open my mouth. "No."

"No?" He steps back, raising his voice. "Is this really what you want? Are you really choosing interrogation over the easy way out? Torment over comfort? More lies over easy, painless truth?"

Yes. But I don't tell him that.

"Don't you get it?" He laughs cynically, running a hand through his hair. "You're going to die by the end of this, anyway. I'd be willing to hand you an easier death if you give me what I want. So tell me, Aaron." He leans closer. His breath is sour. "Where. Is. Your. Base?"

I don't say a word.

Saylor sighs and pulls away. "Alright, this is clearly not working." He rummages through the bag and pulls out a plastic water bottle filled with an amber liquid. It glistens in the lamplight. "Thought I'd bring in a familiar friend."

My eyes widen. *Is that—*

"Gasoline. Thought it might make you a bit more comfortable, since you clearly love it so much."

He uncaps the bottle. I can already smell it, the stench clawing at my throat just as it did outside. But up close, the burning is so much worse.

He steps closer.

"Saylor..."

He walks around to the back of my chair.

"Look, we can talk about this, alright? There are other ways to get an in with the Agency—"

He pulls my head back by my hair, and forces the bottle into my mouth.

Fire. That's all I can think about, all I can see, all I can feel as the liquid scorches its way down my throat. The fumes corrode my nose, my lungs. My eyes water and sting. I jerk my head, trying to pull away, but he clutches my hair to keep me in place. He pours even more. I can feel it in my chest, traveling down my esophagus and into my stomach. Magma carving through rock.

He pulls the bottle away. I gasp for air, coughing and wheezing as I choke out the gasoline.

"Don't worry," he says. "I won't give you enough to *kill* you. Not yet, at least."

I'm already dizzy, voice raspy as I glower at him. "What the hell is wrong with you?"

"So you don't want to answer the base question. That's okay, because I have plenty more." He starts pacing again. "How does your group hide from the Corps? I have a feeling you *are* involved with those Washington Undergrounders. The cowardly ones who hide in the woods and distribute medicine to Chips. As if that really makes them part of a *rebellion*."

Behind my back, my hands tighten into fists.

"As pathetic as your group may be, they are quite elusive, I'll give them that. Those in other areas—like the Southwest Region we stand in, for example—have no large encampments that we know of. The Corps has raided dozens of smaller ones who aren't as skilled at staying hidden as you are. So tell me, Aaron. How do you hide from the Presidency in plain sight? And how can we find the rest of you?"

I bite the inside of my lip to keep from saying anything stupid.

"There must be some secret you all have discovered. We have trackers, by the way. But I'm sure you already knew that. There's talk that the

Undergrounders have discovered this and found a way to disable them. Some sort of surgical operation. Is this correct?"

I only glare.

He slaps me again. I spit out more blood when a second split cracks through my lip. "Still won't talk?"

"Screw you."

"Then I think it's time we begin Phase Two."

He walks around to the back of my chair again. I brace myself for more gasoline, throat still burning from the last dose. Eyes still watering from the stench lingering on my collar. But instead, he cuts off my shirt.

I can't see what he's doing. Even when I crane my head, I can't get a good view—not with the lack of sight in my left eye. The blind spot makes the hair on the back of my neck stand on end. I can only listen, only feel the warmth of his nearness as he leans closer.

The point of the scalpel is cold against the center of my back.

He digs it into my skin—and he drags it down.

Slowly. Carefully. Deliberately. He doesn't even flinch when I call out in pain, leaning my head back and squeezing my eyes shut. He just keeps the blade on its steady path, searing my flesh every inch of the way.

I want this to end and I know it hasn't even begun. But I can't give him what he wants. No matter how badly it burns, I will not break.

I am still Unseen.

He stops. Blood tickles my back, a warm dribble down my spine.

"A five-inch incision really made you squirm that much?" Saylor chuckles. "Oh, Aaron. In another life, maybe I'd pity you."

I brace myself for another slice, but he removes his hands from my back. I ready myself for another onslaught of questions instead. No matter how he provokes me, I can't lose my temper. I think about my home and how desperately I want to keep it safe. I can't let my emotions get the best of me. I have to stay calm. I *will* stay—

Cold liquid pours over my back, seeping into the wound. I cry out. My eyes clench shut so tight splotches of white bloom in the black. It looks like television static. Like stars.

I've never felt a burning like this before in my life. The pain is scalding, and I bite my tongue to keep from crying out again. I taste blood.

"Don't worry. I won't get *too* much in your bloodstream. It won't kill you." I can't see him, but I can hear the cruel smirk in Saylor's voice. "Just enough to really sting."

I hang my head low, eyes still shut. Sweat drips down my forehead.

I am still Unseen. I am still Unseen.

"I am still Unseen," I mutter.

"What did you say?"

I chuckle. Deliriously, maybe, but it still feels like my own cut back. Another taste of defiance. Just like how it felt to play Cobra with the Gamblers, laughing when they want us weak, smiling when they want us broken. Like how it felt to watch the lightning and its sunsets with Raven before she threw everything I felt for her down the drain.

This is rebellion.

"What's so funny?" Saylor snaps.

I manage a fleeting grin. "I'm not telling you shit."

He asks me more questions. He wants to know where exactly my base is located—surely to give the Agency another opportunity for a raid. He wants to know how we've grown so good at hiding, unlike other Unseen groups. He wants to know what we are planning. How we are organizing. How many of us there are. He is desperate for any morsel of information that he can trade to claw his way back to the Corps.

But with everything he asks, I give him the same answer in response. Reassuring him and myself that I will not break. I *refuse* to break.

"I am home where I belong."

I am still Unseen.

I say this so I can pretend. So I can be anywhere but here, anything but the shell of an almost-man, tied to a chair he's too weak to escape from.

And with every reply that isn't what he's looking for, I am burned all over again.

It's a fire of metal and flesh, stainless steel and gasoline. I cry out every time, pinching my tongue between my teeth to keep from screaming my throat raw. Blood fills my mouth. I can't tell if it's soaking my back too, or if that's just the gasoline. Maybe it's both.

Another question. Another cut. More gasoline. "I am home where I belong."

I am still Unseen.

Question. Cut. Gasoline. "I am home where I belong."

I am still Unseen.

This is what keeps me grounded. This is what I tell myself, over and over again, until it's all I remember how to say.

Saylor creates tallies on my back. Every time I refuse to answer a question, I get another one. I'm sure they'll scar. Some marks will certainly get infected. If he keeps this up for long enough, I'll get chemical burns too.

With every incision, I think of home. I think of my father in the garden. My mother pouring coffee in Port Keys. Lori digging for sand crabs on the shore. Beau laughing like sunshine, like music. The Yesterday albums Cecil was always so happy to let us borrow. Viv's guidance. Hugo's intelligence. Noriko's comforting command. Asa's steadiness. I think of everyone who calls themself Unseen, everyone who calls the Cut home.

And I will protect them until the end.

Even if it kills me.

"I am home where I belong." I exhale shakily through my nose as Saylor carves into my back again. Soon he'll run out of room. *I am still Unseen.*

"Cut that out," Saylor shouts. His hands are shaking too. A strand of hair has fallen out of place. This is almost as hard on him as it is on me. He can't stand that I won't crack. "Every time you say that, I'm going to give you another mark. Is that what you really want?"

I manage a breathy chuckle. "I am home where I belong."

I am still Unseen.

Another cut. More gasoline. "I am home where I belong."

I am still Unseen.

I think I'm crying now, but it's hard to tell. "I am home where I belong."

I am still Unseen.

I am Unseen.

I say it until the pain becomes too heavy, and my eyelids can no longer bear the weight. They flutter closed.

Everything fades to black.

39

Tuesday, November 15

♪ BROKEN FINGERS - BLUENECK ♪

I blink the room into place, wishing I hadn't. Wishing I could go back to that endless dark, where there was no fire devouring my back and chest. No gasoline stench.

But I am here again, and gasoline is all I smell. All I taste. All I think.

Saylor sits in front of me, plastered in sweat. His hair is askew, like he's been running his hands through it. He still holds the scalpel. It's covered in my dried blood.

He tilts his head, grinning from ear to ear. "Look who's awake."

I spit at his feet.

"Are you going to talk now, or keep repeating that gibberish to yourself?"

My mouth is dry. Speaking feels like swallowing nails, but I do it anyway. "Go to hell."

"I hope I've made it very clear, Aaron—the kind of pain I'm capable of inflicting upon you." He picks more of my dried blood from beneath his fingernails. They're chewed to the quick. He must have been biting them while I was passed out.

"You're stubborn, I'll give you that. But can you really be *that* stubborn all over again?" He leans forward in his seat. "It will be perfectly easy to retrace each and every one of your cuts. They've already started scabbing, but I can reverse that. I've run out of gasoline, though I'm sure the older doses clinging to your back will still make your wounds burn. I can easily come up with dozens of imaginative ways to make you wish you were never born."

Just the thought of another incision makes my eyes go wide. Like I'm feeling him carve into me all over again. With the throbbing pain infecting every inch of my back, he may as well be slicing me up as we speak. My head pounds from the smell of gasoline.

"You were out for a while, but... I believe the riot is still playing out." He stares at the door, then faces me again. The shark smile returns. "Maybe I'll find a prisoner to carve up. Will that get you to talk? I'm sure I can track down Raven, if she's not already dead. Or that nice Fern girl. Where did she run off to?"

My eyes spring open wider. It feels like my every cell has been set on fire, but I glare at him with all I have. "Don't you dare touch her. Not Raven, not Fern, not any of them."

"But it would be so fun." He extends the scalpel. I flinch, but it never touches my skin—just hovers in place as his eyes darken. "I can't stand prisoners, but I hate the Unseen even more."

Unseen.

Unseen.

All at once, my breathing stops. My heartbeat sputters to a halt. I can't even blink as I absorb the image of the Guard in front of me. His gaze is just as cold as it is blue. His uniform is grayer than mine ever was. The knuckles clenched around Doc's scalpel are so pale with tension they could be snow. He hates me for what I am.

But who is he?

My arms shake. I remember it now. He said the word earlier too—before I lost consciousness. Before he started cutting into me. And I'm so damn used to saying it myself that I didn't think anything of it until now.

The network of rebels woven throughout our country is nowhere near united, but there is one thing we all have in common.

Only *we* call ourselves Unseen.

And when I hone my gaze to study his left eye, I see it. A slightly different shade of blue.

He's wearing a contact too.

I try to keep my hands from trembling, but my body betrays me anyway. I know Saylor can sense it. He knows I'm afraid. He knows I'm catching on. But I can't focus on a single one of the questions swarming my mind. A thousand whys and what-ifs buzz like hornets.

Who is Holden Saylor?

And if he really is what I think he is... why does he despise me so damn much?

He chuckles. "You see it now, don't you?" He tilts his head, pointing to his left eye. "I had a feeling you might notice it eventually. Surprised it took you this long."

His mask of humor falls. He leans forward, twisting the scalpel pinned to my neck. It's still not enough to draw blood, but we both know he would in an instant.

"I caught on fairly quickly. Well, I had my suspicions, but no evidence. I tried being proactive and getting rid of you early on, just in case my instincts were right. Couldn't have you exposing my secret."

"What the hell are you talking about?" I mutter. The trembling is gone. I am dead still.

What secret?

"You Unseen have a way of flocking together. Just like Raven and those Goodwin girls. Just like your precious *Doc*. Rebellious spirits are just too kindred not to cling to one another. It's like a sixth sense.

"Maybe Raven pulling you out of that grave preserved your life, but it also reaffirmed my theory. Why would a prisoner have any reason to save a brand new Guard she hardly knows, unless that Guard wasn't *really* who they were pretending to be?"

I open my mouth to say something, itching to get one of my questions answered. But anything I want to ask will only confirm what he's accusing me of being. What I *am*. And what if he's lying? What if this is just some tactic to get me to confess?

Even Agents don't call us Unseen. How does he know what he knows? And what about his left eye?

My shoulders slump. No matter what his truth may be, I don't think there's any use in convincing him I'm loyal to the Corps anymore. I should save my breath.

If I can confirm my own suspicions, then maybe I can get *him* to crack. Maybe I can talk my way out of this.

"You said you didn't want me exposing your secret." I swallow dryly. "What secret?"

He only chuckles.

"What secret, Saylor?"

"Don't forget who's leading this interrogation." I grimace when he digs the flat edge of the scalpel into my neck. This time, it breaks the skin. Blood clusters around the line before falling as a trickle down my throat. "Don't forget who could easily end your life with one little stroke."

I think about the fork Stokes said he plunged in that Guard's neck, wondering if Saylor will do the same to me. Wondering if he'll even hesitate. I can't imagine he would, given what he's already done to Garth.

My lips part. *Garth*. That Guard he killed in the cafeteria.

I turn the story over in my head.

You don't stick a fork through someone's neck around an entire crowd of people unless you're reacting to something. Acting on some emotion they provoked within you, that you just couldn't tame when it finally boiled over the surface. It wasn't planned like the way I tried to use the rattlesnake poison. It wasn't secretive like the way Saylor tried to kill *me* when he buried me alive.

What did Garth do to make Saylor so emotional that he would risk his own skin to get vengeance?

My gaze flickers back to the contact covering his left eye. Like me, he wouldn't be wearing it if he didn't have something to hide.

Not every debugging procedure goes wrong. But if you don't have access to a practiced surgeon, you're going to get scarred. Even those back home who had scarring didn't cover it with contacts, because they weren't around Chips.

Chips. He said that too, didn't he?

I pin my gaze to his, keeping my voice steady. "Where are you from, Saylor?"

I expect anger. I expect him to walk back around to the other side of my chair and start carving me again, just as he promised. But he simply lifts his chin, face blank. "Fleabane Rock."

Ice runs through my veins. *Fleabane Rock.*

The largest Unseen encampment in the Southwest Region.

That's right here in New Mexico. I've seen it marked on Cecil's maps. It's hardly a fourth of the Cut's size, but it was significant enough to have a pin.

Nausea claws my stomach, threatening to summon up what little I had for dinner. All I can do is stare at the wall behind him, hands shaking. This can't be true. He's lying. He's trying to manipulate me into giving him what he wants. But what good would this do to earn my trust, after carving into me the way he did? What benefit would he get from lying about this? How does he think this will make me crack?

Goosebumps stipple my skin when I wonder if it is simply the truth.

I think back to everything Stokes said. How Saylor couldn't adjust to the food. How he was Corrected for spending too much time with the prisoners. How this place changed him.

And when he looks me in the eye, still clutching that scalpel, I picture the fork again. I see the emotion in his gaze.

Vengeance.

"They took something from you," I mutter.

"*You're damn right they took something from me.*" He rises so quickly the chair falls over behind him. He uses his free hand to clutch the back of my own chair, keeping the scalpel pressed against my neck with the other. His nostrils flare. "Lance was never meant for this place, and they sent him anyway. They didn't give a damn that he was always smaller than the others. Too good-hearted to kill a damn fly. They *stole him* from me."

My eyes peel wider as the realization hits.

He followed someone in here, didn't he?

He was a Double—and he got himself sent here on purpose.

"They took my best friend." His hand curls tighter around the chair, carving into the wood. "They took him, and they *broke him*." His head hangs low. He squeezes his eyes shut, like he's trying not to cry. "He was gone before I even stepped on that bus."

Treachery is the one crime no one can evade. If the Corps knew Lance was Unseen, they would have killed him on the spot, not sentenced him here. And they would have known if he had no tracker. He had to have been a Chip. A civilian contact, like Asa.

For a moment, I almost feel sorry for Saylor. It's quick to pass when another pulse of searing pain reminds me of everything he's put me through in the name of his hatred. Of what he did to Doc. To Jelly. To all of us. Of what he's threatened to do to more prisoners if I can't find a way to get out of this before the Agents arrive.

Vengeance.

"That's why you killed Garth." I swallow. "You talked to the prisoners. They told you what he did to your friend."

"Say his name again and I'll slit your damn throat," he growls.

The pressure of the scalpel draws blood again, and I know he means it.

"You're right. I did talk to them. And you know what they said? They did *nothing* to stop that Guard. *Nothing* to save him, because they were too worried about saving their own skin. And I realized something that day."

He laughs, clutching his hair with one hand. "The Unseen are no different. Every day, someone out there is killed for asking the wrong questions. For stealing a stick of gum, or drinking prohibited alcohol without Immunity, or whatever so-called *crime* they think warrants extermination. And in here? The Unseen don't even know what goes on in here, because they're too caught up in their own hesitation to give a damn. They hide, and they do nothing while another Lance dies, *every single day.*"

"You're no better than they are," I seethe. "How many deaths have you caused with your cruelty? How much suffering?"

The back of his hand cracks against my cheek, snapping my head to the side. I straighten my neck with a glare.

"And you're the only thing standing in the way of making things right." He leans back, running a tired hand through his hair. His eyes look bloodshot, like he hasn't been sleeping. Maybe it's the smoke. Maybe it's a bit of both. "I tried everything I could to run the show around here—to get back to the Corps and climb my way to the top, so I can break them too. *Years* trying to sharpen into who they want me to be. And I'm *this close*, Aaron. All you need to do is talk."

He runs the scalpel over the lines in my neck. He lowers his voice. "This could be so easy if you would just give in."

"If you really were a Double, you already have enough to give the Agents, don't you?" I spit out more blood. "Why go through all this trouble to get anything from me?"

"I won't give up the place I once called home." There it is again—that sinister half moon smirk, and the shiver it weaves around my spine. "But I'm not above handing over yours."

There is nothing I can do when he walks to my chair. I can only close my eyes and cry out as he starts carving my back again. Each and every tally, made as good as new.

I give every question the same answer until I can't speak at all anymore. *I am still Unseen.*

I want to die.

It didn't take long for those four words to replace my previous slogan. What was once a ritual to keep me grounded morphed into a prayer, an internal plea for anything in this universe that might be listening. To hear me and grant my wish.

I don't think it worked, because I'm still breathing. Barely.

I want to break. There is no more room on my back or chest, nowhere he can carve that hasn't been sliced already. I can't even bring myself to think about what he might try next. He will ask more questions and I will bite back the answers, and that will compose my final hours.

He was right when he said my death would be slow.

It's morning, I think. Daybreak. Faint orange light seeps in through the holding cell's one minuscule window. The Gamblers are probably gone by now. The delivery truck too. Once the Agents arrive and finish sorting through the aftermath of the riot, the fires, they'll come looking for me. The Guard who made it all happen.

If they get to me, I will break.

Saylor paces back and forth, eye twitching. He can't stand that I won't speak. That no matter how many times he retraced every tally with that scalpel, I still haven't given in.

Maybe it's time. Maybe there is something I could tell him. Something that won't be devastating to the Cut, but will get him to stop. Something that will finally make him get around to killing me.

I don't even remind myself that I'm Unseen aloud anymore, because I'm afraid that if I open my mouth, something will slip out against my will. So I keep it melded shut, dry bits of my chapped lips sticking together. It will hurt to pry them open again.

Saylor stands in front of me, leaning in so I can see the redness in his eyes, the twitching of his neck. "I'm going to extend you a generous offer."

I don't even have the strength to glare.

"If you can answer this one question for me, I will kill you. A simple slice across the neck. It will be quick and painless and we can both be done with this whole ordeal. Does that sound like something you want?"

I don't have the strength to keep myself from nodding either.

Yes.

I want this to be over. Over so it doesn't hurt anymore. Over so I won't be breathing when the Agents get here, ready to do so much worse to get me to speak.

"Would you like to hear the question?"

I close my eyes, sighing heavily. I nod again.

He leans over to whisper in my ear. "Where is your base?"

That's it. That's the question.

Four words. I can end this with just as much, if not less.

I want to give up.

"You seem a little out of it, Aaron. That's probably my fault. Gasoline will make you delirious. Can you at least describe it for me?"

"Trees..." I mutter.

"Trees? Now we're getting somewhere." He leans in closer. "Tell me more."

I can barely keep my eyes open. "Meadows."

"Meadows! Yes, all *very* good information. What else?"

My eyes flutter closed. "Fields with flowers. Lupine. Fireweed." I cough. "Harebells."

"Harebells?" Saylor laughs. "Surely you don't mean Harebell Hill. They were raided ages ago."

Harebells.

My eyes snap open.

The word stirs something within me. In a blink, I am no longer here, but there—in that dingy room with Raven and the others, watching Jelly hold her baby for the first time. I can hear her crying, and the lullaby her mother sang to her. It painted pictures of purple harebells and mountains like the ones near my home. It spoke of lakes and dragonflies, birdsong and dewdrops and...

Daybreak.

Just lifting my eyes takes effort, but I bring them to the window. More light filters in now, brighter than it was a moment ago. The sun can shift so quickly sometimes. It paints the walls with honey. The room may as well be filled with it, given how slow everything feels. Like time has stopped, and here we are, suspended in pain and nectar and the glow of a morning I have yet to meet.

I made it through the night.

There is another shift, but this time, it's not the light changing. The memory of Jelly's lullaby fades away, and I am left with my father's voice instead.

"Bring the morning with you."

It's faint, at first. I've heard the phrase countless times growing up, but its memory is thin. I always despised it—shoved it to the back of my mind where I didn't have to think about it, and that's where it's resided all this time.

But that night with Raven on the porch—when I saw that lightning bring a hundred mornings with it—I thought of him. I rediscovered his words, like pulling an old book off the shelf and blowing away the dust.

"Bring the morning with you."

I can hardly hold my head up. I keep it lowered to save my strength, but I drag my gaze upward, settling on Saylor's glare. His eyes are so cold, so blue. It startles me when I see my reflection within them. Like blinking mirrors, mottled red with exhaustion.

My face is so bruised and swollen it takes a moment to recognize myself. Strands of sweaty hair fall over my gaze, but in my own eyes, I see my pain so clearly. My fear. I'm too weak to even mask it, because afraid is exactly what I am right now. I'm afraid because I failed. Because I'm weak, and always have been. Because I always think with this damn heart of mine instead of letting my brain take the lead. And now, the people I love are at risk. When those Agents get here, they *will* break me. I don't think I've ever been this terrified in my entire life.

I can't even think about what they'll do to my home when I give them what they want.

That is my weakness. My stupid, stupid heart.

I pull my focus away from me, back to the eyes I saw myself mirrored in. In Saylor's stare, there is just as much pain, just as much fatigue. But there is something different to the hurt I see in him.

There is a callus around his wounds. Like the gnarled wood that grows over lesions in a tree, harder and crueler so nothing can get in and hurt the soft parts of its core again. When that wasn't enough, he grew thorns. Because if he can become the one inflicting wounds, then maybe his own won't hurt so bad. That is his illusion of control.

If things had gone differently on my path, maybe I'd be exactly like him. We were the same once. In another life, he could have been my brother. My Beau. But I don't think he has anyone to protect anymore beyond himself.

That is where we are different. He doesn't have my weakness. My heart.

I still have people I need to protect.

I stare at the light again. *"Bring the morning with you."*

I think I get what Dad means now.

Morning is the rise of a new dawn. It is the hope that today will be different from yesterday, and maybe tomorrow will be even better. It is a snake shedding its skin. It is a monarch traveling thousands of miles with wings it wasn't even born with.

Change.

Morning's coming whether I tag along or not. *Change* is happening whether I adapt or not. Last night is enough to prove that true.

Maybe Raven's methods were wrong, but she had a point. People hurt every day. People *die* every day, while others sit by and do nothing but watch. That is the very problem the Unseen exists to unravel. If I give in like Saylor wants me to, who will fight in my place after I'm gone? Who will pick up the shovel I can no longer wield?

Saylor stopped trying to be good a long time ago. If I give up now, I'll be no different from him.

Screw that.

We all carry mornings within us. Even if I've made mistakes—even if I've done things I can never take back—it's never too late to try to be good. To start over, again and again, and the next morning and every tomorrow after.

There are people I love. People I want to protect. And they deserve my every last tomorrow.

I conceal a smirk, and I close my eyes.

"You're finally done now?" Saylor asks. "Still won't tell me anything useful?"

I keep my mouth shut one more time.

He chuckles. "So I didn't get any information from you after all. That's okay. I had fun, while it lasted. I'll let *them* handle the unholy work. At least the Agents will be pleased I got you warmed up for what they have in store for you." He leans closer to whisper in my ear again. "Their job will be much easier now that I've stolen your fighting spirit."

My back and chest are bleeding. Burning. My skin feels like it's on fire from the gasoline. I can still feel it stuck in my throat. I'm not sure the smell will ever really leave me.

But I pull my head back—and I crack it into his.

My forehead slams against his nose, crunching the cartilage. He calls out in pain, stumbling into the table with his eyes squeezed shut, clutching what I've broken with both hands. The scalpel falls to the floor.

"*God dammit*!" He's still closing his eyes. Blood drips from his hands. "You'll pay for that!"

This is going to hurt like hell.

I take a deep breath, tip the chair over to my right, and throw all of my strength to the left. My shoulder slams into the ground as the chair topples over. Something pops. I bite my tongue to keep from crying out, using my unaffected arm to reach for the fallen scalpel.

By the time Saylor opens his eyes, I'm already cutting the rope around my wrist.

The bonds fall right when he kicks my hands. I yell when a bone in my pinky cracks, now bent at an unnatural angle. The scalpel flies across the room, far from my reach. Saylor doesn't waste a second before hurrying after it.

That gives me the time I need to stand.

Dragging myself off the floor feels like I'm carrying ten of me on my back. My drying wounds crack and sting with every bit of movement, but I swallow the pain. There is no room for me to feel it right now. *One thing at a time.*

My legs are still tied to the chair, but now that my arms are free, I can balance myself.

I remember a story my father told me once.

Before I left, we sat on our porch, drinking tea as we did almost every night. He told me about he and Asa's recklessness. About the friend they lost to a Chaser—and the chair Dad used to avoid the same fate.

And when Saylor approaches with the scalpel in hand, I use that story to knock him over.

The chair cracks into his knees, sending him back. The blade falls from his hands again. I dive to his side, grabbing for it frantically. I use it to cut the bonds on my legs. The rope falls away.

Standing is a challenge. My knees buckle, begging me to drop to the floor. If I'm on my feet for any longer, I just might. I've lost so much blood. My skin is clammy and sticky with gasoline. I can't take Saylor on in a hand-to-hand fight.

But I'm still not done with this chair.

I pick it up by the legs. And when Saylor finally rises to lunge at me, I use every last bit of strength I have left to hit him across the head.

He collapses.

I freeze. For a moment, all I can do is stand here, breathless, still clutching the chair in case he attacks me again. I wait another second. Two. Five.

He's still not moving.

The chair drops from my hands, clattering to the floor. I lower to my knees, wincing as my dislocated shoulder pinches. I extend a trembling hand. Slowly, my knuckles press against his neck.

There it is. The softest flicker of a pulse. He's out cold, but he's not dead. Now's my chance.

My gaze shifts to the scalpel on the floor. It glints in the morning light, which makes my blood look more like rust. I stretch for it, biting my lip as my skin pulls taut, every wound stinging until I finally grab it.

The blade shakes in my grip. I turn it over in my hands, thinking about how many times it made me scream. About all the times it made me wish for death. Funny, how one little piece of metal can steal so much blood from your veins.

It could draw so much from his too.

I press it against his neck, arm trembling. It would be so easy to run it across his throat. So easy to end his misery and rid the world of the Chaser he wants to become. I could even tie him up in that chair if I wanted to, while he's unconscious. And when he wakes, I could make him feel *exactly* what he inflicted upon me. Or worse.

Vengeance.

My shoulders slump with exhaustion. There isn't even time for that. If Agents aren't already here, they will be soon. I look over my shoulder. The door is closed. I can't see the aftermath of last night from here, but I know there will be many bodies to burn and bury.

I stare back at Saylor, scalpel still poised against his neck. He's fast asleep. He won't be able to hurt me anymore, if I get away quickly enough.

Do we really need another body?

If I give in—if I let vengeance consume me and stoop to his level—

doesn't that make me just like him?

If I let myself callus over, I'd be no better than Saylor.

I clench the scalpel tighter. There is a rage buried beneath the weight of my exhaustion, and if I uncover it, I'm not sure I'll be able to tame it. All I can think about is plunging this blade into his throat, just as he did with that fork. It would be justice for Doc. For Jelly. For *me*.

But I am not like him.

My arm falls to my side.

I am Unseen.

I leave him unscathed and limp out of the building.

The delivery truck is gone.

I can hardly stand or see straight. Tendrils of smoke curl around my legs, left over from last night's fire. It smolders in the distance behind me. I guess they finally put it out. Most of the buildings are gone.

Agents have already arrived. Chasers of all divisions are swarming the place. It's a miracle I managed to sneak through the commotion.

For nothing, it seems.

I stand in front of the locked gate. If I weren't in so much pain, maybe I'd laugh about how thoroughly this sucks. After everything I went through in that holding cell, I am still just as trapped. And the Gamblers are nowhere in sight.

They left me here.

I wonder what Raven said to convince the others to leave me behind. Maybe they didn't need convincing. Maybe they always meant to use me.

"Where do you think you're going?"

I freeze.

For a moment, I wonder if this is it. Maybe this is where I'll finally meet my end. This Agent will take one look at me and assume I'm a survivor from the revolt, not the Guard who helped start it. And when they see the condition I'm in, they'll shoot me on the spot. There is no use in wasting valuable resources on the recovery of a prisoner in my situation.

But the voice behind me is low and raspy, just like a smoker's.

Slowly, I turn around. Agent Finch holds up a set of car keys. "That's not the way out."

I don't have time to ask what he means before I finally collapse.

My eyes flutter, threatening to close as his footsteps crunch in the dirt. He stands over me with a chuckle. "Looks like your rainy day finally arrived, Rusty."

The world goes dark, and it is quiet.

Thursday, November 17

I never thought I'd be happy to see Ansel Schneider, but when I open my eyes and see his own staring back at me, all I can think about is that they are green.

I can't remember the last time I saw anything that color.

I blink my surroundings into place with a grimace, rubbing my pounding forehead. My pinky throbs. It's caged in a splint. Ansel sits in a chair to my left, shuffling a deck of cards in boredom. Lily sits cross-legged in her own chair, focused on whatever it is she's drawing in her tattered sketchbook.

I can't tell if I've just woken from a nightmare, or if I'm still dreaming.

I'm in my room back at Whitestag. The bed is soft and comfortable. The air is crisp and clean, scented with something like pine. There is air conditioning. My clothes are not gray and scratchy, but a soft set of dark green silk pajamas. My skin is bandaged beneath them.

I bring a hand to my eye. I can tell the contact isn't in. I get the feeling I've already been debugged.

They could pay a Corps healer to fix anything.

I study Ansel again, noticing something new on his wrists. There is a large *X* on either tattoo, covering each Card. Just like Ruth's. *When did he get those?*

"He's awake."

A low voice I recognize draws my attention to the back of the room. I hadn't realized Agent Finch was leaning against the wall, hands in his pockets.

Lily gasps. She sets her sketchbook down and makes a move like she's going to hug me, but stops when I flinch. She sits back down, worried, but forces a grin.

Ansel doesn't seem to care. He just keeps shuffling his cards. "Morning, sunshine."

I look over at Finch again. I open my mouth to ask him something, but no words come out. My throat is too dry.

"You remind me of my son," he says.

I nod. He answered my question.

"And I get free drinks for life at Prairie Pit now, so..." He shrugs. I almost laugh. "See you around, kid."

He gives me one small salute before leaving me alone with the Schneiders.

After he leaves, I turn to Ansel, lips parted. They're cracked and dry. I have so many questions, but I can't seem to get a single word out.

To my relief, he seems to understand my confusion. He lets out a bored sigh, still shuffling his cards. "Uncle commissioned Agent Finch to get you out of that place weeks ago. It should have worked out perfectly; Finch would have been there for Evaluation regardless. But you *refused* to go home with him."

I study my hands. The reminder makes my stomach churn.

"An idiotic choice, if I do say so myself."

Lily swats his arm, glaring. "Stop that."

Ansel shrugs away, shaking his head. "Naturally, as Head of House, he was called to address the... *situation* you stirred."

Images of fire flash through my mind. Beneath my bandages, every wound throbs. Burns.

"You were lucky enough to cross paths with him. He saw an opportunity to get on Uncle's good side—it's not like you could refuse to leave with him *then*, in your condition. So he debugged you and drove you home." He nods toward my battered state, nose twitching in disgust. "Now here we are."

Home. The word makes me flinch.

Ansel squints at me, dissecting my silence with his gaze. He sets the cards down and turns to Lily. "Would you mind leaving us alone for a moment?"

She looks at me, brows creased. "Is that alright?"

I nod. Ansel doesn't scare me anymore.

Lily is hesitant, but exits anyway. She leaves her sketchbook behind on the bed.

Ansel leans back in his chair, arms folded. "My uncle is off negotiating your return to the Cut."

I nod.

"But... he asked us to take care of something for you while he's away." Ansel looks over his shoulder. "You can come in now, Ruth."

The Viper walks in, carrying a black leather bag. She doesn't say anything, but she gives me a small smile as she takes a seat in the other chair.

I wait in silence. She retrieves gear I don't recognize and fidgets with it. It's a large handheld device, fitted with a needle at the end.

I don't flinch when she uses it to cross out my Cards with ink.

The needle is nothing compared to the lines still burning my chest and back.

None of us speak as Ruth works. Her hands are steady and gentle, but she works quickly. Like she's trying to be careful not to hurt me. I wonder if she knows about my wounds. When she finishes the tattoo, she wraps it in a clear, plastic-like sheet that clings to my skin.

She spares me one last pitiful glance before taking her leave too.

Now, it's only Ansel and me, alone in a room I never thought I'd see again.

"Do you remember the conversation we had before your last day?" he finally asks, cutting through the silence.

I nod.

He rises to his feet. "Looks like I was wrong about you after all."

I nearly laugh.

"Welcome to the family, Aaron." He pulls up his own sleeves, revealing the *X*s I noticed earlier. He lowers his sleeves and reaches out to give me a pat on the back, then decides against it. He holds out his hand instead. "Here's to an old skin shed."

I take it.

I glance down at my own new tattoos. I wonder if it's illegal to do such a thing. Then I remember who the Serpent is, and that I don't live in a place where it matters anymore.

"Think of these as a calling card of sorts. They mark you as his. And don't you worry, Becky." Ansel grins. I can't decide if I should shudder or smile back. "The Serpent always protects his Vipers."

And with that, he leaves.

I reach over to pick up Lily's sketchbook. I flip through the pages, smiling at the familiar artwork until I reach the last page—the one she was working on.

It's me, asleep in this bed. There are no fangs. No horns. No demon eyes.

Just me, exactly as I am.

I'm not sure why it makes me cry.

Friday, November 18

My dad shattered his foot while I was gone.

He has a crutch when I meet him in the woods, like the one he made for Beau so long ago. I look around for a sign of Asa or Cecil or Noriko. It's just him.

Ruth is the one who dropped me off at the rendezvous point. I can hear her walking away behind me, beginning her hike back to the car. When the sound of snapping twigs fades to silence, I know my dad and I are alone.

His hair is longer, past his chin like mine. His beard is grown out. We both look like a mess.

As if reading my thoughts, he clears his throat. "You need a haircut."

"You too."

It's quiet for a long time. Neither of us know what to say. Which is funny, because I've spent the past few months going over everything I'd say to him once I got back. The apologies I'd give. The gratitude I'd express. I didn't tell him I loved him enough while I was around.

Instead, I point to his leg. "You came all the way out here like that? What the hell is wrong with you?"

He drops the crutch and wraps his arms around me.

I hold him tighter than I ever have. I'm already crying when I close my eyes and bury my head in his shoulder. I'm an inch taller than him now. I breathe in his smell—pine and wood dust and something smokey. Like a fireplace, not a furnace. Like home.

"I'm sorry," I choke out between sobs.

"You don't have anything to be sorry for." I feel something hot against my neck. A tear. I've never seen him cry before.

"I failed, Dad. I screwed up."

"You didn't fail." He holds me tighter. "You came home."

"But I was stupid."

"You are not stupid, Aaron." He cups my face in his hands. "You are the sharpest person I know."

When he hugs me again, I know he means it.

The leaves are shriveled now.

There are few that still manage to cling to the milkweed's brittle stems. The ones that haven't fallen are no longer green as they were before I left, but dry and brown as the plant prepares for dormancy. Large, pointed pods live in spaces once occupied by flowers. Some of them have already started splitting open, revealing fluffy white seeds waiting to be stolen by the wind.

This is the guardian of Gooseberry's grave.

It's a shame I never got to see it bloom this year.

Dad and I stand in front of the tombstone, steeping in the gilded glow of evening. November runs cold, but the setting sun casts our backyard in warmth. A gentle wind coaxes my hair. The grass. The evergreen needles around us, which seem to be whispering my name.

I'm not sure how many times I've read the words carved into the marker at my feet, or how long we've been rooted here in silence. But I read them again and again, committing every carefully etched letter to memory.

HERE LIES A SON.
EARTH BE KIND TO HIS BONES.

My throat burns. I never realized I missed Dad's handwriting this much. Not until seeing it here, remembering what it felt like to read through the notes he always scrawled in the margins for me. Every textbook and encyclopedia we own has been touched by his ink.

I can't wait to read them again.

"The monarchs visited this year." Dad's words slice through the quiet.

I nod, shifting my focus back to the milkweed. Trying everything in my power not to think about what happened last time I saw a butterfly.

"I wish you could have seen it." His lips flicker with a hint of a smile, but it's quick to fade. "You loved them as a kid."

I remember, I want to say. But the sentence won't come out. No words have—not since I broke down crying during our reunion.

"The plant will regrow soon enough." He lets out a tired sigh, burying his hands in his pockets. "No dormant season lasts forever. As long as it has its roots, it'll come back around every spring."

Roots. Doc's words echo in my head. *"There's always a root."*

I glance over at Dad, who can't bring himself to look me in the eye. And when he does, I notice his real one is watering. He reaches out a hand. I flinch at first, making him freeze—until slowly, it makes its way to my face. He traces my cheek with his thumb, as though he's checking to see if I'm really here. Like I could have been a ghost.

It's just how he looked at me when he first brought me to the Cut, all those years ago.

He lowers his hands, staring at the goat's grave instead. "I took good care of him while you were gone."

I nod. *Thank you*, I want to say—but still, nothing comes out. It's like my tongue and brain no longer know how to communicate with each other. The words are stuck. Trapped. *Fenced in.*

"Cleaned the dust and dirt off. Gave him fresh flowers every week." He nods to the dried bouquet of lavender I hadn't noticed before, resting beside the stone. "I kept him company. Read beside him. Cecil even joined us for a drink."

I'm not sure why a lump is forming in my throat, but I can't seem to swallow it down.

"After we heard—" His voice cracks. He can't finish the sentence. "When you didn't come home, staying by this grave was all I wanted to do. All I *could* do."

He looks at me again, and my heart sinks. "We just wanted you to come home."

Home.

The word does something to me. It feels like a blanket, like plaster being scraped over every crack and flaw etched within me. Because for the first time in so long, I am standing in the only place in the world worthy of that title.

No, I correct myself. I glance at Dad. *He makes this place home.*

Mom and Lori, Cecil and Beau, Noriko and Asa and the strategists and Lily—all of them are my home. *People* are home.

As long as I carry them with me, I could stand anywhere in the world and be exactly where I'm meant to be.

Pines continue to bend with the breeze as I watch my father study the grave. And when I see the way he looks at that stone, just as he always looked at me, I see the way I once looked at Gooseberry. And for the first time I can remember, I finally feel like I understand him.

Even though I separated that goat from his old world, from his family, I did what I thought was best for him. For his survival. Didn't Dad do the same for me?

I lean my head back and stare at the sky, not a plume of smoke in sight.

And it *was* best for me. If I'd grown up out there—in the world that soured Ansel and silenced Lily and hardened Saylor into the monster he became—I would be different. I would be on the wrong side.

The Unseen—the Cut, my father—this is the right side.

"Thank you," I finally manage to say, looking my dad in the eye.

He huffs. "Don't thank me. If anything, it makes my life easier. I have big plans for our garden this year. Would hate to dig up the wrong spot—"

"For bringing me with you," I interrupt.

For a moment, our gazes lock. Then he turns away, wiping his eye with the back of his hand.

"And you brought the morning," he says.

The breeze returns. It runs cold fingers through my hair, snaking around my neck before reaching the milkweed in front of us. We watch it grab a seed. And when it's carried away into the sky, it looks like a feather until it finally disappears. I wonder where it will be planted, what new growth will sprout from this loss.

One thing at a time, Aaron.

For now, I am here.

I am home, and we enjoy the quiet together.

CAUTERIZED

EPILOGUE

Monday, May 8

♪ BROKEN EYES - TWO GALLANTS ♪

I don't talk very much anymore.

It's not a choice. I'm not being negative or making a statement. It's not that I don't have the words, because I do. I think the issue is having more words than I know what to do with.

I say things when I need to, when my brain decides to let me say them. But usually a shrug or a nod is enough to let someone know I'm listening or get my point across.

It's been months since I've participated in a full conversation.

I'm not around enough people to talk much, anyway. Most of my days are spent in my room or the library, scouring over Dad's encyclopedias and anatomy books until every word is ingrained in my memory. There is so much to learn and it keeps me busy. The people who care know not to bother me.

Dad takes me wherever he goes, when he can. His foot bothers him a lot, so usually he'll ask me to do things for him. Even if it means going out to the city to deliver something or pick up a package on his behalf.

Noriko and Cecil do the same. They help me stay busy. I deliver letters to the cabin so she and Cecil can focus more on their plans for the Cut's future. The write-up I gave them helped more than I thought it would. There is lots to study about how the revolt went down, and how we can avoid mishaps like that in the future. Even Beau has taken an interest to the Cut's new plans. Apparently, he's a strategist now, just like Viv and Hugo and Cecil. Dad says my disappearance was the tipping point for him. He wanted to do more to help the rebellion. To get justice.

We smuggle for the Syndicate now. I guess that's one productive outcome that emerged from this whole ordeal. I'm not sure if it's a good thing or a bad thing long-term, but it's one step closer to a good relationship with them. They ensure we have a steady stream of supplies, and we help them store and trade their contraband. Medicine and weapons manufactured beyond our borders. Moonshine and Yesterday guns. Information.

I'm not sure why Noriko decided to compromise her old morals and start this whole smuggling thing. She always seemed so insistent on staying out of their work. She and the others keep quiet about the *why*, but I think they owe the Serpent for what he did to get me out of that hellhole alive.

Maybe we have debts to pay that I don't know about.

I try not to think about it too much. Which is easy, because I do stay busy. I educate myself. I've taken up most of Dad's healing responsibilities around the Cut so he can work in his labs. I'm fixing up the greenhouse a bit. I still do handiwork for Miss Hart when she's not looking.

Staying as quiet and distracted as I want to be is easiest in the woods. I spend a lot of time out here by myself, venturing back and forth from the cabin and even farther if needed. I love the silence of it all. But it's a noisy kind of quiet. Not the quiet of an empty desert. The quiet of soft birdsong you can hear when you pay attention, or a waterfall in the distance, beckoning you with its whispers. And you take the detour, and the whispers grow louder, and you've found the waterfall just by listening. And it's loud there, with rushing white water and mist that pricks your skin when you get close. There is no one else around to enjoy the view but you.

So you close your eyes, and you feel the water's touch, and you let the rush drown out the noise in your head, just for a little while.

There are no screams. No cries. No distressed conversations that stop when you enter the room. Just an empty forest that is somehow still so full of life and sound.

There is no sand in the woods. You are not trapped in emptiness but surrounded by trees and scampering rabbits and bucks with towering antlers who are not scared by your headlights. Like you belong in the evergreens just as much as they do.

I never feel lost here.

I stand by the waterfall a moment longer than usual, just to feel the mist on my skin. Today, I'm supposed to meet Asa at one of our rendezvous points out here. I have medicine for Margot and I want to catch up with him.

Well, catch up with him as much as I can without talking.

I read a book he recommended. It was ass. I wrote him an angry essay about it.

A bluebird chirps, pulling me back to my senses. *I should get going.* I nearly slip when I turn away from the waterfall, but I catch myself.

I hike to our usual spot, next to a mossy boulder and a hollowed-out fallen log. Sometimes there are snakes in there. I hate snakes. I'm almost to the spot and just about ready to pull out the essay folded in my pocket when I freeze in my tracks.

The girl sitting on the log is *not* Asa.

Her curls are dark brown, cascading over her shoulders in a frizzy mess. There's a leaf caught within them that I don't think she notices. She swats away a bug, crinkling her nose in disgust. Her tanned skin is rosy across the bridge of her nose and cheeks. A sunburn. Like she's just spent a day out at the pool, or maybe a river.

My face warms.

I think she's the prettiest girl I've ever seen.

The realization makes me clumsy. I step on a twig, sending a snap echoing through the trees. I scramble to hide behind a trunk just as she whips her head around. She narrows her eyes, looking for the source of the sound. She slides off the log.

She hasn't noticed me yet. A wave of relief floods through me. That's good.

I have no idea who she is. She could easily be a threat—especially considering the fact that Asa is nowhere to be seen. I need to keep my cool so I can maintain the upper hand.

I take a deep breath, letting it cool away my flustered blush. *Get your shit together.*

I watch her take a few steps forward, scanning her surroundings. She almost looks... scared. *Is she lost?*

Given the leaf still stuck in her hair, which she seems to be oblivious to, I wouldn't put it past her.

I close my eyes and release a long, strained sigh. *Is this why Asa isn't here? Did he see her in our regular meeting spot and take a rain check?*

While her back is turned, I slowly make my way toward the log. I climb on top of it, sitting exactly where she was only a moment ago, waiting for her to turn around. It doesn't take long.

She stifles a gasp when she sees me in her place. I slide off the log and walk up to her, pausing two feet away. "You're not supposed to be here."

"And here I am."

I frown. *Okay, attitude.* Then my eyes widen.

I just talked.

I *talked*.

Whenever I break from periods of silence, it happens without warning. There's usually a trigger of sorts—like something that got on my nerves, or a joke I want to tell.

The girl is glaring at me now. I glare back, because it's rude. *What could I have possibly done to piss her off so soon?*

My shoulders relax a bit. *Maybe that's it*, I wonder. I'm annoyed that she's here, and judging by the looks of it, something about me is bugging her too.

I hide a smirk. Everyone back home is too afraid to be rude to me, given all that I went through. To her, I am simply a stranger who's getting on her nerves. Not broken. Not fragile. Not volatile.

It's refreshing to be seen as an annoyance again.

I shove my hands in my pockets, studying her. Something about her feels familiar in a way I can't place. Like I've seen her somewhere before.

"You lost?" I ask.

Oddly enough, she doesn't seem lost at all.

Lost Island
PRESS

Get Lost. in bonus content for
Deadwood Burning

Explore deleted scenes, author interviews, artwork, and more

LOSTISLANDPRESS.COM

LONE PLAYER
BOOK ONE

CUT DECK
BOOK TWO

DEADWOOD BURNING
AARON'S PREQUEL

DEALER'S GRIP
BOOK THREE

ACKNOWLEDGMENTS

DEADWOOD BURNING has been my most challenging book yet, but it would have been a whole lot tougher without some very amazing people.

First, I'd like to thank my publisher Mel Torrefranca for her unwavering patience, support, and faith in my writing (and listening to me ramble about my book ideas). As always, I'm incredibly grateful for the Lost Island Press team and all the hard work they put into every project.

I'd also like to thank Aidan Hill for offering such valuable insight and attention to detail throughout the editing process. You're a rockstar! Huge thanks to Aleksandra for blowing me away with yet another stunning cover. Nikki Kahl—I'm obsessed with your illustrations!

Reed Podoll, thanks for talking me through all that big-brain engineering stuff about electric fences. I'm not sure how you managed to comprehend my very illegible sketches, but that alone deserves an award.

To my buddies—thanks for being patient every time I said, *I can't, I've gotta work on DB*. And yelling at me to meet my daily goals. Whenever I need a good laugh, you're always there to lift me up and recharge my creativity. Love you all to death.

I'd also like to thank my family for being so patient and supportive, not just during the creation of *Deadwood Burning*, but always. You all mean so much to me. Special shout out to my brother Michael for listening me yap about my ideas for hours on the phone and helping me make the Serpent extra spooky. Now it's time to stop procrastinating and write your book.

I'd also like to extend my gratitude to 1000mods, Old 97's, Mark Lanegan, Black Rebel Motorcycle Club, and Crippled Black Phoenix for giving me delicious music to write and cry to. And that one Peet's Coffee with the great lighting that I spent most of last winter haunting. Sorry for draining your matcha supply.

And thank you, reader, for giving me and this book a chance. Until next time.

ABOUT THE AUTHOR

JULIA ROSEMARY TURK is the author of the *Lone Player* series and winner of the 2021 Lost Island Writing Contest. Born and raised in Northern California's wine country, Julia currently lives with her family (and two adorable dogs) as a full-time content writer and avid indie music enthusiast. She also has chronic Lyme disease and co-infections and is passionate about raising awareness. When she's not working on her next novel, Julia enjoys spending time outside, going on long drives, and brainstorming book ideas with her brothers.

JULIAROSEMARYTURK.CARRD.CO

Learn more about Lyme and how you can make a difference

About the Publisher

LOST ISLAND PRESS publishes dystopian, sci-fi, and fantasy books. Unlike mainstream presses, we don't publish everything for everyone. We publish for *you*. Our catalog offers grounded, character-driven stories that linger long after the last page. The kind you get lost in, that keep you up at night. And because our books have the same vibe, if you enjoy one, you'll enjoy them all.

LOSTISLANDPRESS.COM

Join our newsletter to claim a free ebook